"A sure-footed, swift-paced race against time, *Foul Days* brings Slavic folklore to terrifying life. This is a brilliant modern fantasy that's not afraid to show its teeth."

—Ed McDonald, author of The Redwinter Chronicles

"[An] energetic, witty debut . . . This twisty, fast-paced fantasy adventure feels like what would happen if Delilah S. Dawson and Naomi Novik teamed up to rewrite *The Witcher*."

—*Library Journal*

"*Foul Days* is a phenomenal blend of danger and delight from an exciting new voice in fantasy. The characters, the world, the magic, and the monsters are all compelling, but the deft way in which Dimova brings them all to life while weaving in heavier themes of classism and abuse will leave you breathlessly awaiting the sequel long before you reach that final page."

—Kamilah Cole, author of *So Let Them Burn*

"A fast-paced thrill ride with immersive world-building and a snarky but realistic main character who you just can't help but root for."

—Frances White, author of *Voyage of the Damned*

"An immersive, thrilling read which will stand as a classic of Slavic folklore among the likes of Katherine Arden's Winternight Trilogy."

—Laura R. Samotin, author of *The Sins on Their Bones*

BY GENOVEVA DIMOVA

THE WITCH'S COMPENDIUM OF MONSTERS

Foul Days

Monstrous Nights

GENOVEVA DIMOVA

MONSTROUS NIGHTS

The Witch's Compendium of Monsters

BOOK 2

TOR PUBLISHING GROUP
NEW YORK

MONSTROUS NIGHTS

Copyright © 2024 by Genoveva Dimova

Interior illustrations by Rhys Davies

A Tor Book
Published by Tom Doherty Associates / Tor Publishing Group
120 Broadway
New York, NY 10271

www.torpublishinggroup.com

Tor® is a registered trademark of Macmillan Publishing Group, LLC.

Library of Congress Cataloging-in-Publication Data

Names: Dimova, Genoveva, author.
Title: Monstrous nights / Genoveva Dimova.
Description: First edition. | New York : Tor Publishing Group, 2024. |
    Series: The witch's compendium of monsters ; book 2
Identifiers: LCCN 2024024456 | ISBN 9781250877352 (hardcover) |
    ISBN 9781250329714 (ebook)
Subjects: LCGFT: Fantasy fiction. | Witch fiction. | Novels.
Classification: LCC PR6104.I49 M66 2024 | DDC 823/.92—dc23/
    eng/20240604
LC record available at https://lccn.loc.gov/2024024456

Our books may be purchased in bulk for promotional, educational,
or business use. Please contact your local bookseller or the Macmillan Corporate and
Premium Sales Department at 1-800-221-7945, extension 5442, or by email at
MacmillanSpecialMarkets@macmillan.com.

First Edition: 2024

Printed in the United States of America

0 9 8 7 6 5 4 3 2 1

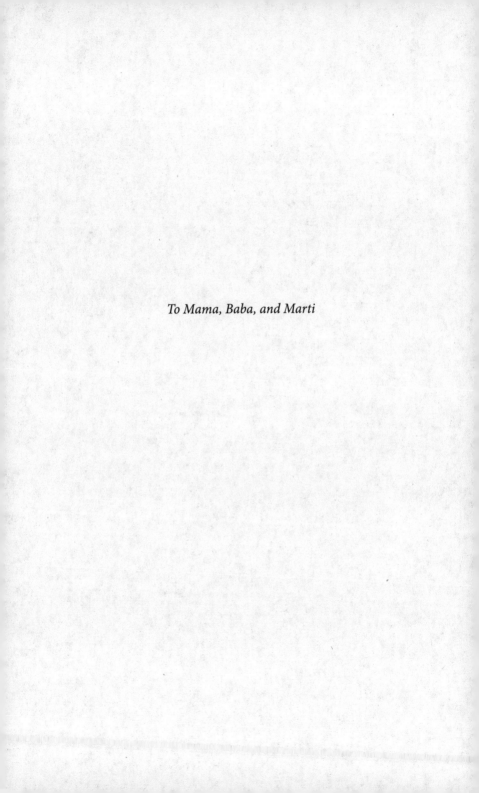

To Mama, Baba, and Marti

MONSTROUS NIGHTS

1

Kosara

It was just after midnight, and the chimes of the clock tower still echoed in the empty streets as Kosara rushed down a dark alleyway. The air smelled of coal fire and coming snow, and if she hadn't known it was the last week of spring, she could have believed it was December. The tips of her ears burned from the cold.

Finally, she reached her destination, an imposing salon on the main street. Kosara was used to seeing its large windows bright and inviting, with their velvet curtains pulled back to reveal the cosy inside. Tonight, the place was dark. The sign above the door swung on its squeaky chains: "The Witch's Rest."

The salon wasn't named after its clientele. In fact, no self-respecting witch patronised it. It was named after its owner, Sofiya Karajova. Sofiya's shtick was summoning long-suffering spirits back from the dead, so their relatives could ask them all sorts of stupid and invasive questions.

Kosara firmly believed death should excuse you from family reunions, but that wasn't the main reason she disliked the other witch's business model. Sofiya made a fortune during the Foul Days, when the realms of the dead and the living were closest. Most other witches were too busy protecting the city from the monsters—Sofiya was more concerned with her profit margins.

Kosara knocked on the door of the salon. When it opened, Vila was on the other side, which wasn't a surprise. It had been the old witch who'd summoned Kosara there in the middle of the night.

What *was* surprising was how tired Vila looked. Her skin had lost its glow. Her eyes were bloodshot and rimmed with purple.

"Come in," Vila said. "Quickly. It's not good news, I'm afraid."

Kosara followed her down the salon's corridor. Their steps were muffled by the deep pile of the carpet. The scent of incense filled the space, but beneath it, Kosara detected a smell that made her nauseous. Blood.

"What's happening?" she whispered. She wasn't entirely sure why. The salon was so quiet, it felt inappropriate to raise her voice. "When you told me it was urgent—"

"It is. Once the coppers sniff out something's wrong, they'll turn up with their little bags and little tweezers and little vials, and they'll scrub the place clean. I need you to see it before that."

"See what?"

Vila turned around so suddenly, Kosara nearly bumped into her. The crystal chandelier illuminated her face, causing the bags beneath her eyes to appear even deeper. "Sofiya's dead. Murdered."

It took Kosara a second of standing there, blinking with her mouth hanging slightly open, before Vila's words fully sank in. "How?"

"Beheaded." Kosara flinched, but Vila's tone remained even. "Her shadows are gone."

"Both of them?"

"Both."

Kosara's hand instinctively found the necklace of shadows around her neck. She'd tried leaving them behind in the house, but no matter how many protective spells she drew around them, they never felt safe alone. They'd told her as much.

Sofiya's two shadows weren't like Kosara's twelve. Kosara's own shadow was the only one she knew how to control. The rest had minds of their own. And no wonder—they hadn't been given to Kosara by their owners. She'd convinced them to help her defeat the Zmey, but that didn't make them *hers*.

Sofiya, on the other hand, had perfect control over her shadows. That made her murder even scarier.

"You see why I called you," Vila said. "Someone's on the hunt for witches' shadows. Again."

"How is this possible?" Kosara asked. "If they're gone, Sofiya must have given them away willingly. And then . . ."

"And then, she'd been beheaded like a common upir."

"Why would they behead her? Unless they were worried she might turn?"

Even then, a pair of silver coins on her eyes would have sufficed. Or an aspen stake through her heart. Or, hell, burying her with a sack of rice, so she got too distracted counting the grains to crawl out.

Beheading her seemed like overkill.

Kosara bit her lower lip. It had started to peel from the cold. "Show me."

Vila took a deep breath before she opened the door. A second later, Kosara understood why. The stench rushed her, thick and putrid.

The room was warm. Bright fire burned in the hearth, painting the walls in yellow and orange, reflecting off the pools of dried blood caked on the parquet floor. The body was naked, save for the vial hanging between her breasts, where Sofiya had kept her second shadow. It was shattered. Above that was the stump of her neck, bloody and messy.

Kosara's stomach churned. Vila's gaze was fixed on her, waiting, and all Kosara wanted to do was rush back outside and take in a breath that didn't smell like death.

"What do you expect me to do?" she snapped.

"You have experience with things like this. Look for clues."

Kosara scoffed. She'd hardly call her frantic search of Irnik Ivanov's room back in Belograd "experience." It wasn't like she had Asen's years of practice. Still, she tried her best. First, she kneeled next to the body and examined it quickly, pushing down the bile climbing in her throat.

For a desperate moment, she hoped the dead woman wasn't Sofiya, after all. In the dim light of the salon, her skin seemed too dark.

It had been a foolish thought. A rich woman like Sofiya could afford an exotic holiday somewhere sunny. Everything about the body made it obvious Kosara was looking at her dead colleague, starting from her signature bright-red nail varnish and ending with the small tattoo on her wrist: three spirals intersecting in a complicated pattern.

Next, Kosara searched the room. The murderer had been careful not to leave any obvious fingerprints. The floor was spotless, except for the blood: there were no marks, no footprints, and no stray hairs. Kosara checked the ashtray and found it full of the thin filters of Sofiya's cigarettes, all stained with her red lipstick. A single wine glass rested on a shelf. Its rim was marked with the same red.

All clues pointed to Sofiya having been alone tonight. At the same time, the person who'd taken her shadows must have been someone she'd known. You couldn't steal a witch's shadow—it had to be given willingly.

But then, why would they murder her once they'd got what they wanted? What could justify this senseless death?

Kosara took in a deep breath to calm her heartbeat and immediately regretted it when the room's smell took up permanent residence in her nostrils.

"Anything?" Vila asked.

"Nothing, except . . ." Kosara's eyes fell on Sofiya's chest again. Under the broken vial, Sofiya's skin was marred by a mark: old and long faded to grey. Karaivanov's two crossed Ks.

"I noticed it, too," Vila said. "He does make for a pretty compelling suspect, doesn't he?"

"I suppose."

This wasn't the first murder in Chernograd over the last couple of months. Kosara had attended numerous overnight vigils, watching over the bodies of the recently deceased. A murdered person was twice as likely to turn into an upir after their death, or worse, a kikimora. There were many precautions that had to be observed: all the mirrors in the house had to be covered; the candles couldn't be allowed to burn out; the household cats had to be kept away so they wouldn't jump over the body.

Kosara suspected the dramatic increase in murders was related to her spell to weaken the Wall. The relatives hadn't been too willing to talk, but she'd spotted Karaivanov's symbol on several of the victims.

She refused to feel guilty for it—they'd known what they were getting into when they'd agreed to work for Karaivanov. They'd been aware of the risk.

And yet, sometimes, in the middle of the night, while watching over the cold, dead body of another young person, she couldn't help but wonder if she'd made a mistake. If Malamir had been right, and the Wall had been the only thing maintaining Chernograd's fragile social structure.

Kosara sighed, glancing again at the symbol carved in Sofiya's chest. "I didn't know she'd worked for him."

"Me neither," Vila said. "I'm surprised, to tell you the truth."

"Why? Sofiya has always been all too ready to sell her morals for the right price."

"You're judging her too harshly."

"I know, I know, we shouldn't speak ill of the dead."

"It's not that. I've known Sofiya for years. She had no qualms about making a quick profit off rich fools, that much is true, but I'd never have expected her to mix up with the smugglers. She had *class*."

Kosara snorted, then felt guilty. The woman was dead. It certainly wasn't an appropriate time or place to laugh.

"She didn't have class," Kosara said. "She had the money to buy herself enough fine clothes and jewellery to appear classy."

"Even that's a good enough reason to believe she'd avoid the smugglers. She didn't need the money."

"But maybe when she was younger, before she got her second shadow—"

"Maybe. God knows we've all done stupid things when we were young."

Kosara shuffled from foot to foot, but she didn't reply. Vila knew exactly what stupid decisions Kosara had made in her youth. All of Chernograd did. She wished her relationship with the Zmey was as easy to hide as an ugly tattoo on her chest would have been.

Vila was silent for a moment, and then she said, casually, "I see you still have the shadows."

Kosara played with her necklace. The shadow beads were warm beneath her fingertips. "I do."

"You were going to find their owners."

"I did. All dead."

"Shadow sickness?"

"The Zmey."

"Oh," Vila said flatly. "Did they tell you?"

"In their own way."

Kosara had painstakingly interrogated each of the shadows until they'd revealed the truth. It hadn't been easy. A shadow wasn't a person, and she couldn't converse with them like they were. Instead, each was stuck on a different fragment of its past, and each communicated it in a mixture of visions and whispers.

Kosara was worried a few of them had gone mad during their time with the Zmey. Their mutterings made little sense.

Still, the truth hadn't surprised her. She'd suspected it as soon as she'd noticed all eleven shadows had belonged to young women. The Zmey had forced the shadows, patiently, over many years and many trips to Chernograd, out of his brides.

"What are you going to do with them?" Vila asked, a bit too quietly. If Kosara didn't know her better, she'd think the realisation had rattled her.

That was impossible, of course. Nothing rattled Vila.

"I don't know," Kosara said. "I'll have to hold on to them for now. I can't figure out a strong enough spell to keep them safe when they're away from me."

"They will make you a target."

"They also mean I can protect myself."

Vila's eyes darted towards Sofiya's dead body. "Be careful. As far as I'm aware, no witch has ever collected this much power. Don't let it get to your head."

Kosara looked down at her boots. She'd never admit it to Vila, but she sometimes thought she heard the shadows' whispers still, even when they were all folded into beads around her neck. Occasionally, she was sure she spotted a familiar figure in the corner of her vision, plucked straight from the shadows' memories.

His hair was gold, and his eyes were flame blue.

She thought she had rid herself of the Zmey once and for all when she'd trapped him in the Wall. She was starting to suspect she'd been wrong.

2

Asen

The blood was everywhere. Rusty red, it splattered the golden wallpaper and the stucco ceiling. A few drops had landed on the crystal chandelier and hung there, suspended in midair, like flies in amber.

"Mondays, eh?" said Lila. The magic detector in her back pocket quietly beeped. She took her notebook out. "What did you say her name was?"

"Natalia," Asen said without looking up from the victim. "Natalia Ruseva. She owned the Witch's Cauldron boutique."

Lila raised her eyebrows. "Isn't that the shop you suspected of dealing with illegally smuggled magical objects?"

"That's the one."

Natalia's body was sprawled on the blood-soaked sheets—pale, bloated, completely naked. A depression in the pillow indicated where her head would have lain. Except, all that remained was the bloody stump of her neck.

That was what almost pushed Asen over the edge. He rushed to the open window and breathed in deeply. The spring breeze carried the smell of blossoming linden trees. It made a putrid cocktail, mixed with the stench of death.

"She looks like she's been dead for a while," Lila observed, turning over the victim's arm to look at the small tattoo at her wrist: three spirals interconnecting in a complicated pattern. "Certainly more than a few hours. What do you think?"

"We'd better leave the precise estimates to the pathologists."

Lila harrumphed, making it obvious what she thought about their colleagues from the pathology department. She quickly dotted all the visible marks on the body in her notebook. "She gave them a good fight."

Asen muttered something in agreement, though his eyes weren't on the bruises dotting the victim's skin. They were on the symbol carved on her chest.

Two crossed Ks. Konstantin Karaivanov's sign.

"What do you think?" Lila asked. "Konstantin? Or an imposter?" Without giving Asen the chance to reply, she continued, "I suppose it would be pretty stupid, wouldn't it? If it was Konstantin, I mean. For him to leave her like that. Your eyes are instantly drawn to that symbol."

"What does he care?" Asen tried to keep his tone casual. "What's one more murder on top of everything else he's done?"

"But still, what would be the point of stripping the body naked?"

"Maybe it's a warning."

"For who?"

For me. Asen didn't say it out loud. He licked his lips. They were trembling.

Get a grip, he thought sternly. He couldn't let Lila see how much this murder had rattled him, because then she'd start asking questions, and before long, she'd find out the truth. She was like a bulldog: once she'd sunk her teeth into a clue, she never let it go.

Lila's eyes narrowed as she kept inspecting the victim. "Her shadow is missing."

"I know."

That had been one of the first things Asen had noticed. It made him shudder, the thought that someone was on the hunt for witches' shadows again. He hoped Kosara was safe. "We'd better get a team in here."

"Yes, boss." Lila flicked her radio open, extended the antenna, and frowned at the crackling coming from the speaker. Asen had known she wouldn't get signal this deep in the house.

She left the room, her blocky heels clicking against the marble floor, but he lingered.

His fingers found the velvet pouch hidden in his pocket. At first glance, it appeared to be nothing but a simple, good-dreams charm. It was stuffed with herbs—a handful of lavender, valerian root, and lemon balm—but it also held a note. An invitation to an illegal auction held in a secret location, penned in Karaivanov's own hand.

The day before, Asen had paid an informant handsomely to retrieve the pouch from under Natalia Ruseva's pillow. He'd been just in time.

"Are you coming?" Lila shouted from the hallway.

"I'm coming." Asen made sure the pouch was safely buttoned inside his pocket and left the room.

Asen should have handed the velvet pouch to the investigative team. He should have, at least, told his boss about it. It only strengthened the connection between Ruseva and Karaivanov, which made it an important clue in the murder case.

However, parting with the pouch would have required explaining how he'd acquired it. It would also mean that this—his one lead to where Karaivanov might have holed up—would be lost forever.

Asen couldn't afford to reveal his cards. Karaivanov undoubtedly had people in the police. In fact, Asen was starting to feel as if he couldn't trust any of his colleagues. There had been so many murders around the city lately, and no one, not even his boss, seemed particularly perturbed by them.

The only logical explanation was that Karaivanov was greasing the police machinery with money, making sure the cases got filed as "unresolved" faster. And the smuggler himself? No one had seen him for months. With every passing day, Asen grew more and more worried he'd fail to fulfil the promise he'd made to Boryana.

He kicked at the ground, dislodging a tuft of grass growing in the mud between the cobblestones. It was a beautiful afternoon on one of the last days of spring, and the linden trees' pollen coated the windows of houses and automobiles. In a week, summer would arrive, and it would be a scorching hot one if the meteorology witches were to be trusted.

He wondered what Kosara's plans were for the solstice. He knew they celebrated it as St. Enyo's Day in Chernograd—the first day of summer, when the herbs were most potent, and picking them would ensure they kept their powers all year.

Asen often caught himself thinking of Kosara lately. How she was, what she was doing. Whether she thought of him.

It was foolish. They hadn't spoken since that day she'd left him in Belograd. The Wall could be crossed now—if she wanted to see him, she could have done so at any time. She obviously didn't. He'd invited her for dinner, and she'd refused.

Could he blame her? She was one of the most powerful witches in Chernograd, and what was he? A crooked Belogradean cop.

At last, he entered the police station and climbed the steep staircase to his boss's office. He didn't get the chance to knock before her voice came from the other side.

"Come on in, Bakharov." His steps on the creaky stairs had obviously alerted her to his arrival.

Asen opened the door. "Hi, boss."

Chief Constable Anahit Vartanian sat behind her desk, cradling a mug of hot chocolate between her fingers. She was a short woman in her mid-fifties who always wore frilly floral dresses and long dangly earrings, even in the depths of winter. Asen had never, not once, let her cheerful demeanour fool him. Under the silk glove, Vartanian ruled the Belogradean Police with an iron fist.

"What have you done now, Bakharov?" she asked as soon as she saw him.

"What? Nothing!"

"I can always tell when you're guilty. Your whole face sags." She pulled her cheeks down to demonstrate. Her nails were painted in a vibrant pink. "Well?"

He sat on the chair she indicated. "I've done nothing. Lila and I stumbled upon a murder."

"'Stumbled upon'?"

"You know how it is. With the Wall gone—"

"Last I checked, the Wall was still very much there. And thank God for that."

"You know what I mean. Karaivanov's underlings have gone berserk. His whole organisation is eating itself from the inside."

"Sounds like a good thing to me."

"People are dying."

Vartanian shrugged. "Criminals. So, who have they got now?"

"Natalia Ruseva. She owns the Witch's Cauldron boutique on the main street."

Vartanian raised her eyebrows. "Well, what can you tell me?"

Asen described the crime scene as he and Lila had found it. Vartanian listened without interrupting.

"So, her head was missing," she said at length. "Any ideas why?"

"Maybe the murderer was worried about her turning. Ruseva is from Chernograd—"

Vartanian's voice was sharp. "We don't have people turning on this side of the Wall, Bakharov."

Asen remained silent. He'd heard the rumours, just like everyone else in the city. Since the Wall had become permeable, there had been reports of corpses rising from the graveyard and suspiciously large wolves roaming the streets when the moon was full.

Except, that was all they were—rumours. No one had managed to photograph these sightings, nor provide other proof. For now.

"We'll have to get someone to ID the victim," Vartanian said. "Just so we can say we've done it all by the book. Did Ruseva have a partner?"

"Not as far as I'm aware." Asen knew, however, that Ruseva had several young lovers, including his informant.

"Family?" Vartanian asked.

"I haven't had a chance to check yet."

"Get one of her staff, if all else fails."

"Yes, boss."

Vartanian sipped on her chocolate and licked her lips. "Didn't this happen in the river district last month? A beheading with the head missing? And there was one in the Docks, I'm pretty sure."

Asen ran a hand through his hair. "Pretty sure" didn't cut it for him, and neither did the detached tone of Vartanian's voice. The murders had happened, and Asen could recite every tiny detail about them—except, he didn't think his boss would care.

"There have been so many corpses lately," he said dryly.

"Popping up like mushrooms after the rain, aren't they? Well, you'd better note it down. There's probably a connection. Any ideas about motive?"

To Asen, it seemed obvious. Natalia Ruseva was involved with Karaivanov's gang. She'd been invited to his secret auction tonight, as the pouch in Asen's pocket attested. Then, something between them had gone wrong, and the smuggler had decided to get rid of her. It could have been Asen's fault, for all he knew, for stealing the invite to the auction from Ruseva. If Karaivanov had somehow discovered she'd lost it, he'd have probably been angry enough to order her killed. The thought made Asen's stomach turn with guilt.

In any case, one thing was clear: Ruseva wasn't Karaivanov's first victim, and she wouldn't be the last.

And while, sure, the criminalists would do their magic and discover a clue at the crime scene—a smeared fingerprint or a tiny eyebrow hair—and they'd catch the hit man Karaivanov had sent to do the job . . . did it matter? Did it matter if they took one of his henchmen off the streets, when he had hundreds? What difference did it make for them to remove the tool he used to commit the murder if *he* still walked free?

Asen knew he'd stayed silent for too long because Vartanian's gaze had acquired a steely edge.

"Not yet," he said. He couldn't tell Vartanian he suspected Karaivanov, not without risking his whole plan falling through. He couldn't be certain whether his boss was in the smuggler's pocket.

Vartanian paused. "Something here doesn't add up, Bakharov."

"About the murder?"

"About you. Ever since you returned from your holidays in the winter, covered in scrapes and bruises—"

Asen's heartbeat quickened. "What can I say, I'm not a great skier."

Vartanian slammed her fist against the desk. The hot chocolate splashed in its mug. "Do you take me for an idiot? It's not just the bruises. Your whole demeanour has changed."

Asen shuffled uncomfortably in his seat, but said nothing.

Vartanian stared at him for a few seconds. "I need you to promise me something."

"Yes?"

"I want you to go home, and I want you to look in the mirror, long and hard. Tomorrow, I want you to come in and tell me if you saw an officer of the Belogradean Police Force looking back at you, or if you saw someone else."

Asen opened his mouth to argue, but Vartanian put up one finger in the air. "I'll see you tomorrow."

Asen sighed. "See you tomorrow, boss."

When he got home, he didn't look in the mirror. He knew all too well what he was.

He found the velvet pouch in his pocket and fished out the note. It smelled strongly of lavender.

Looking at the symbols drawn on it, he couldn't tell where they'd take him. He wasn't even sure if the magic circle was safe to use without knowing a spell or incantation of some kind. If only Kosara was here, she'd have been able to read it, but he'd be damned if he turned up at her doorstep after six months of silence with a request like that.

What he knew for certain was the circle would work only once. It was an invitation for one specific event: an auction for magical objects to be held this evening. He'd have one chance at this.

He'd better not squander it.

3

Kosara

Kosara wasn't going to put the fire on. No way. It was June. And while, yes, her breath came out in thick plumes in the frigid air and her fingers felt like icicles, frozen and clumsy, she couldn't justify the cost. Firewood didn't grow on trees. Figuratively speaking.

After returning from Sofiya's salon, she poured herself a glass of wine to calm her nerves and sat in the living room, which she'd rearranged to serve as her workshop. Colourful bottles, vials, and jars were scattered on every surface. From the roof beams hung herbs, rabbit paws and dogwood branches, yuda feathers and strings of karakonjul ears.

In an attempt to liven up the space, she'd bought an enormous crystal ball from a junk shop in Belograd. It stood prettily atop the table, the mist inside it swirling. As far as she could tell, it did nothing else.

Kosara noticed she'd left a red smear of lyutenitsa on it, from when she'd eaten dinner. She was scrubbing it with her sleeve when there was a knock on the door.

It was nearly two in the morning, according to the grandfather clock ticking quietly in the corner, and Kosara's eyes were already shutting. She crossed the dark hallway, her shadow following at her footsteps, stretching demonstratively and pretending to yawn.

I know, I know, she thought at it. *But that's how it is.* Chernograd never slept, so why should she?

Before she opened the door, only for a brief second, she allowed herself to consider the possibility it might be Asen on the other side. Maybe he'd found himself in trouble in Belograd and needed her expertise. Or maybe he just wanted to see her.

Instead, she found a tall man standing at the threshold, wrapped tightly in a thick coat. She felt the pang of disappointment, but she didn't show it. It had been a foolish hope, anyway. Why would Asen suddenly visit her in the middle of the night, after he hadn't so much as phoned in the past six months?

It was obvious: Asen didn't want anything to do with Chernograd. He didn't want anything to do with *her.*

And could she blame him, really? The last time he'd visited the city, he'd barely made it out alive.

"Kosara, I'm so glad to catch you at home," the man breathed out, his teeth clattering. A woollen hat was pulled low over his head, covering his eyebrows. Only the tips of his ears stuck out, bright red.

Kosara squinted, as the man's face finally clicked in her mind. The baker's apprentice. "Ibrahim? God, I barely recognised you. What happened?" She shivered and added, "Come on in, you can tell me everything."

On the way to the living room, Kosara clicked her fingers and mumbled the magic words. There was a loud crack. Fire loomed in the hearth.

She had a guest now, after all. It was the perfect excuse for some warmth.

"Sit down," she told him, and Ibrahim shuffled to a chair. "Would you like some wine? Or something stronger?"

"Stronger, please."

Kosara poured him a glass of apricot rakia, home-brewed and so sharp, her eyes watered from the smell alone. Ibrahim downed it in one go.

Kosara topped him up. "What's going on? You're pale as a ghost."

Ibrahim looked at her for a long while with eyes framed by dark circles. "I think I'm dead."

Kosara barked out a laugh, but his face remained serious. Her laughter died on her lips. "Dead? How?"

"I electrocuted myself tinkering with the radio. You know I've been trying to catch signals from the monster realm?"

Kosara had heard of his mad idea before. As if the monsters would simply sit around listening to the radio, like humans did. "Yes."

"Well, I thought I finally got something. I swear I heard his voice."

"Whose voice?"

"The Zmey."

Kosara laughed again, this time slightly higher pitched. Her hand holding the bottle trembled and the amber liquid swished inside. She was tempted to pour herself a glass as well. "The Zmey's gone, Ibrahim."

"Well, I'm telling you I heard him. And then the screwdriver slid, and it made a connection with something it shouldn't have, and it electrocuted me. And I died. My partner—Dancho, you must know him? Dancho Krustev." Ibrahim paused, then added, with a tinge of pride in his voice, "He's a doctor."

"I know him."

"Well, he found me slumped on the desk, covered in soot. Look!" Ibrahim took off the hat, revealing his bushy eyebrows and his messy hair, sticking in all directions.

"Right," Kosara said and topped his glass again. If he continued like that, he'd be under the table soon, whether he was dead or not. "I understand you got a fright, but you seem to be all fine—"

"You don't understand. Dancho found no signs of life. No pulse. I was dead, Kosara. Dead as a doornail!"

"Well, it happens sometimes that you die for a few minutes, but you can be revived again. Dancho knows what he's doing when it comes to CPR."

"That he does, but it had been hours, not minutes. I died in the morning and woke up in the evening, absolutely starving."

"Right. You'd skipped lunch."

"Starving *for blood,* Kosara."

Kosara frowned, taking in Ibrahim's pale skin and his bloodshot eyes. He could pass for an upir, she had to admit, but he could just as well have been a man who'd had the fright of his life and was still recovering. Shock did a lot of damage to a person.

"You can't be serious," Kosara said. "I've witnessed upirs awaking before. The mere fact you're here, having a civilised conversation with me and not trying to suck me dry, shows you're not one."

"But aren't there upirs who keep some of their senses?"

"Not right after awakening! Sure, maybe twenty, thirty, a hundred years down the line—if they survive that long—a handful of them recover some of their personality. Or develop a new one, I've never been certain. But hours? A young upir is as senseless as a rabid dog."

"And yet, here I am."

"Ibrahim," Kosara said, keeping her voice level. "I'm telling you, as a witch. Believe me. You're not an upir."

"But I want to drink blood, Kosara! You know what I did, right after I woke up? We keep chickens, you know. Hens. I walked right over to the henhouse. Dancho caught me squeezing a chicken, about to bite its head off!"

"Shock does strange things to people. Maybe you lack iron."

"I lack blood!"

"Have you tried pricking yourself? Upirs have black blood."

"All of them? I thought some—"

"Well, yes, some retain the colour of their blood, but most don't. Did you try?"

"We tried. Dancho poked my finger with a needle." Ibrahim showed her his index finger, where a little red dot marred the skin. "It's red."

"See?"

"But some of them—"

"Listen, I'll brew you a potion, what do you say? Spinach, walnuts, and karakonjul liver. Full of iron. Try drinking that for a few days and see if you improve, all right?"

Ibrahim sighed. "All right. It's not as if I have a choice. Dancho will kill me if I hurt the hens." He laughed without humour. "Though he might have to pierce my heart with an aspen stake to manage it!"

Kosara brewed the potion quickly as her eyes were starting to close. It had been a long day. She'd had her usual customers, needing her potions for various aches and pains, but recently, more and more people came after an ill-fated trip to Belograd. The Chernogradeans weren't used to the exotic food and alcohol, and many needed a hangover cure or something for stomachaches. On top of that, there were allergic reactions to foreign cosmetics, seasick travellers who'd never been on a boat before, and people who'd got into silly fights over some cultural misunderstanding.

It wasn't only Chernogradeans who visited her, either. The Belogradeans flocked to Chernograd. In only a few months, she'd treated more upir bites and varkolak scratches than she had for years. Wannabe monster hunters, wide-eyed tourists, lovers of extreme sports, second- and third-generation immigrants trying to find their ancestral home: the queue in front of her workshop was never-ending.

Once the potion had finished bubbling, Kosara poured it into a vial and handed it to Ibrahim. "Come back in a couple of days and tell me how you're getting on."

"Thanks. I sincerely hope it helps. How much do I owe you?"

"Three grosh."

Ibrahim inhaled sharply. "Three?"

"Is that a problem?"

"Well, we just got back from a holiday in Mesambria, and money is a bit tight. You know them foreign prices. Plus, if we have to organise a funeral . . ."

"For who?"

"For me."

Kosara sighed deeply. "For the last time, Ibrahim, you are not dead. Give me a grosh and get out of here."

"A grosh? Are you sure? That karakonjul liver alone costs more than that."

"Believe me, I know."

Once Ibrahim left, Kosara decided not to go to her cold bedroom. The fire in the workshop was nice, and besides, the upper floor was always too quiet now, with Nevena gone.

Kosara hadn't heard her sister's voice since that night last winter, right after she'd trapped the Zmey in the Wall. She was more and more certain she'd imagined it.

It had been a traumatic twelve days. It was no wonder she'd been hearing voices by the end of them.

However, as she snuggled on the sofa under a pile of blankets and watched the coals smouldering in the hearth, there was one voice she couldn't deny she was hearing.

My little Kosara, the Zmey whispered. *Where are you? It's so cold out here. So, so cold.*

She was going mad. That was the only explanation for it. Loneliness had driven her insane, and now she was hearing voices. It wasn't normal, being completely alone in a big, creaky, haunted house. She'd started conversing with the household spirits a lot more often, too, even though outside of the Foul Days, she saw them as nothing but shadows occasionally darting past.

"Nazdrave, Aunty," she'd toast the kitchen spirit as she downed another glass of wine in the evening.

"Good morning, Uncle," she'd greet the bathroom spirit when she went to brush her teeth in the morning.

She knew she had them to thank for the fact that the house hadn't fallen on top of her yet, burying her in a grave of rotten wallpaper, dust, and rusty nails. She'd been so busy these past few months, she'd barely had time for cleaning or maintenance. Between taking care of her clients and poking around the dodgier parts of the city for signs of Karaivanov, there simply weren't enough hours in the day.

"Good morning, Uncle," she said, as usual, when she entered the bathroom that morning. It was so cold, frost flowers bloomed on the tiny circular window above the bathtub.

Frost. In June!

She'd just finished brushing her teeth and was getting ready to jump into the shower when there was a knock at the door. Kosara sighed. They couldn't even let her have a moment of peace first thing in the morning.

The knock sounded again, so loud it startled the swallows nesting on the roof, making them chirp angrily.

"Coming, coming!" Kosara shouted and shrugged her jumper back on as she ran down the stairs.

When she opened the door, she found Ibrahim standing outside. He looked worse this morning—more tired and so nervous, his hands shook.

"The hens!" he shrieked. "Kosara, the hens have all been murdered!"

Chernograd was never particularly cheerful, even in the summer. This June, however, the city was greyer and gloomier than ever. Usually, the cafés and restaurants on the main street set up tables outside, and an ice-cream vendor circled the city on his bicycle. Not this June. Most eating establishments were boarded up, unable to compete with their counterparts on the other side of the Wall. Kosara heard the ice-cream vendor had emigrated to Belograd.

Ibrahim lived nearby, in a block of flats tucked in a grimy alleyway off the main square. He opened the front door and led Kosara through the dingy hallway.

"I woke up early to get ready for work," he explained while he searched for the keys to the back garden in his coat pocket. "We usually start on the dough at three A.M., to give it plenty of time to rise. Then, there's the filo that takes forever to stretch . . . Anyway, I got up and went downstairs to feed the hens. Dancho is working the night shift today." As Ibrahim twisted the key in the lock, his fingers shook. He ran a hand through his dark hair. "God, he'll be so upset with me! He loved those hens like children. He named all of them, can you believe it?"

"Don't be silly," Kosara said. "He won't be angry with you. It wasn't your fault."

"What if it was, though?" Ibrahim turned to face Kosara, his eyes panicked. "What if I sleepwalked there in the middle of the night and did it?"

"Surely, you'd have noticed the blood on your hands when you woke up."

"Maybe I washed it."

"Do you still crave blood?"

"No." Ibrahim paused. "No, I don't think so."

"So, the potion helped."

"Or maybe I sated my hunger in the middle of the night."

Kosara reached over his shoulder and pushed the door open. "Let's have a look around the crime scene."

She'd said it in jest, but soon realised the situation was no joke. The back garden was a scene of carnage. Little feathery bodies lay over the grass and piled high in the henhouse. Their beady eyes stared at her, unseeing.

There was no blood, though. Most of the hens looked as if they'd simply fallen asleep, never to wake. Only the cockerel appeared as if he'd tried to fight: his wing hung at an unnatural angle, and his talons were all broken.

"What the hell . . ." Kosara looked around. "This garden isn't shared? No one else has a key?"

"Not as far as I'm aware."

Kosara turned the cockerel's body around with the tip of her boot, careful not to touch him with bare hands. She couldn't tell if his injuries were caused by a fight with an intruder, or if he'd hurt himself, crashing against the walls of the henhouse in a blind panic. But what could cause such panic in a bird?

"The neighbour suggested we pluck them," Ibrahim said, his voice hollow. "And make chicken soup. But I just couldn't bring myself to. How could I feed Dancho chicken soup made from his hens?"

"Don't. Don't touch them. We don't know what killed them. I'd get the vet to look at them."

"You think they were ill?"

Kosara hesitated. There had been plenty of bouts of chicken flu in

Chernograd over the years—it was what happened when you kept a lot of animals close together. But this . . .

Her eyes fell on the cockerel with the broken wing. This didn't seem right. Her sixth sense was screaming at her that nothing about this was natural.

There was something terribly familiar about the pressure hanging over the henhouse, making the air quietly, almost imperceptibly, crackle. A scent floated in the wind, one Kosara recognised from somewhere, if only she could put her finger on it.

Ibrahim was still looking at her with his brows furrowed.

"You didn't murder them," Kosara told him firmly. "No one's been drinking their blood. It must have been something"—or some*one*— "else that got them."

"Are you sure?"

"Don't you live with a doctor? Do they look like their blood has been sucked?"

"Well, I thought I maybe drank from a couple until I was sated, then killed the rest since they were witnesses."

Kosara fixed him with an even stare. "Are you joking?"

"I don't know, Kosara! I haven't been myself."

"Get the vet in here. I bet they'll be able to solve the mystery." Kosara was a witch, after all, not a henhouse slaughter investigator. If only Asen was here, he'd probably crack the case in no time.

Kosara shook her head. She had to stop thinking about him.

"Let me know what the vet says," she said on her way out the door. "I'm sure there's some logical explanation for all this."

Except, as she walked back to her house, she couldn't shake the feeling she was missing something. There had been something in the hens' empty stares. Something in the cockerel's broken talons. Something in that familiar *smell*.

As soon as she got home, she took her bestiary from the shelf and cleaned the dust off it with her hand. It had been a few years since she'd encountered a new monster in Chernograd. Not counting Lamia, of course.

Kosara flicked through the pages quickly, looking at the drawings.

All the usual monsters were there, neatly arranged in alphabetical order: chuma, hala, karakonjul . . .

Her gaze fell on a drawing of an enormous black cockerel with gleaming eyes.

Mratinyak, read the elaborate script above the bird's head. "Causes illness in domesticated birds," the text explained.

And under it, "The great harbinger of plague and death."

4

Asen

Teleportation magic wasn't for the weak of stomach. Asen's every organ was turned inside out. His intestines unravelled. His blood felt light and bubbly, and his heart rushed to pump it into his fingers and toes, inflating them like balloons.

A second later, his body righted itself and his feet painfully hit a hard surface. Bright light blinded him. A wall of noise slammed against his eardrums—a large crowd. He'd only half-materialised when a stranger pushed him out of the way and shouted at him to look where he was going.

Still disoriented, Asen stumbled to a tall column and leaned on it, breathing deeply. He blinked fast, allowing his eyes to adjust to the light.

He stood in what looked like an old opera house: a spacious hall with wide corridors running between many tiers of red velvet seats, overlooking a stage. Expensively dressed people milled about, pulled on imported cigarillos and cigars, and downed glasses of sparkling wine with a speed that would impress the most seasoned drunkards in the local tavern. On the balconies above, Asen caught the glint of theatre binoculars and the flutter of hand fans.

Asen hesitated, unsure where to go. Everyone else seemed to know each other. He spotted no familiar faces, which was a relief:

it minimised the chance he'd be quickly recognised by Karaivanov's cronies. He'd grown a beard in the last few weeks in preparation for this. He'd also done his best to dress inconspicuously, which in his case involved buying a simple black suit. It had been a mistake. In the sea of pearls, feathers, precious stones, and imported fabrics, he stuck out like a sore thumb.

The first step to fitting in with the crowd, he decided, was to grab a glass of sparkling wine from a nearby tray. Asen deliberately didn't acknowledge the waiter holding it. He had the feeling the people gathered here were not ones to say "please" or "thank you."

"You're new here," came a voice behind him.

Asen turned around. A woman watched him intently through a pair of ruby-encrusted handheld glasses.

He prided himself in being able to accurately estimate a person's age: it was a part of the mental description he always noted down when he met new people. In this case, however, he struggled. The woman had plump cheeks and wore a lot of colourful makeup, which made her appear younger, but her hair, elaborately braided into a tall updo, was salt-and-pepper.

There was also something terribly familiar about her. Asen frowned, trying to remember whether they'd met.

"My name is Maria," she said. "Maria Hajieva."

Oh, bollocks.

They *had* met, several times. Except, her hair had always been gathered in a tight bun, her makeup had been light, and her clothes— professionally conservative. He'd never have recognised her in this frilly red gown.

Maria Hajieva was the mayor of Belograd.

"Ah, it's a pleasure to meet you, Maria," Asen said, putting on an accent that sounded embarrassingly fake even to his own ears. "My name is Kostas Dimitriades, and I'm a rich merchant trading in silk from the great city of Stambul across the Marble Sea."

Asen swore internally. The hell was he doing? Nobody spoke like that. Who introduced themselves as a "rich merchant"? He'd practised his fake story, of course, but his delivery in the mirror at home had been far smoother.

He had to pull himself together. It seemed obvious the mayor hadn't recognised him. He was still in the clear.

"A drink?" he said, rolling his Rs. What was this accent supposed to be? It wasn't from Stambul, that was for sure.

The mayor accepted the flute of sparkling wine from his hand. "So, Kostas, what brings you here tonight?"

"Ah, you know, idle curiosity. I'd heard of the great magical treasures of the city of Belograd, and I wanted to see what the fuss was about."

"There are a lot of downsides to living next door to our poor neighbour," the mayor said dryly. "But I have to admit, the magic that pours into our city over the Wall is not one of them."

"Why are *you* here, M . . ." *Dear God, Asen, get a grip!* He'd almost called her "mayor." "Maria?"

The mayor leaned to whisper in his ear, and the citrusy scent of her perfume filled his nostrils. "I heard tonight's auction will be particularly special. Apparently, our generous patron has prepared a surprise for us."

"What surprise?"

Maria laughed, playfully hitting Asen's shoulder with her fan. "Well, it wouldn't be much of a surprise if he'd told me, would it?"

Asen looked at his shoulder, then up at the mayor's face. She was *flirting.* That was why his improbable accent and his even more improbable story hadn't rang alarm bells to her. She didn't care who he was, she only cared about snatching a rich foreigner in a well-tailored suit.

This was good. Asen could work with this.

"Listen, Maria." Repeating her name was always a good strategy, Asen knew from his interrogation manual. It put people at ease. "You seem like a generous woman. You might be able to help me. The truth is, me being here tonight isn't mere coincidence. I was sent here on an important mission."

"Oh?" the mayor curved an eyebrow. She'd glued rubies along it, and they glinted every time her face moved. "What mission?"

"Do you know the padishah of Stambul?"

"We've met."

"I work for him. He's aware of your city's reputation for magical artefacts. If a magic exists, it can be found in Belograd, they say."

Asen's attempts to appeal to the mayor's patriotism obviously worked. She beamed at him. "So, what is it that your padishah wants?"

"As you know, he's rich beyond imagination. He's got everything a man could wish for . . ." A dramatic pause. "Except for one thing."

"Which is?"

"Love. His young wife died a few years back. He'd give anything to hear her voice again."

"Oh, that's terrible."

Asen's smile widened. He'd got her hook, line, and sinker. "So, you see, that's why he sent me here. He'd heard of the witches from Chernograd who can speak to the dead . . ."

"He'll have to travel to Chernograd and look for Sofiya. During the Foul Days, when the boundary between the realms of the living and the dead is thinnest—"

"He's, as you're aware, an old man now and not fit for travel. Isn't there anything else that can be done? There must be some amulet out there."

"I've never heard of such a thing."

"But maybe if you ask around . . . I've heard there is a man in Chernograd who can get you any magic you can dream of."

The mayor's mouth quirked. "So, you're requesting an audience with our illustrious patron, is that it?"

Asen hesitated. This had been way too easy. "I admit, I'd hoped to meet him here tonight."

The mayor opened her mouth again, but a loud voice interrupted them. "Mayor!"

A large man placed his hand on her shoulder. He looked to be in his forties, well over average height, with a thick black moustache, almost a twin to his black unibrow.

The mayor looked up and smiled at him, though Asen had caught how, for a split second, her mouth twisted in annoyance. She hadn't revealed her job to Asen. He suspected she'd been angling for a quick fling without it ever getting too personal.

"Anton, lovely to see you here," she said. The man leaned in, and they exchanged pretend kisses on both cheeks. "This is Kostas. He's made a fortune trading silk in Stambul, he tells me."

"It's a pleasure to meet you," Asen said, adding several extraneous syllables to "pleasure." God, his accent was getting hammier and hammier with every exchanged line.

"Silk, eh?" Anton asked, shaking Asen's hand vigorously. "Spider silk or sea silk?"

Asen, who knew next to nothing about silk, thought it safest to pretend he hadn't understood. "I'm sorry, I'm having trouble with your accent. Could you repeat the question?"

Thankfully, the mayor didn't let them get any deeper into the particularities of the silk trade. "Forget about that. Kostas had been hoping to see Konstantin tonight, apparently," she said to Anton. "Do you know if he's coming?"

"I'm afraid not, Mimi."

Now that Asen had the time to take him in, it was obvious Anton was one of Karaivanov's cronies. His sheer size suggested as much, and so did the gun, badly concealed under his suit jacket.

Asen barely resisted the urge to roll his eyes. Publicly, the mayor of Belograd had taken a hard stance against the smugglers. In private, she rubbed shoulders with them.

"Oh, why not?" the mayor asked.

"Well, you know. He barely shows his nose outside these days."

Asen hadn't been expecting a different answer. Konstantin Karaivanov was known for being evasive, which was how he'd escaped the police for so many years. He'd never simply stroll into a large gathering like this.

"You know what I heard, though?" Anton said. "He's found a way to leave his lair."

Maria raised an eyebrow, making the rubies glint. "What is it?"

Anton threw a quick look at Asen, who did his best to look like a clueless foreigner, too busy staring absently into the distance to pay attention to the conversation. Anton hesitated, but then, his desire to show off his connection to Karaivanov in front of the mayor won.

"He says he's found a way to make himself unrecognisable. I'm not sure if I believe it. He's become very . . . hmm, superstitious in his old age. He keeps bringing that witch around to tell his fortune, too."

"He's planning to alter his appearance?" Maria asked, obviously all ears. "With surgery?"

Asen tried not to show how interested he was in the answer to that question.

Anton opened his mouth, but before he'd said anything else, he was interrupted by a loud voice coming through the loudspeakers. "Take your seats, everyone!"

Asen had been so engrossed in Anton and Maria's conversation, he jumped about a step in the air.

"Oh, excuse me," Maria said, holding on to Anton's extended arm. "I hope we'll see each other again at the end of this, Kostas?"

Asen gave her his most charming smile. "I hope so too, Maria."

He watched as Anton took her to the staircase leading to one of the balconies. *Damn it.*

Still, not all was lost. The mayor seemed keen to see him again later. That gave Asen time to calm his nerves and try not to ruin everything with his bad acting.

He shuffled to a seat in the middle of the row, hoping if he entrenched himself deep enough, no one would ask him to leave. As an old lady started making her way towards him, Asen's heart skipped a beat.

Her skin was so pale, it looked almost translucent. Her eyes were a bloodshot red.

It couldn't be, he told himself. What would an old upir from Chernograd be doing here?

But then, she settled into the seat to his left, and he realised her skin wasn't naturally that pale. Particles of bluish-white face powder were caught in the fine hairs on her cheeks. From a certain angle, her eyes were glossy, indicating she wore contact lenses.

Asen resisted the urge to roll his eyes. It had recently become a bizarre fashion among the upper echelons of Belogradean society to dress as Chernogradean monsters. Now that he was paying attention, Asen couldn't even count the amount of samodiva hair wigs gleaming in the crowd, not to mention the upir teeth necklaces and rusalka scale tiaras. The man on Asen's right sported a high-crowned karakonjul fur hat, while a few rows ahead, someone wore a varkolak fleece vest.

Funny, Asen thought. On the other side of the Wall, crafting a hat out of karakonjul fur was a necessity. Here, it was a sign of wealth.

He couldn't examine the people surrounding him for much longer, because the lights in the hall dimmed. After several seconds of expectant silence, a tall man walked out on the stage, waving to the crowd. Asen frowned, recognising him immediately. It was his new acquaintance, Anton.

Asen considered applauding, but nobody else did, so he put his hands back down.

"Welcome, welcome, friends." Anton stood behind the mahogany stand and picked up the gavel resting on it. "How wonderful you all look. Didn't you see on your invites where it said this was to be an informal occasion?"

The crowd erupted in laughter. Asen stayed silent.

"We've got a great selection of prized objects tonight, including, of course"—Anton winked at the crowd—"our big surprise. Let's begin!"

This time, there was applause. Asen was a second too late to join it.

What followed was a long procession of magical objects which Anton brought to the stage, each received by oohing and aahing from the crowd. There was everything, from simple good-luck charms crafted from rabbit paws to ancient curses sealed in jars. Asen shuffled uncomfortably when a heart-shaped bottle of blood-red liquid came up for sale. A love potion.

Love potions were nasty business. Not only because of their effect, which was, of course, unconscionable, but because of the way they had to be prepared. He'd heard of several different recipes, all involving "virgin" this, and "maiden" that, and "innocent" other.

Asen made sure to note down the description of the elderly gentleman who won that particular auction, so he could pass it over to Vartanian.

Finally, just when Asen was growing restless, the spotlights on the stage grew even brighter. Nearly complete darkness swallowed the audience. Anton waited until the hall was perfectly silent, and then pronounced, "And now, for the surprise!"

Several of Karaivanov's cronies dragged a cage onto the stage. Asen stood straighter in his seat, straining to make his tired eyes focus on the silhouette inside it, awash with light.

A loud wail sounded, as if from a bird of prey, and Asen immediately knew what—*who*—was in the cage. As if his eyes had refused to see it before, deeming it impossible, the contours of a large figure began to take shape, covered in waxy feathers.

She screeched again, high-pitched and terribly familiar. Asen would recognise this sound anywhere, after spending a full night listening to it, trapped in the cage on top of the Zmey's tower. A yuda.

The audience had been silent as the cage appeared onstage, but soon a low murmur spread among them. Then, they grew louder.

Asen watched as the yuda thrashed in her cage, hitting the bars with her chest. Through the crowd, her eyes caught his. They were bright, full of pleading, and disturbingly human.

She seemed completely real. Which, of course, she couldn't be. Firstly, because a yuda couldn't have stayed in the human world after the end of the Foul Days. And secondly, because a yuda couldn't have crossed the Wall.

Except, hadn't Malamir brought a karakonjul to Belograd only a few months ago? He'd coaxed it into jumping in the teleportation circle.

Asen had wondered how long it would be before someone else got the same idea. It all had to do with how good those teleportation spells of Karaivanov's were getting. Asen still remembered back when he'd worked for the smuggler, and they'd first developed a ring that could take you across the Wall. It worked roughly half the time. The other half, it tore the wearer apart from within. Asen and the rest of Karaivanov's thugs had spent many an afternoon scrubbing blood, guts, and brains off the walls.

Nowadays, the teleportation artefacts seemed to not only be a lot less dangerous, given how willing the smugglers were to use them, but could also transport multiple people at the same time. What was next? Entire families? Would public transport become obsolete if instead of taking the train or the ferry, people could draw a chalk circle and mumble a few magic words?

The only issue was, Asen knew how the teleportation spells were made. They required not only a skilled, experienced witch, but also her shadow. The only way to craft an artefact that powerful was to convince a witch to sacrifice her magic and die a slow death.

This was something all Chernogradeans instinctively knew, and Belogradeans often failed to understand. All magic had a price, and it never came cheap.

"Silence!" Anton shouted from the stage. "Silence, please!"

Slowly, the conversations died down. All that was left were the yuda's screeches.

Anton walked over to the cage. "She's beautiful, isn't she?" He extended a hand and reached through the bars to touch the yuda's head. She hissed and snapped her teeth at him. He quickly withdrew. "She's a bit wild, but that's half the fun, isn't it? Taming her yourself."

Bile burned in the back of Asen's throat. Even if this was some kind of a trick, and the cage didn't contain a real yuda, it held a living, breathing person. Karaivanov must have trapped a woman inside it, and then—who knew? Used some perverse combination of potions and surgery to create this disturbingly convincing disguise.

"So, dear guests." Anton clapped his hands. "May I hear your opening bids?"

Next to Asen, the man in the karakonjul fur hat raised his hand in the air. The spotlights, which must have been enchanted to detect movement, swirled towards him.

"Two hundred grosh!" Anton shouted. "Come on now, this is a real yuda. A prophetic bird from Chernograd. You can't let her go for any less than four hundred, can you?"

The spotlights shifted their position again, illuminating the mayor on her balcony. She waved her handheld glasses.

"Four hundred from the lady in red!" Anton announced.

What would the mayor of Belograd do with a yuda? She was known for collecting exotic birds in her aviary—but taking care of a flock of parakeets was one thing, feeding a yuda was something completely different.

Not to mention, a yuda was much closer to a human being than to a parrot. This was all wrong. All of it.

Asen knew he shouldn't draw attention to himself, but before he could think better of it, he'd lifted his hand in the air.

"Six hundred from the dark-haired gentleman in the middle row!" Anton proclaimed.

This was fine. Asen had savings. He'd been with the police for years, and he rarely splurged for extravagances, save from the occasional tailored piece of clothing. Other than that, his salary piled up in his bank account every month.

"Eight hundred from the lady in red!" Anton shouted. "A thousand from the man in the fur hat!"

With a sigh, Asen lifted his hand. There was a living being in that cage. He couldn't leave her there.

"A thousand five hundred! Two thousand!"

The next minute was a blur as the numbers kept growing, and so did Asen's dizziness. He couldn't even imagine that much money in one place.

"Five thousand from the lady in red!" Anton shouted.

The mayor looked down at Asen through her handheld glasses and winked at him.

He didn't have this much money. Even if he scraped every last grosh from his vault in the bank, even if he sold all his possessions, he wouldn't have this much.

With a sigh, he gave up.

Anton lifted his gavel in the air. "Going once, going twice . . ."

Asen didn't think he'd imagined the look of disdain in the yuda's eyes as she looked at him.

"Sold!"

5

Kosara

Kosara was asleep at the table again. Her neck was stiff. The tablecloth was cold and slightly damp beneath her face—she must have been drooling on it.

"Kosara!" Vila's voice echoed in the room. What was the old witch doing in Kosara's house? "Kosara, stop lazing about!"

Kosara opened one eye slowly, then the other one faster. She stood up straighter in her seat. Vila's face floated in the enormous crystal ball in the middle of the table.

"How the hell did you get in there?" Kosara asked, suddenly aware she wore nothing but a fluffy dressing gown with embroidered daisies and stains from the tripe soup she'd had for lunch.

She felt something stuck to her cheek and peeled it off. A playing card. The rest of the deck was spread on the table in front of her. She'd fallen asleep while trying to read the future.

"Never mind that." Pink smoke curled gently around Vila's face. Her forehead appeared distorted as she pressed it closer to the glass to peer at Kosara. "We might have a problem."

Kosara was suddenly completely awake. "What is it? Another murder?"

"Multiple. I met Ibrahim, the baker's boy. He told me about his henhouse."

Kosara tried to laugh. She wanted to dismiss whatever nonsense Ibrahim had spewed.

But then she saw Vila's face and realised the situation was more serious that she'd anticipated.

Kosara shuddered, remembering the page from her old bestiary. *The harbinger of death and plague.* Could this be related to Sofiya's murder?

No, that was nonsense. Even if some monstrous infestation had caused the hens' demise, Sofiya was a human being, and she'd most likely been murdered by one. There was no need for mythical monsters here. Not when people could do just as good a job.

Kosara asked, "Vila, have you heard of a monster called a 'mratinyak'?"

"I have, though not for many years. What made you think a mratinyak was involved?"

Kosara hesitated. What had, really? There had been nothing supernatural about the scene she'd found in Ibrahim's henhouse. All the hens had died peacefully in their sleep. Only the cockerel had appeared as if he'd fought for his life—but what? A monster? Or his own panic?

There had been something, Kosara realised. Something only her subconscious had registered, hidden deep under the stench of chicken shit and rotting fodder.

"The smell," Kosara said. "I smelled magic in the henhouse."

She expected Vila to dismiss her. Making outrageous claims about the presence of long-forgotten monsters based on nothing but a smell was ridiculous.

Instead, the old witch's frown deepened, burrowing grooves in the corners of her mouth. "What kind of magic?"

"Not ours. From the monsters' realm."

"Are you sure?"

"I am. At least, I think so." Kosara paused. "But that's not possible. It's almost the summer, nowhere near the Foul Days. I must have made a mistake."

Except, Kosara couldn't deny the weather had been awfully strange for June. Was it possible that was a symptom of a bigger problem? Were the Foul Days closer than she'd thought?

"I think you're right," Vila said grimly. "I don't think you're mistaken."

"But Vila—"

"Last night, I was awoken by a great commotion. My house shook. I ran outside, thinking it must be an earthquake, and what do you think I saw? A huge chicken footprint in the mud."

"Vila," Kosara said gently, "your house has chicken legs."

"Do you take me for an old fool? Don't you think I considered that? It was bigger than my house's feet."

A shiver ran up Kosara's spine. A monster bigger than a house? That didn't bode well.

"I believe," Vila continued, "the mratinyak tried to claim my house, but it fought back. The next time, it might fail in scaring the monster away."

Kosara swore under her breath. "How is this possible? How could the mratinyak find its way down here outside of the Foul Days?"

"Someone must have summoned it. Someone must have dragged it out of the monster realm by the tail, and that's why it's so angry."

"Who?"

Vila sighed deeply. "I have no idea."

Kosara looked at her for a long while, expecting some kind of clarification, which never came. Vila knew everything that happened in Chernograd. Her seer powers were legendary, and she kept tabs on every witch and warlock in the city. Kosara couldn't use a pimple-concealing spell without the old witch finding out.

"The person who's summoned it must be very strong." Vila ran a hand through her hair. It fell down her shoulders, stark white. "Or maybe I'm getting old."

Kosara stopped her eyes before they'd traced the deepening lines on Vila's face. The old witch was ancient, of course—she'd seen things Kosara had only read about in dusty tomes. Yet, Kosara had never considered she might actually age. For as long as Kosara could re-member, she'd been there. She'd always looked the same, the one thing in the city that never changed.

"Don't be silly," Kosara said quickly. "You must have got a fright, that's why your spells aren't working properly. You should rest."

"You're probably right," Vila said, which was worrying on its own. She never admitted someone else was right this easily. "Let me know if you discover something."

And then, she was gone. All that remained in the crystal ball was rolling pink smoke.

Kosara stretched and the chair beneath her groaned. The fire in the hearth had long died, and the cold had sunk deep in her bones, making her stiff.

She needed to go to bed and catch up on sleep. It promised to be another long day, with her first appointment set for the early morning. A tourist from Belograd had got too drunk on home-brewed rakia and had lost his vision temporarily, but he was convinced he'd been cursed and wanted Kosara to find the perpetrator. At least he paid well.

Her eyes fell on the playing cards spread on the table. She was going to go to bed, but first, she had to figure out what was happening to Chernograd's chickens.

Kosara tried laying down the cards as she always did, in a cross: one side for the past, one for the future, one for her choices, one for the possible outcomes. She got nothing, other than a series of clubs and spades, foretelling some vague danger.

"Tell me something new," Kosara muttered, and tried again.

Once more, the cards showed her nothing useful. They wouldn't even reveal what danger she faced, let alone point her to its source.

Kosara sighed. She knew what she had to do.

With numb fingers, she undid her shadow necklace. The beads were smooth, waxy, and warm to the touch, about the same tempera-ture as her skin.

She slid them off the chain one by one and rolled them between her palms. They morphed in her hands, becoming larger and less corpo-real, leaking darkness between her fingers.

Once finished, she was surrounded by shadows. They spilled over the walls and surfaces like ink. Some floated several steps in the air and circled her curiously. Others twirled and whirled around her fast, obviously relieved to be free again. Their whispers echoed in Kosara's mind. In the tumult, she could barely make out a single word.

"Be quiet," she said. "Please."

She knew they wouldn't listen. They never listened.

"I need your help," Kosara almost shouted so they'd hear her.

Finally, it was Kosara's shadow that ushered the rest into some semblance of order. They stopped their dance and surrounded her, towering over her, watching her without eyes. For a moment, a brief but sweet moment, the room was quiet.

"I need to know who summoned the mratinyak," Kosara said.

That got them talking again. Their voices rose like a wave, suffocating her own thoughts. She only made out a word or a phrase here and there, "a monster" and "chickens" and "oh no, not again."

"Concentrate," Kosara ordered them, and most of them quieted down. She had no illusions it was because she had power over them. They were simply being polite.

However, a couple kept chattering quietly in the corners of Kosara's mind. Those were the ones she could never shut up. Their words were muffled, barely audible, but she recognised the Zmey's name coming up over and over again. What was even more disturbing, she saw him in her peripheral vision, a pale figure lurking in the dark.

He wasn't really there, she knew—he was merely a figment of the shadows' imagination, fed straight into her mind. She still found it difficult to ignore him. Trickles of cold sweat ran down her spine under her shirt.

"I need you all to concentrate," she repeated and shut her eyes, so she wouldn't be tempted to look at him.

She grabbed the cards again. Her hands were clammy and awkward, but she managed to shuffle the deck quickly. After many years of practice, her fingers knew how to on their own.

Kosara's magic stirred. The shadows' voices filled her head, an impenetrable wall of sound, but she also felt the shadows themselves, sliding under her skin. If she opened her eyes, she thought she'd see her veins running black with them. Their power poured into her.

She was too afraid to look. If she did, would it be her own eyes she looked out of, or theirs? Would she see the present or their pasts, the ones they'd all been so desperate to show her before?

Kosara couldn't go through it again. She'd sat through their visions once, in an attempt to piece together what had happened to their owners. She'd watched the Zmey from so many angles. She'd seen his eyes, first filled with adoration, then with hatred. She'd felt his touch, first gentle, then painful. His hands had run all over her body, except it hadn't been her body—it had been the bodies of eleven other women.

She'd felt their love for him. And then, their heartbreak. Again, and again, and again.

No, she thought, she wouldn't open her eyes. With them firmly shut, she grasped the cards with trembling fingers. She was going to arrange them, as usual, in a cross. One side for the future, one for the past, one for her choices, one for the consequences.

But her hands shook, and her fingers pulsated with her own magic and that of eleven other witches. She couldn't take it anymore. She threw the cards up in the air.

"Who summoned the mratinyak?" she shouted.

Her ears popped. The fine hairs on her arms prickled. The room filled with the smell of magic.

The shadows' murmur died down. For a long moment, Kosara sat there, in the silence, with her eyes squeezed shut. Then, taking a deep breath, she opened them.

The cards had all landed on the table, face up, arranged in the shapes of letters. Letters that formed a name.

Sofiya.

6

Asen

Once the auction was over, it became obvious most guests had come prepared. Some left immediately, using various enchanted artefacts. Others joined the long queue in front of the stage where Anton had drawn a teleportation circle. They each tipped him, placing several grosh in his extended hand, and he activated the circle for them, making them vanish.

Asen scanned the crowd, trying to spot the mayor. Chances were, she'd been ushered out of the building as soon as the auction had finished. The cage with the yuda had long disappeared.

Feeling defeated, Asen joined the queue. He rummaged through his pockets, looking for change, when he heard a familiar voice.

"So, we meet again." The mayor appeared next to him and wrapped her hand around his forearm.

"Mayor." He nodded at her. He tried to seem vaguely disinterested, playing hard to get, but secretly, he heaved a huge sigh of relief. There was a chance still his trip to the auction hadn't been for naught.

"Please," the mayor said. "Call me Maria."

"*Maria,*" he deliberately lingered on her name. "I thought you'd have been whisked out of here by your admirers by now."

The mayor shrugged. "I came to find you. You seem to be a man of mystery, Kostas, and I can't bear to leave a mystery unsolved. I didn't know you were interested in exotic birds."

"Birds?"

"Well, given how viciously you fought for the yuda . . ."

"Ah, yes, of course. I love birds. Parakeets are my favourite."

"What a coincidence! I happen to keep a large flock in my aviary. Do you want to see them?"

Asen's smile was measured despite the fact that internally, he was rejoicing. "I'd like nothing more."

"Come!" The mayor grabbed him by the forearm and led him through the crowd. Instead of marching to the teleportation circle at Anton's feet, as Asen had expected, they walked in the opposite direction, towards the hall's double doors.

"Where are we going?" Asen asked.

"Oh, Konstantin knows I can't stand teleportation. It makes me dizzy. So, he lets me borrow one of his carriages to come to the auction."

"He's not worried the people accompanying you will discover this building's location?"

"He is. Which is why I have to insist to cover your eyes."

She produced a silk ribbon. Asen reached for it, but she playfully evaded him.

"Let me." She walked behind him, and the heady smell of her perfume enveloped him.

First, she tied the ribbon over his eyes. Then, with swift fingers, she wrapped another one around his wrists.

Her hand found his forearm again, and she dragged him through a squeaky door, along a musty-smelling corridor. Asen had no choice but to follow.

While he'd been looking for the mayor, he'd finally got the chance to examine the building. He quickly realised it wasn't an old opera house—it was an ancient chapel. The velvet seats, the heavy curtains, and the stage were all modern additions. The stone columns and the arched ceiling, however, were original.

Tall windows were hidden behind the curtains, but no light leaked through them. This could only mean one thing: they were underground.

Belograd was an ancient city. Hundreds of generations had inhabited it, building their houses, palaces, and temples on the remains of older, half-buried ones. Under the city, entire streets were preserved.

This was why when the mayor led him into what felt like a closet, then shut the door and pulled a creaky lever, he wasn't surprised as the room shook and began climbing.

"Are we in a lift?" he asked.

"Rich, handsome, *and* smart," the mayor purred. "You're full of surprises, Kostas."

It took them nearly a minute to make it to the surface. Once they walked out of the lift, the mayor didn't remove the ribbon over Asen's eyes. She pulled him after her. He couldn't tell by the sounds surrounding them or the feel of the cobblestones under his feet in which part of the city they were. His only clue was the air, thick and moist, smelling vaguely of seaweed. They had to be close to the Docks.

"Take us straight home, Ivan," the mayor said to someone, and then she guided Asen to climb the stairs to her carriage. She pushed him into a soft seat with both her hands against his chest.

Outside, the coachman shouted at the horses. Their hooves hit the cobblestones, and the carriage wobbled forwards.

The mayor moved closer to Asen, but she didn't make to untie him. He tried to lounge back and appear unperturbed, but on the inside, he was beginning to worry. He was completely alone with one of the most powerful women in the city. What would he have to do to win her favour? How far was he willing to go?

Not as far, he suspected, as she would have liked him to. Asen was aware, in a distant, almost academic way, that she was attractive. He considered her pleasant to the eye in the way a painting or a nice garden would be. Though she was attractive, he was by no means *attracted* to her. There were many qualities Asen found himself drawn to in a person, some of them rather unconventional—but being a corrupt politician did not feature on the list.

He started to prepare an excuse, a fiancée he'd left back home or an old friend he was desperately devoted to, his mind summoning the image of Kosara on its own. But then, he felt the mayor's fingers on the back of his head, untying his eyes. Once the silken ribbon fell in his lap, the mayor was sitting across from him in the carriage. She didn't untie his hands.

Her face had changed. There were no smiles. No fluttering eyelashes.

Maria Hajieva had become all business. "So, the padishah of Stambul, huh?"

Asen froze. Had the mayor recognised him? He should have known this had all gone too well. He'd thought he'd got unbelievably lucky, and he'd been right. It was unbelievable. Why had he believed it, then?

He remained silent. He'd participated in enough interrogations to know silence was usually the best strategy—though, admittedly, he was normally the one asking the questions.

"I happen to be good friends with the padishah of Stambul," the mayor said, matter-of-factly. "We exchange letters regularly. You know who else I like to write to? The padishah of Stambul's wife."

Asen said nothing.

"So, you can imagine my surprise when I heard about her untimely demise. So, tell me, *Kostas,*" she spat out the name. "Who are you spying for?"

Asen tried not to show it, but he relaxed in his seat a little. The mayor hadn't recognised him. She suspected him of being a spy.

"Nobody." He kept up his ridiculous accent. He looked at her through his dark lashes and smiled ruefully, a move which had got him out of sticky situations before. "I'm sorry I lied to you, Maria. I simply didn't think you'd be interested in helping me, had you known I'm nothing but a simple silk merchant with no real connections. The story I told you is true."

"You can't expect me to believe that."

"Why would I lie? The story is true. Except, it's not the padishah's dead wife I want to find a way to communicate with. It's mine."

Asen kept looking at the mayor. He was a good liar, but he was even better at telling the truth.

He missed Boryana every day. He'd have given anything to speak to her again. All he wanted was to apologise to her—face to face.

He could never do that. Part of Boryana had stayed in the realm of the living, but it wasn't a part with which it was possible to converse. Asen had tried before.

The only thing he could do for his wife's spirit was to make sure her murderer was brought to justice. He had to find Karaivanov.

"You must take me for a soft-hearted fool," the mayor said. Her face showed none of the compassion Asen had hoped for. "I will wring your secrets out of you, Kostas, believe me. For now, I have just the perfect place for you."

"Where?"

"As you're aware, I have a soft spot for pretty things. So, I'm going to add you to my collection." She peeked through the curtain of her carriage window, and then said, almost as an afterthought, "Let's hope the yuda I just purchased isn't hungry."

The cage was cramped with Asen and the yuda both in there. Every time he shuffled, trying to find a comfortable position inside it, his shoulder brushed against her feathers. The mayor had replaced the silk ribbon tying his hands with a pair of handcuffs, bright pink and fluffy. He suspected they were usually reserved for more pleasant activities.

To make matters worse, the damned parakeets were small enough to fit through the cage's bars, and they kept sweeping past him, shrieking loudly, and nibbling his ears.

This whole situation reminded Asen of when he'd last been caged, atop the Zmey's tallest tower. Just like then, all he saw were stars, though this time, he watched them through the glass dome of the aviary. The Zmey's cage had been freezing cold—the aviary was oppressively warm.

The feeling of being trapped and helpless, however, was just the same.

Asen's one hope was the fact that when she'd searched him, the mayor had found his gun, but not the lockpick stuffed deep in a hidden pocket. Asen had been working on the handcuffs with it for hours, though he'd had little luck so far. The handcuffs were obviously old, and the mechanism had grown rusty.

"So, how's your night going?" he asked the yuda while he struggled with the lockpick.

She stared at him with her gleaming eyes for a long while, but never replied. It had been a stupid question, anyway.

"You know Sokol?" Asen said. He figured the answer to that question might help him determine whether the yuda was real or some elaborate hoax.

"Sokol?" she croaked.

"Yes, Sokol. You must have met her. A bit taller than you, with more purple in her plumage." Asen paused. "She saved my life once."

Before the yuda could respond, the door to the aviary opened, and a spindly middle-aged man walked in. First, he filled the parakeet's feeders with a mountain of leafy greens, carrots, and cucumber slices. Then, he approached the cage carefully, his eyes fixed on the yuda. In his hands, he carried a bloody cow leg.

"Hi, friend," Asen greeted him. "Have you brought me anything? I'm feeling a bit peckish."

The man ignored him. Without saying a word, he placed the cow's leg on the ground next to the cage.

The yuda wrinkled her nose, but then, her stomach grumbled loudly. The meat was too fresh for her, Asen knew, but beggars couldn't be choosers. The yuda tried to peck at it through the cage's bars, but they were too closely spaced. She couldn't fit her head through them.

Asen narrowed his eyes at her. She could have used her hands to bring the cow's leg inside the cage. She wasn't an animal. He opened his mouth to say as much when she threw him a sharp look over her shoulder. The message in her eyes was clear: be quiet.

He finally realised what she was doing. Asen knew the yuda could use her hands—the other man didn't. He probably saw her as an overgrown parakeet.

Clever. Asen's attempts to free himself from the handcuffs grew more frantic, though he was careful to keep his back turned to the man.

After watching the yuda struggle for a while, the man sighed. He took his revolver out of its holster and held it tightly in his right hand. With his left, he unlocked the cage. When he leaned over to grab the piece of meat, the yuda saw her chance.

She rushed out of the cage and pushed the man down.

He swore as his back hit the ground. He wasn't an experienced shooter. The bullets flew everywhere, crashing against the floor and the bird feeders, ricocheting, and making tiny holes in the glass dome. They flew everywhere—but at the yuda.

At last, the gun ran out of bullets. The man, with a panicked look in his eyes, shook it, as if that would help. When it still wouldn't fire, he threw it at the yuda. This time, ironically, he didn't miss. He hit her squarely between the eyes.

The yuda had been patient with the man, Asen could tell. She'd tried not to hurt him. None of this was his fault—he was simply doing his job.

Except, now he'd gone a step too far. The yuda wailed and hit him with her talons. The man flew through the aviary and slammed his head on the corner of a bird feeder. The parakeets, startled, flew around him, shrieking, but he didn't react. His head lolled, eyes shut.

Asen watched in awe as the yuda prepared to take flight. She stretched out her wings, filling most of the aviary. How did the mayor ever think she could keep a Chernogradean monster caged like a simple pet?

"Wait!" Asen shouted. "Take me with you!"

The yuda turned to look at him, and that single moment of hesitation almost cost her life. A crossbow bolt flew past her ear.

Asen spun towards its source. The mayor stood in the doorframe, in her nightgown, with rollers in her hair. Her green face mask cracked when she smiled a vicious smile. She recharged her crossbow, pointing it at the yuda.

"I heard the commotion," the mayor said calmly. "I thought it would be you, Kostas, not her. Or should I call you 'Detective Asen Bakharov'?"

Asen's heartbeat quickened, but only for a second. So, she'd figured it out. He should have expected as much.

This, of course, meant that even if he made it out of this alive, his days in the police force were numbered. Maria Hajieva would do anything in her power to get him fired and undermine his word before he could expose her connections to the smugglers.

Asen, with mild surprise, realised he didn't care. His days in the police force had been numbered, anyway. His boss no longer trusted him, and he didn't trust her. Worse, he didn't trust himself. Every day, he found it harder and harder to tell right from wrong.

Besides, he couldn't dwell on his future career prospects right now. If he didn't get out of the aviary, there would be no future to worry about. The damned handcuffs still wouldn't budge. He kept pressing on the lockpick in a panic as the mayor prepared to take another shot.

The yuda's eyes were fixed on her, petrified.

"I knew I recognised you from somewhere," the mayor continued. "So, when I got home, I looked through my old newspaper clippings. It turns out we've met three times before, when I've personally handed you letters of commendation." She paused, the bolt still loaded onto her crossbow. "I like the beard."

"Thanks," Asen said through his teeth. *Come on,* he urged the lockpick. *Come on!*

He turned the lockpick once more, and finally, blissfully, the handcuffs clicked open. He caught them before they fell to the ground.

The mayor didn't show any sign she'd noticed. "As you can imagine, I can't let you walk, knowing what you know. It's a shame, really. You sound like a capable officer."

The mayor shifted her aim towards his forehead.

Asen threw the handcuffs in her face. She swore loudly. The bolt she loosed made a wide arc in the air, broke through the glass, and disappeared into the night.

The mayor stumbled to reload, but she was too late. Asen dove out of the cage towards the unconscious man's slumped figure and picked up the gun from the floor. The yuda watched him, neither moving to help him nor attempting an escape.

It was *his* gun, Asen realised. His police-issued revolver. The aviary's staff had never had much of a reason for a gun before, he supposed.

He also noticed something else—when it had hit the yuda, the revolver had broken. The rear sights were misaligned, and the cylinder had snapped off. He could only hope the mayor wouldn't see it in the aviary's gloom.

Asen pointed the gun at her. "Put the crossbow down."

She hesitated, and for a moment Asen worried she'd seen through his bluff. But then, slowly, without breaking eye contact, she placed the crossbow at her feet. She couldn't examine the gun in detail when the barrel was pointed at her face, Asen supposed.

"Will you take me with you?" Asen asked the yuda without moving the gun away from the mayor.

He expected a "no." He knew from Sokol how much yudas hated carrying people—they were too heavy and too clumsy. The yuda would need all her strength and agility to escape the aviary.

Instead of replying, she grabbed him by the collar with one long, curved talon, and helped him climb onto her back. Asen internally thanked his luck, which seemed to have turned yet again.

"You'll regret this, Bakharov!" the mayor shouted, and Asen suspected she was right, in a way. There was a lot of danger involved in owing a favour to a monster. What he'd regret even more, however, would be staying trapped in the aviary. "You won't find a moment's peace in all of Belograd, I can promise you this much!"

The yuda flapped her wings once, rising into the air, making the mayor's nightgown flutter in the wind.

"Hold on tight!" the yuda shouted.

Asen was glad he listened, because the next second, they burst through the glass dome. The noise as it shattered was deafening. In the last moment, Asen managed to hide his face in his hands, though he felt a few tiny shards piercing his skin.

Then, they were flying out into the night. The yuda ascended until the aviary was barely visible, a dark patch among Belograd's lights.

"Why?" he shouted, so she'd hear him over the howling of the wind. "You could have left me there."

The yuda shrugged her shoulder, making Asen lean to one side. He held on to her tighter. Her feathers were cold and waxy in his fingers.

"You said you were a friend of Sokol's."

Asen hadn't said that, not exactly, but he wasn't about to correct her. "You know Sokol?"

"She's my sister."

"I see." Asen paused. Then, because he was brought up to be polite even in the direst of circumstances, he added, "My name is Asen. Nice to meet you."

"I'm Vrana." The yuda was silent for a long while, her gaze fixed straight ahead. Far below, the lights of Belograd flickered. "Was it true, what that horrible woman said? Are you really a detective?"

"I am."

Another pause. "Sokol's missing. She's been gone for days. Can you find her?"

"Find her? In the monster realm?"

"Don't be silly. You won't last a minute in the monster realm. No, she went to Chernograd. She went to look for Roksana."

Asen frowned, sure in his shock he must have misunderstood her. "How? It's not the Foul Days. The monster realm is supposed to be shut to our world."

"*Supposed to be,*" Vrana said mockingly. "Things haven't been like they were supposed to for a good while, copper. Ever since the Zmey disappeared, everything's changed."

"Why?"

"Who knows? All I can tell you is this: cracks have started to appear in the barrier between our world and yours. Sokol managed to sneak through one of them. I followed in her steps. Then, the slavers caught me. I'm afraid something similar must have happened to Sokol. Or worse."

A chill ran down Asen's spine. This whole thing had Karaivanov's greasy fingerprints all over it.

"Do you remember anything about where they kept you?" he asked. "Before you ended up at the auction house?"

"I do. A storage container in the Chernogradean river district."

"And did you see him? Karaivanov himself?"

Vrana seemed confused. "The short man with the glasses? I saw him."

Asen swore internally. Deep down, he'd always known this was where his chase would lead him. Back to Chernograd.

Perhaps it was for the best. It was the perfect place to hide until Maria Hajieva's wrath had subsided.

"Well?" Vrana asked. "Will you help me find her, or did I get you out of that cage for nothing?"

Asen didn't think he'd imagined the threat in the yuda's voice. He wasn't prepared to find out what a yuda could do to a man's body with those scimitar-like talons, and he was even less keen to discover just how sharp her notoriously sharp teeth were.

Besides, Vrana had just given him an important clue. The next step in his endless pursuit of Karaivanov.

"I'll help you," he said.

While Asen could cross the Wall by foot, Vrana could not, and she was unable to fly over it, either. He only hesitated for a second before he took one last confident step down Crooked Cop Lane.

"Where are we going?" Vrana asked, as the two rushed along Belograd's dark streets. It was still the middle of the night, so Vrana didn't attract too much unwanted attention. In the darkness, her plumage could pass for an extravagant coat, while the feathers on her head resembled an elaborate hairdo. Worse fashion crimes had been committed on the streets of Belograd.

"The police station," Asen said.

Vrana frowned. "Why?"

"I'm hoping to find a way to get you over the Wall."

He left her waiting outside, hiding in the dark hallway of a block of flats, while he snuck in. The night shift was only two sleepy coppers, playing cards in the break room, and neither spotted him as he tiptoed to the evidence room.

Once there, he used his key to break into a filing cabinet and retrieve what he was looking for: an amulet recently confiscated from one of Karaivanov's cronies. It was an older model, requiring you to get close to the Wall before it would work, but at least it involved no complicated spells or incantations. He'd be able to use it to transport both himself and Vrana across.

On his way to the exit, as he passed by his office, he considered leaving a note. He could try to explain what had transpired to his boss before the mayor had managed to spread her lies. After so many years with the police, it felt wrong to simply leave.

Screw it. His boss could think whatever she wanted.

He left the police station without looking back.

The first thing Asen noticed once they made it to the other side of the Wall was how bloody freezing it was. The cold cut straight through his linen shirt and his light trousers, soaking deep into his bones and making his teeth clatter.

He'd heard from colleagues who'd visited Chernograd recently that the city was dealing with unusually cold weather. It also seemed to have stayed just as violent as he'd last seen it during the Foul Days. Lila had returned with her ear bitten off by an upir she'd met at the dance hall. Valeri the pathologist now refused to examine a corpse before silver coins had been placed on its eyes.

High above, Chernograd's spires towered, their lit windows watching him without blinking. Next to him, Vrana stumbled and fell to her knees near a pile of rubbish. She was heaving, obviously travel sick after using the amulet.

Asen looked at her, and for a single shameful moment, he considered leaving her there. Being back in Chernograd brought too many memories.

What was he doing here, chasing after Karaivanov again? He knew very well he didn't belong in this city. The last time, he'd barely made it out alive. In fact, he wouldn't have, if it wasn't for Kosara.

Kosara. A lump stuck in his throat.

He hadn't had the courage to see her for the past six months, and he was about to turn up at her doorstep and ask for help. What made him think she wouldn't simply tell him to get lost? She'd have every right to.

As if reading his thoughts, Vrana looked up at him. "Don't even think about running away, copper. You said you'd help."

Asen gave her a tight smile. He couldn't run away. He'd made Boryana a promise, and he'd be damned if he broke it. He had to continue chasing Karaivanov, no matter how tiny the crumbs the smuggler left behind were.

There were two things he knew for sure. One, he'd just been dragged into deep trouble by a desperate yuda. And two, when he was in trouble and there were monsters involved, one person could reliably either get him out or sink even deeper with him.

He had to see Kosara.

7

Kosara

Sofiya had summoned the mratinyak. This was bad news—it meant that any chance of convincing her to simply send the monster back to its realm had died with her.

Feeling rather foolish, Kosara unveiled the crystal ball and knocked on it.

"Hello?" she said. "Vila? Are you in there?"

There was no response. Kosara tried again, this time louder. When Vila didn't reply, Kosara grabbed the hand mirror she usually used for calling the old witch and wiped the dust off the surface with her sleeve. It took several taps before Vila's face floated inside.

"What time is it?" she barked instead of a greeting. Her eyes were puffy and red-rimmed, and her hair was tangled.

"Um, about seven. Sorry. I have a client coming in at half past, so I thought we'd better get this out of the way."

Vila waved a hand. "It's fine. You woke me up, that's all. I haven't been sleeping well."

Kosara shuddered, remembering her own restless night. The Zmey's voice still echoed in her mind. *Why did you leave me here, Kosara? It's so dark, I can't see. Are you coming back for me?*

"I'm sorry," Kosara repeated. "I just thought you should know. I asked the shadows to help me find out who summoned the mratinyak."

"And? What did they say?"

"Sofiya."

Vila cursed under her breath. "Peachy. So, what do you think? Someone forced her to do it before killing her?"

"Possibly. Or maybe she'd already summoned it, and they tried to make her send it away. Except, it ended badly."

"Why would she have summoned it?"

"Who knows? Maybe she's got a grudge against someone who keeps hens."

Vila stared at Kosara, unblinking. "You don't get it, do you?"

"What?"

"You haven't stopped and thought about why the mratinyak is such a dangerous beast."

Kosara frowned. Chickens were important for Chernograd's economy, of course. They were perfect to keep in small gardens and on balconies. Besides, they could be brought from Belograd. Bigger livestock was difficult to transport through the Wall, even now that it would freely let them through. Cows and sheep went into a frenzy if you tried to make them approach it.

Eggs were a key source of protein, especially in the winter, and Kosara liked omelettes as much as the next Chernogradean, but—

Then it dawned on her. "Oh," she said, her eyes widening.

"Oh," Vila imitated her.

"The first cockerel's crow on St. Yordan's Day. Without cockerels, there's no one to send the monsters back to their own realm once the Foul Days are over."

"Yes. Precisely. It took you long enough."

"So whoever summoned the mratinyak here is someone who wants the monsters to remain in the city forever?"

"Perhaps. If they truly knew what they were doing. Except, I can't for the life of me figure out who that could be."

The Zmey, was the first thought that crossed Kosara's mind. It was nonsense. The Zmey was gone.

She shuddered. "We're in huge trouble, aren't we?"

"No," Vila said carefully. "Not yet. There's still time. We have half a year until the Foul Days, and plenty of chickens the mratinyak hasn't managed to get its talons into."

Kosara licked her lips. Did they have half a year, truly? Or did this unusually cold summer point to their time quickly running out?

Last night, when she'd got up to use the toilet, she could swear she saw the bathroom spirit, sitting cross-legged in the bathtub—until she blinked, and he was gone.

"But what if more monsters come?" she asked in a small voice.

Vila waved a hand dismissively, but Kosara knew her too well not to have noticed the fear in her eyes. "Let's not go borrowing trouble, all right? We should concentrate on solving Sofiya's murder."

Kosara shook her head. She couldn't worry about one part of this mess, but not another—the mratinyak, Sofiya's murder, the barrier between the realms of people and monsters crumbling six months too early. It was all connected.

"I've been thinking about the murderer," she said. "It must have been someone she knew. She must have given them her shadows voluntarily."

"Not necessarily. Aren't you meant to be good at this whole investigative business? We don't know if her shadows are related to her murder. I haven't seen Sofiya in ages. Maybe she traded them for something months ago."

"Like what?"

"An ingredient necessary to summon the mratinyak, maybe?" Vila paused. "No, you're right. It doesn't sound much like Sofiya to trade her shadows."

Kosara was about to remark that from what she'd seen, Sofiya would have traded her own granny for the right price, but she swallowed it. It was tasteless, speaking ill of the dead.

The grandfather clock in the hallway banged once. Kosara's client would turn up at any minute. "Listen," she said, "I need to go now, but I will . . ."

Kosara trailed off. What could she possibly do to find a murderer who'd committed the perfect murder? She had no clues to follow. She didn't even have half a bloody fingerprint.

But then, she realised, she was approaching this from the wrong angle. She didn't need fingerprints and blood splatters and stray hairs found at the crime scene. She wasn't a goddamned copper—she was a witch.

"I'll ask my shadows to help," she said.

She hadn't expected Vila's reaction. The old witch flinched. "You be careful with those shadows."

"Why?"

"Have you looked at yourself in the mirror today?"

"I . . ." Kosara frowned. "I haven't. Why?"

"Kosara. Your left eye." Vila licked her lips. "It's green."

"My what is what?" Kosara touched her eye, as if that would somehow help her see it. She waved Vila away in the mirror. "Step to the side. I need to see."

"I'd better go," Vila said, obviously uncomfortable. "You're not the only witch who's got a busy day planned. But listen to me: every time you use those shadows, they use you. Be careful."

Then, she disappeared. The mirror became just a mirror once more.

In its silvery surface, Kosara saw herself. Her left eye wasn't its usual dark brown. It was bright green, rimmed with yellow.

She swore loudly and threw the mirror across the room. It didn't shatter. Instead, it slid gently under the sofa, disturbing a family of spiders who rushed out, wobbly on their many legs.

The trouble was, Kosara recognised that green eye. She'd seen it before, looking back at her from an old painting glued to a crumbling headstone. It belonged to Smirna Koleva, who'd married the Zmey one New Year's Eve forty years ago. Smirna's shadow was currently strung as a bead around Kosara's neck.

Kosara had watched Smirna die at the Zmey's hands through the visions the shadows had manifested. She swore again and rubbed her eye until it hurt, as if she could simply wipe the green off it.

Someone knocked loudly on the front door, making Kosara jump. She straightened her shirt and dusted it with her hand. While she walked down the hallway, she ran her fingers through her hair, since she hadn't had time to brush it. If only she'd had a couple more minutes to dab some concealer on her under-eye circles—

Another knock. God, he was impatient. "Give me a second!" Kosara shouted. "Looking for my keys!"

She finally found them in her pocket, in among several dirty handkerchiefs, and unlocked the door. "I'm sorry for the delay, but—"

Except, it wasn't the Belogradean tourist she found on the other side. It was Roksana.

"What the hell?" Kosara tried to slam the door in Roksana's face.

The monster hunter was faster. Her leather boot landed between the door and the frame. "Please hear me out!"

It was only then that Kosara noticed Roksana wasn't alone. A slumped figure leaned on her shoulder. His dark hair fell in front of his face, but even so, Kosara recognised him. Malamir. The two made an unexpected pair, given what Kosara knew about their last encounter, when Malamir had ended up in the hospital.

Roksana had one large hand around his shoulders, gently supporting him. He appeared to be asleep—or, what was more likely, unconscious.

"I see you two have made up," Kosara spat out. She was about to ask if Malamir had maybe had a few too many, but then she realised she didn't care. She leaned her shoulder against the door, trying to push Roksana's boot away.

"Kosara," Roksana said without budging. She took a deep breath, as if the next words pained her: "I need your help."

Kosara barked a laugh. "You need my help? After everything you did? You have the audacity to come here—"

"Please. I didn't know who else to go to."

Kosara rolled her eyes. As if she'd fall for this obvious guilt trip. "Roksana, I don't know what mess you've got yourselves into this time, and, frankly, I don't care. Now, leave before I turn you into a frog."

"You can do that?"

"Why don't you wait and find out?"

Roksana waved a hand. "It doesn't matter. It's not me. It's Sokol."

Kosara hesitated, still holding the door. Sokol had saved her from the Zmey's cage. Sokol had found the rakia and the rags Kosara had used to disinfect Asen's wounds. Kosara owed her, and a witch always paid her debts.

"Please," Roksana repeated. "Can we come in? Just for five minutes? Malamir's not well, and it's fucking freezing out here."

Kosara sighed deeply and stepped back. Roksana stumbled in, supporting Malamir. He hung off her shoulder like a limp piece of meat. The only reason Kosara was certain he wasn't dead was that his chest rose and fell in quick succession.

Roksana dragged him to the sofa and dumped him there, on top of a pile of clean laundry Kosara had never got around to folding and putting away.

"What's wrong with him?" Kosara's every instinct screamed at her to check on him, but she resisted. Neither Roksana nor Malamir deserved her help.

"He tried to give me information."

"About?"

"About Sokol." Roksana played with the end of her braid, letting it slide between her fingers. "Listen, here's the deal. Sokol and I planned to run away together."

"Run? Where?"

"I don't know. Mesambria? I heard they have great beaches. Or maybe Irinopol."

Kosara frowned, imagining Sokol's feathery body, clad in a swimsuit, sunbathing on the beaches of Mesambria. "Roksana, Sokol is a yuda."

"I know that. I found someone who can take care of it."

"How?"

"Have you heard of the face merchant?"

"I can't say that I have."

Roksana leaned in closer, her eyes intense. "They say the face merchant knows magic that can transform someone completely. Make them unrecognisable."

Kosara rolled her eyes. This was just like Roksana, falling for an obvious scam. "That's nonsense. There's no such magic."

"That you know of. Believe it or not, you don't know everything."

Kosara scoffed. She certainly knew more about magic than Roksana. "As nice as this all sounds, how were you planning on getting Sokol out? She's trapped in the monster realm until the Foul Days. And then, once the first cockerel crows on St. Yordan's Day . . ." Kosara trailed off. The way things were going, there might not be a single cockerel left in Chernograd by then.

Roksana waved a hand. "I'll worry about the bloody cockerels when the time comes. Who knows if they can affect her if she manages to leave Chernograd?"

"That still doesn't solve the obvious problem. Sokol is trapped in the monster realm until the Foul Days." Kosara hesitated, her dread growing. "Isn't she?"

"She found a way to escape."

"How?" Kosara asked, even though she suspected she knew the answer.

"You know Sofiya?"

"Of course I know Sofiya." It had been a stupid question. There weren't that many witches in Chernograd, and they all knew each other.

"Well, Sofiya had figured out a way to break through the barrier between our two realms. She promised she'd get Sokol out. But then . . ."

Kosara swore internally. This was all coming full circle. "But then she died."

"Yeah. Except, she got murdered after Sokol would have already arrived. Sokol told me she was coming a few nights back. I went to the agreed place to meet her. She never showed up."

"Maybe she's been delayed."

"That's what I thought, but she would have found a way to contact me, you know? She must have known I'd be worried sick. And then, Malamir turned up." Roksana threw him a worried look. "He knows something, but he can't tell me."

"Why?"

"That fucking symbol on his chest. Karaivanov's mark. It keeps hurting him."

Kosara shuddered, remembering how Asen's symbol had burned him.

She wasn't surprised Karaivanov was involved in this. If Sofiya had somehow broken through the barrier between the human world and the realm of monsters, the old smuggler would have likely been very interested in it.

Kosara remembered the symbol carved on Sofiya's chest. The witch had worked for Karaivanov. Was it possible it had been him who'd paid her to drag monsters down to the human world? First the mratinyak, and then Sokol? Had Sofiya never planned to reunite the yuda with Roksana at all?

Or had Sofiya tried to go behind his back, which was why she'd been murdered?

"You know, Karaivanov tried to brand me, back in the day," Roksana said. "When I did a few odd jobs for him. I told him, 'No fucking way.' Frankly, I can't believe Malamir agreed to it."

"His mum's ill," Kosara said absent-mindedly. "He'd have agreed to anything."

"Is she? What's wrong with her?"

"He never told me. All I know is she requires an operation, and the waiting list at the hospital stretches years. She'll die waiting unless he slides a few hundred grosh into the right hand. And guess what the easiest way to obtain a few hundred grosh in this damned city is?"

"This makes a lot more sense all of a sudden." Roksana looked at him again. "I figured you might come up with some way to help him. Since you know your curses . . ."

"I have practically zero experience with curses. You need Vila."

"If Vila sees me, she'll bloody kill me. Please, Kosara. Do something."

Kosara sighed. Neither Roksana nor Malamir deserved her help— but she'd help them, soft-hearted fool that she was. It was her job, after all, wasn't it? Helping ungrateful bastards get out of whatever mess they'd got themselves into.

She kneeled on the floor next to the sofa. Malamir's eyes were shut, and little droplets of sweat rolled over his eyebrows and onto his cheeks. One of his hands grasped his chest through the wide neckline of his shirt. The symbol carved on it was aglow beneath his fingers, as if fresh from the branding iron.

With a sigh, Kosara got back up, hung the cauldron over the fire, and selected a few herbs hanging off the ceiling beam.

"What are you doing?" Roksana asked.

"For starters, an anaesthetic. Then, we'll see."

Kosara encouraged the fire with a click of her fingers and a few magic words, and soon, the water was boiling. The scent of eucalyptus, willow bark, and valerian filled the room.

She spread the mixture over a piece of cloth and waved it about for a minute so it would cool faster. Then, she leaned over Malamir and slowly, with great difficulty, pulled away his hand from the glowing brand. When she pressed the herbal mixture onto it, the brand pulsated under her fingers.

Malamir inhaled sharply through his teeth. For a second, the pain must have been unbearable. But then, the herbs began working their magic and Malamir relaxed. His breathing normalised. After a few seconds, his eyes fluttered open.

"Kosara?" he croaked. "What are you doing here?"

"You're in my house."

Malamir hesitantly lifted himself up on his elbows and looked around. His eyes fell on Roksana. "Roksana, what are we doing here?"

"You passed out. I didn't know what to do."

Malamir looked down at his chest where Kosara firmly pressed the cloth. It was starting to grow hotter under her fingers.

"What's that?" he asked.

"Anaesthetic," Kosara said. "The strongest one I could brew you in a hurry."

He licked his dry lips. "What happens when it loses its potency?"

"You'll probably pass out again."

Malamir groaned. "I promised I'd never betray him when he branded me. Can you believe it? What an idiot."

"I suspect he left you no choice."

"He didn't." Malamir looked at Kosara again and squinted. "Kosara, doll, why is one of your eyes green?"

Kosara, who'd momentarily forgotten about that, shook her head so her hair would fall in front of it. "Long story. So, Karaivanov's brand can do that now, huh?"

"He was very chuffed with it, believe me. The old model could only hurt you if you were within an arm's reach of him."

"Oh, I know. I've seen it."

"This one works over distance. 'A true magical innovation,' he called it."

"So," Roksana said impatiently. "Can you tell me where Sokol is or not?"

Malamir's fingers flinched towards the symbol on his chest. Kosara used this opportunity to grab his hand and make him press his own compress, so she could get up. Her knees were starting to hurt on the hard floor.

"Karaivanov is keeping her in an empty storage unit near the river," Malamir said. "I can take you there."

"Right." Roksana did up her coat. Then, with a murderous look in her eyes, she rushed towards the door. "Let's go."

"Wait." Kosara stepped in her way. "You can't possibly plan to take Karaivanov's entire gang alone."

"And who's going to help me? You?"

Kosara chewed on her lower lip. She remembered the promise she'd made Asen's dead wife very well. Perhaps, finally, this was her chance to locate Karaivanov. "Maybe I will. Just . . . Just sit down for a minute, will you? Let's take this one step at a time."

"Who knows what they're doing to Sokol while we're sitting around chatting!"

"Fair point, but—"

"They're doing nothing to her," Malamir said. "Karaivanov won't let a feather fall off her head; he told me as much himself. She's too important." Then, his face twisted in a grimace. "I think your poultice might be starting to lose its potency."

"Already?" Kosara shoved his hand away. The cloth resting against his chest burned. "Damn it."

"This isn't working," Roksana snapped. "Can't you remove it?"

Kosara gave her an even look. Roksana always got angry when she was scared, Kosara knew that, but she still didn't appreciate the monster hunter's tone of voice. "Remove what?"

"The symbol."

Kosara laughed. "If a random witch could erase Karaivanov's symbol, there wouldn't be much point to it, would it?"

"But you're not a random witch anymore, are you?"

Kosara's smile froze on her lips. She knew what Roksana was implying. Kosara's fingers found her left eye on their own—except, it wasn't her eye at all. It felt foreign beneath her fingertips. Too big, too round.

But that was nonsense, wasn't it? An eye was an eye. Green, brown, purple, who cared?

"I'll try," Kosara said. "I can't promise anything."

Under Malamir's pained gaze and Roksana's concerned one, she repeated the now familiar ritual: she took the beads off the chain one by one and placed them on the table. Then, she rolled them between her palms until every shadow had woken up.

Their dark forms filled the room. Their voices rushed inside her mind. Their visions flooded her eyesight.

It happened so fast, Kosara lost her balance. She managed to hold on to the table so she wouldn't crumple to the floor.

"Kosara?" Roksana's voice sounded like it came from very far away.

Kosara waved in her general direction to stay away. She didn't know what the shadows would do to the monster hunter.

"I'm okay," Kosara said with more conviction than she felt. "This always happens."

Except this time, it was different. This time, her own eye, the brown one, saw the shadows' visions like ghosts running past her gaze.

The green eye saw something else, something a lot more corporeal. A familiar figure with golden hair. Kosara shut the green eye firmly. She had no time for this.

She had to ask the shadows if they could lift the curse over Malamir. But first, because she was certain all of this was connected somehow, she asked a different question: "Can you tell me who killed Sofiya?"

The shadows' muttering grew louder, but no answer followed.

"Who killed Sofiya?" Kosara repeated.

Kosara couldn't catch a single word they said, but she gathered their general sense of confusion. Her own shadow turned its ink-black face towards her and shrugged.

"Sofiya, the witch with two shadows?" Kosara specified, hoping it might help. "Sofiya, who could speak to the dead? You know Sofiya! Sofiya who summoned the mratinyak!"

No answer.

Exasperated, Kosara pulled the deck of playing cards out of her pocket. She threw them at the table, just like she'd done before. They rained onto the surface. A couple gently floated to the floor. As far as Kosara could see, they didn't arrange themselves in any discernible pattern.

She caught Roksana's eyes in between the shadows' bodies. The monster hunter looked genuinely worried for Kosara's well-being.

Kosara sighed. Her skin felt prickly, as if the shadows were pushing against it, impatient to do the magic she'd summoned them for. Her temples pulsated, faster and faster, in rhythm with the shadows' whispers. It hurt.

Perhaps she was wasting her time. Whoever had killed Sofiya now owned two witches' shadows. It was more than likely they protected the murderer from Kosara's badly behaved twelve.

"Fine, fine," she said, as if speaking to an impatient dog waiting at the door for its morning walk. "Let's do some real magic."

She didn't need to say anything else. The shadows rushed her, pulling at her arms, leading her to Malamir. They pushed her until she kneeled next to the sofa. Then, they grabbed her hands and lifted them to his chest.

They were around her, but they were also inside her head, pressing against her skull. Her veins ran with their magic. They floated behind her eyelids every time she blinked. When her brown eye was open, it saw the room.

Briefly, only for a second, Kosara risked opening the green one. Unsurprisingly, it saw something else. A hall fashioned from white marble—no, Kosara corrected herself, a hall carved of melted bone. She saw him, too. The Zmey.

Her own reaction surprised her. A flutter in her stomach she hadn't felt for him in years.

Kosara shut the green eye tight again. She couldn't afford the distraction.

She let the shadows guide her hands, shaping magic symbols over Malamir's chest. They took control of her tongue, twisting it into a spell. Kosara had no idea what she was saying. She didn't even know what language she spoke—the sounds felt foreign in her mouth. Her body wasn't her own anymore, it was the shadows'.

In many ways, she mused while watching her fingers weave a spell she'd never thought possible, it was a reversal of how shadow magic usually worked. Usually, the witch would tame the shadows. In this case, the shadows had claimed the witch.

Malamir screamed, a choked, ugly screech, and for the first time, Kosara thought that maybe this hadn't been the smartest idea. The shadows were keen to do magic, but it mattered little to them whether it would help or harm its subject. To them, he was nothing but a means to an end.

Then, one of the shadows reached for Kosara's face, and she was *certain* this had been a bad idea. Its fingers dug into the green eye, grasping at its eyelashes, forcing it open.

Kosara swore as the room blurred. The next time she blinked, she wasn't in her house anymore. She was back in the Zmey's palace.

8

Kosara

It was all so familiar. A hall of bone, melted together, carved by the Zmey's fire. High above, the chandeliers fashioned from yuda wings clicked and clacked, swinging from their chains. The windows were framed with human teeth and every gust of wind sent them clattering. The sky outside was dark and full of stars.

It was freezing cold, and the lights were dimmed, which meant the Zmey was in one of his moods again. When he was happy, the halls were pleasantly warm, and fire crackled in every hearth. But the palace getting too hot wasn't a good sign, either. This usually meant he was angry, which caused the fireplaces to burn too bright, threatening to engulf anyone who was careless enough to get too close to them.

Kosara knew all this because she'd spent months in this place, even though back in the human world, it had been mere days. She'd got used to the palace's every peculiarity, becoming an expert at reading the Zmey's moods. She also knew it because Smirna Koleva knew it, and Kosara currently observed the hall through her bright-green eyes.

She—Smirna, Kosara—sat at one end of the long table, her freckled hand curved around the stem of a glass of moon wine. Her fingers trembled, making the base of the glass rattle against the embroidered tablecloth. Despite the ripe berries, perfectly round red apples, and large, dark grapes piled high in gilded bowls, the plate in front of Smirna was empty.

The Zmey wasn't there, but she felt him with every gust of freezing air hitting her bare arms and snaking under her linen shift. He was furious—a cold, cruel fury.

Smirna lifted the glass to her lips, then thought better of it and put it back down. Her heart galloped in her chest, sending the blood swooshing in her ears, and Kosara thought it so funny: in this foreign body, watching these foreign hands, her heart sounded just the same.

Her heartbeat masked his footsteps until it was almost too late. She heard him—the heels of his boots against the bone floor, and his deep, angry inhales—at the same time his scent hit her. A familiar mixture of smoke, magic, and something sweet and primal. Her stomach twisted in a way that was familiar, too.

If Kosara was in her own body, she would have bolted for the door. Stuck inside Smirna's mind, all she could do was silently beg her to run.

Smirna didn't run. Instead, she turned and faced him.

The Zmey didn't age. Yet, Kosara had expected him to have changed in the forty years that separated her and Smirna. He hadn't. His hair was the same shade of dark gold, and his eyes were just as blue as Kosara remembered them. His skin was unlined, though he had carefully allowed for a few small imperfections here and there, in his desperate attempt to appear human: a tiny scar on the bridge of his nose, fine crow's feet in the corners of his eyes.

He wore his coat, the one Kosara had stolen from him last winter, and it swished against the floor. Under it, his shirt was covered in elaborate embroideries. In her panicked state, Kosara felt a foreign thought, one coming from Smirna's mind: it would be a shame if, in his anger, he took on his monster form and shred the beautiful coat to pieces.

"She tried it again," the Zmey said, accusation in his voice. The glass in Smirna's hands trembled and the wine almost escaped it as it splashed.

"Who?" Smirna asked sweetly. It only added to Kosara's sense of déjà vu: though the voice wasn't hers, the tone was recognisable. Slow, careful, aware one wrong word would send the Zmey into a rage.

"Your friend Vila." He spat out her name as if it was a thorn in his mouth. "I can smell her, you know. I can smell her trying to sneak in here and steal you from me."

Smirna's heartbeat thundered in her ears, but her voice remained calm. "Silly woman. She knows I'd never leave you." A measured smile, a flutter of eyelashes. "Come on. Sit down. Let's have dinner."

The Zmey reached for her face and cupped her chin in his pale hand. His touch sent a shiver down her spine, and as much as Kosara wanted to pretend it had been caused solely by fear, she had to admit something else also stirred in her stomach. Something warm and pleasant. He simply *cared* so much.

Kosara hated it. She hated every second of it, because it was all too familiar.

"Are you mine, Smirna?" the Zmey asked, and Kosara startled at the unfamiliar name. For a second, she'd completely forgotten this wasn't her own past.

"I'm yours," Smirna said immediately, leaning into his touch.

His grip tightened, his nails digging painfully into her skin. "I want you to prove it to me."

She took a deep breath. "I'd do anything for you," she said, and even Kosara heard the lie in her voice. "Just ask."

"You know what I want."

A wave of panic washed over her. Again, Kosara could have sworn she was in her own body: she remembered the way her skin prickled, and her lips grew numb, the blood draining from them. She remembered the fast thunder of her heart, and the feeling that her stomach was filled with lead, and that horrible, bitter taste in the back of her throat.

"You want my shadow," Smirna said quietly.

The Zmey must have sensed the hesitation in her voice because he stepped closer, towering over her. He pushed her chin, so she'd keep looking at him, even though it hurt to have her neck twisted back at an unnatural angle. Smirna fought back tears.

"Why do you need your shadow when you have me?" he asked. "Am I not enough for you?"

The words tumbled fast from her lips, "You are, of course you are . . ."

"Have you ever wanted for anything since you met me? Is there anything I haven't given you?"

Understanding. Compassion. Love.

Kosara knew Smirna wasn't going to say any of it. What did the Zmey understand of compassion or love?

She tried to push her chair back away from him, but he held her tight. "You've given me anything I could have asked for, and more. Please . . ."

"Have I ever asked for anything in return?"

Everything. You've asked for everything, and I gave it all willingly, the fool that I was. "No. Never. Nothing."

"Now I ask you for this one simple thing. A useless trinket you'd never need again as my wife. Give me your shadow. Let me take care of you."

"If I give you my shadow, I'll die."

The Zmey laughed, a sharp sound that cut straight through Smirna's resolve. "Smirna, my Smirna. Trust me. I'd never let you die."

Kosara's stomach twisted from the betrayal in his words. Smirna didn't know it, even if she suspected it, but Kosara was certain: the Zmey was lying. He'd let her die. Like all his previous wives, Smirna had died at his hands.

His touch felt even more nauseating now.

"I'll have to think about it," Smirna said carefully. "Give me time."

"Fine. You know I'm an understanding man. Three days. After that, I'll kill her."

Smirna frowned. "Who?"

"Vila. Didn't I mention I caught her sniffing around the castle?"

The Zmey's bloodthirsty grin filled her vision as he leaned in for a kiss, and Kosara wanted nothing more than to run. She couldn't move. She was trapped in this foreign body, feeling his familiar tongue separating her lips and running down her teeth. Her scream was stuck in her throat.

"Kosara?" she heard a familiar voice.

This wasn't possible. Nevena couldn't be here.

She'd never visited the Zmey's palace. And besides, she was dead. This time, she was dead for certain. There were no remnants of her spirit floating around in the human world, trapped.

She was gone. Kosara had made sure of that.

And yet, her voice sounded so real. "Kosara, you need to wake up."

"Kosara?"

She recognised this voice, too, but she didn't dare open her eyes. It could be another of the Zmey's tricks, just like Nevena's voice must have been. Kosara still heard the Zmey's cruel laughter, echoing in the back of her mind. She still tasted his tongue in her mouth.

If she looked up, would she find him looming over her?

"Kosara?" A gentle hand, shaking her by the shoulder. This gave her a pause. The Zmey was rarely gentle.

Kosara peeled her eyes open. She was lying on the floor of her living-room-turned-workshop. This wasn't the first time she'd woken up with her head resting on the creaky floorboards, though, admittedly, it usually happened after a few more glasses of rakia.

It wasn't the Zmey she found watching over her, and it wasn't her sister. It was a dishevelled Asen, staring at her with big, worried eyes. Her relief was so sharp, it was almost painful.

He was warm, but not scalding hot like the Zmey. He smelled of smoke—not from the Zmey's fire, but from Belograd's docks and Chernograd's chimneys. For a second, she felt so safe, she almost laid her head back down on the floor to finish her nap.

"Kosara!" He shook her by the shoulder. "Wake up!"

"Mm?"

"How many fingers do you see?" He waved two fingers in front of her face.

"I might be a simple girl from Chernograd, Bakharov, but I know how to count." She slapped his hand away. "Let me sleep."

"Here, doll." Malamir floated into view, holding a cup of something steaming hot.

Asen helped Kosara up from the floor until she sat down with her head resting against his shoulder. Malamir lifted the cup to her lips and the scent of coffee hit Kosara.

She drank and coughed. "What's this?"

"Coffee." Malamir blinked innocently. "From your cupboard."

"Which jar?"

"The red one."

Tears filled Kosara's eyes as the liquid burned her throat. It wasn't only coffee she'd mixed into the ungodly concoction she kept in the red jar, but she'd be damned if she admitted what else was in there in front of a copper.

In any case, the brew finally woke her up. The room sharply came into focus.

Kosara coughed again and stood up straight, separating herself from Asen's warmth. She glanced around: at Malamir, standing over her, still holding the cup; at Roksana, lounging on a chair with her legs spread wide, pulling on her long-stemmed pipe; and at Asen.

A swarm of treacherous butterflies flapped wildly around in her stomach. Kosara wanted to pluck away their goddamned wings one by one.

She'd done her best in the last six months to convince herself she didn't care about him. That whatever she'd thought she'd felt last winter had been the result of a few too many close brushes with death. Danger tended to make people feel closer like that.

Now that he was right there, it proved a lot more difficult to keep pretending. Despite herself, she was happy to see him.

He looked better than when she'd last seen him, which, in fairness, wasn't a great achievement. His scrapes and bruises had healed, and his dark circles had melted away. He'd grown a short beard, and though Kosara didn't usually like facial hair on men, it looked good on him. She resisted the urge to touch it, to find out what it would feel like against her skin.

Being away from Chernograd seemed to agree with him. Or maybe, Kosara thought with a pang of bitterness, being away from her did.

"What are you doing here?" she asked, carefully standing on wobbly knees, supporting herself on the table.

"I . . ." he mumbled and got up after her. "I, well, um . . ."

"He's with me," said an unfamiliar voice.

Kosara turned around and found a yuda looking back at her.

Someone less experienced with monsters would have probably screamed, or at least swore out loud. Instead, Kosara blinked, and then, with the politest tone she could manage, "And you are?"

"Vrana. I'm Sokol's sister."

Kosara wished her head didn't feel like it was stuffed with cotton wool. She'd worked some difficult, taxing magic. Even the mixture from the red jar couldn't combat her sheer exhaustion.

Her thoughts were sluggish, which meant she had to spend a few moments standing there, trying to connect the dots in her mind: Malamir was here because he'd gone to see Roksana. Roksana was here because Sokol was missing. Asen was here because Vrana was Sokol's sister . . .

"Did it work?" she said, turning to Malamir.

"Did what work?" Asen asked.

Instead of replying, Malamir unbuttoned his shirt. Karaivanov's symbol was still there on his chest, but it had faded, like an old sailor's tattoo. It looked similar to Asen's—in fact, Kosara noticed Asen's fingers twitching towards his own faded brand.

"It doesn't hurt anymore," Malamir said. "At least, not for now."

"I can't promise it will stay that way."

"I figured." Malamir shifted from foot to foot. "I'm sorry."

Kosara frowned. "Why?"

Roksana exhaled a large plume of smoke, drawing Kosara's attention. "Kosara. Your hair . . ."

Kosara reflexively lifted her fingers to the strand falling in front of her eyes. Except, it didn't feel right. No matter how many oils and creams she used, her hair was always coarse and frizzy, especially when the weather was this damp. Today, it felt silky smooth between her fingertips.

Swallowing a juicy swear, Kosara rushed to the mirror hanging above the fireplace. Most of her hair was still hers, dark and wavy. Two strands, however, framed her face in a pale, straight curtain.

Kosara immediately knew which shadow these had come from: Sevda Yordanova, who'd married the Zmey on a stormy winter night thirty-seven years ago.

Kosara turned her back to the mirror. "Yes, well. Magic sometimes has unexpected effects." She tried to ignore the pointed looks everyone in the room gave her. "Who'd like a drink? We have a lot to talk about."

Roksana never said no to a drink. She opted for a large glass of dogwood rakia Kosara had bought from a neighbour—it was a foul-smelling, nose-hair-burning ferment, normally reserved for warm compresses to treat chest infections and fever. It seemed to suit the monster hunter's tastes just fine.

Asen brewed a pot of linden blossom tea for himself and Vrana, from a pouch he'd brought from Belograd. In Chernograd, the spring had proven too cold for the linden trees, and their branches were still naked.

Malamir poured a thimble-sized cup of coffee from the cezve, and his eyes widened when he tasted it. Kosara shrugged and took a sip from her own brew. The mixture from the red jar slid down her throat, tingling on the way down.

For a while, they sat around the table and talked. Asen started by describing Natalia Ruseva's murder, and then explained how he'd met Vrana. Vrana filled the gaps in Roksana's story of how Sokol had snuck away from the monster realm. Kosara listened without interrupting until Vrana fell silent.

"So, Sofiya helped you cross the border between our realm and yours?" Kosara asked.

"No," Vrana said. "She helped Sokol. I simply followed in Sokol's steps."

Kosara played with the cup, moving it between her fingers. She'd been right in her guess that this mess was all Sofiya's doing. Unfortunately, that didn't make solving it any easier.

Even worse, the fact that Vrana had been able to simply follow her sister to Chernograd only confirmed Kosara's suspicions. The barrier between the realms of monsters and humans was growing weaker.

However, all this didn't explain the mratinyak. If Sofiya had been looking for Sokol, how come she'd instead summoned an enormous, bloodthirsty cockerel? Had it been a simple mistake? Had Sofiya performed her ritual to summon monsters, rummaging inside their realm with her eyes closed until she'd felt something large and feathery, and dragged it out hoping she'd found the yuda?

"What's the problem?" Asen asked, noticing Kosara's silence.

Kosara avoided looking at him. She knew she couldn't succumb to any of the warm and fuzzy feelings he stirred in her. She was acutely aware he'd only returned to Chernograd because he'd made a promise to Vrana. He'd come to Kosara because he needed help.

But then, wasn't this their whole arrangement? She'd promised him, and his dead wife, that she'd help them get rid of Karaivanov, once and for all. She owed him. She owed both of them, since without Asen's enchanted ring, they would have never survived last winter.

Last winter, Kosara had allowed herself to believe there might be something deeper there, between Asen and her, after what they'd gone through during the Foul Days. She'd been wrong.

"The problem is," she said, "Sofiya is dead."

Vrana's already large eyes grew even larger. "Do you mean to tell me Sokol and I are trapped here?"

"You might not be," Kosara said quickly. She didn't want a panicked yuda in her house. "I might be able to figure something out. I've got my shadows—"

With the corner of her eye, she caught Roksana flinching.

"Are you sure using them is safe?" Asen asked.

Kosara tucked a blonde strand behind her ear, ignoring how foreign it felt. Her green eye was somehow more tired than the brown, and she had to stop herself from rubbing it. "Perfectly safe."

Asen looked unconvinced. "You passed out . . ."

"I was exhausted, that's all. I let them get out of control."

"But—"

"But it worked, didn't it? Malamir's healed."

"For now," Roksana muttered.

"Listen." Kosara looked around the table. "How about we take things one step at a time? First, we'll rescue Sokol from Karaivanov, then we'll worry about how you two can return to the monster realm."

"If Sokol wants to return," Roksana amended.

Vrana stared at the monster hunter. "After how your city treated her? I believe she'll be keen to come back home."

Kosara hurried to steer the conversation away from these treacherous waters. That was the last thing she wanted, ending up in the middle of a family quarrel. "There's one thing I still don't understand," she said. "How did Karaivanov capture Sokol? How did he capture Vrana?"

"I can answer that question," Malamir said. "Karaivanov wanted a yuda. He told me he's got a witch who could drag one to Chernograd."

Roksana slammed her tankard on the table, startling everyone in the room. "Sofiya," she hissed. "I knew it. That sneaky bitch. She was going to double-cross us."

"No." Malamir shook his head. "No, it wasn't Sofiya. Her name was Natalia."

Kosara frowned. Natalia, as in Natalia Ruseva? Natalia who'd lost her head on the same night Sofiya had lost hers?

Asen had mentioned he suspected the two cases were related. There were too many similarities for it to be mere coincidence.

Malamir continued, "Word got out he's looking for a yuda, and you know what his minions are like. They'd do anything to get into his good graces. When a second yuda happened to just fall from the sky, they took her straight to him."

Vrana laughed without humour. "That would be me."

"Of course, he didn't need any more yudas, especially since Natalia had convinced him Sokol is a famous seer back in the monster realm.

But Karaivanov would never say no to some hard cash, especially now that smuggling is a lot less profitable than it once was. Hence, the auction."

"But why?" Kosara asked. "Why did Karaivanov want a yuda in the first place?"

"Well." Malamir leaned forwards. He was using his dramatic voice, the one he'd learned at the theatre back in the day. "What I heard is, Karaivanov had a brush with death. He's grown paranoid. So, he wants a yuda . . ."

Kosara gasped. "To tell his fortune! A yuda can see how you die."

Vrana exhaled through her nostrils. "Sokol would never tell him. She couldn't, even if she wanted to."

"Why?" Kosara asked.

"We can't control our visions."

Kosara swore internally. If Sokol couldn't give Karaivanov what he wanted, he'd tire of her soon. He was likely to auction her away, just like he'd done with Vrana.

She turned to Malamir. "You said you knew where they're keeping her?"

"Yes. A storage unit in the river district."

Asen was frowning, that familiar line between his eyebrows deepening. "How did you find out? Surely, Karaivanov wouldn't share such sensitive information with someone outside his closest circle."

Malamir looked down at his hands. His fingers, wrapped around his cup of coffee, trembled. "I've been working for him for a while now. Maybe he's starting to trust me."

Asen leaned back and crossed his arms. "Well, *I* don't trust you. Your boss finally shares some important information with you and the first thing you do is run here and betray him? I don't buy it."

Kosara cast him a glance. He'd never been this quick to dismiss a change of heart before. The Asen she knew believed in the good in people.

He caught her looking at him and shrugged. "Copper intuition."

Malamir turned his pleading eyes to Kosara. "I swear I'm telling the truth. I've done a lot of regrettable things in my past, but one thing

I draw the line at is human . . ." He shot Vrana a look. "Or, I suppose, yuda trafficking."

Kosara chewed on her lower lip. Her instinct was to believe him, as she knew how much he'd cared for his karakonjul pets. She could imagine his sympathy extended to other monsters. But was she simply letting her guard down because she'd once considered him something akin to a friend?

"There's one thing you're forgetting," Roksana said. "Malamir almost died betraying Karaivanov."

"Good point," Kosara admitted. It would have been one hell of a performance if he'd been faking it, and she knew him. Even back when he'd made his living as an actor, he'd been hammy at best.

Instead of replying, Asen let out a grunt. He couldn't argue with that.

"I feel like there's something else you're all forgetting," Vrana interjected. "While we're sitting here chatting, Karaivanov's got my sister."

"Believe me, I'm well aware of that," Kosara said. "Well, Malamir? What's the plan?"

Malamir startled, as if he'd thought his role in the conversation was over. "I can show you where he's keeping her. After that . . ." He shrugged.

Asen and Roksana both started talking at the same time.

"How many guards?" asked Asen.

"How are the guards armed?" asked Roksana.

"Three guards," Malamir said. "Guns."

"Only three?" Asen was frowning again.

"It's not like he's expecting problems. Only a handful of people know of Sokol's location." Malamir checked his watch, the one hanging on a long silver chain, which Kosara strongly suspected had hypnotising powers. She avoided looking at it, just in case. "We'd better hurry if we want to catch the time when the guards change. What do you say?"

Roksana and Vrana both stood up. Asen and Kosara shared a look. Kosara could easily interpret the face he was making, with his eyebrows inquisitively curved and his mouth in a thin line. He still thought this was a bad idea.

But did they have a choice? Karaivanov had Sokol. Even if he hadn't hurt her yet, Kosara knew him. His patience would wear thin soon.

Kosara still owed the yuda for saving her from the Zmey's cage. Now, Asen owed her sister. And Kosara still owed Asen . . . They were all tangled together in this web of obligations, and God knew there were very few things a witch hated more than a debt. A debt had to be paid.

"Let's go," Kosara said, and she didn't think she imagined Asen's frown deepening.

9

Asen

This whole situation stank. Not only because they were currently weaving their way through the river district's narrow alleyways, jumping over piles of fly-infested rubbish and starving stray cats fighting for scraps. It wasn't the coat he'd borrowed from Kosara's dad's wardrobe, which reeked of mildew and lavender, either.

There was something Malamir wasn't telling them, Asen could feel it in his bones. Something was rotten.

However, Kosara had refused to listen, and he needed her help if he wanted to survive this city. He knew as much from experience.

Besides, he had no better plan. If they dallied too much, Karaivanov would sniff out Malamir's betrayal and move Sokol elsewhere. There were a thousand dark, secluded nooks and crannies one could hide a monster in Chernograd. They'd never find her.

So the best Asen could do was stay vigilant, keep on high alert, and hope that if it came to an altercation, he'd be fast enough to grab a gun from one of Karaivanov's minions.

The hip where he usually carried his revolver felt naked. He'd discarded the broken gun once it became obvious fixing it wasn't an option. His only weapon was a knife hidden in his coat's inside pocket—in his youth, he'd known a few moves that would cause quite a bit of damage. Nowadays, he was more familiar with how to use it to julienne carrots.

He was their little group's weak link, he was well aware. Roksana had her pistol, and he could spot at least a dozen knife handles poking from her pockets, tucked in her boots, and strapped to her belt. Malamir looked scrawny, but his knuckles were raw and bloody—and anyway, he was from Chernograd. He'd hold his own in a fight. Vrana was a monster. And Kosara, well . . . Kosara was a witch with twelve shadows, but even without them, she'd been fearsome.

Asen was a copper with a kitchen knife.

He deliberately lingered last in the group, watching the flank, and Kosara slowed down to walk next to him.

"What's wrong?" she asked.

He shrugged. "You trust Malamir."

Kosara paused. Asen knew she would never admit to trusting anyone easily, especially someone who'd betrayed her once. "You didn't see him when Roksana brought him to me. He was barely standing up. He was in agony."

Asen made a noncommittal sound. Perhaps Kosara was right. Perhaps he only distrusted Malamir because he'd seen how much his last betrayal had hurt her, and he didn't want to see her hurt again.

He stole a quick glance at her, unable to help himself. She seemed exhausted and fidgety, and her lips were raw from biting. She watched him with two different-coloured eyes, one brown and one green, framed by two limp strands of pale hair.

He'd always liked her hair. It was wild and untamed, like her. He also liked her dark eyes.

The green was pretty, but it wasn't *her*. It made him worry. He'd broken out of the habit of biting the soft skin around his nails years ago, but he caught himself doing it again, chewing on them until he tasted blood.

That was his problem—he kicked one bad habit, only to introduce a new one. He'd stopped drinking, but he'd started smoking like a chimney. He'd stopped smoking, and now he was biting his nails.

"Asen?" Kosara brought him out of his thoughts. "What's wrong? Do you have concerns about the plan?"

"No. It's a good plan."

It was nice and simple. They'd wait until half an hour before the guards were supposed to change. Malamir, Asen, and Roksana would go to the door, while Kosara and Vrana hid in the shadows. Malamir would explain the three of them were the new shift, there to relieve the guards of their duties. Then, they'd get Sokol out and be on their way before the real new shift turned up.

The guards wouldn't suspect anything, Malamir had assured them. They knew him, and they knew he couldn't betray Karaivanov without risking his life. They also wouldn't see anything amiss in the arrival of two new recruits. Karaivanov's associates were dropping like flies. New blood was always needed.

It helped that Asen had been marked with Karaivanov's symbol. He'd undone the last couple of buttons of his shirt, so the top of it peeked over his neckline.

"I'm sorry," Asen said, since Kosara was still watching him. "I've been out of sorts lately. I'm sure it will all go well."

Kosara pursed her lips. He knew how much she hated it when he said things like that. She was certain he'd jinx them.

As they approached the end of the street, Malamir gestured at them to be quiet.

"It's behind this corner," he whispered. "Are you ready?"

"I'm ready," Roksana replied immediately. Her large hand casually rested on the handle of her gun.

Asen threw one last look at Kosara, and she squeezed his shoulder in a way he thought was supposed to be reassuring. Her eyes, however, were full of worry.

He placed his hand on top of hers and squeezed back. For a second, as they stood there in silence, their eyes locked, he forgot everyone was watching them. There was so much he wanted to tell her, so much a single touch couldn't communicate: "Don't worry," and "I've got your back," and "It's so good to see you," and "I missed you."

What he wanted the most, however, in that single moment before he'd walked into whatever danger Malamir was leading them to, was to draw her close and press his lips to hers.

He did nothing of the sort. He was too much of a coward—and, perhaps, he hadn't forgotten about everyone watching, after all. He couldn't bear the embarrassment of them seeing her reject him. It was all very well and good when the protagonists of romantic novels planted a wet kiss onto their beau's faces before going to war: those bastards never got pushed away and questioned where the hell they'd been for the last six months.

Something else stopped him, too. He felt another pair of eyes on him, one that made the fine hairs on the back of his neck stand on end. When he turned around, for a second, he was certain he saw a redheaded silhouette watching them from the shadows. Boryana.

Then he blinked, and she was gone.

His first instinct was to touch the wedding ring at his throat. He was seeing things in his nervousness, that had to be it. Boryana's ghost had been banished last winter, when they'd promised her they'd catch Karaivanov.

Knowing this didn't help him feel less guilty. He detached himself from Kosara, mumbling some weak excuse under his breath, and, without looking back, followed Malamir through the puddles.

The storage unit was a low building made of steel, so rusted a strong gust of wind threatened to make it crumble into dust. A lantern swung on a chain above the entrance. The three guards sat at a table under it, playing cards, betting loudly and swearing even louder.

Asen and Roksana hung back while Malamir approached them. They exchanged a few words, accompanied by grunts and more swears, and then the three of them got up, packed up their cards, packets of cigarettes and the half-finished bottle of rakia, and were gone. It took less than a minute.

Malamir had been right. The guards were keen to go home, have their dinner, and snuggle into their warm beds. It was another bitterly cold night, and Asen's teeth were clattering.

Nevertheless, this had been easy. Too easy.

"Kosara!" Malamir whispered once the guards' broad backs disappeared from sight. "Vrana! It's all clear."

Roksana was already kicking the door open.

"What did you do that for?" Malamir muttered, as it collapsed backwards in a pile of dust. "I have a key . . ."

Roksana didn't listen. She rushed inside, shouting, her voice echoing in the large space, "Sokol! Are you there?"

"I'm here." The yuda's voice was hoarse, barely more than a whisper.

Asen stopped at the door, with Malamir, Kosara, and Vrana behind him. The storage unit was empty, save the spiderwebs glinting in the corners, the dust bunnies rolling on the floor, and the chair placed in the centre. Sokol was shackled to it by her wrists and ankles, and several lengths of heavy chain were wrapped around her wings.

Karaivanov hadn't kept his word that he wouldn't hurt her. Her lower lip was swollen and bruised, and a single, deep cut ran across it. Asen flinched. He'd seen the same injury on a dozen different faces. He knew exactly what had caused it: the diamond ring Karaivanov wore on his middle finger.

Roksana kneeled in front of the chair. "I'm going to kill him," she muttered under her breath, gently running her finger over Sokol's lip. "I swear, I'm going to kill him."

"I'm happy to see you, too," Sokol said.

Malamir rushed to her with the set of keys he'd retrieved from the guards, trying them one by one. Asen watched him without saying anything, though he suspected none of them would fit. Knowing Karaivanov, he kept the key for Sokol's shackles somewhere only he could access it.

Soon enough, Malamir swore and threw the keys at the floor.

Asen felt a hand on his shoulder and jumped, before turning around and seeing Kosara. She'd never been particularly touchy, so it had come as a surprise she'd reached for him twice in the same evening. He still saw the redheaded silhouette every time he blinked, watching his every move.

She took a step back, realising she'd startled him. "Can you help?"

Asen was already rummaging in his pocket for his set of lockpicks. "Probably."

"You'd better hurry." Malamir checked his watch. "We don't have long."

Asen didn't need the reminder—his fingers were already shaking. He selected the lockpick he thought would be the best fit and got to work. It wasn't the first time he'd had to unlock a set of Karaivanov's shackles. Roksana didn't move, still kneeling in front of the chair and holding Sokol's bruised hand.

After a few seconds of everyone staring at him while he was trying to break the lock, including two pairs of gleaming yuda eyes, he couldn't take it any longer. "Could someone go outside?" he said over his shoulder. "If the new guards turn up, we'll need someone to distract them."

"I'll do it," Malamir said immediately.

Asen's hand froze for a second, the chiming of the lockpick growing silent.

Kosara must have caught his hesitation because she turned to Roksana. "You should cover his back. You're a better shot."

Roksana grunted, still squeezing Sokol's hand, until the yuda shook her off.

"Go," Sokol said. "I'll see you in a minute."

Roksana sighed and unsheathed her gun before following Malamir. At the door, she turned around. "If anything happens to her while I'm gone, copper . . ."

Instead of responding, Asen groaned. He was risking his skin saving Sokol, and instead of gratitude, all he got were threats.

"I'll be here." Vrana's tone was just as hostile. "Don't you worry."

"Stop it, both of you," Sokol said. "Let the man work. Roksana, go help Malamir."

Roksana finally left. The door she'd kicked in was beyond repair, so she balanced it in the frame.

"Did you see him recently? Karaivanov?" Asen asked Sokol, trying to distract himself. He always worked best when he let his fingers follow the familiar moves while his mind was busy elsewhere.

Sokol licked her wounded lip. Her voice was surprisingly calm, even casual, but Asen felt her tremble every time the shackles brushed against her bruised skin. "Not since the first day. I don't think he enjoyed our conversation."

"Why?"

"He wanted to know how he'd die. All I could tell him was that it wouldn't be pleasant. That's all I saw every time I looked—blood, pain, and anger."

"Do you know how long you've been here?"

Sokol shook her head. "It's always so dark. Five days? Six? I'm starving."

"Did he not feed you?" Vrana interrupted.

"Rats. A stray cat or two. Not enough."

Kosara cleared her throat, and though Asen could feel the discomfort in her voice, she suggested, "Malamir's got connections at the graveyard. Maybe we can get you a fresh corpse . . ."

"We don't need handouts," Vrana snapped. "I can feed my sister, thank you very much."

"I was just trying to h—"

Voices sounded from outside. Malamir's pleasant and warm, Roksana's grunting, and then a third one, low and threatening.

Of course. Asen had known this was going too well. He tried working faster, but breaking locks was a slow, finicky process. It couldn't be rushed.

"Goddamnit." Kosara looked around, as if they weren't trapped in an empty room with no other exit. Swearing under her breath, she sat on the ground, undid her shadow necklace, and began to methodically unfold her shadows.

Asen was so busy watching her, he was surprised to hear the shackles around Sokol's wrists click and open.

"Finally!" The yuda straightened out, making a low, pained sound. Asen had forgotten how tall she was until she loomed over him.

More voices joined the conversation outside. Their words were muffled through the door, but their tone was unmistakable. Malamir's distraction wasn't going well.

A gunshot, a thud, and for the second time that night, the door collapsed inwards. The first thing Asen saw on the other side was the barrel of a gun pointed straight at him.

Karaivanov's underling wasn't a police officer. There wasn't going to be a "Freeze!" or a "Keep your hands where I can see them!" He'd simply shoot.

Before Asen had even attempted to take cover, Vrana screeched and landed on top of the man, scratching his face with her talons. She threw him across the room. His screams reverberated between the metal walls of the storage unit. The space filled with the stench of blood.

A few seconds later, Vrana stood, long intestines dangling from her completely human mouth, while the man at her feet stilled forever.

She spat out the bloody mess, wiped her mouth with the back of her hand, and muttered, "Dinner is served."

Disturbingly, Asen heard Sokol's stomach rumble, and then the yuda was on the floor, her mouth buried inside the man's stomach.

Asen had to turn away before he was sick. It had been easy, while chatting with the two yudas and listening to their very human words, to forget that at their core, they were monsters.

Outside, Malamir shouted, and Roksana's gunshots rang. Kosara clicked her fingers. A blue flame danced on top of her fingertips. In its light, her shadows appeared enormous, circling the door, waiting for more prey.

That first thug to make it past Roksana and Malamir had been only the beginning. They came in a swarm, squeezing through the door, armed people in dark clothes.

Then, they hesitated. Clearly, they hadn't expected to find not only two Chernogradean monsters, but a witch with twelve shadows on the other side.

"There's no need for more bloodshed," Kosara said, nodding to the body on the floor. "Let us go, and no one else will get hurt."

One of the men spat at the floor. His saliva landed on the ground, pink, bloodstained, with a single white tooth glinting in it. He'd obviously had a run-in with Roksana or Malamir outside.

"I really don't think so," he said. Asen recognised that tone of voice. The man was too angry to simply let them go. He craved blood.

It all happened within seconds. The man charged towards Kosara, swiftly evading the two yudas. For all their impressive size, they were slow. Before he'd reached Kosara, however, her shadows surrounded him, holding him tight in their inky arms.

His eyes grew wide, not only in surprise, but in pain. He tried to scream, but they filled his mouth, stilling his tongue.

"It's not like I didn't warn you," Kosara said to the group at the door. "A single step, and I'll kill him."

One of the thugs, a girl with straight dark hair, barked a laugh. "Kill him. He's an idiot."

Kosara raised her eyebrows. She clicked her fingers again, making the flame between them grow bigger. The shadows in the man's mouth swelled, suffocating him. He let out a gagging sound.

She wasn't going to kill the man, Asen knew. It wasn't like her to hurt a helpless person. She was simply trying to scare Karaivanov's minions away—she'd always been excellent at bluffing.

Except, he'd rarely seen that look in her eyes before. In fact, he'd only seen it once, on the day they'd met Karaivanov on the bridge, when Kosara had seemed ready to incinerate the smuggler with a click of her fingers.

He realised that her mouth was moving. At first, he thought she was mumbling a spell, but then he read her lips. She repeated the same words over and over again. *Please shut up. Please shut up. Please shut up.*

Suddenly, Asen realised who she was talking to. He knew whose voice she heard in her mind. The only voice she always fought against.

The Zmey.

With a mocking smirk, the girl at the door unsheathed her gun and spun it around her finger. She looked so young, barely twenty, and Asen was left with the impression she considered this nothing but a game. He remembered being that young, running around with Karaivanov's gang. He remembered being that stupid.

Kosara took a step forwards, her brows furrowed, and opened her mouth. Asen thought she'd threaten the girl again—tell her to stop playing with that gun and put it away.

Instead, Kosara screamed.

10

Kosara

Kosara heard her own screams echoing in her ears. Her every muscle ached, as if a pair of enormous hands gripped her tightly, preventing her from moving. Her blood slammed against her eardrums.

"Kosara!" It was Asen's voice, but she couldn't focus on him through the pain.

The flame she'd been holding melted away. With it, her shadows retracted, growing smaller and weaker, surrounding her in a tight circle. She crumpled to her knees.

It was only then that her eyes fell to the ground.

Below her, on the floor, a magic circle glittered, barely visible amid the dust. The symbols were rough and angular, penned in a hand she didn't recognise.

"Kosara!" Asen tried to reach for her, but his hand slammed against the circle's invisible barrier.

Kosara gasped, the scream finally dying on her lips. The thugs still watched her, not daring to take a step. The one who'd been captured by her shadows inhaled deep, pained breaths.

Kosara clicked her fingers. Nothing happened. Her shadows swirled around her in a panic, unable to escape the circle's confines.

She clicked her fingers again. Still nothing.

Kosara swore under her breath. They had been led straight into a trap, just like Asen had suspected. The circle had been drawn on the floor hours ago, waiting for Kosara's arrival.

Malamir had betrayed her. Again.

I told you, you should just burn them all, the Zmey's voice purred in her ear.

Shut up, she snapped at him.

Karaivanov's minions had been watching her carefully, ready to pounce if the magic circle hadn't proven strong enough to contain her. Now, their posture relaxed. Vicious smiles split their faces.

Kosara opened her mouth to say something—to bargain or to threaten, she wasn't entirely sure. She knew what the Zmey wanted her to do.

Tell them they'll regret it if they ever touch you. Say you'll burn their houses to the ground with their families still inside. You know you want to.

She didn't get a chance to say anything before a gunshot sounded. The bullet flew through the open door and sank straight into the dark-haired girl's shoulder. She yelped, grasping at her arm, and her fingers came back red.

Roksana stood at the threshold, her broad shoulders taking up most of the doorframe, her gun at the ready.

"Sorry I'm late," she said. One of her eyes was purple and swollen shut, but it didn't seem to have affected her aim. "Who's next?"

Except, something wasn't right. Roksana was a formidable sight even when she wasn't swinging a gun with a bloodthirsty grin. The thugs, however, looked unperturbed. They hadn't so much as flinched when their comrade got shot. She, herself, was still smirking despite the blood seeping through her shirtsleeve.

Roksana shot again. This one pierced the back of the girl's head. The girl hissed in pain but didn't so much as wobble on her feet. She brought her hand to her head, dug inside until she found the bullet, and pulled it out.

Roksana's eyes widened as she took a step forwards, allowing Kosara to see the street behind her. It was the middle of the night, but it was light enough to make out the outlines of shops and houses. A moon hung on the horizon, low and heavy, perfectly round.

A chill ran over Kosara's spine. The moon was full. Roksana's lead bullets hadn't hurt Karaivanov's underling. This could only mean one thing.

You should have burned them when you had the chance.

Kosara couldn't find it in herself to argue.

11

Asen

The dark-haired girl threw her head back and wailed. The rest of the thugs—even the half-dead boy the shadows had attacked—answered her in turn.

Her canines elongated. Tufts of soft fur blossomed all over her face.

The knife's handle was slick in Asen's palm. He could do nothing but watch, his mouth hanging open, his brain stuck on a single thought: *Now we're fucked.*

Without ever stopping the constant stream of muttered curses under her breath, Roksana fell to one knee, emptied her gun's cartridge, and reloaded it, this time with silver bullets. Vrana and Sokol let out loud screeches as they prepared for the attack.

They all seemed ready for a fight, which gave Asen some courage.

They all seemed ready, that was, except for Kosara. Her eyes were panicked, and she kept clicking her fingers and mumbling magic words, as if she expected with enough determination, she might break the circle's hold.

This was bad news, because Kosara was obviously the one the wolves had been sent for. They ignored everyone else and swarmed her. The circle must have been designed to let them in, because they passed through the invisible barrier as if it was nothing but air.

Roksana fired again and again, bullet after bullet sinking into the varkolaks' flesh. The stench of burnt fur and meat penetrated the air, mixing with the smell of blood.

Vrana and Sokol grabbed a varkolak each, dragging them away from Kosara. It wasn't going to be enough. Several wolves still surrounded her. As valiantly as her shadows fought, they were too weak without her fire magic to strengthen them. They let a wolf past, and Asen watched in horror as two rows of sharp teeth snapped centimetres away from Kosara's face.

For a second, he forgot he was a useless copper with a kitchen knife. He forgot this was a Chernogradean monster, many times stronger than him. All he wanted to do was to hurt the bastard.

Asen couldn't allow himself to get distracted by impotent rage. He had to *think*. There had to be some way to break the circle and restore Kosara's magic. There had to be something he could do, something obvious . . .

His fingers found the wedding ring hanging at his neck. That was it. Evading the varkolak's jaws snapping at him, he pulled sharply on the chain, unclasping it.

For a second, he was sure he spotted Boryana's ghost watching him from the corner, pale and still among the commotion. Her brows furrowed. Her mouth turned downwards.

"I'm sorry," he mumbled. "I have no choice." And then, louder, "Kosara!"

When Kosara turned to him, he threw the ring. At first, he worried in her panic, she'd miss it and it would fly straight past her.

She reached and caught it by the chain.

Just in time. The next moment, the varkolak slashed at her leg and she lost balance, tumbling to the ground.

She screamed, and Asen screamed, too. At first, he thought his connection to Kosara must be so strong, he felt her pain as if it was his own. Then, he looked down, and noticed the dark-haired varkolak with her teeth around his own calf.

Asen lashed out with the handle of his knife between her eyes, and she stumbled back. He prepared to attack, gripping the knife with both hands, but then Kosara screamed again, and this time, she didn't sound like she was in pain. She sounded furious.

She got up from the floor. With one hand, she held Asen's wedding ring high, so the wolves couldn't reach it. With the other, she clicked her fingers. The flame she produced was large, crackling, and so hot, Asen felt its warmth on his skin.

She balled it in her hand and shot it at one of the varkolaks, setting his fur on fire.

His wails were deafening. He rolled on the floor, trying to extinguish the flames, but Kosara didn't give him the chance. She kept shaping fireballs with her fingers and sending them, indiscriminately, after the wolves. She missed as often as she hit them, and her fire sank into the storage container's metal walls, making them hotter and hotter.

Asen struggled to inhale, sweat rolling down his face. His eyes watered. He was certain if they didn't get out of the room soon, they'd die.

The wolves must have had the same realisation, because they scrambled for the door, leaving a trail of smoke and the stench of burning fur behind them.

"Kosara." Asen stumbled to her, uttering her name between coughs. It was ridiculous, because she was terrifying, but he couldn't help but notice how beautiful she looked with the fire glittering off her hair. What was it with him and women prone to angry outbursts? "Kosara . . ."

Her lips moved, shaping a spell, and another blue flame formed between her hands.

"Kosara!" He grabbed her hand. It was blisteringly hot, and he had to clench his teeth so he wouldn't scream. He closed her fingers until the flame inside it suffocated. "Kosara, it's time to go."

She turned to face him. The fires burning around the room reflected deep inside her eyes, painting them bright blue. Her mouth stretched in a snarl.

As much as he wanted to, as much as she reminded him of the Zmey in that moment, he didn't flinch away from her. She wouldn't hurt him. She wouldn't.

"Kosara!"

For a moment, he thought she might hit him with a fireball after all. But then, she shut her eyes, and when she opened them again, the fire was gone. She staggered, her head lolling.

Asen caught her, leaning her against his shoulder.

"Come on," he said. "Let's get out of here."

Outside, Roksana and the two yudas waited for them. Asen let Roksana put Kosara's other arm around her shoulder, and the two carried her home.

The entire way, Kosara mumbled, "Shut up. Shut up. *Shut up.*"

12

Kosara

This time, Kosara was in the Zmey's enchanted gardens. She sat on a swing suspended from a tall oak and listened to its golden leaves clank, just like real gold would. Her hands lay in her lap, holding a book, but she wasn't reading. She was waiting.

A gust of wind made the grass beneath her feet chime. The air, which until a moment ago had been pleasantly warm, turned frigid. The smell of snow drifted in.

At first, Kosara thought she was in her own memories, as the hands in her lap were just as scarred as hers. But then, the wind brought a strand of hair in front of her eyes, light blonde.

Sevda Yordanova's hair. Kosara had been dragged into another memory.

Just as before, she sensed the Zmey approaching. Sevda didn't turn around when his smell engulfed her. His hands landed on her shoulders, ring-encrusted and pale, and his hot breath tickled her ear. "I caught her sniffing around the palace again."

Kosara shuddered internally. She knew how the conversation would go because she'd heard it all before. The same questions, the same answers. A minor variation here and there to account for Sevda having a quicker, more analytical mind than Smirna Koleva, and not needing nearly as much guidance from the Zmey until she reached the obvious conclusion.

He wanted her shadow. If she didn't give it to him, he'd kill Vila.

"Give me a minute to think," Sevda said, and Kosara felt those hands she knew so well slide from her shoulders, down her side, until they cupped one of her breasts. It was freezing cold, and her nipples were painfully hard. The Zmey playfully pinched one, and it hurt so bad, tears prickled at Sevda's eyes.

That was his way, she knew, of letting her know her time for thinking had ended.

If Kosara had been in her own body, she would have sworn, shouted, pushed him away. Sevda, with her analytical mind, knew none of it would help. It would hurt less if she agreed to everything he asked.

Whether she fought or not, he'd get what he wanted in the end. He always did.

"Fine," Sevda said. "Fine. You can have my shadow, but on one condition."

"I think you'll find, my dear, I set the conditions here."

Sevda grabbed his hand and moved it until it rested on the curve of her waist, away from her swollen nipple. "I need you to promise me something."

The Zmey must have decided to hear her out because he didn't interrupt.

"Promise to leave Vila alone," Sevda said. "This is all about her, isn't it? You're obsessed with the woman."

"Please, my dear Sevda. I only have eyes for you."

"I didn't say you want her, I said you're obsessed with her. This is why you always pick her students, don't you? To taunt her. I checked the wedding registers in the library. Yes, you take an ordinary girl here and there, you'd starve if you didn't, but every few years, you manage to lure a witch. And you know what they all have in common?"

"What?"

"Vila's students. Every last one."

The Zmey's hand moved, and Sevda watched it without blinking.

Kosara was aware how it felt, needing to be on high alert whenever he was this close. You never knew when he'd strike.

He didn't hurt Sevda. Instead, he used his thumb and index finger to flick her temple. "I've always been in awe at how that mind of yours works. Remember all the names of Vila's previous students, do you?"

Sevda shrugged. "I have a good memory."

"Sevda, my dear Sevda, you know I can't lie to you. Yes, it's true. I happened to have married a few of her students, but it's mere coincidence. We both happen to have a similar . . . type."

"And what type is that?"

"The city's strongest witches."

"Why? Her, I can understand. She wants to train the best the city has to offer. You? What do you need us for? Our shadows?"

The Zmey exhaled through his nostrils. "Your shadows? I need no such trifles. I pick the strongest of you because I want you to survive. Do you think I enjoy this pointless chase, year after year? Marrying someone, only to bury her a few months later?"

"But my shadow—"

"I want your shadow because you're using it as a crutch. I can show you how to wield true magic, but only if you let go of all the nonsense Vila has been teaching you."

"How about I keep my shadow until that happens?"

"That is a foolish idea, and you know it. I need your shadow for safekeeping. Just in case."

"In case of what?"

"Well. In case you don't survive."

"That's the point," Sevda spat out. "None of us ever survive."

"Now, you know that's not true, don't you? You would never have married me if you believed that."

The Zmey finally came into view, walking in front of Sevda and kneeling so he could look her in the eyes. The wind died down, and the sun peeked from behind the clouds.

Kosara wondered if he'd done it on purpose—if he'd rearranged the sky so the sunlight would hit him just right, making his golden hair glint and his eyes sparkle. If he'd done it so she wouldn't be able to help but think how handsome he looked, kneeling in the grass in front of her.

He took one of her hands in his. "You don't love me, Sevda," he said so gently, even Kosara who was used to his trickery was surprised. "I know that, and I've made my peace with it. A marriage is a partnership. It doesn't need love. None of my gifts and flatteries worked on you, did they?"

"They didn't," Sevda said evenly.

"You have me figured out, haven't you? The source of my power?"

"I believe I do."

Interesting. Throughout their entire exchange, Kosara had been wondering how the Zmey had managed to lure Sevda to marry him, since, by all accounts, she saw straight through him.

Right then, Kosara knew. The Zmey always found his victim's biggest weakness. Kosara had been full of teenage insecurities, so he'd preyed on them. Sevda thought she was smarter. She thought she was safe from the Zmey because she didn't love him.

What she craved was power. And in her young foolishness, she thought she'd be the one to trick *him.*

She hadn't succeeded, Kosara knew. If she had, Kosara wouldn't have found her grave, overgrown with thorns.

"So you know you can survive, if you're strong enough," the Zmey said. "You know there's been someone who's done it before you."

Sevda's laugh was sharp and piercing. "Yes. Vila. That's why you're so obsessed with her."

The Zmey's eyes narrowed. Kosara immediately knew Sevda's mockery had been a step too far, and she strongly suspected Sevda knew it, too. Her whole body tensed. Pins and needles prickled at her skin.

If I die in this dream, Kosara wondered as she watched the Zmey's fists clenching and unclenching, *would I die in real life, too?*

She wanted to run, but she had no control of her body. Sevda was frozen in place.

"Kosara!" came a familiar voice, completely unfitting for the scene. Nevena had never been in the Zmey's palace. Yet, it was definitely her voice Kosara heard calling her. "Kosara, you have to wake up!"

When Kosara woke up, her first thought was that she hated all of it. She hated the smell of burning flesh stuck in her nostrils. She hated how her fingers smarted where the fire had licked them. Most of all, she hated that Asen had been right.

Malamir had led them into a trap.

Was it any wonder? Malamir had repeatedly proven he couldn't be trusted, and yet, Kosara kept giving him chance after chance to disappoint her. Neither Malamir nor Roksana deserved her faith in them.

She'd never admitted to herself that she saw them as friends, but it *had* been some form of friendship they'd developed, built on nothing but familiarity, loneliness, and the closeness that comes from surviving too many dangers together. The sort of friendship that thrived in a city like Chernograd—the sort of friendship that made their betrayal unsurprising, yet still hurtful.

Kosara peeled her eyes open. She was in her bedroom, tucked in the blankets up to her chin. Whoever had brought her here had taken her boots and coat off but left on everything else. Her clothes stank of smoke. The wire of her bra poked painfully at her side.

The events from the previous evening were hazy, though she remembered one thing clearly: the Zmey's voice, whispering in her ear, urging her to *burn*. To her shame, she'd almost listened.

Then, she recalled seeing him in Sevda's vision, holding her hand and admitting a marriage to him was not always deadly. Something he'd also told Kosara when he'd desperately needed her help last winter. Apparently, he'd married Vila and let her go, something the old witch had most certainly never mentioned before.

Just how much was Vila hiding?

Kosara shook her head to clear it, before she got up and stumbled down the stairs. The living room was dark, the only light coming from the window, where the full moon hung low over the frosty roofs and icicle-clad spires.

The first thing Kosara did was drink thirstily straight from the tap, letting the cold water calm her sore throat. The second thing was light the fire so she could warm up.

She clicked her fingers, wincing when her blistered fingertips touched. The wood she'd stacked in the hearth came alight.

A figure moved on the couch.

Kosara swore and clicked her fingers again, summoning a flame in her hand. In its light, she noticed she hadn't put her shadows away, and they surrounded her, swirling at her feet.

Kosara shuddered looking at them. She'd been so close to using them as a deadly weapon last night.

"It's me!" Asen shouted, lifting his hands in the air, slowly rising to sit on the sofa.

"Oh." Kosara closed her fist around the flame, extinguishing it. Her shadows faded again in the gloom. "Sorry."

"It's fine. I didn't mean to startle you."

"What are you doing here?"

"I didn't know where else to go."

Kosara frowned. "You couldn't go home?"

He looked like he needed a good night's sleep, not a nap on her rickety sofa. After only a few hours in Chernograd, the purple circles under his eyes had started to return. He was tightly wrapped in all the extra blankets Kosara kept in the dresser—a fact she noted immediately. As she clearly remembered from last winter, he liked to sleep in nothing but a pair of impossibly tight boxers.

He ran a hand through his hair, attempting to smooth it down. It didn't work. "I thought you might need someone to keep an eye on you."

"I don't," Kosara croaked. *How dare he?* As if she hadn't been just fine without him for months. "I feel great."

She didn't feel great. She was sore and tired, and her head hurt, but she didn't see how that was any of Asen's business.

Had he stayed because he was afraid *for* her, or had he stayed because he was afraid *of* her? Another memory from the previous night surfaced in her mind—the look in his eyes when she'd let her shadows nearly suffocate a man.

What did Asen think she'd do if he wasn't around? March straight to the river district and incinerate any thug she stumbled upon?

"You don't look great," he said, echoing her thoughts.

Kosara crossed her arms. "Did you stay here to insult me?"

"I didn't mean it like that," he said quickly, obviously flustered. "You know I always find you beautiful."

Did he?

Kosara was speechless, but only for a moment. "Trying to overcompensate with pointless flattery now, are we?"

Asen fidgeted in his seat. "Have you seen yourself in the mirror?"

"No," she said, confused, and then she remembered her shadows' recent habit of tweaking her appearance. "Oh no. What now?"

"You'd better see it for yourself."

Kosara tried to remain calm as she walked over to the mirror hanging above the fireplace. With the light coming from underneath, her face was covered in deep shadows. Her two blonde strands framed it in ghostly white.

At first, she couldn't figure out the difference. Her skin was slightly darker in places, but it was a subtle change, like getting a sunburn on only half your face.

But then, Kosara lifted her fingers to her cheek, searching for something that wasn't there.

"My scars." In the mirror, her eyes, both the green and the brown, watched her in horror. "My scars are gone."

Asen said nothing.

Tears filled Kosara's eyes. The rest of the changes she'd gone through had been purely cosmetic. People changed their hair all the time. When she'd been a teenager, enchanted lenses had been all the rage, and she'd spent a few weeks with red eyes, like an upir, until they'd given her a ghastly infection.

Erasing her scars was something else. It was like the shadows were attempting to erase her past. It was as if her last tangible connection to Nevena had been wiped clean.

Kosara wanted to cry, but she couldn't do it in front of Asen. So, she took several deep breaths, trying to calm down, pushing the tears away.

She was overreacting, surely. The shadows' magic was unpredictable, and it had manifested in an unexpected way this time, that was all. She was still herself—the differences in her appearance didn't change that.

She still remembered Nevena. She didn't need scars to remind her of her sister.

Kosara blinked fast, diffusing the tears in her eyes. Then, she sat at the table, her hands folded in front of her, trying to appear unperturbed. "Where are Roksana and the yudas?" she asked in an attempt to steer the conversation in a different direction. Her voice came out hollow even to her own ears.

Asen still looked at her apprehensively. "At Roksana's. I said we'd contact them once you feel better."

"I told you, I feel fine. I have to figure out how to send Sokol and Vrana back to the monster realm."

"You should rest."

"There's no time. I have to repair the breach between our realms before more monsters have found it. Before the entire city has frozen to death."

"Why you?"

Kosara laughed. "Who else? I'm the best witch this damned city's got."

"The best? Or just the most powerful?"

Kosara waved a hand. "It's the same thing." Except, she knew it wasn't.

"Kosara, I'm sorry, but you look exhausted. Karaivanov is obviously after you. You need to preserve your strength in case—"

"What the hell would you have me do, Bakharov?" Kosara snapped. "Sit here and wait for him to show up? You think Karaivanov is after me? Fine. Good, even. Because I'm after him, too. Or have you forgotten the promise we made your wife last winter?"

Asen didn't reply, but his eyes darted to the side, obviously trying to avoid hers. Kosara realised that when she'd raised her voice,
her shadows had moved closer behind her, looming threateningly
over Asen. She urged them, internally, to back off. Thankfully, they
listened.

"Don't you see how this is all connected?" Kosara said. "Karaivanov's
paying witches to tear holes in the barrier between our two worlds
and pull monsters down. I need to know how, so I can stop him."

Asen was silent for a moment. "You can't do it alone."

Kosara gave him an even look. He was the one to talk, after not
showing his face in Chernograd for months. After leaving her to deal
with the fallout from last winter alone.

"Get Vila to help," Asen added. "Get the other witches."

He had a point. The only issue was, Kosara wasn't sure she could
face Vila after what she'd learned in Sevda Yordanova's memories.
The old witch had kept it all a secret: her relationship with the Zmey,
her many failed attempts to save her students from him.

If things had gone only slightly differently, Kosara would have
never managed to escape his palace. She'd seen how that exact sce-
nario would have played out twice already.

There was also something else—something she found difficult to
admit, even to herself. Kosara couldn't help but feel a tiny, shameful
pang of jealousy. All these years, she'd thought the Zmey was obsessed with *her*.

When it came to asking for help from the other witches, there was
a different issue. There weren't that many of them left, and they all
thought she was the strongest magic user in the city. A witch with
twelve shadows.

If she went to them for help, she'd have to admit the truth. Kosara
couldn't control her shadows. She couldn't even control herself, what
with the Zmey's voice getting louder in her head every day.

She didn't know how they'd react. She didn't know if she could
trust them not to betray her, if they were to find out how weak she
really was.

"I can't go to the other witches," she said. "Not yet."

"Why?"

"I told you about Sofiya, didn't I? Her shadows were missing. You said Ruseva's was gone, too."

"You suspect a witch is involved in the murders?"

"I simply don't know who I can trust. After what happened with Malamir . . ." Kosara trailed off.

"Fine," Asen said. "Then let me help."

Kosara blinked. She hadn't expected him to volunteer. After so many months avoiding her, she'd started to believe he didn't care much about what happened to Chernograd. Or to her. "How?"

"I know I'm not a witch, but I have experience investigating murders. Besides, I think you're right. It's all connected: the mratinyak, Karaivanov's secret auctions, Sokol and Vrana getting trapped here, the breach between our realm and the monster one. The first step to untangling this whole mess would be solving the murders."

"And the second?"

"Hopefully catching Karaivanov. We both made a promise."

"What do you suggest?"

"Do you have access to the results from Sofiya's autopsy?"

Kosara snorted. "What do you think?"

"Right, it was a stupid question. I'll see if I can pull some strings."

"Can't you go to your boss back home and request them to be sent to you?"

"I'm afraid not."

"Why?"

"Two reasons. One, I don't work for the police anymore."

She frowned, unsure she'd understood him correctly. "As in, you resigned?"

"Something like that."

Kosara heaved a sigh of relief. She'd associated with her fair share of dodgy characters over the years, but she never could get over making friends with a copper. People would talk. "Oh, thank God. But why? I thought you loved your job."

Asen shrugged. "I love investigating. The rest of it? I found it didn't suit me anymore. If you know anyone who's looking for help, I'm all ears, by the way. I've got savings, but—"

"In Chernograd?"

"Yeah."

Hope fluttered in Kosara's chest and she quickly, decisively, smothered it. He wasn't here because of her. She knew that. "You don't plan to return home?"

"Ah." Another attempt at smoothing his hair, another failure. Kosara resisted the urge to try to help him. "This brings me to the second reason. What can you tell me about varkolak bites?"

For a few seconds, Kosara was unsure what to say. She looked at him, blinking slowly, trying to process his question.

The events from the previous night were still a blur. She remembered Karaivanov's varkolaks swarming her, but not much else after.

"Did you get bitten?" she asked, dreading the answer, the blood slowly draining from her face.

Instead of replying, Asen rolled up the blanket and showed her the fresh bite mark, bright red among the dark hair. It was barely a scratch. It didn't even seem to be bleeding anymore.

Except, Kosara knew that was all it took. She swore out loud.

"That bad?" Asen asked. "I'd hoped you'd say it wasn't deep enough."

"There's no such thing as 'not deep enough' with varkolak bites."

"I'd kind of expected to turn, what with it being the full moon . . ."

"It normally takes a few days for the infection to develop. I suspect you're safe until the next full moon, provided you avoid stressors. Stress can make it manifest quicker."

Asen looked at her as if she'd gone mad. Avoiding stressors was easier said than done, she supposed, given the situation they'd found themselves in.

"I'm sorry," she added helplessly.

"There's nothing you can do?" he asked.

Kosara bit her lip. The last time she'd researched varkolak bites, it had all seemed hopeless. However, that had been years ago. She was much more experienced now. Not to mention, she had twelve shadows.

She still didn't want to give him false hope. "I'm afraid not."

Asen sighed. He was trying to put on a brave face, Kosara knew, but internally, he must have been devastated. He hated Chernograd, that much was clear. His whole life was in Belograd. What did he have here?

Her?

He doesn't want you, a voice said in her head, and she recognised the Zmey's warm baritone. *He's afraid of you.*

She couldn't argue with that. She'd seen it with her own eyes.

You know who's never been afraid of your power? Who'd never try to smother your magic?

"Be quiet," Kosara muttered under her breath without thinking.

Asen raised his eyebrows at her. He must have realised she wasn't talking to him, but hopefully he didn't know *who* she was talking to.

"All might not be lost," she said quickly, attempting to smooth over the fact she was conversing with someone who only existed in her head. "What about your wedding ring? It might protect you from turning."

Asen looked away from her, fixing his eyes somewhere over her left shoulder. Kosara turned back to find nothing there but the room's dark corner.

"You have my wedding ring," Asen mumbled.

Of course. Kosara remembered now. That was how she'd escaped the magic circle's confines. Sheepishly, she took the ring off and handed it to him. Without saying a word, he clasped it at his neck and hid it under his T-shirt.

This was her fault. She'd insisted they follow Malamir to the river district. She'd needed Asen's wedding ring to get out of the magic circle she'd walked into like a complete idiot.

What was worse, the fact that he was trapped here was her fault, too. She'd made it so people could pass through the Wall, not monsters.

She looked at him, sitting on the sofa and carefully trying to rearrange his hair so it would stop falling in front of his eyes, and she could hardly believe this man was a monster.

For the second time that night, she had to swallow back tears. It all felt too familiar. Looking at the bite mark on Asen's calf sent her back to the day Nevena had been bitten. It had been Kosara's fault then, too.

"I should make you a poultice." Kosara used it as an excuse to turn her back to him. She started gathering her herbs, reaching to separate a twig of thyme from the bunch hanging from a roof beam.

"It's just a scratch, Kosara. I don't need a poultice."

"I'm making you a poultice."

He didn't understand. This was another debt she now owed him. She needed to do something, so she'd feel less rotten about it.

"I don't need a poultice," Asen said again, and Kosara continued to ignore him. "But there's something I have to ask you."

"Yes?" Kosara looked over her shoulder while picking mint leaves.

"I have no way of contacting my mother, and she must be starting to get worried. We have no phone. If I send her a letter, I'm not sure it'll ever get to her."

Kosara nodded. The Chernogradean Post was notoriously slow and unreliable.

"So," Asen continued, "I was wondering, can you deliver the letter straight to her?"

"Of course. Is that all?" The truth was, she didn't want to deliver a letter to his mother. What would Kosara even say to the poor woman? "You don't know me, but I made sure you'll never see your son again unless you follow me to my monster-infested hellhole. Cheerio!"

Asen looked even more uncomfortable than he had earlier. "Well. If I'm trapped here for the time being, I have nowhere to stay—"

"You can stay here."

"I'm not sure that's wise."

"Why?"

"Didn't you tell me a story once about your sister turning into a varkolak and attacking you?"

Kosara shuddered. Evidently, she wasn't the only one who'd been reminded of that night. "That was before I'd finished my apprentice-ship with Vila. I can handle a varkolak now, believe me."

"Are you sure?"

"Certain. We'll set up a cage in the basement for you."

Asen considered her for a long moment. "You're only suggesting this because you feel guilty I got bitten, aren't you?"

"I'm suggesting this because you're my friend and you need help." The words came out of her mouth before she'd had the chance to think them over. If she had, she'd have probably decided to swallow them.

Were they friends, really? She'd be the first to admit her perception of what counted for friendship was completely off-kilter—but unlike Roksana and Malamir, Asen had never given her any reason to doubt him.

Besides, she knew he was right. She couldn't do it all alone.

Rather, she couldn't do it with her shadows circling her like sharks, waiting for her to slip up, and she absolutely couldn't do it with the Zmey whispering in her ear.

She was going to help Asen get rid of this curse if she could. Get rid of the curse, get rid of Chernograd, get rid of her.

But first, she'd allow him to help her, and all the while, she'd have to learn to control herself around him. She couldn't allow herself to turn into the Zmey.

She heard him, even now. *You should have burned them all. They'll never take you seriously if you don't show them your power.*

Burn, my little Kosara. Burn.

13

Asen

A varkolak. Asen could hardly believe it.

It had been nothing but a quick brush of the wolf's teeth against his calf. The bruise was almost gone now. The dots where the canines had broken his skin had stopped bleeding.

Such a trifle, but it changed so much.

He tried not to dwell on it, at least for now, as he walked down a dark Chernogradean street towards the police station. It helped that he was about to do what he did best: investigate.

It was still the early morning, and the city awoke slowly and grumpily. Grim-faced people strode past, clutching steaming cups of coffee and stinking cigarettes. Someone beat their carpet on the balcony of a tall block of flats—the rhythmic thuds echoed, startling the stray dogs and making them bark.

Asen stopped at the bakery for a buttery filo pastry stuffed with cheese and a bottle of sour Chernogradean ayran. After several bites, he decided his situation wasn't that bad, after all. He had warm clothes on his back and a solid roof over his head.

You have Kosara, a hopeful voice in his mind chimed in, and Asen dismissed it with a wave of his hand. Whatever chance he'd had with her last winter, he'd squandered it out of cowardice: fear of rejection, fear of not being worthy, fear of losing her like he'd lost Boryana.

Fear that the redheaded silhouette he kept seeing in the corner of his eye wasn't simply his imagination, but Boryana's vengeful kikimora, watching him after he'd awoken her last winter. It filled him with guilt.

You have her as a friend, the hopeful voice amended, and with a shrug, Asen admitted it might have a point. She hadn't told him to get lost yet, anyway.

In any case, his situation wasn't that dire. Yes, he was trapped in Chernograd, but did he really have a right to complain, when most Chernogradeans had spent years unable to leave the city? He couldn't be sure how many of the people he passed in the street were still imprisoned within the confines of the Wall. How many were just like him. Monsters.

One thing still gave him hope. When he'd asked Kosara if there was a cure for lycanthropy, she'd hesitated before answering "no." Asen knew her. If there was any way she could break the curse over him, she'd find it.

Until then, Asen was determined to make the best of his precarious position. Maybe this was what he'd needed all along. A fresh start, away from Belograd. Away from the mayor's influence and his boss's all-knowing gaze.

His fingers automatically found the scar on his forearm, where a karakonjul had bitten him within minutes of arriving the last time he'd visited Chernograd. He'd been a clueless tourist then. Now, he was more prepared.

For example, as he walked up the steps of the Chernogradean police station, he came armed not only with confidence and arguments, but also with a thick wad of banknotes.

"My name is Asen Bakharov," he introduced himself at the entrance.

An old man in a scruffy uniform sat on a folding chair, rolling a cigarette between yellowed fingers. His bushy eyebrows twitched when he looked up at Asen. "And?"

"I am here on urgent business related to a murder case currently under investigation by the Belogradean Police Force."

"And?"

"Can I speak to Chief Constable Darina Chausheva?" Asen had

dealt with Darina before. She'd been unusually helpful for a Chernogradean police officer.

"Right," the man said. He finished rolling his cigarette, tucked it behind his ear, and, with a lot of huffing and puffing, got up from the chair. "I'll show you to her office. I'll have to search you first."

Asen submitted to the most perfunctory pat down he'd ever experienced before he followed the old man inside, along a series of dank narrow corridors. When they reached the door to Darina's office, the man didn't feel the need to introduce Asen. He simply nodded and walked away.

As soon as Asen knocked and opened the door, a mass of cigarette smoked rushed him.

"Darina, hello," he said, holding the door half-open. After many years of working with Vartanian, he was used to not entering unless given explicit permission.

Darina Chausheva looked up from the pile of papers on her desk. In many ways, she was the polar opposite of Vartanian: tall, skinny, with high cheekbones and slicked-back hair. Her dark uniform was a size or two too big for her, which Asen thought might be on purpose— just like how cats made their tails bushy to appear larger.

"Who are you?" she barked.

"Asen Bakharov. We've spoken on the phone before. I investigate Karaivanov's ring over in Belograd."

"Bakharov!" Darina's face split into what seemed to be a genuine smile. "Of course, of course. Please come in, why are you hanging about the door? Sit down."

Asen sat in the chair she indicated. When she offered him a cigarette from a gilded case, he couldn't resist it. He was a Chernogradean now, wasn't he?

Besides, from what Kosara had told him, varkolaks were known for their good constitution. Surely, he didn't need to worry as much about his lungs anymore.

Chernogradean cigarettes were putrid. The smoke was thick and stinking, almost greasy as it slid down his throat. He still thought it tasted wonderful.

"What brings you to Chernograd?" Darina asked.

"The usual."

"Karaivanov?"

"There's been a murder we believe he's responsible for. A witch involved with his gang has been beheaded."

Darina inhaled through her teeth but said nothing.

Asen continued, "I believe you've had a similar case in Chernograd recently?"

"You've seen it in the papers, I gather? I tried keeping the journos away, but they're like vultures, always circling." Darina sighed. "Yes, it was ghastly. A beheaded witch, just like yours. I'm surprised I hadn't heard about your case if it so strongly resembles ours."

"I'm sure Vartanian would have contacted you soon . . ."

"Please, Bakharov. You know as well as I do Anahit would rather cut off her own ears and eat them than cooperate with me. Even if it means leaving a murderer at large."

Asen shuffled in his seat. He was aware Vartanian didn't trust Chausheva, though he didn't know the history between the two. Vartanian likely had her own informants in the Chernogradean police, circumventing its chief constable.

"Good thing you've always been more sensible than her," Darina said. "I suspect I know why you're here. You want our case files, don't you? Well." Darina smirked. "I'll show you mine if you show me yours."

Asen paused, but not for long. He couldn't let her see his hesitation or his whole story would fall through. "As you can imagine, Vartanian would never let me bring any hard copies to Chernograd . . ."

"Of course. We can do what we did the last time. I'll tell you what I know, and then you tell me what you know."

This worked for Asen. He hadn't had the chance to read the report from the pathologists, but he could make a few educated guesses. The rest of it he'd seen with his own eyes: the blood splatter, the wounds on the victim's body, Karaivanov's mark.

Darina asked a few questions that nearly tripped him. Had they recovered any fingerprints? Had any witnesses come forwards?

Asen managed to brush it all off. There had been many murders in

Belograd lately, and resources were stretched thin. They were still to compare the fingerprints against their database. He wasn't aware of any witnesses they'd managed to locate. He'd let her know as soon as he found out anything new.

Then, it was Chausheva's turn to speak. "So, I suspect you know most of it already. The victim was attacked late at night. Beheaded. Tonnes of blood. Here's where it gets interesting . . . At first, we'd assumed the victim was the salon's owner, Sofiya. There had been some effort made to leave that impression. The woman was of similar height and weight, similar in age—"

"But?"

"But we compared the fingerprints. We had Sofiya's on file after she'd been arrested for petty theft as a young girl. They didn't match."

Asen frowned. "So . . ."

"So, the victim's not Sofiya."

Asen kept his face professionally neutral even though his heartbeat quickened. If Sofiya was still alive, she might know how to repair the breach between the realms. If they found her, they'd be one step closer to resolving this mess.

He couldn't wait to tell Kosara.

But then, another realisation hit him.

"I know this face," Darina said. "What are you thinking?"

"Well, if the murderer went to all this effort to fake Sofiya's death, chances are . . ."

"The murderer is Sofiya? I can tell you she's certainly a strong suspect."

Asen swore under his breath. "Why haven't you released this information to the public? She must be easy to spot. She's a witch with two shadows."

"Three, at least. The victim's shadow was missing, remember?"

"Even more notable. Someone must have seen her."

Darina extinguished her cigarette and squeezed it in the overflowing ashtray, before immediately lighting a second one. She threw her head back and exhaled a cloud of smoke upwards. "I don't want Sofiya to know I'm coming for her."

Asen leaned forwards in his seat. "So, you know where she's hiding?"

Darina watched him evenly for a few seconds, obviously weighing whether she should tell him. "Let's say, I have an idea how to bring her out of her hidey hole."

"How?" Asen asked, unable to hide the eagerness in his voice.

Another long stare. Then, Darina leaned closer, too.

Before she'd opened her mouth, a loud shout interrupted them from the hallway. "Chief Constable Chausheva!"

"What?" Chausheva barked without making to get up from her seat.

"We've got Lila Levi on the phone here from the Belogradean Police. She says she's got something important to discuss. It's about the beheading on the main street."

Chausheva raised her eyebrows at Asen. He shrugged, trying to appear nonchalant, but under the desk, his leg trembled in a nervous tic.

Damn Lila. Asen had taught her too well. She'd been there the last time he'd gone behind Vartanian's back to exchange information with Darina, and now, she was copying his strategy.

"Tell her Bakharov is here," Chausheva said. "We're already discussing it."

A long pause, and then, just when Asen was starting to hope he might have got away with it, "She says Bakharov doesn't work for them anymore!"

Damn Lila, Asen thought again with frustration, but also a certain amount of pride. She'd acted exactly how he'd trained her to.

Chausheva's eyes narrowed. Asen, out of pure habit, tried for the charming smile that had got him out of many a hot water before. He knew it wouldn't work on her. She was too smart to fall for it, and besides, he suspected he wasn't her type. Judging by the framed photo of her wife on her desk, Chausheva preferred blondes.

"Tell Lila I'll phone her back in a minute," Chausheva shouted towards the hallway.

She didn't say a word to Asen. She simply watched him.

With a sigh, he found the roll of cash in his pocket. He counted three bills and looked up to find Chausheva's face hadn't softened. So, he counted three more. And three more.

God, this woman was determined to bankrupt him.

Finally, after she'd made a considerable dent in Asen's savings, she gave him a tight smile, leaned over the desk, and plucked the notes from his hand.

"Get out of here, Bakharov." She stuffed them in her desk drawer. "And pray I don't tell Vartanian about this."

Asen hurried to leave the police station, grateful for his forward thinking to bring the money. Grateful, as well, that Chausheva and Vartanian hated each other, so his secret was safe with the Chernogradean chief constable. Vartanian would have had no issue with him impersonating an officer to get information out of Chausheva, of course—but she'd have had a huge issue that he'd got caught.

He regretted nothing. His gamble had paid off. He'd found a golden nugget of information.

Sofiya was alive—and Chausheva believed she knew how to locate her.

As Asen walked out into the damp, grey Chernogradean morning, several uniformed police officers darted past him, carrying stacks of papers and jars of glue. One of them stopped in front of a nearby building and proceeded to attach the papers onto the wall, obscuring old theatre posters, lost pet notices, and obituaries.

"Excuse me?" Asen approached her. "Do you mind if I take one of these?"

The police officer shrugged and handed him a piece of paper from the pile in her hands.

"AUCTION," it read in big red letters. And underneath: "To raise money for funeral expenses, and since no living relatives have been located, the Chernogradean Police Department is hosting an AUCTION for all items remaining in the Witch's Rest after the proprietor's death. All are welcome."

14

Kosara

All in all, the conversation with Asen's mother didn't go terribly. Even if Rosa Bakharova blamed Kosara for her son's unfortunate condition, she didn't show it. She spent a few minutes lamenting what had happened and asking all the usual questions: "Is there a cure? Are you sure? Are you completely, absolutely sure?"

Kosara had managed to avoid it all, humming and hawing and relying on half truths.

"I haven't seen a cure work yet," she'd said carefully.

Then, Rosa had declared what was done was done, and insisted Kosara stay over for lunch, which had quickly led to a card game and several thimbles of Rosa's best brandy.

"You should come to visit soon," Kosara said at the door, after Rosa had loaded her with a bag of Asen's favourite sweets, teas, and trinkets. "I'm sure Asen would love to see you."

"I don't know, Kosara. I've never been over the Wall before, and I've heard it's dangerous . . ."

"Nonsense. I'll bring you over. How about next Saturday? I can come and get you first thing in the morning."

"Ah, all right. But don't tell Asen. I want to surprise him."

"My lips are sealed," Kosara said with a laugh.

On the way home, Kosara stopped at the market. It was a mild day, and she felt even more conspicuous than usual in her thick clothes. Asen had warned her not to overdress, but she'd still donned her thermals, unable to imagine what the heat felt like after a year without it.

Of course, unlike last winter, she wasn't the only Chernogradean around. Multiple unsuitably dressed people walked past, sharing a sympathetic look with her.

The Belogradean fashion had shifted with the season. The people passing by still wore pastels and multiple layers, but of linen and tulle, not cashmere and lambswool. Their sandals slapped loudly against the cobblestones as they mulled around, carrying bags of shopping.

The market stalls were overflowing with stock: brightly coloured fruits and country wines, vials of exotic oils and jars of spicy pastes, strings of dried chillies and garlic the size of Kosara's fist. A procession of donkey carts snaked up the street, filled with rose blossoms destined for the city's best perfumeries and pharmacies. The air was thick with their heady scent.

Kosara compared it all to the empty shelves in Chernograd and thought it little wonder people were leaving for Belograd in droves. The price of eggs had been going through the roof in the past few days since a quarter of the hens in Chernograd were now dead. She'd heard people in the street talking—they were worried it was bird flu.

The city had been on the brink of bankruptcy for many years, but the mratinyak might have just finished the job.

As Kosara got closer to the Wall, the square grew louder. She knew from experience something was always happening in Belograd: a free concert, a performance of a street theatre, or a full-blown carnival. She elbowed her way past the crowd to get a better look.

It wasn't a carnival, that much became clear immediately. As Kosara waded deeper into the rabble of frowning, angry people, she grew increasingly uncomfortable. It wasn't only the tension hanging thickly in the air. It was the looks they gave her—scornful, almost disgusted.

Several people were holding placards. She craned her neck to read them, and her blood ran cold. "Belograd for the Belogradeans," said one of them. "Go home, Chernogradean scum," another proclaimed in big angry letters.

Many years of living in a monster-infested city had trained Kosara to immediately recognise when she was in danger. Slowly, step by step, she separated herself from the crowd, angling towards the mouth of a dark alleyway where she could disappear.

Just as she'd stepped into it, she heard a voice rising over the crowd's tumult. Against her better judgment, Kosara risked peeking around the corner.

On a stage erected in front of the Wall, high above the crowd, a woman stood with a loudspeaker in hand. She wore a strict business suit, tailored to fit closely to her body, and her hair was tied in a tight bun.

"Dear citizens of Belograd," the woman shouted, and the crowd quieted to listen. "Dear friends. Thank you for coming today on this first day of my reelection campaign."

As the crowd erupted in applause, Kosara squinted, trying to make out the woman's features. She was sure she remembered this particular politician from somewhere—a photo in the newspaper, possibly, or a poster on a wall. It took Kosara a few seconds to recognise her, and when she did, she gasped.

The woman standing on the podium was the mayor of Belograd herself. Maria Hajieva. The woman Asen had narrowly escaped only days earlier.

"We have a lot of hard work ahead of us to make Belograd the grand city it once was," the mayor continued. "I know we're all tired of feeding foreign mouths and giving our hard-earned money to foreign hands who never stop begging. It's time for us to say, 'Enough!' It's time for us"—she made a long, deliberate pause—"to rebuild the Wall."

The crowd went wild. The placards flapped in the wind as people jumped, screamed, and cheered.

With relief, Kosara noticed not everyone gathered in the square was taken with the mayor's promises. There were other people in dark clothes there, watching grimly from street corners. There were Belogradeans too, heckling the mayor.

"How will you do that?" a man with a Belogradean accent asked loudly, his deep voice carrying over the crowd's din. Whether he used magic to project it, or he'd trained it just for such occasions, Kosara couldn't know.

"I'm glad you asked," the mayor said with a practised smile. "Until recently, we assumed the secret to how the Wall was built had died with our illustrious Grand Master Kliment last spring. However, we recently heard from the generous donor who had been tasked with rehoming Kliment's large library. The schematics for the ritual have been uncovered once more, and a team of the best witches money can hire are currently working on deciphering them. All thanks to none other than my dear friend, the famous businessman, Konstantin Karaivanov."

The mayor paused again and the crowd, knowing what was expected of them, enthusiastically applauded her.

Bile climbed up Kosara's throat. Chernograd was full of corrupt politicians, but she hadn't realised how similar Belograd was in that regard. Here was the most powerful political figure in Belograd, openly admitting Karaivanov was her "dear friend" to a crowd of cheering idiots.

What was more, the mayor's words only confirmed Kosara's worst fears. Karaivanov and his witches were working on making the Wall whole again, trapping everyone within the city once more.

It was hardly a surprise. Of course Karaivanov was keen to restore the Wall and make smuggling as profitable as it once had been.

The mayor shouted into her loudspeaker, "If you reelect me, dear citizens, I'll make sure the Wall stands strong again!"

Kosara had heard enough. She turned around to leave.

She'd barely made a couple of steps deeper into the alleyway when the sounds drifting from the square abruptly changed. The cheers died down, followed by a moment of silence. Then came the screams.

Kosara paused, her fists clenching and unclenching at her side. She wouldn't turn back. Whatever happened to the crowd, they deserved it. It wasn't her problem. She wasn't going to help them.

She wasn't.

A few seconds later, with a deep sigh, Kosara turned back.

In the brief time it had taken her to return, the square was unrecognisable. The people pushed against each other in a frantic bid to get away. Their placards lay on the ground, soaking in the mud.

The mayor still stood on her podium. She used her loudspeaker as a weapon, bashing the head of something small and furry. A fox? Or a dog?

No. *A karakonjul.*

Even from afar, Kosara recognised its donkey-like ears, its curved horns, and its eyes shining like lanterns.

She rushed through the crowd. It wasn't easy, going against their relentless tide. On several occasions, she almost stumbled to the ground. It would have been a death sentence, falling down when everyone around her was in such a panic.

Eventually, out of breath and sweating profusely, Kosara made it to the podium. The mayor was still alive, somehow, still repeatedly hitting the monster's face with the loudspeaker.

The karakonjul let out a roar, but it stayed back. Kosara narrowed her eyes. She'd witnessed plenty of karakonjul attacks before. The beasts couldn't be stopped with a couple of badly aimed thumps with a loudspeaker.

She didn't get the chance to analyse the monster's behaviour in any more depth. The next second, it turned its gleaming eyes in her direction.

Kosara was prepared. She put her bags on the ground and cupped her hands in front of her face to make sure it would hear her: "What has ears like a donkey, horns like a ram, and a big ugly face?"

The karakonjul stared at her with its mouth open, drooling radioactive-green saliva onto the podium. Kosara prepared a fireball in her hand, just in case things went sideways fast.

The mayor used this moment of distraction to lift a crossbow from the floor, aim at the karakonjul, and shoot.

The monster didn't even have time to scream. First, it looked down at the bleeding hole in its torso, then it turned back to Kosara, as if it expected her to do something. Then gently, peacefully, it collapsed onto the ground.

Kosara extinguished the fireball in her hand and blinked at the dead monster, trying to process what she'd just witnessed.

It took the crowd a few moments to realise the danger had passed. Eventually, most stopped their panicked rush away from the square. Some turned to look at the podium: at Kosara standing over the karakonjul, her hand still smoking, and at the mayor, whose face looked more and more like she'd smelled spoiled milk.

Slowly, the cheers and applause began again. Kosara, who was un- used to being in the limelight, did a little bow. The mayor didn't move.

"You're welcome," Kosara said as she walked past the mayor, but the other woman didn't answer.

Belogradeans, Kosara scoffed. *You save their life, they do nothing but glare at you.*

She collected her bags, climbed down from the podium, and walked towards the Wall. The crowd let her pass. Some shouted en- couragement at her. Others remained silent, watching her with wide eyes.

They are afraid of me. The realisation hurt. She'd just saved their mayor's life.

I'm not a monster! she wanted to shout at them, but protesting too much would only leave the wrong impression. She'd conjured fire out of thin air. Everyone had seen her do it.

Maybe she was a monster, after all. If Asen was one, then why wouldn't she be one, too? She was just as dangerous, and just as foreign to these Belogradeans.

Kosara exhaled deeply when she crossed through the Wall and found herself in the familiar streets of Chernograd. Here, no one looked at her as if any minute, she might incinerate them where they stood.

The change in temperature made her shiver, and yet, she walked slowly, enjoying every cold breath. The pavements were perfect and white, and the snow kept falling, hiding her steps behind her.

It was only now, as the adrenaline rush ended and her heart stopped galloping in her chest, that she got the chance to review what had just happened on the other side of the Wall.

The first unusual thing had been the karakonjul. Not only the fact that it was there, in Belograd, but its behaviour. It was impossible to keep a beast like that at bay armed with nothing but a loudspeaker. The mayor hadn't even reached for her crossbow, obviously prepared beforehand in case of trouble, until Kosara had arrived.

Besides, that confused stare on the monster's face? Kosara had seen it before—on Button, Malamir's pet monster.

It seemed obvious. The karakonjul had been trained. The mayor hadn't been in any real danger. It had all been political theatre to strengthen her cause.

"Look!" it was meant to communicate. "If we don't shut the Wall again, more monsters will come. Look at your brave mayor bravely defending you from one!"

Kosara had interrupted the performance. That was why the mayor had looked as if she was ready to strangle her.

Kosara's teeth sunk into the inside of her cheek. She was furious at the mayor for taking her entire city for fools, but she was also angry at herself for not realising it earlier. She could have grabbed that loudspeaker and revealed it all to the crowd.

But then, would they have believed her? She was nothing but a Chernogradean to them. By definition, she couldn't be trusted.

The mayor wouldn't simply let her do it without a fight, either. Maria Hajieva obviously had important friends. After all, who was the only person who could have provided her with the karakonjul for her little display? Who was the man who knew how to pull monsters through the barrier between the realms outside of the Foul Days?

Konstantin bloody Karaivanov.

15

Asen

Asen had been reading by the hearth, but he looked up when the door opened and Kosara rushed in.

His eyes ran over her oversized coat and thermal tights. Despite his best efforts, he could spot no hints that there was a woman hiding under all the layers. She looked, for all intents and purposes, like a shapeless woollen blob. He'd be damned if he knew why this didn't detract from his attraction to her—on the contrary, it seemed to only fuel it. There was obviously something not quite right with him.

What was next: Would he start frequenting the dodgy nightclubs around the Docks, but instead of tipping dancers for taking their clothes off, he'd ask them to pile on layer upon layer?

Asen somehow doubted it would have the same effect if it was anyone else but Kosara, which was the crux of the issue. He had to get a grip.

He cleared his throat. "Look at you!" he exclaimed. "How did you manage not to melt on the other side of the Wall?"

"I took the coat off," Kosara said, as if it were obvious. Her hair had grown more voluminous from the damp outside—all but her two blonde strands, which hung straight down, surrounding her face. "Your mother sent all this." She handed him several bags.

He couldn't help but grin as he pulled out box after box of sweets.

"How is she?" he asked, unwrapping a packet of hazelnut lokum.

"She seemed well. I managed to convince her you're well, too, I hope."

"How's Belograd?"

"It was quite tense, actually. You'll never believe what I saw."

Kosara told him what had happened: about the crowd gathered in the square, the karakonjul attack, and her suspicions of how the monster had found its way to Belograd.

"Karaivanov," Asen said flatly.

"Karaivanov," Kosara agreed.

Asen sighed deeply, running a hand through his hair.

"How was your trip to the police station?" Kosara asked.

"It went well, actually." Despite his worries, Asen smiled. He had enjoyed stretching his investigative muscles, even if it had required him parting with what little remained of his savings to do it. "I've got some interesting news."

"Oh?" Kosara was still standing, holding a bottle of Belogradean brandy his mother must have given her.

"You might want to sit down."

"Stop being dramatic, Bakharov. Spit it out."

"Sofiya is alive."

A loud clank. The bottle shattered, spilling brandy all over the floor. The sharp smell of alcohol and apricots filled the kitchen.

"Shit," Kosara said, her hand still trembling.

Asen grabbed the brush and pan and hurried to collect the shards of glass. Kosara kneeled down to wipe the brandy with a rag.

As the two of them worked, she asked, "How? I mean, how can she be alive? Her head was missing. That would be one hell of a magic trick, even for a witch with two shadows."

"Chausheva compared the fingerprints she had on file for Sofiya with those of the victim. They didn't match."

"Ah." Kosara grimaced. "The bastard. She completely fooled me."

"I think she fooled everyone. For a bit, at least."

"Do they know who the victim is?"

"Chausheva didn't say."

"Of course she didn't." Kosara rolled her eyes, then turned to rinse the rag in the sink. Asen threw away the shards. Finally, they sat at opposite ends of the kitchen table.

Kosara rubbed the bridge of her nose with her thumb and index finger. It was an unfamiliar gesture, and Asen frowned.

He hadn't truly paid attention to how much she seemed to have changed recently—he should have. It wasn't just the superficial differences—the eye, the hair, the skin. Her mannerisms had subtly shifted. Her accent kept fluctuating. Even her voice occasionally acquired an unfamiliar ring to it.

He suspected it had something to do with her shadows.

"This makes no sense," Kosara said. "Why would there be someone who just happens to have the same bloody tattoo on her wrist as Sofiya—"

"Wait," Asen interrupted her, images of Ruseva's dead body flashing in his mind. "What tattoo?"

"Three swirly things. Sofiya's had it for years. Why?"

"Ruseva had the same tattoo. You never mentioned it before."

"I didn't think it was important. Everyone and their grandma's got a magic tattoo these days. You can get one for spare change at the market. Whether it would do what it's supposed to is a different matter entirely."

"Do you know what Sofiya's tattoo was meant to do?"

"I've never thought about it, to be honest. Three interlocking spirals? A spiral is usually used to symbolise infinity. Three infinities?"

Asen was struck by an idea. "Maybe it's the three realms. You said Sofiya used to talk to the dead? And now, she's poking holes through the barrier between the human and the monster realms."

"Maybe," Kosara said, but she looked unconvinced. "I suppose we can ask her once we see her. If we see her. I still can't believe she's alive."

"Chausheva is organising an auction for her possessions." Asen pushed the poster for the auction across the table to Kosara and waited while she read it, her eyes narrowing. "I think she hopes that if Sofiya hears all her precious treasures might get plundered, she'll show up. Do you think it will work?"

Kosara shrugged. "It might. Sofiya is the materialistic type. I'm not sure it will work exactly how Chausheva is imagining it, though. Sofiya wouldn't simply stroll through the door during the auction in some cheap disguise. She's smarter than that."

"What would she do?"

"What *I* would do is go to the house tonight, before the auction, and save as many of my treasures as I can."

"I'm sure Chausheva has stationed officers to guard the house tonight."

"Yeah, but Sofiya is a witch with two shadows—"

"Three. At least."

"Oh?" For a second, Kosara looked confused. "Oh, yeah. Of course. Anyway, I suspect Chausheva is underestimating Sofiya. Which is good news for us because we won't underestimate her."

Asen paused. He recognised that look on Kosara's face. She was about to do something reckless. "You think we should also stake out the house?"

"Of course. We can't let Chausheva have Sofiya if we ever hope to solve this."

Asen knew she was right. They had no choice but to intercept Sofiya before she'd be arrested.

Yet, it seemed like such a risk to get themselves stuck between Sofiya, a dangerous and likely desperate witch, and the entire Chernogradean Police Department. Asen was aware it was a bit too late for him to worry about breaking the police code of conduct, but purposefully sabotaging a stakeout seemed like a step too far, even for him.

"What?" Kosara asked, eyes fixed on him. She'd sensed his hesitation.

"Sofiya won't let herself get captured easily. She's dangerous."

"So? I'm dangerous, too."

"She's got at least three shadows—"

"I've got twelve. There's nothing to worry about, Bakharov, I promise you."

Asen looked away from her. When they'd first met last winter, he'd have believed her. She tried so hard to sound casual.

By now, however, he knew all her tells. Her fingers kept playing with the corner of the auction poster: folding, unfolding, folding again. She'd bit her lips so hard, little beads of blood had formed between the cracks.

Kosara was scared. And if Kosara, the witch with twelve shadows, was scared, Asen knew he ought to be terrified.

16

Kosara

Kosara licked her lips and tasted blood. She had to stop chewing on them, or no amount of beeswax would keep them from bleeding.

Thankfully, Asen didn't seem to have noticed. Why would he? Her fear of facing Sofiya made no sense. Kosara had the clear advantage—it was three shadows against twelve. Child's play.

If only Kosara could rely on her shadows to behave.

"What's the plan?" Asen asked.

Kosara, for once, was prepared for the question. "Chausheva's got people at the back and the front door, right?"

"I'd guess so."

"Except Sofiya has a secret. You know how she does séances with the dead?"

"Yes?"

"Well, some dead are deader than others. No matter how much you prod them, they don't wake up. So, when Sofiya gets a client who wants to speak to someone who's refusing to be dragged back to the world of the living, instead of giving the client a refund, she pays one of her apprentices to come in, rattle the table, and whine."

Asen furrowed his eyebrows. "Which is important because?"

"It means there's a third, secret way into Sofiya's salon. It's been a great source of jokes in the witch community ever since we found out, but I doubt Chausheva knows about it. Witches are no snitches."

"Where does it lead?"

"Under the table, of course. From the gutter in a nearby alleyway."

The corners of Asen's mouth twitched. "So, if we make it past Chausheva's minions and into the séance room . . ."

". . . we'll ambush Sofiya as soon as her pretty head pops out of the gutter. I might take a page from Karaivanov's book and prepare a magic circle to trap her. If only I'd had time to decipher it fully . . ."

"What, while getting attacked by varkolaks?"

"Anyway, I do have a few ideas." In fact, Kosara's mind was already whirling with them. "I'll use rusalka ink, that stuff's practically impossible to smear, and then if I throw a few drops of upir saliva—"

"You should take my wedding ring," Asen said.

"What?"

"My wedding ring. You should take it if you're to face Sofiya."

Kosara shook her head quickly. "Oh no. No way. After what happened the last time you lent it to me? I'm not touching that thing again."

"Kosara." Before she could react, Asen took her hand in his and pushed the ring into her palm. It was still warm from where it had sat against his chest. He closed her fingers around it firmly and continued speaking without ever letting go of her hand. "I'll come with you, but once we've got Sofiya, you'll be on your own. I'm helpless when it comes to magic. The only thing I can help you with is this. Please let me help."

"You can help me by coming with me, watching my back, and sweet-talking any copper who might catch us." Kosara pushed the ring back into his hand. "You need to keep the ring. I'm not sure, but I hope it might prevent you from turning."

"Oh," Asen said. "Oh, I see."

"It might not," Kosara hurried to add, so he wouldn't get his hopes up. "It all depends on how strong that ring actually is."

"I understand." Asen smiled at Kosara, that smile she'd always liked so much, but for a moment, his eyes flicked past her. He quickly let go of her hand.

Kosara glanced over her shoulder. For a second, she could swear, she saw a redheaded figure standing in the corner, dressed in white. The look in her eyes was murderous.

Kosara blinked, and the figure was gone.

Getting past the two police officers stationed at the back door was surprisingly easy. Kosara and Asen found them hiding in the bushes. Asen introduced himself and offered them each a cigarette, making sure, as per Kosara's instructions, to select the one marked with a red dot on the filter for himself.

After a few long drags on the cigarette and some small talk about the weather, both officers slid to the ground, sound asleep. Kosara and Asen hid them deeper into the bushes before leaving them.

The lock on the back door wasn't much of an obstacle, either. All in all, it took Asen less time to break it than to finish his cigarette.

"Since when do you smoke?" Kosara asked, watching him inhale deeply, pure bliss spread over his face.

"I don't," he said firmly and extinguished the cigarette on the wall of the building.

The séance room was dark. The fire in the hearth had long died down, and the only light came from the window, where the full moon shone, painting everything in ghostly silver. The stench of death still lingered, though it was less sharp, having acquired an earthy, musty undertone. Only a faint chalk outline denoted where the body had lain.

Kosara clicked her fingers. She needed more light—magic symbols were tricky little buggers, and even a single line slightly slanted in the wrong direction could change their meaning completely. The blood dried onto the parquet floor reflected her flame like a dark mirror.

Kosara tried not to touch the blood as she kneeled down. She dipped a brush in the jar of enchanted ink and muttered the spell under her breath. Her pockets were heavy with charged talismans and amulets—as precaution, in case the magic circle didn't work as planned.

As she drew, she noticed something she hadn't during her last visit. The house was alive with noise. In the kitchen, a pot clanked loudly. High up in the attic, the floorboards creaked, as if someone paced back and forth. A low purr came from the corner. When Kosara turned to look, all she saw was an empty cat bed.

A rhythmic clicking drifted from the walls, like hundreds of tiny feet. Rats, Kosara had originally thought, what with there being a secret tunnel in the room leading directly to the sewers. But then, there were too many of them. How many rats could a single wall hold?

When one of them ran past her peripheral vision, a pale little figure on pale little feet, it dawned on her.

The house wasn't alive with noise—it was *dead* with it. Ghostly rats filled the walls. The ghost of a cat purred in its bed in the corner. Ghosts haunted the kitchen and the cellar, and most likely, the house's every room.

Sofiya had interrupted their slumber, and now, some of the dead had settled here, like unwanted guests overstaying their welcome. The rats had most likely awakened accidentally, caught in the afterglow of Sofiya's magic. The cat, Kosara wasn't sure about—a beloved pet summoned back from the dead, perhaps.

The ghostly figure who'd just walked through the wall, though? Definitely an intruder.

Asen spotted the ghost a second after Kosara. He made a strangled noise and reached towards his hip, most likely looking for his gun. A moment later, his fingers fell helplessly at his side, empty.

"Go away," Kosara made an impatient gesture at the ghost. He was an elderly man, surprisingly vivid for someone who must have been dead for a while. Kosara could swear she smelled the fustiness of his old-fashioned suit and the tobacco filling his clay pipe. "Shoo!"

The ghost assessed the situation: Kosara, her twelve shadows circling her, and the flame in one of her hands. Then, he melted back into the wall, muttering something about young people having no respect these days.

"You told me ghosts are only visible during the Foul Days," Asen said accusingly. His fingers still trembled.

"Did I? It's not strictly true."

"You don't say!"

"See, ghosts are always around, but they get more active during the Foul Days. Denser. More corporeal. Usually, they can't interact with the human world much. But, like with every monster, there are exceptions."

"Like what?"

"You just met one. Sofiya's magic has permeated the building so deeply, séance after séance, all her ghosts are very much awake."

As if in response, the invisible cat in the corner meowed loudly.

"It gives me the creeps," Asen said, his eyes darting to the wall where the rats' feet kept tap-tap-tapping.

Kosara shrugged. "Get used to it." A second later, she realised that hadn't been the most sensitive thing to say, since he *would* have to get used to it. He was trapped in Chernograd. "They're not dangerous," she added quickly.

"I know. It's just . . . it's not normal."

"Not much is, on this side of the Wall. I thought you knew that." *You're not entirely normal anymore, either,* Kosara thought, but she didn't say it out loud. Asen was already in a mood.

Finally, Kosara finished drawing the circle and wiped her inky hands on her trousers. Good thing she was dressed in black or else the stains would have shown.

"Ready?" Asen asked.

"Ready." Kosara plopped herself in one of the tall-backed chairs arranged around the séance table. "Now, we just have to wait."

"How long do we have until the two coppers in the bushes wake up?"

"Oh, hours. I gave them an extra strong dose of sedative."

Kosara had prepared for a large variety of possible pitfalls and problems tonight. The last thing she'd expected to deal with was awkward silence. For a few minutes, she and Asen sat at opposite ends of the long table. Kosara played with one of the velvet tassels of the tablecloth. Asen stared out the window at the full moon.

Kosara remembered, only a few months back, when their silences had started to become companionable. They'd lost it again now, that sense of comfort around each other. Part of it was Kosara's guilt. She hadn't forgiven herself for Asen's varkolak curse, and she doubted he'd forgiven her, either.

Part of it was Asen. Ever since he'd come back to Chernograd, he'd been distant. He kept avoiding her gaze. Whenever she tried to touch him, whether it was a friendly pat on the shoulder or an accidental brush of her fingers against his when she handed him something, he flinched away. As if he'd been burned.

They were to be stuck together for the time being, at least until she'd found a way to cure his lycanthropy. He didn't want to be more than friends, and she could accept that, although it hurt. Maybe he didn't want to be friends, either. This, too, she could live with. She was used to rejection.

Still, even if they were to be nothing but reluctant roommates, Kosara couldn't take this tension. It made her want to crawl out of her skin. She had to say something that would fix this, make some attempt to go back to how things had been last winter.

"Listen . . ." she said, unsure how she intended to finish the sentence.

She didn't have to. A floorboard creaked in the hallway. Then, several seconds later, another one. It sounded like someone tried very hard to be quiet, but the floor betrayed their every step.

Behind Kosara's back, the door opened with a groan. Asen's eyes, pinned over her shoulder, widened. Kosara turned around, expecting to see another ghost.

It wasn't a ghost.

"Oh, thank God," Sofiya said. "It's you."

Kosara made an embarrassing sound in the back of her throat. She prided herself in never losing her nerve in a tense situation—even so, it took her a few seconds of staring and blinking before she managed, "Who were you expecting?"

"Karaivanov," Sofiya said simply.

She wore a silken turban, decorated with feathers and precious stones, and a fur coat, covering her from neck to ankles. Kosara shuddered, unsure what spells and amulets she hid underneath. Her three shadows stretched behind her, long and black.

Kosara's fingers slowly inched towards the talisman in her pocket.

Sofiya continued, "I thought I'd find him here as soon as I heard the coppers snoring in the bushes. Though, I suppose if it had been him, they'd be dead." Her eyes flicked to the symbols inked at her feet. "Oh, a magic circle. Was this for me?"

"I expected you to come through the secret passage," Kosara admitted, her hand now gripping the talisman firmly.

"What? In these shoes?" Sofiya wiggled her toes, clad in silk slippers. Then, she turned to Asen. "I'm Sofiya, by the way."

"I know who you are," he snarled.

Sofiya curved a thin, painted eyebrow. "So, to what do I owe the pleasure?"

Kosara had prepared for an altercation, not for a friendly chat. Sofiya was obviously stalling, trying to distract them so she could strike at the opportune moment, and Kosara didn't intend to give her the chance.

"I think you know," Kosara said, pulling the talisman from her pocket. It was a simple thing, a red string tied around a boiled egg— though given the way things were going, a boiled egg would cost its weight in gold soon.

"Oh, a talisman," Sofiya observed with the same flat tone with which she'd noted the magic circle. "Are you going to fight me?"

Kosara assessed the situation. Her twelve shadows unspooled around her. By now, she'd become used to ignoring their constant whispers, but sensing her attention on them, they grew louder, their chatter filling her ears.

Sofiya's three stood behind her, unmoving like well-trained soldiers. One of them was the same as Sofiya, complete with the bulbous turban. The second was an old woman, hunched over a walking cane. The third—the shadow of the murdered witch—stood straight, prepared for a fight.

Kosara had hoped the third one would be susceptible to her

influence, the way the eleven she'd stolen from the Zmey had been. Now, looking at the shadow's confident stance, it did not look likely.

Kosara glanced over her shoulder and waved at Asen to step back. Unsurprisingly, he didn't listen.

"I don't want to fight you," Sofiya said, despite the fact that behind her back, her shadows grew taller.

"You should have thought about that before you murdered that poor woman. Who was she anyway?"

"I know that no matter what I say, you're not going to believe me—"

Kosara didn't let her finish. She gripped her talisman and muttered the magic words. The egg in her hand turned to ash, coating her fingers in a grey, sticky mess.

Sofiya choked. Her throat bulged, like a snake attempting to swallow too large a rat. She tried to inhale, but she only produced an ugly, whizzing sound. Another minute or two, and she would have lost consciousness.

Sofiya's shadows had other plans. One of them, the old woman, hobbled over to Sofiya.

Kosara tried to command her twelve shadows with her mind—*Go, stop her!*—but they ignored her, floating around the room. Only Kosara's own shadow turned its head towards her, but it was too busy working the curse together with Kosara, an egg-shaped hole gaping in its chest. That was the issue with talismans this powerful—they required the full attention of both the witch and her shadow, leaving her completely vulnerable.

Stop her!

Finally, a couple of them meandered to the old woman, but they were easy targets. The old woman batted them all away with her walking stick. Then, without much ceremony, she plunged her dark arm into Sofiya's mouth up to the elbow.

Sofiya gasped. When the shadow retracted her arm, she held an egg-shaped ball of shadows—the essence of Kosara's curse. The old woman released it and it floated to Kosara's shadow, who dutifully stuffed it back inside its chest.

"That was nasty," Sofiya said with tears in her eyes. Her voice came out barely a whisper. Her ring-encrusted fingers held her bruised throat.

"I've got plenty more where that one came from," Kosara tried to sound threatening, but even she heard the hesitation in her voice.

Why wasn't Sofiya fighting? Was she waiting for Kosara to run out of talismans and amulets? Kosara could play that game all night. She'd come prepared.

"Kosara, please," Sofiya said. "I said I don't want to fight—"

A scream.

Kosara turned to find Asen enveloped in a tight embrace by two shadowy arms. The knife at his throat, however, was fully corporeal.

Sofiya's third shadow had managed to sneak away while the old woman had distracted Kosara.

Goddamnit, Kosara swore internally, though she had to admit she was impressed. It took a lot of control to get a shadow to hold an object heavier than a playing card.

"Will you talk to me now?" Sofiya asked.

Kosara made a noncommittal sound. She wanted to talk, of course, but she'd have much preferred to do it on her own terms: with Sofiya tied up and helpless, not with a shadow threatening Asen's life.

His Adam's apple bobbed as he swallowed hard. The knife left a pinprick of blood on his skin.

"Fine," Kosara spat out. "Talk."

"Firstly, I have to tell you, I'm not a murderer."

Kosara barked a laugh. That was rich, coming from a woman whose shadow currently held a knife to someone's throat.

I think you should burn her, the Zmey said conversationally in Kosara's head.

If I burn her, her shadow will kill Asen.

The Zmey paused. *And?*

Sofiya pulled a small vial from her pocket, filled with a pink, bubbling liquid. "I knew you wouldn't believe me, so . . ."

"Truth serum," Kosara said. It was the real thing, she was sure. She had more than a passing familiarity with the substance at this point.

"I've always admired your powers of observation. I'd hoped to use it to convince Vila, but you're, I suppose"—Sofiya's eyes darted to Kosara's shadows—"the next best thing."

"Convince Vila of what?"

Sofiya waved at Kosara to wait, uncorked the vial, and downed the serum in one go. She moved her tongue around her mouth, making her cheeks bulge. "I need help."

"With what?"

"I'm in big trouble, Kosara." Sofiya opened her arms, as if inviting Kosara's mockery. "Yes, I know, *me*. The witch with three shadows. I've found myself in deep water."

Kosara didn't mock her. Several drops of serum were caught in the fine hairs above Sofiya's lip. This wasn't a trick. "Why don't you tell me what happened?"

Asen coughed delicately, obviously trying hard not to let the knife touch his throat.

"But first," Kosara added, "release my friend. He's not dangerous."

Asen coughed louder, an offended look on his face. Kosara supposed, she'd just told a lie. If Asen was to turn, he'd be very dangerous indeed.

"And you?" Sofiya asked.

"I won't attack you. I promise."

Sofiya hesitated, but only for a second. Then, she gestured at her shadow to stand down. It dropped the knife, letting it clang against the floor, and returned to Sofiya's feet.

"I'll tell you what happened," Sofiya said. "Why don't we sit down?"

"I prefer to remain standing. Get on with it."

"Right, right." Sofiya tucked a lock of dark hair that had escaped her turban behind her ear. "So, I made a mistake. In fact, I made several mistakes. The first one was sticking my nose in magic I didn't understand."

"Unsurprising," Kosara muttered under her breath.

"No, wait," Sofiya said. "Actually, my first mistake was trusting Natalia Ruseva."

Kosara was going to ask why, but she wasn't fast enough. She knew very well that once the truth serum had loosened your tongue, it was impossible to regain control over it.

"It happened like this," Sofiya continued, talking faster. "I'd sensed the cracks in the barrier between our realm and the one of monsters."

"You sensed them?" Kosara managed to interrupt while Sofiya took in a breath. "You didn't cause them?"

"Of course I didn't cause them! I'm powerful, but I'm not *that* powerful. Anyway, I knew, if I used my magic just right, I could pluck a monster out of there, like a skilled midwife performing a complicated birth."

"What for?"

"I'd heard of Roksana and Sokol's plight and I wanted to help them..." Sofiya's tongue obviously fought against her. "And, fine, Roksana might have buried me in gold."

There it was. Kosara would have never believed Sofiya had done it simply out of the goodness of her heart, truth serum or not.

"As I said," Sofiya continued, "I knew I could do it, except, my power alone wasn't going to be enough. I did the research. Every ancient tome I read was adamant: you needed three witches. So, it was time to get the old coven back together."

"The coven?"

"Me, Natalia Ruseva, and Irina Sotirova. We used to be best friends at school. We even got that stupid tattoo." Sofiya lifted her sleeve to show the three interconnecting spirals. "Friendship forever, it's supposed to mean. But it didn't work out that way, did it? Irina's dead." Sofiya sniffed loudly, wiping her nose with a silk handkerchief. Her eyes had grown glassy.

Kosara would have accused her of faking her sudden onset of grief, except she felt it, too. She'd known Irina—all the witches of Chernograd knew each other. They hadn't been friends, but they'd fought countless karakonjuls together over the years.

Kosara would have thought after so many decades of monster attacks, she'd be used to losing colleagues. It still hurt.

Sofiya blew her nose. "Excuse me, where was I?"

"Irina," Kosara said. "How did she die?"

"Well. That's the thing I couldn't believe. Natalia, my childhood friend, my sweet Natalia—she murdered Irina."

"Natalia Ruseva murdered Irina?" Kosara asked, rather pointlessly, struggling to see how this piece of the puzzle fit. "How?"

"Irina came to me that night a few days ago—that horrible, cursed night—just as I was having a glass of wine after my last séance. She was terrified. She begged me to take her shadow because, she said, someone was after her and she was worried she'd die soon. It was the mratinyak's curse, she told me. When we'd summoned it, we'd brought its curse onto ourselves. 'The bringer of plague and death,' they call it."

Kosara opened her mouth, but she couldn't get a single word in.

"Irina was a seer, you know," Sofiya added for Asen's benefit, "so I believed her. Except, I promised her, I'd give her shadow back as soon as the danger had passed. Until then, I'd protect her." Sofiya took a deep breath. "But when push came to shove, I couldn't protect her. I couldn't do anything."

"Protect her from Ruseva?"

"Yes. How could I have expected Natalia to do this? She used a talisman. A more powerful one than I'd ever seen. If I had to guess, several witches had given up their shadows to create it. Natalia said the magic words, and off Irina's head went."

"And then?"

Sofiya shrugged, wiping her nose with her handkerchief. "How am I supposed to know? I ran. Have you ever seen your best friend's head flying off their neck? I bet you'd run, too."

"Sofiya," Kosara said, "are you aware that Natalia is also dead?"

"I heard."

"The circumstances of her death are very similar to those of Irina's murder—"

"So? What do you expect me to do? Cry for her?"

Asen cleared his throat. "If Natalia is the murderer, how come you haven't explained it all to the police?"

"What a brilliant idea!" Sofiya snorted. "Hand myself over to the police and end up a sitting duck for when Karaivanov decides he'd like my head, too. How long do you think it would take him to bribe one of our valiant police officers to hand me over?"

Kosara had to admit that was a good point.

"Do you know why?" she asked. "Why Ruseva murdered Irina?"

"I have no idea," Sofiya replied. "I'd heard rumours that Natalia works for Karaivanov now. I never believed it, but it must be true. I know Irina used to run errands for him, back when we were in school, but Natalia? She'd never lacked for anything."

Kosara shuddered. This was the way of money, she supposed: the more you had, the more you craved.

Sofiya sniffed again. "In any case, whatever Natalia's motive, I truly believe the mratinyak is to blame for it ending the way it did. Had it not been for that monster, we could have worked something out. We were childhood friends, for God's sake. But once you accidentally unleash a death curse onto yourself . . ."

"So, you didn't bring the mratinyak here on purpose?" Kosara asked. She had to admit, that was a relief. If Sofiya hadn't intended to murder Chernograd's hens, that made her a much more sympathetic figure.

Sofiya, for the first time that evening, looked uncomfortable, her eyes avoiding Kosara's. "I promise you, I didn't. I think it must have been sealed there, in the monster realm, a long time ago, by witches far greater than you and I. When the three of us tried to perform the rite to help Sokol escape, something went wrong, and it got unleashed on the city."

"And then? You didn't try to send it back?"

"We tried, but we weren't strong enough. It was a mistake. We should never have played with such powerful magic."

Asen cleared his throat. "Do you think that maybe it wasn't an accident?"

Sofiya scrunched her face. "Listen, copper, I told you. I never meant to—"

"Maybe you didn't. Maybe it was Natalia who did. If she worked for Karaivanov . . ."

"What's Karaivanov to do with a huge bloodthirsty hen?" Kosara asked.

"Well." Asen waved a hand in the air. "It's just a pet theory, but I've been thinking. Now that people can cross the Wall, Karaivanov's business is suffering. Maybe he was trying to upset the status quo. Maybe he'd hoped that by bringing more and more monsters over to Chernograd, he'd give the Belogradeans the final push they need to demand the Wall be restored to how it was. Or maybe his plan didn't extend far beyond making sure he had plenty of monster parts to sell to rich fools on the other side of the Wall."

Kosara frowned. She had to admit it made sense.

"What have I done!" Sofiya wailed, hiding her face in her hands.

As much as she didn't care for the other witch, Kosara couldn't help but feel sympathy towards her. Sofiya had made one single bad decision, cast a single poorly thought-out spell. As a result, her best friend was dead, and Sofiya herself had to live in hiding.

Besides, Kosara couldn't stand it when people cried.

"There, there." She made to touch Sofiya's shoulder, but changed her mind in the last minute, and her hand awkwardly hovered over it. "Not all is lost, I'm sure."

Sofiya looked at Kosara through her fingers.

"We'll figure something out," Kosara added. "We'll have to."

"You're right," Sofiya said. "Of course, you're right. I'm so glad I decided to ask for your help."

"You haven't actually asked . . ."

"We need to send the mratinyak away. If we don't, we'll only face more death. We need to seal it back into the monster realm. Will you help me?"

Kosara and Asen looked at each other. They both knew Sofiya couldn't be lying. Ruseva had been the one who'd murdered Irina before facing a similar end. And, just like Asen suspected, Karaivanov was behind it all.

However, the fact that Sofiya was telling the truth still didn't mean she could be trusted.

"What did you come back for?" Kosara asked, trying to fill the silence while she decided on her next step. "What in this house is so precious that you risked getting caught by Karaivanov for it?"

The corner of Sofiya's mouth twitched. Kosara wasn't sure what answer she'd expected: the golden candleholders? The finely woven carpets? The paintings and statues decorating the hallway?

Sofiya walked over to the corner and tucked the cat bed under her arm. The ghostly cat inside it meowed.

"She's a lazy oaf," Sofiya patted the cat's invisible head. "But I couldn't leave her. Well? Will you help me?"

Goddamnit. Sofiya had managed to tug on Kosara's heartstrings. If only she'd come back for the golden candleholders or the statues in the hallway . . .

"What do you suggest?"

"You, me, Vila," Sofiya said immediately, like she'd planned this whole encounter. "Tomorrow, St. Enyo's Day, at midnight. On the hill where the old graveyard used to be."

Kosara saw the logic in the suggestion. They needed a third witch they could trust, and Vila's experience and skill would surely come in handy. St. Enyo's Day was, doubtlessly, one of the most magical days of the year: the time when herbs and potions were at their most potent.

And the old graveyard? Kosara supposed that was where Sofiya felt the most at home, surrounded by ghosts.

"Well," Sofiya said. "Are you in?"

Kosara sighed. "I'm in."

17

Kosara

Vila did not look pleased. This was no great surprise, since "not pleased" was her default expression, but given how readily she'd agreed to help, Kosara had hoped she'd show a bit more enthusiasm.

Part of the problem could have been that they'd arranged to meet Sofiya at the top of the old graveyard hill. The climb had proven steeper than either of them had anticipated. Vila quietly swore under her breath as she climbed. Her bony fingers had gone white around the head of her walking cane.

Kosara kept throwing worried looks at her every few minutes, until Vila snapped at her to stop staring. She didn't look well. Her hands trembled in a way Kosara had never seen before. Her breath came out wheezing, like she fought a bad chest infection. Drops of sweat rolled down her forehead, settling into the lines around her eyes.

She looked old, that was what it all came down to, and Kosara was ashamed of how uncomfortable it made her feel. Of course Vila was old. She was *ancient*. If she'd decided to stop hiding her age with potions and enchanted creams, that was her prerogative.

The only issue was, if Vila was to show her true age, she wasn't going to be a cheerful granny with dentures and a bad perm. She'd be a pile of bone dust.

You're overreacting, Kosara told herself firmly. Vila was tired, that was all. Tired, old, and unused to exercise. In fact, Kosara had barely managed to convince Vila that a walk up the hill would do them both good and they didn't need to teleport there.

It was a nice evening—cold, but dry. Frost glistened on the branches of shrubs and trees. Snowdrop flowers nodded their white heads in the breeze, obviously unaware their season had long passed. The soil was plenty fertile, Kosara supposed, since the hill was built on the bones of generations of Chernogradeans. As the dead piled up, the hill grew taller.

Vila's single shadow trudged after its owner. Kosara's twelve followed at her feet, eager, almost skipping with enthusiasm. They must have been able to tell she was preparing to do magic.

They kept reminding Kosara of the visions she'd had of the Zmey's palace. She tried to come up with a way to broach the subject without Vila cutting her off—and failed. If Kosara wanted answers, she'd have to catch Vila in a good mood. Tonight, that seemed unlikely.

Ask her, the Zmey kept taunting Kosara in her head. *Ask her and see if she can explain why she kept letting me take her students year after year.*

"I can see you've been using your shadows," Vila said, startling Kosara out of her thoughts.

"I . . ." Kosara played with a strand of blonde hair. "I have. Only a few times, but—"

"I told you to be careful. You can't let them run circles around you."

"I am careful. Nothing bad has happened."

Vila scoffed, making it obvious she considered what the shadows had done to Kosara bad enough. "Where's Asen?"

The question came as a surprise to Kosara. She didn't think Vila remembered Asen's name, given that whenever she talked about him, she called him "your copper." What had the old seer seen that had made her ask after him?

"Home," Kosara said.

"How come? He didn't insist on coming along?"

"He did. I convinced him I didn't need him."

"How?"

"Well, I told him he has no reason to be present at a witch's ritual." Kosara paused. "I might have strongly implied we'd be dancing naked."

Vila lifted her eyebrows. "You mean we aren't?"

"Certainly not in this weather." Kosara buried her nose deeper in her scarf. She hesitated, and then said, "He got bitten. Asen. By a varkolak."

"I'm sorry to hear that," Vila said with the same measured tone she used when she didn't want to admit she'd already foreseen something.

"You don't happen to have discovered a cure—"

"You know there's no cure."

"What about that ritual you mentioned when the clockmaker's daughter got bitten? You said it looked promising."

"It was a dud. They always are. Plenty of charlatans have no qualms inventing all sorts of fake rituals, talismans, and amulets, only to make money off desperate people."

Kosara shrugged. A ritual could be a dud for one witch but work for another. Especially if that second witch happened to have the biggest collection of shadows in the city.

"Where did you get the ritual from?" Kosara asked. "Can I borrow the book?"

"Oh? Oh, it was in the *Magus Liber*. I believe you have my copy already."

Kosara remembered the thick tome she'd used to research embedding magic last winter. The last she'd seen it, she was using it to support the wonky leg of the kitchen table.

When they reached the top of the hill, the wind grew stronger, trying to snatch Kosara's scarf away and billowing Vila's skirts.

Sofiya was waiting for them. She sat on the ground, cross-legged, with her eyes closed. Meditating, perhaps—or simply listening to the whispers of the dead buried beneath. She wore her turban and fur coat again, and between that and Vila's woollen vest embroidered with sequined roses, Kosara felt distinctly underdressed.

Sofiya's eyes opened when she heard them approach. "Good evening. Thank you for coming."

Kosara was unsure how to respond. She'd never been good at small talk, and besides, she felt that arriving at a potentially deadly ritual should be greeted differently than making it to someone's name-day party.

"Well, you didn't leave us much of a choice, did you?" Vila exhaled through her nostrils. "A mratinyak! For crying out loud, what were you thinking?"

"I didn't think—"

"Clearly."

"When we reached through the gap between the two realms—"

"Silly girl," Vila interrupted her again. The old witch evidently didn't plan to let Sofiya finish a single sentence. "Did you stop to think why you were able to do that, all of a sudden? Those cracks between the two realms you felt, did you think why they were there?"

"Well," Sofiya said, because she was never one to admit she didn't know the answer to a question. "I assumed it was something to do with the Wall and how it can now be crossed."

"It's the Zmey," Vila snapped. "Isn't it obvious? It's his absence that's caused the barrier between the two realms to tear."

For a few seconds, the only sounds were the wind's howling and the fast beat of Kosara's heart.

She'd desperately hoped there was some other explanation for Chernograd's strange weather and for how the mratinyak had escaped outside of the Foul Days. Deep down, she'd known there wasn't.

"Are you sure?" she asked.

Vila shrugged. "I've known the Zmey for many years, and as long as he's been alive, the barrier between our two realms has been solid. Now, with him gone, the balance has been thrown, and the barrier is crumbling."

"So, then," Sofiya said, nodding towards Kosara. "Technically, this is all her fault?"

Kosara opened her mouth to argue, but then she shut it again.

When she'd trapped the Zmey in the Wall, she'd been certain she was doing the right thing. That was how the Wall was supposed to work in the first place. She'd repaired it. In doing so, she'd made it possible for the people of Chernograd to leave the city, something they'd been desperate to do for years.

Well, a small voice in her head reminded her, *not all people.* People like Asen were still imprisoned within the Wall. People who were not fully . . . people.

Sofiya looked at her, expecting a reaction.

"I didn't know . . ." Kosara trailed off. The truth was, she hadn't *thought*. She'd made a snap decision, pressed by the Zmey's deadline.

His disappearance had thrown Chernograd into chaos. It had also thrown Belograd into chaos, what with Karaivanov and his cronies growing more and more desperate. And now, it had turned out, it had affected the monster realm, too.

It hadn't been Sofiya's single bad decision and misguided spell that had triggered all this. It had been Kosara's.

"This is on both of you," Vila said, her tone final. "You're lucky I'm here to sort your messes."

"What are we going to do?" Kosara said, realising how young she sounded. She'd messed up again and there she was, expecting her teacher would fix everything.

Vila shrugged. "First, we'll send the mratinyak away. Then, we'll see."

"We need to seal the monster realm shut again."

"Believe me, I know. We have time. The cracks between the monster realm and ours are still small."

"But they'll only grow bigger."

"They will."

Kosara swore. "What happens if we can't shut them?"

"To tell you the truth, I don't know. This has never happened before."

This was bad news. If even Vila's seer powers weren't strong enough to glimpse the future, it meant that truly anything could happen.

"Anyway," Vila clapped her hands, practical as ever. "Should we get on with it?"

Kosara swallowed hard. She had to focus on the task at hand, but she still felt as if she'd been punched in the gut.

"What ritual did you use?" Vila turned to Sofiya.

"We did a summoning. A circle of three. Nothing too fancy, just a lot of raw energy."

Vila nodded. "Sounds like a solid plan. Well, lead the way."

When Kosara had explained to Asen how the ritual would go, she'd embellished the truth considerably. All it involved was the three witches, holding hands under the full moon, concentrating all their skill and power into a single clear message to the mratinyak.

Leave.

Their shadows surrounded them: Kosara's twelve, Sofiya's three, Vila's one. Their magic intertwined between their fingers.

Kosara was more used to working with magic circles, but this was Sofiya's spell, so she followed Sofiya's lead. The three of them didn't draw the words on the ground—they said them out loud, pronouncing them into being. It didn't sound like any language Kosara had heard, but she repeated every syllable dutifully after Sofiya, her tongue twisting in unfamiliar ways.

It didn't matter how a witch directed her magic, through words or images or touch or smell: all that mattered was a clearly communicated intent.

Leave.

They repeated it until the mratinyak heard them. Its croak tore through the night. Somewhere in the distance, its wings flapped once, twice, three times. Its dark shadow covered the full moon.

Leave. Kosara's heart climbed to her throat. *Leave.*

The monster turned its face towards the three witches. It croaked again, a loud, harsh sound, scraping the inside of Kosara's skull. With a great crash, it landed on the other side of the hill. Its talons sunk into the damp mud.

Kosara let out a short, desperate laugh. The mratinyak looked just like the bestiary had described it: an enormous cockerel, with a beak the size of a human arm and gleaming eyes as big as streetlamps. Its stench was thick and pungent, of dirt, blood, and chicken shit. It would have been ridiculous, if only it wasn't terrifying.

Leave.

The mratinyak made it obvious it didn't intend to listen. It dug into the earth with its talons, revealing both roots and crumbling white bones, and then, flapping its wings, it prepared to charge.

Kosara reacted first. Without letting go of Sofiya's hand, only with a flick of her wrist, she shot two fireballs at it. The first one missed, flying away into the dark sky. The second crashed into the mratinyak's body.

It sank into it without leaving a trace. The only sign the bird had felt it was its loud, surprised cluck. It took a step back and shook its head, but its retreat only lasted for a second. The next, gobbling and squawking, it rushed towards them.

Kosara had to do something. She couldn't control her powers with her hands trapped. That had always been how she did magic, the way Vila had taught her: by snapping fingers and clapping hands and drawing magic symbols on the ground or in the air. If only she'd trained to use primarily her voice, like Sofiya . . .

Kosara tried to pull her hands from Vila and Sofiya's grasp, but they didn't let her.

"Kosara," Vila said. "Concentrate on the spell."

"But the mratinyak—"

"Concentrate. Stop it *with words*."

"Oh," Kosara said, finally understanding and feeling silly. Why was it always her first instinct to start throwing fireballs?

She joined the other two again, letting her words interlace with theirs. The air crackled and the smell of magic grew unbearable, making Kosara dizzy. Vila had been right. The fireballs had done nothing. Their summoning circle, however, was working.

Their shadows rushed the mratinyak as one, surrounding it. They held hands, too, and their feet moved quickly in the grass, as if in a dance. The monster tried to fight them, pecking them and scratching with its talons, but it was helpless against them.

Leave, Kosara thought, and for a second, it looked as if this would be all it took.

The mratinyak let out a croak. It grew blurry along its edges, like all monsters did on the morning of St. Yordan's Day.

But then, one of Kosara's shadows broke the circle. It shook itself off the hands of the two holding it and stepped back. The mratinyak, emboldened, flapped its wings, sending several shadows flying.

"No!" Kosara shouted. "What the hell are you doing?"

Kosara recognised the shadow's smooth hair floating in the wind. Sevda Yordanova, the woman whose blonde strands Kosara had inherited. The woman who'd thought she'd be smart enough to outsmart the Zmey.

Kosara tried pouring all her mental energy into the shadow, begging it to rejoin the circle. Doing magic with Sofiya and Vila had been easy. Now, suddenly, Kosara felt the strain of the spell. The blood rushed to her head. Her vision blurred. A familiar golden-haired figure appeared in the corner of her eye.

If she wasn't careful, she'd pass out. If she let this get out of control, she'd find herself in the Zmey's palace again, and the mratinyak would be free.

"Sevda!" Kosara shouted, heat climbing to her cheeks. This was so embarrassing. Sofiya's shadows would have never behaved like this. "Get back in the circle!"

The shadow must have recognised its owner's name. It turned to Kosara, its hands in the air, and then it slowly, deliberately, placed them on its face and out again, like playing peekaboo. It took Kosara a second to understand what the shadow was getting at: it was gesturing at her to open her eyes.

Kosara frowned. Her eyes were wide open.

"Sevda, please!"

Instead of listening, the shadow kept making the same gesture. Watching it, Kosara realised she'd misunderstood it at first. It was opening its left eye, while covering the right with its fingers.

Fine. If this was what it took to make it behave.

Kosara shut her right eye, the brown one, leaving only the green one open. For a second, nothing changed.

Then, colourful spots danced in front of her vision, as if she'd kept her eye shut for too long. When they dispersed, Kosara gasped.

Look around, the shadows whispered in her mind, *look, look, look . . .*

The light was everywhere. Threads of it poured out of her fingers, wrapping around her hands and around Vila's and Sofiya's. Other threads connected Kosara to the twelve shadows. Most were hair-thin and glowing faintly, except for one—the one which led to her own shadow, which was thick and bright.

"This is amazing," Kosara muttered, her eye trailing Sevda's shadow. It returned to the circle, and the mratinyak was trapped once more, bound with many strands of light.

Was this how the witch who'd originally owned Kosara's green eye had seen magic? Was this how all witches but Kosara saw it?

"Kosara . . ." Vila said. It sounded like a warning, except Kosara didn't listen. She was too busy looking at Vila's light, encircling the old witch in a bright halo. Her connection to her shadow was like the beacon of a lighthouse.

Sofiya, similarly, was aglow, and so were her shadows.

"I've never seen magic like this before," Kosara said. "You both look beautiful."

"Kosara," Vila said again. "You're getting spell drunk. Please focus."

Vila was right. Of course she was. Kosara needed to open her own eye. They had work to do.

Look up, the shadows insisted in her mind. *Look up.*

Unable to stop herself, guided by her shadows' will, Kosara did.

The sky was littered with stars, constellations on top of constellations, flickering, moving and shifting, just like they'd done when she'd been in the Zmey's palace. Some died in a flash of light only for more to rise in their place.

Between them, thin cracks had spread, like the hairline fractures on a piece of delicate porcelain, oozing bright light. The gaps between the human realm and the world of monsters. Kosara could see them, and just like the fissures in porcelain, she could glue them shut.

"Kosara, don't you dare," Vila's voice was full of threat. Normally, Kosara would listen. There were very few things more terrifying than Vila when she was angry.

But now, her shadows had grown even louder, their whispers filling her mind.

Let us help. Let us fix this.

Now that Kosara saw her connection to the twelve shadows, she could use the threads of light to control them like a skilled puppeteer.

Yes, let us. Let us.

Once Vila had understood what Kosara was doing, she wouldn't be angry any longer. Who cared about the mratinyak? They'd captured it once—they'd do it again. Next time, they'd kill it. Kosara knew how to control her shadows now. She was unstoppable.

"Kosara," Vila hissed. "You're letting those shadows control you. Stop it."

Kosara didn't listen. She had to repair the barrier between the realms. She had to correct her grave mistake. This was her doing, and it was her job to fix it—now, before more monsters had found their way to the city.

Let us do it. Set us free.

Somewhere in the back of her mind, she realised doing this would mean trapping Sokol and Vrana in Chernograd forever. She didn't let herself hesitate. You couldn't make an omelette without breaking a few eggs, after all.

Sharply, Kosara pulled her hands away from Vila's and Sofiya's. Vila swore loudly. Sofiya muttered a curse.

Kosara pointed both her hands upwards. Her fingers deftly pulled on her shadows' strings, sending them towards the sky.

The mratinyak let out a croak as it freed itself. Kosara heard the flapping of its wings as if from very far away. Vila and Sofiya could deal with it. They were two of the strongest witches in the city. Kosara had more important work to do.

Yes, yes, yes! Her shadows reached for the sky with their black fingers. They pulled on it as if it were fine velvet, pressing one navy end against the other, filling in the gaps between.

It was so *easy*. It would only take a minute. Kosara couldn't believe she hadn't done it earlier. Only a minute . . .

The next moment, bony fingers grabbed Kosara's chin and forced her eyes downwards. Her vision was filled with Vila's furious face.

Kosara gasped. "What the h—"

"The price," the old witch said through gritted teeth, "is too high."

And then, she slammed her forehead against Kosara's.

It all went dark.

18

Asen

Kosara had made Asen promise he'd stay home tonight. She'd made him cross his heart and swear it.

As he rushed to the old graveyard hill, he sincerely hoped breaking a promise to a witch wouldn't have dire consequences.

She couldn't have truly expected him to stay cooped up inside while she fought one of the most terrifying monsters Chernograd had seen in years. He wasn't a witch and wouldn't be of much help during a ritual, but he could still watch her back. If all else failed, he was prepared to use the old kitchen knife on the feathery bastard.

She tried to scare him away with talk of naked dances under the moonlight. Except Asen couldn't imagine Kosara, someone who rarely left the house without at least three layers of thermal underwear, ever partaking in something like that when it was this cold.

Well, he could *imagine* it—fairly clearly, and it was rather distracting. He just doubted it would happen.

As soon as he approached the hill's summit, Asen realised something must have gone terribly wrong. The first thing he heard was Vila's swearing. What followed was a screeching *cock-a-doodle-doooo*. It should have been a ridiculous sound to come from a monster—but something about its eerie, drawn-out quality caused the hairs on the back of Asen's neck to stand on end.

He reached the top of the hill, out of breath and with his throat scraped raw by the cold air, and saw the monster. The first thing that struck him was its sheer size. It was as tall as a three-storey house, with legs thick as tree trunks. It produced that tinny screech again, and the two fleshy flaps hanging on either side of its beak quivered. Its eyes were large, yellow, and completely empty of any thought as they turned to Asen.

Asen stared at it for a few seconds with his mouth hanging half-open. An embarrassing sound came out of his throat.

"What the fuck are you doing here, copper?" Vila's fingers grasped his sleeve and dragged him backwards. She and Sofiya hid in a dog rose bush, crouching low in the mud.

Asen joined them and the three traced the mratinyak through the dog rose's thorny branches. As soon as Asen had disappeared from its view, the confusion in the monster's gaze grew. It let out a frustrated cluck and dug around in the mud with its feet, searching for a victim.

"Where's Kosara?" Asen asked, and then he saw her. She lay curled on the ground with her head resting on her hand. Her twelve shadows slept in a heap around her.

"She passed out," Vila said.

"Why? Did something go wrong?"

Screeching, the mratinyak pulled out one of the nearby shrubs with its foot and threw it at the ground.

"What do you think?" Vila snapped.

Behind her, Sofiya let out a strangled noise. The mratinyak was getting closer with every flap of its wings. It left havoc behind it, a mess of uprooted plants, upturned ground, and disentombed bones.

Asen looked at the knife tucked in his belt, and then back at the bird, and he felt like a fool for ever thinking he stood a chance. It would be like attacking a rabid dog with a toothpick.

"So," he said, trying to sound as calm as Vila looked. "What's the plan?"

"Fuck if I know." Vila spat on the ground. "We had it, you know? We had it captured. All we had to do was seal it back inside the monster realm."

"But then?"

"Kosara lost it," Sofiya said quietly.

"She's letting those shadows run circles around her," Vila said. "She needs to learn to control them."

From the ground, Kosara let out a loud snort. The mratinyak's eyes veered towards the sound.

"Is there nothing you can do?" Asen's voice came out high-pitched. "You've got four shadows between you."

"Don't you think we tried? The damned thing keeps dispersing them." Vila suddenly turned to Asen and wrinkled her nose. "You smell different."

Asen hadn't expected that turn in the conversation. He'd recently started using a new aftershave, but he suspected that wasn't what she meant. There was something in her steady dark gaze pinned on him that he didn't like. At all.

"There is strong scientific evidence," she said casually without breaking eye contact, "of the magic-enhancing powers of varkolak blood . . ."

"Vark . . ." Asen trailed off. For a brief second, he'd forgotten this was what he was now. A varkolak. And by the looks of things, Vila somehow knew.

Asen swallowed in a dry throat, feeling terribly self-conscious. Had she truly smelled him? No, of course not. Kosara must have told her.

This was Vila winding him up, surely. She was doing the same thing she'd done that first time they'd met, when she'd joked about boiling him in her cauldron. She wasn't truly planning to bleed him to death so she could enhance her magic. Surely.

But then, would Vila really joke in such a dire moment?

He imagined her sticking her knife straight into his gut and smearing his blood over her hands as she prepared to cast a spell.

"How much do you need?" he asked tentatively.

No matter the answer, he had to do it, if it meant the mratinyak would be defeated. Except, in that exact moment, Asen wasn't sure where his priorities lay. Was saving Chernograd worth bleeding to death?

No, a pathetic little voice in his mind answered. But was saving Kosara?

Vila opened her mouth to reply, but the next moment, the ground shook.

A screech. A thud. The mratinyak dug its talons in the dog rose bush and uprooted it. Crumbs of mud and dried leaves and little rotten berries rained on top of their heads.

Asen looked up, only to see its gigantic foot coming down again. His first instinct was to duck away. His second—to protect Kosara. Somehow, he managed both, throwing himself on the ground and placing himself in between the mratinyak and her sleeping figure.

A swear. A scream. The sound of a body being dragged through the mud.

Asen looked up. The first thing he saw was Sofiya's face stuck in a grimace of pure horror. Despite the distance growing between them, he watched her, petrified, unable to look away.

The mratinyak threw her body down the hill. Like a rag doll, she bumped against the hard ground again and again. Her turban tumbled off her head and rolled with her until, together, they slammed against a tree. The crack of broken bone was deafening.

Sofiya stilled.

Asen swore loudly. He suspected there was nothing in the police first aid manual that would help save Sofiya after that fall, but still, he stood up on shaky legs to go to her. He couldn't make a single step. The mratinyak turned its gaze back to him and Vila.

Asen's heart climbed to his throat. He felt the old witch's eyes on him and saw the glint of steel in her hand, and he was unsure who she was getting ready to stab: the mratinyak, or him? He'd had many brushes with death, but he'd rarely felt so terrified.

Then, the wind changed direction, dispersing the clouds. The moon shone bright, glittering off the mratinyak's waxy feathers. It reflected, perfectly round, in its black pupils.

With the wind, came a smell. Of frost, mud, and old bones. Of the mratinyak, wild and otherworldly, but also mundane. Like a henhouse in desperate need of a deep clean.

Asen's head spun. Scents rushed him, as if his every nose hair was a tiny antenna perfectly tuned to catch them. He smelled his new aftershave, suddenly too cloying. He smelled Vila—the fustiness of her woollen vest, the herbal oils in her hair, the cold sweat rolling in glinting droplets down her ashen face. He smelled the blood, wafting in thick clouds from Sofiya's slumped body.

The colours melted away. The mratinyak's bright-red comb became a pale yellow. The sequined roses on Vila's vest were a murky blue.

The smells, however, remained bright. Asen could almost see them—trace them with his eyes, not only with his nose.

A loud snap sounded. Asen managed to catch the broken pieces of his wedding ring a second before they'd fallen to the ground. He stuffed them in his pocket with fingers that didn't feel like his. They were too large. And was that . . .

Was that fur covering them?

"Well, fuck," came Vila's voice, but Asen barely heard her.

The moon shone bright above, and he, inexplicably, couldn't suppress the urge to throw his head back and howl.

Asen only registered brief snippets of what followed. He was an observer, trapped in some cramped, dark corner of his mind, watching helplessly as another, more primal part of him took control.

Blink, and he was running through the grass, the scraggly strands tickling the underside of his belly.

Blink, and he was preparing to jump, the tension growing in his hind legs—since when did he *have* hind legs?

Blink, and his mouth closed around tender flesh.

His mouth didn't feel right. It was stuffed full of teeth. Sharp, curved things, crisscrossing in unfamiliar patterns, a dangerous labyrinth through which his tongue had to crawl.

What he'd bitten into didn't feel right, either. Not only flesh, but feathers, getting stuck between his fangs.

He had to stop this. He wasn't an animal, damn it. He was a human being

But then, another blink, and this time, he was at the bird's throat. He was so small compared to it—a tiny, irritating tick. The mratinyak flapped its wings in a frenzy, trying to get rid of him, but Asen held tight.

He sunk his teeth into its throat. It shouldn't have worked. A normal wolf's teeth would have never pierced the mratinyak's thick hide.

But Asen wasn't a wolf. He was a varkolak, and he had a mouth full of scimitars.

He must have hit an artery because the blood rushed out, a curtain of dark, sticky liquid. Surely one varkolak wouldn't be able to defeat a legendary monster? While the beast part of Asen rejoiced, the rational part was certain this wasn't the end. However, he hoped he'd at least managed to distract it while Vila worked her magic.

Vila's voice sounded far below, drawing his attention—except, it wasn't a spell she was reciting. She was swearing loudly.

Kosara's form lay on the ground next to her, completely helpless. It made something in Asen stir. Something primal. The human part of him tried to keep the reins on the beast, but it was no use. For a second, all he wanted to do was taste her. Drink her blood. Devour her flesh.

Then, a bright light blinded him. He saw Vila, a little figure bent over a walking cane, with her hand in the air. From her fingertips, threads of light emerged, wrapping themselves around the mratinyak.

The bird let out a desperate screech and tried to shake them off. All it achieved was dislodging Asen. He rolled onto the ground with more agility than a human body would have ever provided him.

Maybe he was starting to like this, after all. He was faster. Stronger. His sense of smell was far superior. So what if he thirsted for blood?

As the human part of him watched from its corner, the beast stretched out its tongue and licked its fur, collecting the sticky black liquid that had oozed from the mratinyak's neck. It tasted metallic, but it also had that unwashed, grimy quality to it, similar to the beast's scent.

This wouldn't do. It wouldn't do at all. He needed something fresher. His eyes found Kosara's sleeping form again and thick saliva filled his mouth.

No, he thought sternly. *No. Down.*

He was a human being. He was not a beast.

The next moment, the side of his face erupted in pain. His vision blurred.

The last thing he saw before the darkness engulfed him was Vila, standing over him with her walking cane held high, ready to strike again.

When Asen woke up, he was naked. He lay on the ground, curled up near Kosara's feet, surrounded by her shadows. Someone had draped his coat over him, but he still shivered in the frigid air.

He propped himself up on his elbows. The coat slid off his shoulders and the biting wind caused goose bumps to rise on his skin. Asen hurried to cover himself again, which in turn exposed his feet to the cold.

"I've brought you spare clothes," came Vila's voice.

He turned towards her. She sat with her back resting against a scraggly juniper that had somehow escaped the mratinyak's wrath. Her walking cane lay across her lap.

"How did you know I'd need them?" Asen croaked, and immediately realised it had been a stupid question. Vila was a seer.

"Sixth sense." The witch winked and threw a bunch of sequined skirts, patterned socks, and embroidered shirts at him.

Asen grimaced. He and Vila would look like twins who'd had a tragic collision with the charity shop's delivery cart.

"Don't put them on if you don't like them," Vila said. "You can walk home stark naked under that coat if you want."

Asen suspected that wouldn't be an uncommon sight in Chernograd, given how many varkolaks there were, but he still worried what people would think. Besides, it was freezing.

He chose an ensemble of embroidered linen shirt and skirt that were both too wide for him and way too short. He tried hiding behind his coat to put them on, though he suspected Vila's interest in his naked body was marginal at best. Her gaze was fixed somewhere in the distance.

"How do you feel?" she asked once he was dressed. "The first transformation is always disorienting."

"I'm fine." He felt awful. His every muscle hurt, unused to the strain. His mouth still tasted the mratinyak, a putrid mixture of flesh, blood, and feathers. He swallowed hard. "The mratinyak?"

"Gone."

"And Sofiya?"

"Dead."

"I'm sorry," Asen said, unsure what he was apologising for. He didn't know if Sofiya and Vila had been particularly close.

Vila shrugged. "It was her own damned fault. She'd summoned a death curse upon herself. I suspected it would take her death to send the mratinyak away, and I was right."

"So that's why you managed to capture it? I'd thought . . ." His fingers inadvertently found the bump on the side of his head where Vila had struck him with her walking cane. "I'd thought you might have used my blood."

"For what?" For a second, confusion crossed Vila's face. Then, she laughed. "Oh, the varkolak blood nonsense? Did you really believe that? I was winding you up."

"Then why did you hit me?"

"I wasn't sure what your intentions were."

Asen avoided her gaze. He hadn't been sure himself. The taste of the mratinyak was bitter on his tongue.

"But then, you curled up over there like a good puppy," Vila continued. "So, I left you alone." She stood up, supporting herself on the walking cane, and nodded towards Kosara. "Come on, give me a hand. We should get Sleeping Beauty home."

19

Kosara

"No. Do it again."

The first thing Kosara heard was the Zmey's voice. Then, her vision cleared.

She stood in the cage on top of the palace's tallest tower. High above, the stars kept shifting. The wind carried the cloying scent of the garden below.

"Again," the Zmey demanded.

Kosara's head throbbed. At first, she thought it must have been because Vila had hit her. Then, she realised, that wasn't possible. She wasn't in her own body.

The hand that appeared in front of her was unfamiliar. Smaller than hers, with longer nails painted in pink. There was something else unusual about it, too—it wore a simple gold band on its ring finger. On the inside, Kosara suspected, she'd find an inscription with the Zmey's name. It made her sick.

Kosara was still disoriented, so it took her a moment to remember whose body she inhabited. She flicked through her mental catalogue of shadows and found the one that best matched. Svetla Sokolova, who'd married the Zmey twenty-seven years ago.

Kosara had been particularly interested in this young witch's fate. From what she'd uncovered, Svetla had remained married to the

Zmey for over a year. He hadn't returned to Chernograd the following New Year's Eve after their wedding to hunt for a new bride like he
always did.

It had ended badly, of course. Svetla's shadow was the one Kosara
found the most unbearable. It never shut up, mumbling everything
from apologies to accusations. Something about Svetla's time with the
Zmey had broken it.

"What are you doing?" the Zmey snapped, and Svetla turned to
face him, her hand still in the air.

Kosara startled at how close he was. Close enough to touch.

He was looking at her, unblinking, with the stars reflecting in his
eyes, and she thought she'd never seen his face so animated. He was
angry, which was an expression she knew well. Frustrated, annoyed,
ready to break something—all familiar.

But there was something else there. Something careful and fragile.

Svetla sounded confused. "You told me to do the spell again, and
I thought—"

"What? I told you to stop clicking your fingers like some village
witch. You don't need any of this." The Zmey grabbed her wrists and
pinned them down close to her body. "All you need is your mind."

Confusingly, Kosara didn't feel any of what she thought she would
as the Zmey's fingers closed around her wrists. There was no fear stirring in her stomach. No unbearable urge to escape. Instead, her lips
curled in a smile as she shook him off.

Svetla raised her hand in the air again. Now, Kosara noticed something else that was unusual. She didn't cast a shadow.

"This"—she clicked her fingers—"helps me focus."

A light erupted from her fingertips. It flew upwards, snaking between the stars. Svetla's eyes followed it. It was so bright, it made them
water.

It was only then that Kosara looked at the sky properly. It wasn't
as it usually appeared. The stars were there, rearranging themselves
in hundreds of strange combinations every time she blinked, but the
cracks were there, too. The same cracks she'd seen above Chernograd.

As she watched, Svetla's light sank into one of them, filling it like liquid gold.

She turned back to face the Zmey, and Kosara felt one of her eyebrows going up—a gesture Kosara could never achieve in her own body.

"See?" Svetla asked.

Now, the Zmey's face looked completely foreign. Kosara had never seen his mouth twisted in this particular way. It took her a second to recognise it.

Happiness. The Zmey was happy.

He grabbed Svetla in his arms and lifted her from the ground. She melted into his embrace, ignoring how scorching his skin felt through his shirt. His lips rained kisses all over her forehead, her cheeks, her lips. They were hot too, so hot they burned, but Svetla didn't step away. She leaned closer.

"My Tsaritsa," the Zmey purred in her ear, biting on her earlobe gently. "Finally. Finally."

Kosara wanted to squirm. She felt like a voyeur, experiencing someone else's bliss through someone else's senses.

She wanted to leave. Go home. Return to her own body.

"Kosara?" Nevena's voice came as if Kosara had summoned her.

At this point, Kosara suspected Nevena was nothing more than a figment of her imagination—something familiar to cling to so she could find her way back to the real world. She still wanted to weep with joy when she heard her.

"Kosara, it's time to wake up."

When Kosara opened her eyes, she was surrounded by darkness. It was only the familiar smell of lavender and freshly washed linens that indicated she was in her own bedroom.

Her first bizarre, disorienting thought was that she missed the Zmey. His absence was visceral, squeezing her stomach in a tight fist. It made her sick.

It wasn't *him* she missed, of course. It was the feeling of being held so tight, her rib cage hurt. It was that wild, genuine smile she'd seen on his face. It was his warmth, soaking deep into her body.

It had knocked her off-kilter. She'd never seen him like that.

This was yet more proof her relationship with him had been nothing special. She'd been just another woman he kidnapped with the intention of feeding on her. It was only after she escaped him that he'd grown interested in her, since the Zmey craved what he couldn't have. *That* was why he'd chased her for seven years.

But then, maybe that hadn't been about her, either. Maybe he'd done it in an attempt to get back at Vila.

Once she finally managed to shake off the feeling of confusion, Kosara realised she was freezing. Her teeth clattered as she got out of bed, and she pulled her blanket with her, draping it across her shoulders like a cape. When she opened the door, the light from the kitchen downstairs rushed her, momentarily blinding her.

She found Asen sitting next to the cold hearth with a book. It was one of her romance novels, *A Night of Passion With the Upir Lord,* and judging by the deep frown on his face, he was completely engrossed in it.

"Good evening." Kosara ventured a guess, looking through the window at the darkening sky hanging low over the rooftops.

Asen jumped slightly. He hadn't heard her coming down. "Evening."

"What time is it?"

Asen checked his watch. It was one of the models that had become popular recently: when he pressed a button, its light illuminated his face in fluorescent green. "Nearly seven o'clock. You've been asleep all day."

No wonder. She felt as if she could sleep for another day at least, or maybe two.

Kosara almost didn't ask the question, because, in truth, she didn't want to know the answer. "What happened last night?"

Asen didn't meet her gaze. "Vila says you tried to do something above your capabilities."

Kosara considered this. She would have managed to repair the barrier between the realms, if Vila hadn't interfered. It hadn't been "above her capabilities." She remembered Vila's words, just before the old witch had knocked her out: "The price is too high."

Kosara would have to speak to Vila, there was no escaping it. The two of them were long overdue an honest talk.

After the silence had stretched for too long, Asen added, "Sofiya is dead."

Kosara swore under her breath. It wasn't exactly a surprise, given how wrong everything had gone last night, but she'd still hoped they'd managed to avoid it.

"And the mratinyak?" she asked.

"Gone. Vila says Sofiya had to die for the mratinyak to be sent away, but it still seemed so unnecessary, you know?"

Guilt roiled in Kosara's stomach. If she hadn't got distracted, the mratinyak would have never escaped the spell.

But then, they were witches. Dying at the hands of a monster while performing a ritual seemed like a fitting end. Besides, she suspected Vila right. For all their hard work, the monster couldn't have been banished before it had fulfilled its task.

It was a death curse, after all.

"You should be glad you didn't see it," Asen continued. "The way it picked her up like she was nothing but a doll? Nightmarish."

"Wait," Kosara said, narrowing her eyes. Previously, she'd assumed Asen was describing the events as recounted by Vila. "Did you follow me?"

Asen looked down at his book, clearly uncomfortable. "I did, but—"

"You promised you wouldn't!"

"What did you expect me to do? You could have been killed over there."

"You could have been killed, too!"

"Well, I didn't." He paused before adding, conversationally, as if sharing what he'd had for dinner, "I transformed into a wolf."

Kosara shuddered, her anger quickly shifting into worry. Inadvertently, her eyes searched for any signs of the transformation on Asen's face, as if he'd still have tufts of fur sticking out of his ears. "And? How do you feel?"

"Fine. Vila says I'm lucky the infection hadn't spread completely yet, so it was only for a short time. She gave me this." He fished a herbal pouch out of his pocket. "Wolfsbane. It's supposed to have calming effects."

Kosara nodded, though she knew it wouldn't be of much help once the next full moon rolled around, and Asen's infection took over him completely. It could prevent any accidents in the meantime, however.

She shivered despite the blanket still draped over her shoulders. "It's freezing in here. Why didn't you put the fire on?"

"Is it?" Asen said, looking around, like he hadn't spotted the hearth he sat next to. "I didn't notice. I feel quite warm."

Kosara furrowed her eyebrows. She would have thought it was her who was unusually cold after spending hours outside last night, passed out on the ground. However, the thin layer of ice on the inside of the kitchen window suggested otherwise.

She reached and touched his forehead. It was scalding hot.

"You're burning," she said.

"Am I?"

"It must have been the transformation."

"I feel absolutely fine."

"Your body has just been through its very first transformation. You're not fine."

Kosara's eyes ran through the herbs hanging off the ceiling. She could brew him something soothing, out of thyme, ginger, and coriander seed. She'd whip up a quick potion in no time, but first, she needed to start the fire.

She clicked her fingers. Rather, she tried to click her fingers. No sound came out.

Kosara frowned and examined her hand. It was only then she noticed it wasn't her hand at all.

She swore loudly, moving the unfamiliar fingers in front of her eyes. They were too long, too thin, so pale they were almost translucent. A web of blue veins ran along them, like smeared ink on a blank page.

"Whose hands are those?" Asen asked, sounding unperturbed. At this point, he must have grown used to the effect her shadows had on her.

Kosara wasn't used to it. Those strange fingers—they made her want to scream.

"I'm not sure," she said instead. When she'd researched the Zmey's past brides, she'd found yellowed obituaries, creased photographs, and engravings on crumbling headstones. She'd looked at the women's faces—she hadn't spent too much time examining their hands.

Kosara tried clicking her fingers again. Her foreign fingertips slid against each other, producing a quiet whisper of a sound, but no click came out.

"Whoever they used to belong to couldn't click their fingers," Kosara said, unable to hide the frustration in her voice. It was that skin, thin as cigarette paper, that failed to have any traction, and the phalanges, so delicate she worried they might crumble if she pressed too hard.

"Really?" Asen asked. "How did they do magic?"

"How am I supposed to know, Bakharov?" Kosara snapped and immediately regretted it. This wasn't his fault. He was curious, that was all. "They used their voice, or they burned herbs to summon smells, or they simply trained their mind. There are many ways to weave magic."

"But you always use your hands."

"I do," Kosara said through gritted teeth and tried clicking her fingers again. Finally, they produced a faint sound and the world's most pathetic flicker of a flame appeared at her thumb, before disappearing with a hiss.

That was it. Kosara was too tired, too sore, too bloody cold.

She'd just fought an enormous, vicious cockerel. She'd lost a colleague who she'd grieved once already. And now, she couldn't even use her magic properly.

Kosara crumpled to the floor, the blanket coming after and burying her in a pile of lavender-scented wool. Her shoulders shook.

She wasn't going to cry. No matter how tired she was. She didn't cry in front of people.

Except, she'd cried in front of Asen before, and he'd been nothing but understanding.

"Kosara." Asen tentatively lifted a corner of the blanket and peeked inside. She must have looked ridiculous, hiding under it like a wounded animal. "What's wrong?"

"Nothing," Kosara said with all the dignity she could muster. "I'm fine. Let me be."

Asen shuffled closer and wiped a tear off her cheek with his thumb. Then, he shuddered. "You're freezing."

"I'm fine. You're too warm."

He moved the blanket, so it was draped over both their shoulders, and wrapped his arms around Kosara, holding her close. At first, she sat there stiffly, too stubborn to admit this was precisely what she needed. Then, she leaned into him, burying her face in his shoulder. His warmth wasn't oppressive like the Zmey's had been—it was pleasant. His hand rested on her waist, but she wasn't worried it might crawl under her layers and cruelly pinch her if she said the wrong thing.

He smelled nice—familiar, like coffee, smoke, and the sea, though slightly different. Had he started using a new aftershave?

She lifted her head to look at him. He was barely visible in the gloom of the kitchen.

"You've shaved," she said. Except, she'd felt the stubble on her cheek when she'd moved.

"I did. Not that it was much use. It's been growing very quickly. I tried to give myself a haircut as well, but it's not as if you can tell."

"It's the varkolak curse. It does that."

"I gathered. I'll have to find a very good barber."

"This is Chernograd. There are plenty who have the necessary experience." Kosara fell silent. It suddenly hit her how close they were, huddling under the blanket. Their noses almost touched.

The sensible thing would be to step away. There was so much work to do. Always, so much work.

She didn't want to step away. Her eyes were fixed on his, and his were on hers, framed with dark lashes longer than any man had the right to have. Except, for a brief second, when his gaze flicked to her mouth, and Kosara realised he was thinking of kissing her.

This was a bad idea. Their situation was messy already, and getting too close would only make it messier. She had too many problems of her own. Besides, everything about Asen's recent behaviour pointed to him not wanting her. What had changed?

Was this his recent transformation affecting his brain chemistry, his animal side making stupid decisions the human would regret in the morning? Or was it simply the fact that he was trapped in Chernograd now, so he might as well settle for her, given that they were stuck together for the time being?

Her own feelings were all over the place, too. As if in confirmation, a familiar voice rushed into her head. *Is it him you want to be kissing, my little Kosara? Or is it me?*

A nervous giggle escaped Kosara's lips. What a preposterous idea. Asen and the Zmey couldn't have been more different. The only thing they had in common . . .

The only thing they had in common, Kosara realised with a start, was that they were both monsters. The heat radiating from Asen reminded her of it. It sent her right back to the Zmey's palace where only minutes earlier, she'd felt the Zmey's kisses.

No, she thought sternly, forcing his voice in her mind to be quiet. This was nonsense. The Zmey was gone. What she'd seen in the shadow's vision had been the past. It hadn't even been *her* that he was kissing. None of it mattered.

The Zmey was gone. It was her and Asen under an old, tattered blanket. Just the two of them.

She looked into his eyes, soft and unblinking as he took her in, and she couldn't convince herself that this man didn't want her. To hell with all her doubts and worries. So what if this proved to be a bad decision? It wasn't as if she wasn't already drowning in bad decisions.

Kosara leaned closer. She felt Asen's breath as he exhaled, warm against her cheek, and his lips brushed hers. When she didn't pull away, he pressed forwards. She hadn't been expecting it, somehow, and her teeth painfully collided with his.

Great job, Kosara, finally getting to kiss him and making a mess of it.
Instead of pulling away, he gently bit her lower lip. She laughed,
throwing her hands behind his neck and pulling him closer, until her
nose was full of his scent and her mouth was full of his taste. Her
stomach fluttered, half with nerves, half with want. It had been far too
long since she'd been touched like this, and she was all out of practice.

He gently pushed her until she lay with her back on the floor, and
he was on top of her, his hair tingling her face, his stubble scratching
her cheek. She ran a hand down the length of his spine, making a low
groan escape his lips, and then, emboldened, she let her fingers slide
under his shirt, over his stomach, feeling the fine trail of hair on it. He
kissed her mouth, then down her chin and neck, then her collarbone.

Just when Kosara thought he'd move to somewhere even more
interesting next, he braced himself on his elbows above her, messy
haired, out of breath, with his mouth slightly parted. She was grin-
ning at him, unable to contain all the warm feelings inside her, but
his face was serious, his eyes large and dark. He appeared almost
stunned. He opened his mouth to say something.

A loud crash. They both flinched. Kosara let out a strangled sound.

A strong gust of wind ran through the room, smelling of snow, as
if the front door had been slammed open. It made gooseflesh rise on
Kosara's arms. Then, a series of thuds came from the hallway, closer
and closer, as something slammed against the walls in a frenzy.

A high-pitched wail sounded. A woman's voice—one Kosara recognised.

Boryana.

20

Asen

The kikimora stood at the threshold, bringing the smell of freshly spilled blood with her. Her feet didn't touch the ground. They dangled above the floorboards, pale and limp.

She screamed so loudly, Asen's eardrums vibrated, and it was as if the scream propelled her forwards. She flew towards him. He scrambled backwards until his back hit the wall.

At first, he'd thought the kikimora looked nothing like Boryana. Boryana's lips had been full and red; the kikimora's were grey and dry. Boryana's cheeks had been pink; the kikimora's were pale hollows framing her gaunt face. Boryana had always cared for her clothes; the kikimora's white dress was bloodstained and frayed.

Boryana had been very much alive; the kikimora, with its blue-tinged skin and a body that exuded the faint stench of rotting flesh, was not.

Then, the wraith looked at him, and he recognised those eyes. He'd memorised each golden fleck surrounding those irises. He could draw every eyelash from memory. Those were Boryana's eyes.

The hair was hers, too, and it spilled around her face in a halo of bright fire-engine red.

Just like in the graveyard last winter, Asen couldn't fight her. All his love for this woman was still there, and what was worse, his guilt for losing her was, too. Now, he had to add the guilt of her catching him kissing Kosara to it. Had she seen it? Did she know?

He was unsure what she wanted of him. His blood? His flesh? His heart? Whatever it was, he simply couldn't look into those eyes and refuse her.

The kikimora slammed her taloned hands against his chest. The pain made him hiss. The blood quickly soaked through his shirt, colouring it red.

Asen didn't fight her. If devouring him alive was what would give her peace beyond the grave, he'd gladly let her. It was his fault she was dead in the first place.

But then, in the brief second between the kikimora's wails, he heard a different voice. Kosara. His eyes caught hers, watching in horror from behind the kikimora's back. Her lips moved, whispering a single phrase: *Please stay with me.*

As if he was a dying patient. When the kikimora's scalpel-sharp nails struck him again, slicing cleanly through his skin, he supposed, in a way, he was.

Asen moved his gaze from Kosara's terrified face to Boryana's furious one, and then back to Kosara's.

Suddenly, guiltily, he realised he wanted to stay. He didn't want to die.

His death would mean nothing to Boryana, anyway. It hadn't been him who'd murdered her. It had been her father. Devouring Asen's heart would do nothing to sate her.

Or at least that was what he told himself. He *really* didn't want to die.

Unfortunately, the realisation made no difference. He was too weak, after a night of fighting the mratinyak, to resist the kikimora. He attempted to push her back, his muscles straining, but it was like fighting a steam train. If he trusted himself to remain in control, he would have attempted transforming, but he didn't trust himself—and wouldn't have known how to go about it, anyway.

As he ducked to evade the kikimora's nails, he saw Kosara again, swearing loudly as she fished the jar of enchanted ink from her pocket.

She fell to the floor, undid the lid, and started drawing, dipping her fingers directly inside in the absence of a brush.

Asen wasn't sure precisely what Kosara's plan was, but he knew he had to win her time. He sidestepped the kikimora's next attack, causing her to crash against the floor. It didn't slow her down. A second later, she pushed herself up, hissing and spitting, and she was on her feet again. Asen grabbed the copper frying pan hanging from a roof beam and prepared to strike.

The best strategy would be to hit her across the face. Except, he couldn't do it. He couldn't hit Boryana.

This is not Boryana, his mind pleaded. *This is Boryana's anger personified.*

His arms refused to listen. Instead, he pushed her back with the frying pan and ran.

"How long do you need?" he shouted at Kosara as he dashed around the kitchen table, the wraith close behind him.

"Two minutes," Kosara said, and then lifted two fingers in the air to make sure he understood her. "Maybe one."

The kikimora knocked the crystal ball off the table. It shattered against the ground, scattering its pink mist around the room. Asen nearly tripped on the corner of the rug in his bid to avoid it. On the floor, among the glittering shards of glass, Kosara kept drawing.

He hunched down to fit under the roof beams near the hearth, where they slanted at a sharp angle, and the herbs hanging off them tickled the crown of his head. The kikimora followed, leaves of thyme and rosemary catching in her hair. The pink mist dispersed in her wake.

Asen prodded and pushed her with the frying pan, but the monster kept coming, slashing at him with her fingernails. Several bloody scratches bloomed on his arm.

"Asen!" Kosara shouted. She was standing, waving her hands to attract his attention. Who knew how long she'd been shouting for? The kikimora's wails were deafening.

Kosara shouted something else, but he couldn't hear her. Then, she pointed at the floor. The circle was complete.

At first, Asen was worried the kikimora might have traced their exchange and figured out they'd prepared a trap for her. The next moment, she staggered towards him blindly, slamming her forehead against a roof beam, and Asen was certain the monster was blinded by anger.

He sidestepped her, rushing towards the circle. The kikimora was fast. Her fingers grazed his back, where his shirt had stuck to his skin, slick with sweat and blood.

She was fast, but he was faster.

When he reached the circle, Asen leaped over it. The kikimora followed, but she didn't jump. Her feet hovered a centimetre or two above the ground, never touching it.

Come on, Asen pleaded. He was out of breath and his chest hurt. He couldn't keep running forever. *Come on.*

The tip of the kikimora's toe caught on a piece of uneven timber. It was barely a brush of her curved, yellowed nail against the ink-stained floor. It was enough.

The kikimora's screams, somehow, grew louder. She fell in a heap on the floor, holding her head in her arms. Beneath her, the runes of the magic circle glistened, freshly painted, but they didn't smear.

Finally, her wailing stopped.

The first thing Asen heard in the sudden silence was the thumping of his own heart. Then, Kosara sighed with relief. The sounds from outside rushed back in: the howling of the wind and the swearing of the cart drivers as they navigated a busy crossroads nearby.

Asen wavered. On one side of him stood Kosara, with her ink-stained fingers that had just saved his life. On the other, Boryana was trapped, a skeletal creature in dirty rags.

This was his fault. This was what loving him had done to Boryana. He couldn't allow himself to make the same mistake twice.

He stepped towards the circle. "Boryana?"

The kikimora lifted her gaze, and Asen unwittingly flinched. He wasn't used to seeing Boryana's face so full of hatred.

The kikimora kneeled, resting her hands against the floor, and then, like a predator, she pounced. Her body slammed against the circle's invisible barrier.

She whimpered, retreating back to the floor.

"Are you okay?" Kosara asked. He looked to his side to find her standing there, watching him. "Are your wounds deep?"

Asen shrugged, trying not to show the pain on his face. He couldn't handle Kosara's worry right now. He couldn't allow her to get closer, even if it was so she could bandage his wounds, too scared of how Boryana would react. "Just scratches."

"Are you sure? I can—"

"I don't need anything. I'll wash them in the sink."

For a few seconds, they remained silent, while on the floor, Boryana breathed heavily.

"Is the circle hurting her?" Asen asked.

"I don't think so. It shouldn't do."

"How long will it last?"

"Until midnight. Then, I'll have to recharge it."

"Every day at midnight? I can set an alarm." Asen checked his watch. It was barely half past seven, and the streetlights outside were just flickering on. It was right about the time, he thought absent-mindedly, when the monsters usually began to wake during the Foul Days.

Except, it was the middle of June. What was Boryana doing here?

"On your watch?" Kosara lifted her eyebrows. "Is this some kind of magic?"

"Just gears, I think." Asen turned the little crown, setting the alarm for ten minutes to midnight. Then, he looked back at Kosara. "Thank you."

She gave him a tired smile. "You're welcome."

Asen had lost track of how many times the two of them had saved each other at this point. Did he owe her? Or did she owe him?

It didn't matter, he supposed. They'd continue dragging each other out of deadly situations, he was certain. That was what friends were for.

Friends. He scoffed internally. As if he could keep pretending this was all they were while he still tasted her mouth on his. As if this was just the sort of thing friends did—rolling around on the floor, exchanging saliva, and feeling each other up.

"I don't understand," Kosara said, obviously oblivious to his musings. "Why is the kikimora here?"

"I was about to ask you the same thing."

"You haven't been back to the graveyard, have you?"

"I haven't." This was another source of guilt. "I'd meant to, but—"

"You'd meant to? After what happened the last time?"

"Well, now it's not the Foul Days."

"That's just what I was thinking." She chewed on her lip. "Remember, the last time Boryana attacked you, I summoned her away with a promise."

"As if I could forget. You told her we'll bring justice to her killer."

"I told her we'll bring justice to her killer *by the next Foul Days*. We should have had a year to catch Karaivanov."

They both looked down at the kikimora, who showed no signs she intended to dematerialise and wait until December before she attacked again. She fixed them with her terribly Boryana-like eyes and made a low, growling sound in the back of her throat.

"You know, I've been seeing her occasionally, in the corner of my eye," Asen said after a moment. "I thought I was imagining her."

Kosara shook her head. "I've been seeing her, too. She's been waiting. Biding her time. I just can't figure out, what was she waiting for?"

The worst possible moment to interrupt? Asen thought bitterly, and immediately felt awful. Maybe that was precisely it. Maybe if he hadn't kissed Kosara, provoking Boryana's wrath, none of this would have happened. This was his fault, for being selfish.

The Boryana he'd known, his Boryana, would have never wanted him to remain stuck in the past forever. She would have wanted him to move on, so many years after her death. But this wasn't his Boryana— this was her every negative emotion personified. It was mostly anger, but there had to be hurt in there, too. There had to be jealousy.

It was very difficult to move on when your past was staring at you with big, angry eyes.

After a few seconds of tense silence, Asen asked, "Can you leave us for a few minutes?"

Kosara frowned. "If you're going to do something stupid—"

"I won't get within an arm's distance of the circle, I promise. I just want . . ." He hesitated. What did he want exactly? "I just want to try talking to her."

Kosara sighed. She'd had plenty of experience attempting to converse with kikimoras, he supposed. She knew how hopeless the idea was.

Nevertheless, she nodded. "Fine. I'm going back to bed. Make sure to wake me up before midnight." Kosara paused. Asen didn't think he'd imagined her hand reaching to touch him, before she changed her mind and pretended to be tucking a lose strand of hair behind her ear.

She turned on her heel and marched to the door. At the threshold, she looked over her shoulder. "Please, be careful."

Kosara had been right. Having a conversation with a kikimora indeed proved impossible. Every time Asen opened his mouth, she wailed at him. Whenever he stepped closer, she tried to attack him.

This wasn't Boryana. He knew it wasn't. One side of him was fully aware this was nothing but an angry apparition, whose only desire was to devour his heart. She might have donned some twisted version of Boryana's face, but she was *not* Boryana.

The other side of him wanted nothing more than to hug her and tearfully apologise for everything he'd done. Once again, he'd messed it all up.

Eventually, he figured out the best way to spend time with her was to sit there, at the kitchen table, while the kikimora stared at him with accusation in her eyes.

He must have nodded off because the buzzing of his watch woke him up. When he opened his eyes, he found Boryana asleep as well, curled up on the floor. He'd never considered whether ghosts slept, but this one certainly did. She snored, too.

He tiptoed out of the room and up the stairs, where, in the darkness, he nearly bumped into Kosara. Her hair was messy from the bed, and she was in her nightgown, on top of which she'd put on an oversized jumper. Her legs were bare.

She let out a short yelp when she saw him. "Damn it, Bakharov." She held on to her heart. "What are you doing, sneaking about in the dark?"

He had to shake his head to clear his thoughts. It was truly a sign of how far gone he was that a pair of legs managed to distract him this much. Even now, all he could glimpse was an expanse of bare skin stretching between her ankle, where her woollen socks ended, and her upper thigh, where who knew how many layers of thermal underwear began.

What he truly wanted to do at this exact moment was to peel them all off, one by one, like opening a name-day present. Maybe with his teeth.

"Asen?" Kosara asked, frowning.

Christ, what was wrong with him? What kind of a man had those kinds of thoughts while his wife's vengeful spirit slept in the next room? He found the pieces of the broken wedding ring in his pocket, gripping them tightly in his fist until it hurt.

He cleared his throat. "I was coming to wake you. It's midnight."

"I know. I set an alarm too, just in case." She paused. "How is she?"

"Asleep. Do you think we should get her a blanket?" There, this was how a thoughtful haunted widower acted.

Kosara was looking at him as if he'd gone insane. "She's a kikimora. She doesn't feel the cold."

"We can't just leave her lying on the floor without at least a blanket." Asen knew he sounded ridiculous. This wasn't his wife. It was a wraith. A dangerous, bloodthirsty wraith who'd take the first chance to devour his heart.

And yet, it looked so much like his wife.

Kosara sighed. "Wait here." A minute later, she returned with a woollen blanket.

The two of them entered the kitchen quietly. Asen carefully draped the blanket on top of Boryana. The kikimora stirred, mumbling something under her breath, but she didn't wake.

Kosara kneeled down and, using her finger, retraced the symbols she'd previously drawn, meticulously following their dark lines on the floor.

Once she'd finished, she stood up and dusted her hands. Just in time. The grandfather clock in the hallway began chiming.

"I should get back to bed," Kosara said, obviously trying to suppress a yawn and failing. "Do you need any extra bl—"

The rest of the sentence was drowned by thunder. A storm, Asen thought. Not unusual this time of year, though he wouldn't have expected it when it was this cold.

Then, the screams started.

Asen and Kosara shared a look. Without exchanging a word, they rushed to the door. Kosara put on her boots while running forwards to unlock it. Asen followed, checking for the knife tucked in his belt.

They weren't the only people outside. Some stood at their doorways in pyjamas and slippers, with their eyes fixed on the sky. Others peeked from behind the railings of balconies, or opened windows and craned their necks to see better.

Asen traced their gazes upwards, and he wanted to scream, too.

The sky was cracking.

21

Kosara

Kosara blinked, certain she must be trapped in another nightmare. When she looked up, the fractures she'd previously seen were there, except they'd grown into rifts, separating large chunks of darkness. In between them, a foreign sky peeked, grey and laden with storm clouds.

Something glittered, falling down, and at first, she was worried it was chunks of sky raining on the city. Then, it landed on the tip of her nose, cold and wet. It was snow. Just snow.

What she couldn't deny seeing, however, were the monsters. High above, the waxy wings of yudas reflected the moonlight, and the golden horns of the samodivas' deer glinted. On the street below, rusalkas moaned and slithered along the cobblestones on their bellies.

This was her fault. Hers, Vila's, and Sofiya's—or hers alone. Whether her botched attempt to glue the fissures between the realms had led to this, or whether it had been the mratinyak tearing the fragile barrier too much on its way past, she couldn't know. In any case, this was her doing. Once more, she'd got herself involved with magic too complicated for her to understand.

"Kosara," Asen's voice came out almost a whisper. "Kosara, are those . . ."

She traced his gaze. From the roof of a nearby house, a swarm of karakonjuls descended, clicking their teeth and wagging their tails. They were so close, Kosara could count every long hair sticking out of their donkey-like ears.

"Fuck." Kosara grabbed Asen's hand and pulled him back inside. She locked the door behind them.

"What's happening?" Asen asked, his eyes panicked.

"I'm not sure. Something's gone wrong."

Asen only looked at her, his face clearly communicating his thoughts: *You don't say.*

Kosara took in a deep breath, trying to organise her scattered mind. This wasn't new to her. It had never happened in June before, sure, but she'd lived through plenty of monster invasions. She knew what she had to do. "I need to secure the house."

The protective circles she'd drawn around each window and door last year had long faded. It was a good thing she still had plenty of enchanted ink. Kosara undid the jar lid with trembling fingers. Then, methodically, moving from one room to the other, she repainted each circle of runes.

When she returned to the kitchen, she found the kitchen spirit sitting in the corner, fully visible, eating a jar of pickled cabbage with a big wooden spoon.

"Good evening," the spirit greeted her.

"She said she was hungry," Asen explained while he busied himself around the cooker.

Kosara wasn't sure why she was surprised. The rest of the monsters had awoken. Of course her household spirits would follow.

"Hi, Aunty," she said. Then, she turned to Asen. "What are you doing?"

He turned around, cezve and cup in hand, looking sheepish. The smell of freshly brewed coffee rushed her.

"I wasn't sure if you wanted any, but I couldn't think of what else to do to help," Asen said, and Kosara took the cup from his hand and drank a large gulp. Her mind still felt sluggish, too tired after the fight with the mratinyak, and she needed it sharp if she wanted to figure out some way out of this.

Then, she noticed Asen hadn't poured two cups of coffee. He'd poured three. Carefully, he took the third cup, rattling in its saucer, and placed it on the floor next to the kikimora's sleeping body. Boryana stirred, opening her eyes for a second, but thankfully, she didn't fully wake.

Kosara swore internally. She hated seeing him like this. His eyes were red-rimmed and the skin around his nails was raw from biting. *This isn't your wife,* she wanted to tell him, but she suspected he already knew. Logically, he was aware his wife was dead. But emotions didn't always follow logic.

If Kosara was better at this sort of thing, she'd know what to say. She'd hold him and let him cry on her shoulder until he'd run out of tears. She'd come up with some clever joke and make him laugh.

She wasn't good at any of it.

Before she'd said anything, Asen asked, "What are we going to do?"

"You? Nothing. I need to go and see Vila."

"If you think I'm going to simply sit here and wait while you—"

A knock at the door interrupted them. Asen grabbed one of the pans hanging over the fireplace while Kosara crept to the window.

It was too dark outside, and the snow was too thick for her to be certain, but she thought the two silhouettes waiting at the door looked human. In any case, if they weren't, her wards would take care of them.

When she opened the door, it took her a moment to recognise the women standing outside, wrapped tightly in too many layers, their faces hidden behind woollen scarfs.

"Kosara, thank God you're home," one of them said urgently, and her voice helped Kosara place her. Siyana, the girl who'd applied to be her apprentice last year.

And if Siyana was here, chances were, the other formless, woollen blob was Ayshe who'd apprenticed under Sofiya. Poor girl. It must have been difficult, losing her teacher so early.

"It's okay," Kosara shouted over her shoulder at Asen, who was lurking behind her in the hallway, armed with the frying pan. "I know them."

He nodded and retreated inside the house.

Kosara hesitated. "Do you two want to come in?"

"No time," said Ayshe. "We're here to fetch you. We're having an emergency meeting."

"Who is?"

Siyana looked at her as if she'd lost her mind. "The Witch and Warlock Association."

"Ah," Kosara said. "Is Vila coming?"

The two girls exchanged a telling grimace. She was not.

This only made Kosara angrier. Why was the old witch hiding?

Ayshe sounded unsure. "She said she's too old to be traipsing around the city in the middle of the night."

"She said *what*?" Unwittingly, Kosara raised her voice.

"Um, she said she's too old to be—"

Kosara huffed loudly. *Too old.* Vila was one of the only proper witches left in the city.

Sofiya was dead. Irina had been murdered. Several others had disappeared during the last Foul Days, a few had immigrated to Belograd, and Konstantin Karaivanov had recruited many. They'd lost some of their strongest to the Zmey. There was old Ivan, who had some weak herbalist powers, and Yovana the seer who rarely left her house, and then—there was Kosara and a bunch of children.

Siyana and Ayshe were both gifted girls, but they were too young to be dealing with any of this. They weren't experienced enough to work on their own, and the last thing Kosara needed right now was to take on a babysitting gig.

"You two should go home," she said. "Barricade yourselves inside. Leave this to me."

"But the Association—"

"The Association is gone, girls. We've lost too many."

Siyana harrumphed. They both gave her a contemptuous look before turning around and stomping through the snow. Kosara watched after them for a minute, making sure they were gone.

Good, she told herself. She'd dealt with them well. They'd return home to their parents, safe and sound. This wasn't their fight.

Kosara stormed inside the kitchen and downed the rest of her coffee. "I should go. The house is protected, so you should be fine for the rest of the night."

She considered changing into more appropriate clothes but decided against it. Time was of the essence. She shrugged her coat on.

"I'll come with you," Asen said, quite predictably.

"I'd really rather you stay here. With the monsters out there—"

"Kosara, I am a varkolak. Believe me, I can take care of myself."

"It's not that." At least, it wasn't only that. "People might come looking for me. Those two girls might return. You can calm them down. If anyone is injured, you'll know how to patch them up until I'm back. Please, it's important."

Asen sighed, but he couldn't argue.

"Can't seeing Vila wait until the morning?" he asked. "It's the middle of the night. There are monsters outside."

Kosara gathered her shadows around her like a small army, ushering them towards the door. "I'm a witch. I'm not afraid of monsters."

"Fine," Asen said, still sounding unsure. "But you should at least put some trousers on."

22

Asen

Stuck alone in the house, with no one but a snoring kikimora to keep him company, Asen couldn't sleep. Through the window, the cracks in the sky were still visible, and so were the silhouettes of monsters flying over the rooftops.

He should have gone with Kosara. He should have never let her convince him he wasn't needed. What if she got attacked on the way to Vila's house?

She's a witch with twelve shadows, he reminded himself. *Any enemy that can take her wouldn't have any issue going through you first.*

Asen had no doubt Kosara hadn't wanted him there when she spoke to Vila. Whatever the two of them had to discuss, it was witch business, and it wasn't his place to interfere.

A hunger stirred in his stomach, and he was acutely aware of how animalistic it felt. Inside his mouth, his canines elongated, coming to a sharp point.

Bloody hell. Maybe this was why Kosara had insisted he stay home. One less monster out in the streets had to be a good thing. He still remembered how he'd nearly lost control when they'd fought the mratinyak. He couldn't allow for it to happen again.

But then, he realised, it wasn't meat he hungered for. It was sugar.

Before he knew it, he'd demolished the last remnants of the sweets his mother had sent. He'd always been a stress eater, and he craved something so sweet, his teeth would hurt. None of that cheap, bitter chocolate Kosara kept in the cupboard would do.

Perhaps baking wouldn't have been most people's first instinct while trapped inside during a monster-infested snowstorm, but Asen had always found it calmed his nerves. It helped him forget about the gigantic mess he'd found himself in, and concentrate on measuring the ingredients exactly, so he'd achieve the perfect rise.

First, he rummaged through the kitchen until he found the spices, tucked away in a dusty cupboard covered in cobwebs. Soon, he fell into the familiar rhythm, deshelling walnuts, measuring cinnamon, and sifting flour, creating great white clouds floating around in the kitchen. The mixture in the big bowl already smelled divine, and he licked the spatula once he'd finished stirring.

Next, he was going to whip up some kind of icing . . .

There was a knock on the door. Probably Kosara, Asen decided. She must have forgotten her keys.

He opened, already smiling, but it wasn't Kosara he found on the other side. It was a young man in a bowler hat, red-faced and breathless from walking too fast. When his eyes fell on Asen, the man jumped.

Asen realised he must have looked like a ghost, standing in the dark hallway, dressed in a white apron, and covered in flour.

"Can I help you?" he asked flatly.

The man was quick to find his bearings. "Is Kosara home?"

"She's not. Can *I* help you?"

"No," the man said. "I don't know. Maybe." Finally, his manners caught up with him and he extended a hand. "My name is Dr. Yordan Krustev, but you can call me Dancho. Everyone does. I'm looking for my partner."

Asen shook Dancho's hand firmly. "Asen Bakharov. And your partner is?"

"Ibrahim. Ibrahim Kaptan, he works in the bakery? You must have met him."

"He's not here, I'm afraid," Asen said, switching to his professional tone. "When did he go missing?"

"Missing?" Dancho suddenly looked panicked again. "That's a bit of a strong word. It's probably nothing, honestly. He always says I worry too much. See, what happened was, I came home after my shift, just after whatever this is started . . ." Dancho waved a hand to encompass the street with the quietly falling snow. "He wasn't there, and he's been acting a bit strange lately . . ."

"In what way?"

"Well. He might have died. Briefly."

"Right," Asen said, careful not to show his surprise. He was in Chernograd now. He had to get used to the Chernogradean ways.

"He visited Kosara a few days ago, and she prescribed him some sort of syrup to treat severe iron deficiency, which helped for a bit, but then his condition deteriorated again. I thought he might have come for something stronger."

"He hasn't been here. I'm sorry."

"Ah. Oh well. As I said, I'm very likely worrying over nothing. He's probably gone over to open the bakery. It's supposed to be his day off, but he's been so out of sorts lately, he must have forgotten."

Asen considered Dancho Krustev's worried face for a few seconds. Kosara had instructed him to stay in the house. He was supposed to keep an eye on it while she was outside.

On the other hand, she'd also asked him to take care of whoever came looking for her. "Let's go and check," he said. "I'll get my coat."

"Oh, please, you don't have to interrupt your night for my sake. I'm sure Ibrahim is fine."

"It's no problem." The truth was, Asen was itching to do something useful, even if it was solving the disappearance of a baker who was very likely to be found safe and sound in his own bakery. "Actually, you'll be doing me a favour. I was in the middle of making a cake, but I've just realised I've run out of icing sugar for the glaze. Do you think Ibrahim will let me borrow some?"

"I'm sure he will." Dancho smiled, obviously grateful to have company. "The bakery's near the Wall. Not that there's anything scary about the Wall, nowadays—in fact, it's been great for business with all the tourists, but you know . . ." He shrugged. "An old superstition. I'm always nervous when he's at work."

"I know. I'll be back in a minute." Asen hurried inside to change out of his apron and into his coat.

"Bye, Boryana! I'll be back soon!" he shouted as he left the house, and then felt foolish. The kikimora likely cared little when he'd be back, except if she started feeling peckish—then, she might start to wonder where her snack had disappeared to.

The sky had grown darker, and the snow kept falling. The streets were empty of people. The Chernogradeans had plenty of experience with monster attacks, Asen supposed. It was no wonder they'd managed to quickly shut whatever businesses were still open and return home. Now, everyone huddled inside, safe behind locked doors.

For the first time, Asen considered whether leaving the house had been wise. In his peripheral vision, he was sure he saw a pair of gleaming eyes watching him from the hallway of a block of flats. As he jumped over a sewer grate, the sound of rushing water came from below, but also the distinct wheezing of an upir taking in a heavy breath.

He looked up and spotted a monstrous silhouette, perched on the balcony of a nearby building. His hand automatically searched for his pistol before he remembered—he was unarmed. Panic rushed him. A moment later, the lantern of a passing cart illuminated the monster.

It wasn't a monster at all. It was a large woollen coat, swinging from a washing line.

Asen had to calm down. Chernograd was his home now, whether he liked it or not. He couldn't live the rest of his life jumping at shadows.

Besides, it seemed hypocritical of him to be afraid of monsters, given he was one. *He* was the thing that went bump in the night. While, sure, a karakonjul or an upir wouldn't feel any great sense of solidarity towards their monster brethren and would attack him all the same, Asen suspected he would be able to defend himself.

It was entirely possible he was imagining things, of course, but he was certain he saw better in the dark. When he'd heard that upir in the gutter, he'd also *smelled* it.

And now, once the wind died down, he smelled something else, too. Something familiar, vaguely reminiscent of wet fur and dog breath.

"Pardon my curiosity," said Dancho Krustev. "But I don't believe I've met you before."

"I moved to Chernograd recently," Asen replied vaguely, still sniffing the air.

"Oh, you're from Belograd? Interesting. I didn't realise there were many people like us on the other side of the Wall."

Asen finally gave his nose a rest. "People like us?"

"I can only imagine how confusing that must have been for you. It's bad enough here, where we're used to it, but over there? It must have been hell."

"I'm sorry. I don't believe I understand what you're talking about."

"Please, there's no need to pretend." Dancho gave him a wink, which took Asen aback. "I can smell you. I know you can smell me, too."

Asen was so busy gawking at Dancho, he nearly tripped over the flat ground. That whiff he'd caught when the wind had died down— the smell of wet dog? It had come from Dancho Krustev.

"Yeah, well . . ." Asen stammered, the realisation finally hitting him. He'd allowed for the possibility that many of the citizens of Chernograd were monsters just like him, but he hadn't expected to find himself taking a midnight stroll with one.

"We've got a book club, by the way," Dancho added casually.

Asen, once again, found himself at a loss for words. He'd imagined the conversation going in a hundred different directions, but this hadn't been one. "A book club?"

"It's more of an excuse to get smashed, I'm not going to lie to you. We take turns to host. Do you want to join?"

A varkolak book club. Would this city ever stop surprising him?

"Why books?" Asen asked.

"Ah, well. It started as a sort of a group therapy session, but you know what Chernogradeans are like. They hear the word 'therapy,' and they break into hives. So, I thought if I call it a book club instead, they'd join more readily. It sounds all intellectual, you know? And then, it always descends into boozing and crying on each other's shoulders, anyway." Dancho laughed. "It's at mine this Saturday. Seven o'clock. You should come."

"Maybe I will," Asen allowed, even though something about the whole thing made him distinctly uncomfortable.

He didn't need therapy. He was doing just fine. Wasn't he?

"It's *A Night of Passion With the Upir Lord,* by the way," Dancho added.

"What is?"

"The book we'll be discussing. A lot of critics dismissed it as nothing but a sappy love story, but let me tell you, the way the anonymous author tackles the conflict between the two lovers, one of whom feeds on the other . . ." Dancho trailed off. They'd just turned the corner and seen the bakery—a short, white-walled building with frilly pink curtains on the windows. The door was slightly ajar, throwing a line of light over the cobblestones. "Oh, thank God," Dancho said, walking towards the entrance. Then, he shouted, "It's your day off, silly! What are you doing?"

As he got closer to the bakery's open door, several distinct scents rushed Asen. First, the yeasty smell of dough and the sweetness of melting chocolate. Then, blood. A lot of it.

"Dancho, wait!" he shouted, but he was too late. Inside the building, Dancho screamed.

Asen rushed after him. The bakery was a small space with white counters, covered in bowls of dough rising in large, bubbly heaps. One of the ovens was lit and its heat filled the room.

The back door was wide open. Dancho's broad back blocked the view outside.

Asen walked closer to peek over Dancho's shoulder. The door led to a tiny courtyard, enclosed by a wooden fence overgrown with ivy. It must have been where the bakery's hens lived. Asen was drawn to this conclusion based on the evidence: the dozen feathery bodies now resting on the muddy ground.

A man kneeled in the mud. The light coming from the door landed on him like a spotlight. He held a dead hen in his lap and his baker's apron was smeared with its blood. The bird's neck had been broken.

"Ibrahim?" Dancho uttered.

The man looked up. The whites of his eyes weren't white anymore. They were the same bright red as the hen's blood.

When he opened his mouth, his teeth were covered in red, too.

"Dancho?" he said. It came out muffled, since his teeth had grown long and thin, like too many needles stuffed in too small a needlecase. "Dancho, I can explain."

He didn't have time to explain. Dancho Krustev produced a syringe gun from his coat and shot him in the neck.

23

Kosara

Vila's house was, luckily, currently located close to the Botanic Garden's entrance, with its two giant chicken legs resting on either side of the wrought iron gate. Vila must have been expecting visitors.

Kosara knocked on the door impatiently. She was out of breath and her hair was covered in snow. She'd spotted a karakonjul trailing her for the last few minutes of the journey, so she kept looking over her shoulder while she waited for Vila to open the door. The old witch was taking her time.

"Vila!" Kosara shouted, slamming her fist against the oak. "Vila!"

When the door finally opened, Kosara nearly fell forwards through it.

The old witch stood at the threshold with her eyebrows raised. Her outfit was very similar to Kosara's, except instead of a jumper on top of her nightgown, she wore one of her signature tacky woollen vests, embroidered with golden bells and pine trees.

"Good evening," Vila said pleasantly. "Would you like to come in for a cup of tea?"

This is your fault, isn't it? Kosara thought, her eyes fixed on the other witch's polite smile. *This is all your fault, and now, you're trying to pull the wool over my eyes by being nice.*

The only trouble was, Kosara knew very well that Vila was never nice unprompted.

"I'd like nothing more," Kosara said through gritted teeth and followed Vila inside.

"Chamomile, ironwort, nettle, thyme?" Vila asked, going through the bunches of herbs drying suspended from the ceiling.

"It doesn't matter," Kosara said. "Vila, what's going on?"

"Mm?" Vila didn't look at Kosara, busying herself around the hearth.

"The sky has cracked open. Monsters have invaded the city."

"You're acting as if it's your first time."

"Well." Kosara struggled not to raise her voice. "It's never happened like this before. We haven't had time to prepare. I've just crossed half the city. There are drunks peacefully asleep in gutters, unaware of what is happening around them. There are carts trapped in the snow, with people inside them who might freeze to death if the monsters don't get them first."

"You could have helped them."

Kosara had tried. She'd forced the drunks awake by making them swallow a concoction she brewed especially for cases like this. She'd melted the snow around each cart she'd seen with a well-aimed fireball, though it had taken her several tries to summon them, since she still wasn't used to casting spells with her new fingers. It had been good practice, at least. She'd finally figured out just at what angle she had to click her fingers to produce a sound.

But she was a single witch, and Chernograd was a big city.

"I did my best," Kosara snapped. "Did you know this would happen?"

Vila poured two cups of tea and pushed one towards Kosara. "Magic always has its risks."

"Vila." Kosara's voice was measured, but on the inside, she was getting angrier with every exchanged empty line. "I need to know the truth. I'm aware there is plenty you're not telling me. I've been shown things by my shadows that have made that much obvious."

Almost imperceptibly, Vila flinched. She quickly covered it up by pretending to be sipping her tea.

"Please," Kosara said. "I don't know what to do. I can't fix this if I don't know what I'm standing against."

Vila sighed. Suddenly, she looked older than ever, with her snow-white hair and her tired frown. "Silly girl. You can't fix this no matter what. We all made too many mistakes. You know what the problem with witches is?"

"What?"

"We always think we know best."

"I don't underst—"

"I knew sending the mratinyak back to the monster realm might cause this to happen. The barrier between our worlds was fragile as it was. But we had to risk it, didn't we? It was either take the risk now or face the Foul Days without a single cockerel left in the city."

"So, if Sofiya hadn't summoned the mratinyak—"

"There's no use in pointing fingers. We're all in this together, tangled like a pig's intestines. Sofiya wouldn't have summoned the mratinyak if you hadn't caused the barrier to destabilise in the first place. You wouldn't have done that if I'd protected you better from the Zmey when you were a child. And the Zmey . . . The Zmey was the result of a mistake that happened long before you were born."

Kosara opened her mouth to ask a question, but Vila interrupted her with another sigh. "I'll tell you everything. There's no escaping it now, is there? However . . ." She got up from her seat, huffing. "A tale like that can't be told over cups of tea."

She rummaged inside a cupboard until she found a dusty bottle of clear liquid.

"What's that?" Kosara asked, watching the old witch pour two tiny glasses.

Vila squinted at the label. "Vodka. Foreign. I believe my ex left it behind."

She handed one glass to Kosara, then clicked hers against it. "May we live for a hundred more years." She downed it one go.

Kosara drank hers, too. Her eyes filled with tears, and she barely suppressed her coughs. Whatever this foreign alcohol was, it burned as bad as home-brewed rakia.

"Now." Vila sat back down. "I'll tell you a story, but you need to promise me you won't interrupt."

"Vila, I really don't think we have time for—"

"I'll tell you a story," Vila insisted. "I can guarantee you'll find it interesting."

"Fine," Kosara said impatiently. She couldn't for the life of her figure out how Vila was so calm about all this. Had she finally lost her mind in her old age?

Hopefully not. Because if she had, if Kosara had to deal with all this without Vila's help, they were truly fucked.

"Fine," Kosara repeated, because Vila was still watching her expectantly. "I promise."

Vila leaned back, letting the light of the fire cast long shadows across her face. When she started talking again, she used her storytelling voice, deeper than her usual tone. "Once upon a time, beyond nine mountains in the tenth, beyond nine woods in the tenth, as they say in the old fairy tales, there was a village. At a first glance, it looked like any other—mudbrick houses with ceramic roofs, donkey carts rolling along dusty roads, wheat fields and melon patches and gardens full of roses. Except, every New Year's Eve, the world would turn, and another realm would draw closer, and for twelve days, the village welcomed unusual guests."

Kosara made to ask a question, but Vila raised one bony finger in the air. "You promised!"

Kosara made a gesture, pretending to be locking her lips shut. She'd listen to the old witch's story, for now. However, if Vila didn't get to the point soon, Kosara would march straight out of here. She had no time to entertain nonsense.

"As I said," Vila continued pointedly, "strange guests arrived in the village every New Year's Eve. They spoke a foreign language, but the sharpness of their blades needed no translation. The foreigners' ruler was a handsome man with golden hair wearing fine clothes, but he acted like a common thug: if the villagers refused to pay his tax, he threatened to raze the village to the ground.

"Now, I know what you're thinking. Why didn't the villagers move away? The reason is simple. This foreign realm brought not only fear—it brought magic. Amulets and talismans no one had seen before. Scrolls and books of spells people travelled from the world over to get their hands on.

"In the village, there lived a witch. She'd grown tired of watching her people toil all year, only to give it all away to the foreigners' ruler. She'd heard a rumour—the source of the foreigners' power, the key to their strength, was an apple tree. This tree grew in the ruler's garden, and every one hundred years, it would yield a single golden apple. Then, once the apple's seeds had been carefully planted, the old tree would die, and a new one would sprout. Luckily for the witch, she didn't need to wait long. A year later, when the tree was due to bear its fruit, she snuck into the ruler's garden.

"I can see in your face you want to ask how, and to tell you the truth, if I was to describe every mundane detail of this story, we'd be here until tomorrow. She snuck onto a merchant ship and sailed a sea overflowing with monsters, and then she crossed thick woods where horned beasts lurked and prophetic birds nestled in the trees, and when she finally reached the palace, she simply pretended to work in the kitchens, because sometimes the simplest lies are most effective.

"Anyway, she found the apple tree quickly. It had grown taller than the palace's tallest tower and its leaves disappeared somewhere in the clouds. The witch knew she had to make the tree sweet on her if she ever hoped to be gifted its fruit, so, being a witch, on the first day she brought a sacrifice to it. A cockerel, which she slaughtered at the tree's roots, letting its blood sink into the ground.

"The tree did not like that. It lashed at her with its branches and caused the ground under her to shake. The witch learned fast. On the second day, she gave it her gold ring, which she buried in a hollow in its trunk. This time the tree caressed her with its leaves. On the third day, she had to do something drastic, or else she wouldn't win the tree's affection in time. She cut her hair, which back then was black as night and reached to the ground, and she weaved it into a hundred little ribbons which she planned to tie to the tree's branches.

"Once she reached the tree, however, she realised she'd been beaten there by someone. The tree's branches were adorned with a hundred golden bells, ringing in the wind. A young man waited, leaning against the tree's trunk, and his hair was the same gold as the bells.

"'I thought someone had been sneaking in here and trying to woo my tree,' he said. 'Who are you, girl?'

"The witch, who knew better than to converse with strange men bearing daggers at their hips, ran. The next day, she went to the tree earlier, creeping carefully through the tall grass, and she thought she'd avoided the stranger. But as she tied a ribbon to a bell-covered branch, a pair of hands reached from behind her and held her wrists.

"She tried to fight him, but the stranger was stronger.

"'Stop,' he said in her ear. 'I just want to talk.'

"He led her to a table he'd set in the shadow of the tree, and she was impressed by the plump fruit and the sweet wine he'd prepared for her. They talked. He got her story, and she got his. He was a prince, he told her, the son of the ruler of this realm, and he had two older brothers, as well as a younger sister. It was the brothers he was afraid of: he struggled to decide who was the stupidest and cruellest between the two. So, he'd make sure he was the one who'd get the golden apple, and he'd use its power to claim the throne for himself. If the witch would be so generous as to let him have it, that was, since his tree had grown quite fond of her.

"If he'd met the witch now, when she was an old woman, she would have never fallen for his nice smile or his pleasant words. But the witch was young then, and her young heart was easily fooled. For the next several days, until the twelfth day after New Year's Eve, the two met under the tree, drank wine, and talked. The prince's brothers came to the tree, too, they knew, because they'd find their footsteps in the mud and see the gifts left at the tree's trunk. Except, the tree never accepted those gifts. It would be between the witch and the young prince it would choose in the end, the two of them were certain.

"Finally, on the twelfth day, as they toasted each other with straw-berry wine, a great thud sounded. A plump, gold apple landed on the table right between them.

"'Please let me have it,' said the prince, 'and I promise your people will never want for anything. My mother was a human princess, and my father was a great zmey with scales of gold, and so, I love both your world and mine.'

"'Do you promise?' asked the witch.

"'I promise,' said the prince, and she believed him, because back then she didn't know how easily such promises were broken.

"She gave him the apple, expecting him to plant it as she'd heard was done. Instead, he broke it in two, letting its sweet juice run down his forearms and drip from his elbows, revealing a thousand tiny seeds inside it. Then, one by one, he ate them. His belly grew large with the strain. His eyes watered and sweat rolled down his face. Eventually, when he only had a single seed left, with a great sigh, the prince leaned back in his chair and fell asleep, his belly so full, it threatened to make the golden buttons on his shirt pop.

"The witch, who'd watched this display in silence, growing more and more horrified, regretted her decision to give him the apple already—however, she knew there was no point in crying over spilled milk. So, she grabbed the last seed, popped it in her mouth, and ran, and ran, and never stopped running until she reached her village.

"And even then, she kept running. The witch had seen something in the prince's hungry eyes and his greedy hands when he'd eaten the apple. She worried he'd come to claim that last seed from her. She left her village and for many years, she travelled the world. She met many friends and took many lovers, and when she finally returned, she didn't come on foot, but in a house on chicken legs. She'd grown homesick for her village, and so many years had passed—the prince had probably forgotten all about her.

"She found her village had changed. It was a city now, sprawling over the valley all the way to the river. The mudbrick houses were gone, replaced with tall spires. A clock tower stood where the melon fields had once been. One thing, however, remained the same. Every

New Year's Eve, for twelve days, the city had a toll to pay. The foreign realm had a new ruler, she was told, who called himself the Zmey, the Tsar of Monsters. He wasn't satisfied with money or gifts. He demanded payment in blood.

"The witch wasn't a scared girl now. She was a grown woman. She marched to his palace and demanded to see him. When their eyes met, she recognised the boy to whom she'd given the golden apple, and he recognised her, too.

"He had a story for her, like he often did. About how eating the apple had been a mistake. It was too much power for a single man to bear. His realm was fraying at the edges, and he couldn't keep it together. His subjects had grown hungry, and he couldn't control them. If only the witch would help him, maybe the two of them could fix this.

"The witch remembered that last seed she'd eaten, and so, she decided this must be her fault. Nine hundred and ninety-nine seeds weren't enough. His realm needed that last one. So, she stayed. She agreed to marry him. The two of them started to rebuild.

"For a while, all was well. The witch and the Zmey worked their magic, weaving the monster realm back together. Except, it quickly became obvious, the Zmey wasn't the man he'd pretended to be. His moods grew more and more volatile. At first, she tried to excuse him. He was under a lot of pressure. He was frustrated by his past mistakes. He resented needing her help. Soon, a raised voice turned into a raised fist, which turned into many late nights, brewing poultices and bandaging her own hurting body. The witch knew she had to run once more.

"I know what you're thinking. If only she'd stayed—if only she'd been strong enough to survive the Tsar—the monster realm would have been restored to its former glory and the monsters wouldn't pillage Chernograd every year. But, you know, spilled milk. She ran.

"Before she ran, however, she took one final precaution. On the night she snuck out of the palace, she stole the Zmey's shadow."

Despite her promises, Kosara simply couldn't keep her mouth shut any longer. "A shadow can't be stolen. It needs to be—"

"Yes, yes. But the witch had eaten that last apple seed, which gave her more power than any other witch who has ever lived, and besides, she'd had many years to win his shadow to her side. As I said, I had to take some shortcuts in the story. We don't have all night."

Vila finally fell silent. Kosara glanced at the clock, ticking above the old witch's head.

"My mouth's dry," Vila said. Her tired eyes also flicked to the clock. "Another drink?"

"Sure."

They downed another glass of vodka, which gave Kosara time to think. Vila's story sounded like a fairy tale, which made her doubt some of the more fanciful parts, but she had no doubt there was a sliver of truth in there. Vila had married the Zmey, that much Kosara had gathered from the shadows' visions. Their relationship had ended badly. Since then, the Zmey had been looking for a witch strong enough to replace her, unaware that Vila was one of a kind. The only witch who'd taken a bite from the golden apple.

"Is the golden apple metaphorical?" Kosara asked.

Vila waved a hand. "All stories are, in a way, metaphorical."

Kosara harrumphed. She wasn't sure why she'd expected a straight-forward answer.

"Why have you never told me any of this before?"

"It was never relevant."

Kosara chewed on her lip. It had been quite relevant, she thought, when she'd acquired the shadows of the Zmey's past brides. It had been relevant when she'd been enamoured with him as a young woman. Vila could have mentioned her history with him.

"My latest vision was of your student Svetla," Kosara said. "The one who survived the Zmey for a year."

Vila didn't say a word. Instead, with trembling fingers, she poured herself another vodka.

Kosara continued, "I saw her working with the Zmey. It looked like the two of them were doing what I'd attempted to do on my own. Repairing the fractures. But when I tried, you . . . um, strongly objected."

"I hit you on the head, yes. What you were going to do was seal the monster realm shut. The monsters would have been trapped there, in a world that is falling apart. It would have been a death sentence."

Kosara shuffled uncomfortably in her seat. She hadn't even considered what her magic would have done to the monster realm. She'd only thought of Chernograd.

But then, why should she care? The monsters had brought her city nothing but suffering.

"And what was the Zmey trying to do?" she asked.

"He was trying to repair his realm."

"What's beyond his realm?"

"Nothing. Darkness. Given the chance, it would devour his world."

Kosara played with her empty cup. It was barely the length of her pinkie, decorated with drawings of men and women in traditional dress, distinctly foreign in their elaborate headdresses and fur coats.

"Did you really take his shadow?" Kosara asked.

"Hm?" Vila asked, feigning confusion.

"I mean the witch from the story. Did she really take his shadow?"

"Of course she did. Why do you think he's so desperate to steal shadows from other witches? He doesn't have his own. He has no way of controlling all this power he's hoarded."

Kosara was certain she'd seen the Zmey cast a shadow before, back when she'd stayed in his palace, but now that she thought about it, she'd never paid much attention to it. It could have very well been someone else's shadow that had followed at his feet.

"Where have you—" Kosara sighed. She was getting tired of this game, but if Vila insisted, she'd play along. "Where did the witch hide it?"

"Somewhere he'll never find it. Inside a needle, which is in an egg, which is in a duck, which is in a hare—"

"Which is in an iron chest, which is buried under a green oak tree on the island of Buyan in the ocean," Kosara finished. She immediately recognised the diversion. Vila was avoiding the truth by quoting fairy tales again. The island of Buyan was nothing but an old legend.

Vila didn't want anyone to find that shadow. It was probably a good idea, Kosara had to admit. Kosara had managed to do so much damage already with only the shadows of people. What would she do if she got her hands on the magic powers of the Tsar of Monsters?

"So, let me see if I understand your story correctly," Kosara said. "The barrier between our realms is crumbling because the world of monsters is falling apart without the Zmey's magic to keep it together."

"Yes."

"And there is nothing we can do about it because hundreds of years ago, the Zmey ate an apple that was supposed to be planted. Metaphorical apple or real, we can't be certain."

"Well . . ." Vila drawled. "Yes."

Kosara noticed her hesitation. She was getting so tired of Vila's evasions. This had been the issue with their relationship all along—Vila hoarded information like she hoarded ugly woollen vests. It was as if she still saw Kosara as a child who couldn't be trusted with any real knowledge.

"Is there anything we can do about it?" Kosara asked, her voice tense.

"See, the issue is, that power he took, it should have never ended up in the hands of a single person. It was supposed to be for everyone, not for him alone. Those golden apple seeds are still there, churning in his belly, if only he could ever be selfless enough to give them back."

"How?"

"How does anything go back to the earth? Once his body is buried and rotting in the ground, the magic will return to the monster realm."

Kosara took a deep breath. That was it. The subject they'd been dancing around all night. "Kill the Zmey. That's what you're saying we need to do, isn't it? Trapping him wasn't enough. It was a mistake. He needs to die."

Vila spread her arms helplessly. "Kosara, I'm an old woman. What do I know? At this point, you have as much information as me. Draw your own conclusions."

Kosara's mouth became a thin line. What Vila was doing was washing her hands of the whole mess. She was an old woman now, she'd decided, and she didn't care what happened to the realms of humans and monsters any longer.

"You can't leave me to do it all alone," Kosara said, and she hated how lost and helpless she sounded.

For the first time that evening, something sharp glinted in Vila's eyes. "What do you expect me to do? I've fought the Zmey more times than you can imagine. I've lost so much to him."

Kosara shuddered, acutely aware she was surrounded by the shadows of the students Vila had lost. They floated around them like a thick, black fog.

"I almost lost you," Vila continued. "I won't watch it happen again. I'm tired. I've had enough."

"But then what—"

"I thought there must be another way. I thought if only I gave myself time, I could come up with a solution to this."

"But?"

"But I'm running out of time, Kosara. I've grown too old."

Kosara hesitated. "I don't understand what you're saying."

"I'm saying, it's time to do what I've always done best. We have to run."

"Where?"

"Beyond the Wall. This city might fall, but the Wall will protect Belograd. We can forget Chernograd ever existed. Will anyone miss it, really?"

Kosara shifted in her seat. She'd miss it. Chernograd was her home. Besides, there was another issue. "Some people can't run."

"What people?"

"Well. People like Asen."

"You mean monsters."

Kosara couldn't help but raise her voice. "I mean people."

"One day, when you grow as old as I am, you'll realise there are situations in which you can't save everyone. You know what they say— you can't make an omelette without breaking a few eggs. You have to save yourself." Vila raised the bottle of vodka again. "Another drink?"

"I have to go." Kosara stood up from the table. She'd had enough of this nonsense.

"Oh, are you leaving? I have something for you."

Kosara, foolishly, let herself hope the old witch would give her something useful. An all-powerful artefact that would destroy the Zmey on sight. A talisman to protect her from his wrath.

Instead, she returned with an empty cat bed. "Here, it was Sofiya's. I can't take care of it."

"Meow," said the ghost cat.

"I don't want a cat," Kosara snapped. "I'm more of a dog person, really."

"You have to take it. Moth can't stand the invisible bastard. Come on. It will make a fine addition to your zoo."

"My what?"

"Well, you've got a varkolak now, don't you?"

Kosara grunted and took the cat bed from Vila's hands. The animal inside it might have been invisible, but it weighed as much as any cat would.

"Is this all?" she asked. "This is all I'm going to get from you?"

"Well, no." Vila produced a handkerchief from her pocket and coughed into it. Then, she presented it to Kosara.

Kosara opened it. Inside it rested a single gold seed.

"Good luck," Vila said.

"Thanks," Kosara said, unsure what she was supposed to do with it. Eat it? But then, how would she ever retrieve it again if she needed it?

Besides, who was to say this was the real thing? Vila could have been simply winding her up. It wouldn't be the first time the old witch refused to take a dire situation seriously.

For the time being, Kosara stuffed the seed in her pocket.

As she kicked her way through the snowdrifts back to the house, she grew more and more furious. Vila had decided she'd just lie down and take whatever was coming? Fine. She was a grown woman. She could make her own decisions.

Kosara wasn't going to run. She'd had enough of running.

If the Zmey's death was what it would take to fix this, she'd wring the life out of him with her own two hands.

24

Kosara

As soon as Kosara walked into the house, the smell of linden tea and walnut cake hit her. It was nice, after her tense conversation with Vila, to come home to a lit hearth and pleasant scents wafting from the kitchen. It made a change from when she'd had no one to keep her company but spiders and ghosts.

She stomped the snow off her shoes and shook her head to dislodge it from her hair. When she opened the kitchen door, she froze at the threshold. She hadn't expected visitors.

"I brought a cat," she said helplessly, raising the cat bed in her hands.

"I brought an upir," Asen replied, nodding to Ibrahim passed out on the couch.

"Hi, Kosara," said Dancho Krustev. He busied himself with the teapot, pouring three cups, while Kosara positioned the bed in the corner.

The invisible cat meowed, and the kikimora snored on the floor next to the table. Somewhere upstairs, the fireplace spirit stomped on the floor, and the bathroom spirit rattled the pipes. The kitchen spirit sat high above on one of the ceiling rafters, knitting a long, semi-visible scarf.

Kosara remembered what Vila had called her house: a zoo. It still made her angry.

The cat didn't like Asen. As soon as he approached it, it started hissing. Kosara couldn't see the paw striking him, but the scratches on his skin bled all the same.

"It must be able to smell you." Dancho laughed, but Asen didn't look ready to join in.

"What happened?" Asen asked, as soon as the three of them sat around the table. "What did Vila say?"

Kosara glanced at Dancho. She grabbed a piece of walnut cake from the tray since she couldn't resist the smell. "Oh, she said a lot. First, what happened here?"

While Kosara ate her cake, Asen quickly recounted how they'd found Ibrahim, deep to the ankles in hen blood.

Kosara clicked her tongue. "He was right all along, wasn't he? He's an upir."

"How is that possible?" Asen asked. "I thought you said it was the mratinyak killing all the chickens."

"Well, it was the mratinyak the first time around. This time, it was obviously Ibrahim."

"But how can he be an upir?" Dancho threw a worried look at Ibrahim. "I've seen plenty of resurrections at the hospital—"

"And who's fault is that," Kosara muttered under her breath, loud enough for him to hear.

Dancho chose to ignore the slight. "When they first wake up, they're feral."

"Usually, yes. But lately, things have been strange."

"In what way?"

Kosara waved to the window where the snow now covered the street and piled on the roofs. "The fact it's snowing in June might have something to do with it. The monster realm is closer than ever before." She sighed. "What do you plan to do with him?"

"What would you prescribe?"

"I can give you something to keep him asleep."

Dancho took a deep breath and continued with an even tone, "I'm not going to have the love of my life permanently sedated. That's worse than killing him."

"He'll need a steady supply of blood."

"Would pig's blood do? Our butcher does excellent black pudding."

"It would do, for a while. Occasionally, he'll need to feed on humans. There are no two ways about it."

"How often is 'occasionally'? How much blood will he need?"

Kosara shrugged, exasperated. "How am I supposed to know? My speciality is preventing upirs in the first place. If that doesn't work, I know how to kill them. I've never fed one." She narrowed her eyes at him. "You seem to have an idea, though."

Dancho threw a glance at Asen. Whatever had gone down between the two while Kosara hadn't been there must have made Dancho trust him, because he leaned in closer and whispered, "You promise not to tell anyone?"

"Swear on my heart," Kosara said, and Asen muttered in agreement.

"Do you know Dr. Yancheva? She's in charge of the blood transfusions ward."

"We've met," Kosara said. "Her husband was bedbound for a few years, so I brewed him potions for blood circulation."

"The official story is he was bedbound. The truth, and you didn't hear it from me, is he is dead."

Kosara frowned. "An upir?"

"I heard it from her cousin," Dancho said, and yet again, Kosara was surprised how quickly rumours spread in Chernograd. "He'd died peacefully in his sleep. They'd even started organising the funeral: the gravestone had been commissioned, the mourners had been hired, even the big pot of boiled wheat was on the go. Then, they got told to cancel it all. It was a false alarm. Miraculously, old Mr. Yanchev had woken up again. It all sounds a bit suspicious, doesn't it?"

"It does."

"Well, nobody saw or heard of Mr. Yanchev for a few years. Ill, supposedly. Bedbound. Until, last year, he shows up again, completely cured, but pale and with bloodshot eyes."

"He'd been ill for a while. Of course he was pale."

"It all seems too convenient to me, that's all. She is in charge of blood donations."

"Surely, she wouldn't steal blood. They never get enough donations."

"The thing is, though, an upir doesn't care about blood types. They're immune to human diseases. I have a theory they can handle a slightly out-of-date batch, though I haven't tested it, obviously. There would be plenty of blood going to waste in a blood ward. Donating it to upirs is such a good way to recycle."

"There are dozens of upirs in the city," Kosara said. "You can't feed all of them with discarded blood."

"That's true. And those dozens of upirs come with hundreds of worried relatives. That's always what's worked for us, even for the living. Some people donate blood out of the goodness of their hearts, but most don't. But when they've got a relative in the hospital in need of a donation? They all queue up." Dancho leaned back with a smile on his face. "I believe we can make this work."

Kosara wanted to return his smile. However, experience had taught her to be careful before relying on the Chernogradeans' goodwill. If blood was secretly getting smuggled to upirs out of the hospital, that was one thing. If Dancho Krustev planned to make this public and beg for donations, she could only imagine the uproar.

Some people had relatives who'd been affected by the upir curse— many more didn't. Many more had known only the upirs' victims.

She looked at Asen and saw the same scepticism on his face.

"It will take time," she said carefully.

"Of course. What doesn't." Dancho finished his tea in one big gulp and got up. "I should get Ibrahim home and let you enjoy the rest of your night. Thank you for the tea and cake." He plopped his bowler hat onto his head and, with unexpected strength for such a short man, gently picked up Ibrahim's body in his arms. Varkolak strength came in handy, occasionally.

"Do you need help getting him home?" Asen asked, while he and

Kosara walked the couple to the door. Asen had prepared them a tin of cake to take home.

"Don't worry, we'll be fine," Dancho said, accepting the tin and putting it in his bag. Then, at the threshold, he added, "Saturday at seven, remember? I hope to see you there."

"I don't know . . ." Asen said, obviously struggling to find an excuse. "I'll think about it."

"What is it?" Kosara asked.

"It's a varkolak book club," Asen replied.

Kosara moved her gaze from him to Dancho and back. She hadn't expected Asen to have shared his condition with a near-stranger so openly. She hadn't expected Dancho Krustev to have turned out to be a varkolak, either.

It made sense on reflection. It explained why Dancho had been so accepting of Ibrahim turning into an upir. They were both monsters.

She looked at the doctor in his bowler hat and his pale partner quietly drooling on his shoulder. They didn't look like monsters.

"Oh, I know this face," Dancho said, looking at Asen. "I know what you're thinking. Believe me, we all go through it."

"What?" Asen asked.

"You think there's some way out of this. That there must be a cure. I've seen it all before. So many people lose so much money and time chasing empty hope."

Asen remained silent, and so did Kosara. She suddenly found it difficult to meet Dancho's gaze.

"Listen to me," Dancho said. "There's no such thing. There is no cure."

"Well," Kosara chimed in. "I thought there wasn't a way for an upir to live a normal life until about half an hour ago, but . . ."

"There's no such thing," Dancho repeated, raising his voice. "And you"—he stabbed Asen's chest with his index finger—"would do well to remember it. Stop trying to escape this. Learn to live with it. I'll see you on Saturday."

Without saying another word, Dancho Krustev walked out the

door and disappeared in the snow, cradling Ibrahim in his arms. Asen watched after him for a few seconds before shutting the door.

"Nice guy," he said, "but his fuse seems a bit short."

Once they were alone, Kosara told Asen everything she'd learned from Vila: about how the monster realm was falling apart, and Chernograd would soon follow. About how the only way to prevent it was making sure the Zmey dies.

The fine line between Asen's eyebrows deepened. "Do you think you can do it?"

"I'm not sure yet," Kosara said truthfully.

"I understand you and the Zmey have a complicated history—"

"I didn't mean it like that. I'm fully prepared to kill him."

In Kosara's head, the Zmey laughed his chiming laugh. *I don't believe you.*

"Emotionally, I'm ready to do it," she insisted. The trouble was, she could talk all she wanted, but the Zmey lived in her head. He knew all her doubts and hesitations. "Logistically, on the other hand . . ."

"Oh. I see. Is there a way to get him out of the Wall?"

"Not without destroying it."

Asen paused. "You can destroy the Wall?"

"I don't know. Maybe. You know the Council of Magicians who erected it in the first place? There were twelve of them. I have twelve shadows. If I manage to find the exact instructions for the ritual they used . . ."

"Didn't you say Karaivanov's witches have managed to reconstruct it?"

"If the mayor of Belograd is to be believed. Except, I don't see how this helps us. It's not like we've had any luck finding him."

The truth was, they'd barely had the time to try, between the mratinyak and the monster invasion. Perhaps this had been the smuggler's plan all along: to keep distracting them with monsters, winning himself time until he was ready to strike again.

"Fair," Asen said, but Kosara knew the thoughtful look on his face.

He was planning something. His eyes darted to the sleeping kikimora on the floor. "Though maybe it's time for us to renew our efforts."

"What are you thinking?"

"Karaivanov's cronies tend to frequent the bars and casinos around the river district, don't they? I have very good hearing nowadays, and drink tends to loosen people's tongues. Maybe if we go out there one night . . ."

"No chance," Kosara said. "They all know who I am, and they'd recognise you're a copper as soon as you open your mouth in one of those places."

"Perhaps. What about if I can figure out a way to penetrate one of their usual haunts? I've done it before when I worked for Karaivanov."

"Right, and how did that end?"

Asen paused. "It was just an idea. I might hand in a few job applications around the river district tomorrow, on the off chance it works. I need a job anyway. Except . . ." He trailed off.

"Yes?"

Asen sighed. "Are you sure destroying the Wall is a good idea? It's not that I agree with it ever being built—but making it so people could cross it caused quite a bit of chaos already."

Kosara understood his worries. Destroying the Wall would mean the monsters would be unleashed on Belograd, a city that was unprepared to fight them. Deep down, some petty little part of her felt that the Belogradeans deserved it for allowing the Wall to be built in the first place—and for the spectacle she'd witnessed in the square during the mayor's speech.

She couldn't let herself listen to that part of herself. That was the part that the Zmey liked to prey on.

"I'm not sure," she said. "Perhaps you're right. Perhaps Vila has a point, too. I've caused enough problems already."

"But?"

"But I don't feel like I have a choice. This is all my doing. I need to fix it." Kosara reached for the book of spells propping the table's wonky leg and pulled it out. She flicked through the pages slowly, looking for the ritual she'd used last winter to trap the Zmey.

Instead, her eyes fell on the ritual Vila had mentioned, the one she'd originally thought might cure lycanthropy.

"When I embedded him in the Wall, I thought I was doing the right thing," she said. "I thought I was repairing the mistake the Council made all those years ago. I was wrong. Their mistake was building the Wall in the first place. We're not monsters." Kosara paused, lifting her gaze to Asen. "You're not a monster."

For a moment, he remained silent, staring somewhere past her to the snow piling outside. "But there are monsters. The city is full of them."

"Yes," Kosara admitted. "Believe me, I know."

"How will you prevent them from ransacking Belograd?"

"The same way we prevent them from ransacking Chernograd. With a lot of precautions."

"You have repeatedly said yourself there aren't enough witches left to guard Chernograd. Belograd is much bigger."

Kosara waved her hand. "I never said it was a fully formed plan."

"Kosara . . ." Asen looked exasperated. He kept tapping his fingers on the tabletop, faster and faster. When Kosara couldn't take it any longer, she reached and grabbed his hand to make him stop.

Asen looked down at her hand grasping his and deflated, the tension leaving his shoulders. He weaved his fingers through hers. "I'm sorry if I sound combative. I just worry."

"I worry, too. If what Vila says is right, killing the Zmey should make the monsters a lot less dangerous."

"And you trust her on this?"

Kosara hesitated. She'd have never hesitated when answering this question until only a couple of days ago. "On this, yes."

"All right. Fine." Asen ran a thumb over her palm. "Except, correct me if I'm wrong, but destroying the Wall won't only free the Zmey, would it? It will also release Lamia. That sounds quite dangerous to me."

"Talk about an understatement."

"Do you know how she could be dealt with?"

"I have a few ideas," Kosara said noncommittally. "I'd like to have a look at the rune circle I used last winter when I trapped the Zmey in there. If I base something on it . . ." She trailed off, remembering how difficult it had been back then to control her magic. That had been when she and the Zmey had shared the twelve shadows.

Now, on her own, the idea seemed particularly risky.

However, it was either that or let Chernograd perish, together with the monster realm. The people could escape, true, but how long would they remain Chernogradeans without anything tangible to connect them to the city?

Chernograd was the city of magic and monsters. Without the monsters, the magic would soon dissipate. And without either, Chernograd, which had been struggling for many years to stay alive, would finally die.

As if reading her thoughts, Asen said, "I've asked you this once before, and you never gave me a satisfying answer. Why you? Or rather, why you alone?"

Kosara let out a tense laugh. "Vila said she'd rather run than help me. I asked her."

"I don't mean Vila. Chernograd is full of witches. You should ask them for help."

Kosara hesitated. There were other witches in the city, that much was true, though their numbers were quickly dwindling. What would they do if she told them she planned to tear down the Wall and release Lamia?

They'd probably laugh in her face. Or they'd try to stop her. Or, since a lot of them were in Karaivanov's pocket, they'd betray her.

"What about the Witch and Warlock Association?" Asen asked.

"The Witch and Warlock Association was Vila. Without her, the Association doesn't exist."

"But those two girls who came to the door—"

"They were children, Bakharov. They can barely pick the correct herb to wipe their arses, let alone carry out a potentially deadly ritual."

"You can't do this alone."

Yes, I can. Kosara had always been alone. The vast majority of people she'd trusted to help her had ended up betraying her.

The only one who hadn't was Asen.

She looked down at their joined hands, and he followed her gaze, slightly surprised, as if he couldn't remember when she'd reached for him. His fingers curved around hers, fitting perfectly in the gaps, like he'd fit right back into her life.

In the dim light of the lamps casting his features in shadow, she remembered how when they'd first met, she'd thought he looked like Orhan Demirbash, her favourite actor. Except, his eyes were different, too soft and warm. His jaw was obscured by a layer of stubble.

Nowadays, he didn't look like anyone else, he looked like him. If anything, he was more handsome than Orhan Demirbash. To her, at least.

She considered kissing him again.

Then, Boryana let out a loud snore from the floor, and the moment was ruined. Asen pulled his hand away from hers sharply, his eyes full of guilt.

The two of them sat there for a few awkward moments, neither making to get up.

"You can sleep in Nevena's room tonight, you know," Kosara said. "You don't need to stay on the sofa."

Asen's eyes darted to the kikimora, nestled under her blanket on the floor. "I think I'll stay here."

"Suit yourself." Kosara shrugged, feigning nonchalance. She got up from her seat.

At the top of the stairs, she looked down. The kitchen door was open. Asen kneeled next to Boryana, carefully tucking her in under the blanket. Kosara's nails sunk into the soft skin of her hands.

This was ridiculous. She couldn't be jealous of a kikimora.

Yet, as she snuggled into her own cold bed, she couldn't deny it. She was jealous. It wasn't a logical reaction—it wasn't as if Asen would remarry the ghost of his dead wife and the two would disappear into the sunset. It was deeper than that. Kosara wished someone would gently tuck her in and watch over her as she slept, even after she'd threatened to pull their heart out and eat it. She longed for that type of unconditional affection to be turned on her.

She cursed her own foolishness internally. It *was* ridiculous.

Kosara had thought the events of the previous day would prevent her from sleeping. She'd imagined herself lying awake, trying to figure out the ritual she had to use to tear down the Wall. She was so tired, she drifted into a fitful sleep immediately.

Only somewhere in the back of her mind, in the margins between sleep and wakefulness, the Zmey whispered, *Are you coming for me, Kosara? Are you finally going to free me from this prison?*

25

Asen

When Asen woke up, Kosara was already gone. He found a note from her on the kitchen table, explaining she was going to scour the Witch and Warlock Association's library for a book of spells to help her figure out the ritual.

Boryana stirred on the floor, and Asen prepared for her screaming to start again. The kikimora simply turned to the other side and continued snoring.

Maybe it was something to do with the power of the circle, sapping her magic away. It seemed to have exhausted her, and Asen was grateful for it. Boryana finally looked at peace, even if it was only temporary. Without thinking about what he was doing, he took the empty coffee cup from the floor near the circle, washed it, and refilled it with more coffee, prepared how Boryana liked it: strong and black.

The next time he turned around, the coffee was gone, even though the kikimora still appeared asleep. And was she . . . was she smiling?

He'd just finished his morning routine when there was a knock at the door. It was a hesitant sound, so quiet Asen wasn't sure if he'd truly heard it, until he found Ibrahim standing on the other side.

"Good morning," Ibrahim said, and Asen struggled to reconcile this well-dressed, polite gentleman with the blood-covered upir he'd seen last night. Ibrahim extended the cake tin towards Asen. "I've come to bring your tin back. And to apologise."

"There's no need," Asen said. "There's nothing to apologise for."

Ibrahim shuffled from one foot to another. His bloodshot eyes were pinned to the ground. "In any case, I'd like to make a proper introduction. I'm Ibrahim."

Asen shook Ibrahim's hand. "Asen. How do you feel?"

"Much better. Dancho got some blood sausage for breakfast. I had to eat it raw. But yes, much better. I had some of your cake too, and I was wondering if I can ask you for the recipe? It's delicious."

"Of course," Asen said, unsure where this was going. He could tell something troubled Ibrahim. "Is that all?"

"Well, Dancho mentioned you'd moved to the city recently, and I was wondering . . . Feel free to say no, of course, but . . ."

"Yes?"

"My old boss recently retired, and I've inherited the bakery from him. It's already a lot of work, but now with my . . . poor health, I've been having trouble keeping up with demand. Since you're new to the city, I was wondering, are you looking for a job?"

Asen hesitated. He'd never considered baking as a career before, but he knew his way around the kitchen. Except, he'd planned to find work in the river district, hoping that would give him access to Kara-ivanov's minions.

"You don't have to decide right away," Ibrahim said, sensing his hesitation. "I only thought I'd ask because I've got a big order for today commissioned for a very important client, and I could really use the extra pair of hands. It's a Garash cake, and well . . ."

"Is it complicated?"

"Not really. But it requires seven to eight eggs."

"Ah," Asen said, remembering the unfortunate fate of the bakery's hens. "You know, my mum makes a great no-egg chocolate cake for when her friend is keeping lent. I can give you the recipe."

"I don't know. This client is very important."

Something in the way Ibrahim said it, and the way he kept wringing his hands, made Asen's intuition prickle. He narrowed his eyes. Ibrahim's bakery was, after all, rather close to the river district.

"How important?" he asked.

"Well, I can't be sure, but the men who ordered it were all shoulders and no necks, guns hidden under expensive coats, you know the type. And I do happen to know it's St. Konstantin's Day today . . ."

Asen swore at himself for not making the connection. Of course. Konstantin Karaivanov's name-day.

"You know what?" he said. "I'd actually love a job."

"Really?" Ibrahim looked genuinely surprised. Asen supposed a lot of people would have thought twice before accepting a job offer from a man they'd recently seen biting the head off a chicken. "Great. We'd need to do a few weeks of training—fully paid, of course—and then, we can decide if we're a fit. Are you free to start this afternoon?"

Asen looked behind his shoulder at the sleeping kikimora. Every time he saw her, the guilt twisted his stomach. He'd put the promise he'd made to her on the back burner for way too long. "How about we start right now?"

Asen had to admit, he was in his element. It only took a few minutes for him and Ibrahim to find a working rhythm, kneading dough, mixing batter, and cutting little heart-shaped honey biscuits.

"Behind you," Asen shouted, carrying a large tray of sweet banitsa, and Ibrahim stepped out of the way.

The snow outside reached almost to the windowsill, but the bakery was warm. The air rippled as it escaped the hot ovens. Most of the tables were already taken by people waiting for their order, and more clients queued out the door, craning their necks to see inside.

Asen revelled in it. He'd always liked being busy, and Ibrahim obviously appreciated his help. It was a feeling he'd missed, being good at his job.

Perhaps if back in the day he'd become a baker and not a copper, he'd have saved himself and the people around him a lot of heartbreak. But how would a poor boy from the Docks even think of that as a viable career? Most of his friends had become thugs—others, like him, got recruited by the police, lured in with promises of growing up to be heroes.

Those were his choices back then: a thug or a copper. Even still, occasionally, Asen couldn't figure out the difference between the two. "It's just a few bad apples," his boss always used to repeat, but for whatever reason, she never mentioned how that saying usually ended.

Working together, it only took them a few hours to bake and decorate the orange and chocolate cake for Konstantin Karaivanov's name-day.

Briefly, for a shameful second as he prepared the icing, Asen considered the bottle of rat poison he'd spotted under the counter. It would be so easy to slip a few drops inside the icing . . .

He shook his head, dispelling the idea. Firstly, he couldn't be sure who'd end up eating the cake. Secondly, he couldn't go around mixing poison in the cakes on his first day on the job.

The important clients arrived as Asen applied the icing. He recognised them immediately, not by name but by appearance: two young, broad-shouldered men dressed in black, with guns at their hips, barely concealed by their coats.

Just as Ibrahim had described them. Asen would eat his certificate from the police academy if those two didn't work for Karaivanov.

Before Asen could react, Ibrahim rushed towards the door. "Gentlemen! I'm so happy to see you. You're here for the cake your colleagues ordered the other day, I presume? We had a bit of a mishap with the eggs, and—"

"What colleagues?" one of the men barked. His eyes fell to the cake in Ibrahim's hands in all its orange glory. "You spoke to me."

Ibrahim furrowed his eyebrows. "Believe me, friend, I never forget a face. Yours is new to me."

The other man rolled his sleeves. "Are you trying to swindle us, baker boy? We explicitly told you we need a Garash cake."

"Ah, yes, but—"

"Is there a problem?" Asen stepped next to Ibrahim with his arms crossed. Hesitation flashed across the two thugs' faces. They suddenly seemed a lot less willing to fight, now that it wasn't going to be two against one.

"Yes, there is a problem," Thug Number One snapped.

"We ordered Garash," explained Thug Number Two.

"There was a change of plan," Asen said. "We wanted to do something special for you. Chocolate, coffee, and orange cake. A brand-new recipe, it will be the talk of the city."

They looked unconvinced.

"The boss likes Garash . . ." said Thug One.

"If your boss doesn't like it, we offer a full refund."

Their faces lit up. The boss could have liked Garash, but he liked money more.

Thug One grabbed the cake from Ibrahim's hands. "Well, if you put it that way . . ."

Next to Asen, Ibrahim exhaled loudly.

Pacified, the two men prepared to leave. Asen frantically tried to think of some way to trail them. He couldn't leave his new workplace during his first day, but this seemed like too important an opportunity to miss.

He'd been tracking Karaivanov for months. If the thugs gave him at least an inkling of where the old smuggler was hiding, it would be worth it.

Asen had made Boryana a promise. Now, more than ever, he wanted to see it through.

"Thanks, pal," Thug One said, patting Asen's shoulder with his large hand on his way past. "Rest assured, you'll hear the boss's feedback on your new cake recipe."

Asen couldn't be certain if the man had meant it as a threat, but it certainly sounded like one. He bit the inside of his cheek. Something Ibrahim had said earlier nagged at him. *I never forget a face . . .*

It reminded him of the conversation he'd overheard back in Belograd, at Karaivanov's secret auction. Back then, it had been easy to dismiss it as a silly rumour, but now, any lead could prove important.

"Listen, boys." He wiped his flour-covered hands on his apron.

They'd started to sweat. "Just for my piece of mind, you work for Konstantin Karaivanov, don't you?"

"Maybe we do," said Thug Two, obviously seeing no point in denying it. "Why? Have you changed your mind about the cake?"

"Is it true what they say?" Asen asked casually. "That he's changed his face?"

The thugs shared a look. Thug One stepped forwards. "You'd do better not believing rumours, baker boy."

Asen had to resist smiling because he knew the thugs wouldn't like it. Their sudden anger had told him all he needed to know.

He raised his hands in the air. "My apologies. It was mere curiosity. I hope Konstantin enjoys the cake."

"Right," Thug Two barked. "You'd better."

Before Asen could do anything else, Thug One turned the gold ring on his pinkie three times, mumbled the magic words, and the two men melted away.

Asen watched the empty space where they'd stood with wide eyes. At his side, his fingers searched for a weapon he no longer carried.

He *should* have put rat poison in that cake.

"Thanks for this," Ibrahim said. "I honestly thought they might not take the cake. Now, can you help me get this tray of tikvenik out of the oven? It's too heavy."

"Yes, boss." With a sigh, Asen returned to his day, trying to shake the feeling he'd missed an opportunity to follow the two men. He wasn't a copper anymore. He couldn't go running after criminals, unarmed, in his baker's apron.

He was in Chernograd now, and Karaivanov's henchmen were everywhere, crawling over the city like cockroaches. This wasn't the last opportunity he'd get to wriggle information out of them.

Besides, the whole thing hadn't been a complete waste of time. He'd all but got confirmation to the rumour he'd heard. Konstantin Karaivanov had a new face.

26

Kosara

When Kosara arrived home, she found Asen in the kitchen, reading by the hearth. For someone who'd insisted he wasn't going to the varkolak book club, he surely seemed determined to finish *A Night of Passion With the Upir Lord* in time for Saturday.

"Any luck?" he asked, lifting his eyes from the page.

"No." Kosara took off her wet coat and hung it next to the fire to dry.

"Really? I would have thought the Witch and Warlock's Association's library would be full of useful ancient tomes."

"Well." Kosara pulled her boots off and arranged them next to the hearth, too. "When I said 'library,' I might have exaggerated a bit. It seemed like a good idea back in the day, but what it ended up being is a few boxes of old paperbacks stored in Ivan's basement. Half of them are so mouldy, the pages have fused together."

"And the other half?"

"The other half have nothing to do with magic at all, it's Ivan's collection of novels about men with guns snogging sexy aliens."

Asen laughed, but Kosara was serious. She could happily live without ever reading another paragraph lovingly describing the green-skinned, three-breasted empress of Karena Six.

"Did you tell Ivan why you needed to access the library?" Asen asked.

"Of course not."

He sighed deeply. She knew what he was thinking: she should have asked for help. But what help would old Ivan be? His herbalist powers were nothing compared to Vila's.

Kosara sat down next to Asen. "How was your day?"

"Quite interesting, actually."

He told her about his new job and the conversation he'd had with the two thugs in the bakery.

"A new face?" Kosara sounded horrified even to her own ears. This changed everything. Karaivanov could be anywhere—hell, she could have passed him on the street on her way home, and she'd never know. "You didn't tell me this before."

"The henchman I heard it from didn't seem particularly trust-worthy. He said he wasn't sure himself if Karaivanov's plan would work. He mentioned something about surgery—"

Kosara shook her head. "I don't think so. Knowing Karaivanov, he'd probably use magic. Except, I've never heard of such a spell before." She frowned. It dawned on her that this wasn't exactly true. She'd heard of someone who possessed the magic to change a person's appearance, hadn't she?

"The face merchant!" she exclaimed. "I remember now! Roksana mentioned they could make Sokol look human. That's how she and Sokol were planning to escape the city."

It was Asen's turn to look indignant. "You never told me that."

"It didn't seem important at the time. I never believed such magic possible, to be honest. But now . . ."

Kosara cursed herself internally. She should have investigated this earlier. Of course, whenever a new magic turned up in Chernograd, Konstantin Karaivanov was involved.

"Do you think Roksana might know where that face merchant is located?" Asen asked.

Kosara pulled her coat down and put it on again. "There is one way to find out, isn't there?"

Roksana gave them the face merchant's address without arguing. She didn't even ask for a bribe. The monster hunter seemed exhausted. While they talked at the door, inside the house, Sokol and Vrana had a loud argument carried out entirely in high-pitched screeches.

"Have you found a way to send her back to the monster realm yet?" Roksana said.

"Sokol?" Kosara asked, taken aback.

"Vrana! I swear, I can't take this for much longer. She's driving me mental. Nothing in my house is good enough for her. The towels are too scratchy, the slippers—too slippery. She made me cover all the mirrors in the house because, apparently, it's painful for her to see her own reflection. Yesterday she complained the pillow was too high for her head, and when I got her a new one, she decided that one was too low!"

"You can ask her to hire a room elsewhere," Asen said.

Roksana scoffed. "Don't be bloody ridiculous, Belogradean. She's family now. I might be an uneducated brute, but I've got manners. Please, you two need to find a way to get her out of here."

"We'll see what we can do," Kosara said.

As the two of them walked away, Asen asked, "Can't Vrana return home?"

"Of course she can." Kosara pointed up with her thumb, to where the cracks between the realms gaped wide open. "If the monsters can come down, she can fly up. She's obviously enjoying having Roksana at her beck and call."

"You could have told Roksana that."

Kosara shrugged. "Let her stew for a while. She deserves it."

Asen laughed. Then, he fell silent for a few seconds, his face growing grimmer and grimmer, as more and more snow caught in his hair.

"Is the face merchant far?" he asked in the end.

"No," Kosara said carefully, knowing he had something on his mind. "Why?"

"I've been thinking, maybe you should go without me."

Kosara's mouth gaped so wide, a few lost snowflakes made their way inside it and melted on her tongue. "Are you joking? When I warned you to stay away from the mratinyak, you didn't listen. When

I asked you to guard the house, you went outside and found an upir. Now that I'd actually like you there on the off chance I might need back up . . ."

"I'd like to be there." Asen tried to run a hand though his hair, obviously realising too late he wore a hat. "It's just, I'm not sure how reliable a backup I would be. It's the Foul Days, isn't it?"

"Not technically."

"But in practice. All the monsters are here. I have been doing some reading."

"I can't imagine what useful information you gleaned from *A Night of Passion With the Upir Lord*—"

"Kosara, I'm not joking. I've been reading up on varkolaks. Your bestiary says they grow particularly unpredictable during the Foul Days. More aggressive."

"Oh." Kosara finally understood his worries. "You're concerned you might turn."

"I'm more concerned about what happens *after* I turn."

Kosara chewed on her lip. She had been meaning to try that ritual Vila had mentioned, but she'd found herself constantly putting it off in her mind, finding one excuse after another. What if it didn't work, and that only made Asen more desperate about his situation? What if he'd been taking things so calmly until now because Dancho had been right, and Asen still held some faint hope she might find a cure for him?

And then, if she dug deeper, she found another reason why she hesitated. What if it *did* work? Would Asen ever choose to stay in Chernograd with her if he wasn't trapped here?

He wouldn't, the Zmey's voice whispered in her mind. *Everyone always leaves you in the end, don't they? I'm the only one who's ever stayed.*

Kosara wished he wasn't living in her mind, because had he been corporeal, she would have slapped him. *I swear, if you're not quiet . . .*

"Kosara?" Asen asked.

She realised she'd stopped in her tracks and the snow falling from above was slowly, patiently, burying her boots.

"I have an idea," she said. And then, she hurried to add, "It might not work."

Once they were back in the house, Kosara retrieved the book from under the table and flicked through the pages until she found what she was looking for.

"This is it!" she said, pointing at it.

The page showed a complicated diagram of a varkolak's body, both in their human and wolf forms, with multiple arrows, lines, and circles indicating different parts. It looked simple enough, except where the author specified: "The ritual requires at least seven witches." Then, they'd crossed out "seven" and written "nine."

Kosara couldn't imagine a situation where she'd gather nine witches in the same place that wouldn't end in bloodshed. In the absence of nine witches, however, she hoped her twelve shadows would do.

What followed was a long list of ingredients, all written in an archaic language Kosara barely understood. She shaped the words with her mouth, trying to decipher them.

"It asks for all sorts of nonsense," she said. "Eye of an upir? Fine. I've got a whole jar. A karakonjul ear hair? Not a problem. But then, what the hell is *merudiya*?"

"It's an old-fashioned word for fenugreek."

"What about *chelebitka*?"

"Black cumin. Is this a recipe for koftas?"

"It's meant to be an anaesthetic for varkolaks. Fenugreek, did you say?"

It was a good thing Asen had made quite a few additions to her spice cabinet recently, or else she'd never have had the right ingredients.

She crushed the herbs and spices for the anaesthetic with her mortar and pestle. The concoction smelled like a good stew, but its brownish-green colour was less than appetising. When she presented it to Asen on a spoon, he made a face, but ate it without protest.

Kosara looked around the kitchen, unsure what came next. "Would you like to lie down on the sofa?"

Asen sensed her hesitation. "Is the ritual dangerous?"

Not for you. "It's not."

While she waited for Asen to fall asleep, Kosara couldn't shake the feeling there was something distinctly awkward about this. This was a complicated, ancient ritual. She was one of the most powerful witches in the city.

The atmosphere in her kitchen wasn't right. Asen lying down and staring at the ceiling with his feet sticking over the sofa's armrests wasn't right, either. The smell of herbs and spices that penetrated everything was completely wrong.

Kosara compared Asen's body to the diagram in her book, trying to keep the process professional rather than allowing her eyes to linger on the sliver of stomach visible between his belt and the bottom of his shirt. Seven pairs of hands were drawn in a complicated pattern, each placed on a different part of the varkolak.

Remaining strictly business-like, she chose the most innocent placement for her own hands, the one marked "1" in the book. If she was about to put her hands anywhere close to where the numbers "7" or "9" were located, she'd much rather do it after receiving enthusiastic consent. Certainly not while he was falling asleep. And ideally when the ghost of his dead wife was no longer in the room.

"I'm going to touch your wrists," Kosara told him.

He replied with a noncommittal sound. His eyes finally started closing.

Kosara waited a few seconds to make sure he was asleep before she urged her shadows to join in the ritual with a nod of her head.

The shadows surrounded him eagerly. Their hands hovered over his ankles, his forearms, his stomach, his thighs. Kosara, as usual, was on edge when she let them close to someone she cared about—but for once, they seemed to follow her every instruction diligently. Perhaps they were just as curious to find out whether the ritual worked.

Kosara pronounced the magic words slowly, careful not to make any mistakes. This wasn't the sort of magic she was used to. It felt older and more powerful. In her mind's eye, she saw a group of witches in white robes performing the ritual under the full moon, in a time before spells were written down, only passed from mouth to mouth.

Once she'd finished speaking, she gasped quietly. With her eyes shut, she felt the infection crawling through his veins, like thousands of tiny ants.

The ants weren't truly there, Kosara knew. The human mind had a way to visualise magic that helped it comprehend, even when that magic was beyond comprehension. In any case, it made no difference whether the ants were real or not: she had to crush them one by one all the same.

She began plucking them out and squishing them until they died under her fingertips. The shadows killed twelve times more. Kosara couldn't imagine how the ritual would have worked with only seven witches—or even nine. With every passing second, she grew weaker.

She was certain hours had passed, but the clock in the hallway hadn't chimed. Or maybe it had, and Kosara hadn't heard it. Her ears felt stuffed with cotton wool.

She risked peeking at Asen. His chest rose and fell quickly. His shirt had twisted to the side, revealing the tattoo carved on his skin. Karaivanov's symbol appeared distorted through the tears filling Kosara's eyes.

She let the tears roll down her cheeks. She'd nearly done it. The ants still crawled through his body, but there were fewer now. The ones that remained were frantic: running around, trying to escape her hands and those of her shadows.

She'd nearly done it, but she struggled to keep going. Her vision moved in and out of focus. Her heartbeat grew faster, sending blood rushing to her ears. Every intake of breath hurt.

When she closed her eyes again, she saw the ants everywhere, crawling over the backs of her eyelids, tickling her hands, and disappearing deep into her own veins.

"Keep going," she told herself through gritted teeth. "Keep going."

Asen was relying on her. This was his only chance.

She couldn't keep going.

The last thing she saw before her head slumped over Asen's chest were the ants, pouring out of her, sinking back into him.

Kosara wanted to scream—she couldn't. She wasn't in her own body. She wasn't in Svetla's body, either, even though she stood in that cage atop the Zmey's tallest tower.

A pair of hands floated in front of her vision, weaving a spell. The fingers were short like Kosara's had been before the shadows had replaced them, but plumper, with black hairs growing on them. Kosara didn't recognise those hands, but she recognised the witch's voice.

"I can't do it," she pleaded, and Kosara knew she'd heard that deep, velvet-like timbre before. Tsveta Vulkova had been a young woman when Kosara was a toddler, and everyone used to say she'd become a singer when she grew up. She had such a beautiful voice.

Such a waste, they'd said once the Zmey had claimed her. *Such a waste.* As if all the other women he'd murdered hadn't mattered because they weren't as talented as Tsveta.

"You can do it," said the Zmey from behind her back. Tsveta didn't turn to face him. "You have to."

Tsveta looked up, and through her eyes, Kosara saw the sky. It was crumbling. Great chunks of it fell down, the stars on them glittering. Behind them peeked complete darkness.

Nothing, Vila had said when Kosara had asked what was beyond the monster realm. Now, Kosara saw it. Complete and utter emptiness, threatening to consume.

"You have to stop it!" the Zmey shouted, and Tsveta tried as hard as she could, but her golden rays of light weren't enough to glue the pieces back together. They shot out of her fingers, one after the other, melting in the darkness.

The Zmey's hands closed around Tsveta's wrists. He was behind her, his body pressed close to hers. Kosara felt her relief. It was visceral, a wave of warmth spreading over her. The Zmey was here. He'd help.

His magic intertwined with hers. The next shot of light coming from her fingers was a lightning bolt, blindingly bright. It picked up pieces of sky on its way up, glueing them back together. Tsveta laughed, a piercing sound disappearing into the night, and the Zmey laughed with her.

Soon, the sky was alight with Tsveta and the Zmey's magic. The two fit so well together. Hers fed his, and his fed hers.

Or did it?

A jolt of panic shook Tsveta. Something was wrong. She was terribly tired all of a sudden, so tired she thought she'd collapse. In fact, she felt just like the sky—cracked, fractured, a broken vessel. Her magic was seeping out of her.

And, hungrily, the Zmey devoured it.

Tsveta tried to twist out of his hold. His fingers burrowed deeper into her wrists, sinking into her soft flesh. With every jolt of light coming out of her body, she grew weaker. The Zmey kept feeding.

He didn't let go of her until her body fell to the ground with a loud, painful thud. She shook a few times, her pale light surrounding her like a halo, and then, she grew dim. Her eyelids were closing on their own, but she fought with them to look up at the Zmey looming over her.

"May you die a painful death," she cursed him with her dying breath.

The Zmey lifted his eyebrows and watched her until she stopped breathing. Then, he dusted off his shirt, as if the curse was something he could wipe away with his palm, and turned to leave. He seemed so calm. As if committing a murder had been nothing but a minor inconvenience.

Kosara traced him with the corner of her eye while he descended from the cage. She was relieved she wouldn't have to watch that unnervingly blank, mask-like face of his any longer, but at the same time, she grew increasingly nervous.

Even after the Zmey was gone, she didn't wake. She was trapped in this dead body, with her gaze fixed above at the now repaired sky. The stars stirred, like foam on the crests of invisible waves, and Kosara couldn't look away from them. She couldn't even blink.

"Kosara." Nevena's voice. If Kosara was in her own body, she'd have heaved a sigh of relief. "Kosara, wake up."

For the first time, Kosara felt her sister's fingers, shaking her shoulder.

"Nevena?" Kosara said, unable to look around. "Where are you?"

Nevena's face appeared above her. Her brown eyes were on Kosara, full of worry. Her hair was long and pin-straight, tickling Kosara's face.

This was impossible. Hearing voices was one thing. Kosara was used to voices by now. Seeing Nevena? Feeling her touch? It couldn't be happening.

"How did you come here?" Kosara asked. And then, realising she was pointing out the obvious but unable to stop herself, she added, "You're dead."

"That's not important. You have to wake up. It's nearly time."

"Time for what? Nevena, where the hell are we?"

"You are in your kitchen. Me? I'm trapped."

"Where?"

"On the one hand, between the realms of the living and the dead. On the other . . ." Nevena paused. Kosara wished she could reach up and touch her, just to make sure she was truly there. "On the other, I'm in the Wall. With the Zmey."

"What?" Kosara asked, sure she must have misunderstood.

"When you trapped him there, you also trapped me. His death is my justice. Him still existing, even if it is a pitiful existence, means I can't leave." Nevena cupped Kosara's cheek and leaned closer, her eyes large and intense. "You have to wake up. It's nearly time."

"Time for what?" Kosara repeated, exasperated.

The next moment, she woke up with a jolt.

27

Asen

The ritual hadn't worked. Asen knew it before he'd even opened his eyes.

He touched his chin, covered in coarse hair which hadn't been there a few hours ago. His nose worked fast, painting a vivid picture of his surroundings: the charcoal smouldering in the hearth, the half-forgotten cup of coffee, now grown cold, and Kosara. He smelled her rose-scented shampoo and the lavender in her woollen clothes, tinged with a strong whiff of magic.

When he looked up, he found her standing at the mirror, studying her face intently.

"Are you all right?" he croaked, and she spun towards him fast. He must have startled her.

"I can't figure out what they've changed."

Asen was still disoriented, so it took him a few seconds before he asked, "Who?"

"The shadows. They change something about me after every vision. I can't figure out what's different this time."

Kosara walked across the room, stepping over Boryana as if the sleeping kikimora was nothing but a part of the furniture. In the corner, the invisible cat quietly snored. The household spirits had also fallen silent for once, and it made the monster-stuffed house unusually still.

Kosara sat on the sofa next to Asen and bumped his shoulder with hers. She took a deep breath, as if she was afraid of his reaction, before she said, "The ritual didn't work."

"I know. I can tell. Perhaps Dancho was right. I should stop fighting this and learn to live with it."

"We can try again."

"No." Asen was surprised by the conviction in his own voice. He looked at Kosara, searching her face for what was different. Was that freckle under her eye new, or was he just unused to seeing her face from so close? "You shouldn't have let the shadows show you another vision. If I'd known the ritual might trigger it, I'd have never asked you to do it."

She waved a hand. "It doesn't matter. And besides, the visions have been . . . informative."

Asen caught the hesitation in her voice. "What did they show you this time?"

"I saw a woman die. It shouldn't have been a surprise, should it? They're all dead." She laughed bitterly. "Then, I saw Nevena. She said she's trapped in the Wall with him."

Asen didn't need to ask who "he" was. There was only one man who made Kosara's voice sound so hollow.

He hesitated, unsure what to say. He didn't want to imply Kosara was seeing things. However, she'd been exhausted from the ritual, with a head full of shadows. Seeing things was the most likely explanation.

"Are you sure you really saw her?" he asked.

"She was as real as you are right now." Kosara ran a hand through her hair, making a whiff of rosewater hit Asen. He resisted the urge to bury his face in it. "I know what you're thinking, and I don't blame you. You think I'm going mad."

"I didn't say—"

"But it doesn't matter, does it? Whether Nevena is really in there with him or not, the Wall has to fall." Kosara glanced at the mirror again. "I just wish I'd known what they changed. What if it's something on the inside this time? Maybe they've given me a weak heart or the liver of a drunk."

"Maybe they've given you a big ugly tattoo on your lower back."

Kosara's eyes widened. "They wouldn't." She twisted her back to him, lifting her shirt, and Asen tried to politely look away, because he was a gentleman—and failed, because he wasn't made of stone.

Kosara urged him. "You have to check."

He laughed, his eyes tracing the skin on her back, covered in burn scars delicate as cobweb. Asen wondered how they'd feel under his fingertips. *For God's sake, you pig.* Boryana's ghost was right there, sound asleep on the floor. "There's nothing on your back."

"Oh, thank God." She laughed too, but it was short-lived. The next second, she looked grim again. "Are you sure you're okay? The ritual wasn't too taxing?"

"I'm fine. I probably needed a good nap." Asen checked his watch. He'd only been under for a couple of hours. "What happens next?"

"We should probably get a good night's sleep."

"And then?"

"Then, we can visit the face merchant and try to convince them to sell out Karaivanov."

Asen hesitated. All his doubts were still there, but he'd be damned if he allowed Kosara to do this alone. This was his fight.

"Maybe I need a new pouch of wolfsbane."

"Done," Kosara said immediately. "Anything else?"

"I was thinking, if we were to penetrate Karaivanov's defences, we should try to do it around midnight."

Kosara frowned. "Why?" Then, she followed his gaze to the sleeping kikimora on the floor. "Oh."

"In case we need reinforcements."

"Asen—"

"She'd come wherever I am, wouldn't she? I woke her up, and now she follows me, whether I am on this side of the Wall or the other. Somehow, she always knows where I am."

"Yes, but—"

"If we lead her to her father, then maybe she'll realise what she needs to do. I know her. I know how she'd act."

Kosara's eyes were full of worry. She must have thought he'd gone mad. "She's a kikimora, Asen. There is no logic behind their actions. No one knows how they'd act."

"Nevena never attacked you, did she? She only went for me that one time I broke into her room."

"Boryana has already attacked you. If we hadn't managed to trap her, she would have killed you."

"Only because her father wasn't around. Kosara, believe me. I've spent so much time with her these past few days. I truly believe I'm getting through to her."

Kosara still looked unconvinced. Perhaps this was just wishful thinking on Asen's part. Perhaps Kosara was right, and all Boryana would do was wreak more chaos. But was that such a bad thing? An angry kikimora could cause one hell of a distraction in case they needed to run away. The worst that would happen was they'd need to trap her again.

Besides, his every instinct—both the human and the animal ones— screamed at him that he was right about this. Boryana, his Boryana, would have never hurt him. There had to be something left of her in that bloodthirsty beast that kept following him. Otherwise, he could not explain the kikimora's taste for coffee.

Kosara nervously chewed on the skin around her nails, and Asen took her hand to stop her, grasping it between both of his. "Kosara, trust me on this one. Will you trust me?"

The snow seemed to never stop, continuing to fall relentlessly, deep into the night. By the time Asen and Kosara reached the address Roksana had given them, Asen's eyelashes had started freezing and his stubble was covered in ice crystals.

Like most illegal businesses, the face merchant operated from the river district, snuggled between an unlicensed casino on one side and an illicit brothel on the other. There was no sign over the door. Nothing about the unassuming low building indicated what they'd discover inside.

Kosara tried the door and, unsurprisingly, found it locked. She knocked and waited.

A moment later, a latch creaked, hinges moaned, and a tiny door viewer opened. A single eye peeked out. It must have had a mouth attached to it somewhere in the dark, because next came a rasping voice: "Yes?"

"The cat eats mackerel at noon," Kosara carefully pronounced the password Roksana had given them. Asen quietly prayed it hadn't been changed in the last few weeks.

"The dog nibbles on chicken wings at sunset," the voice replied gravely, and the door opened, revealing a little old lady in a lab coat. "Come in."

The two of them shuffled inside. They found themselves in what appeared to be a lab with sterile white floors and sterile white surfaces. Strips of fluorescent lights ran across the ceiling and reflected off the many jars arranged along the walls, full of murky green liquid.

Asen flinched when he made out what was stored in the closest jar. A pair of unseeing eyes stared back at him. He turned around and saw hundreds of them, looking out from pale faces with open mouths. Here and there, a tongue protruded—a piece of spongy flesh floating gently in the green.

Human heads. The walls were covered top to bottom with jars stuffed with human heads.

Asen would have to make sure he passed on the location of this place to Chief Constable Chausheva at the first opportunity.

"We're looking for the face merchant," Kosara said, her voice level. Either she hadn't noticed the jars' contents, or she was much better at keeping her composure than Asen.

"You're speaking to her," said the old lady.

Asen had been a copper for long enough to know criminals came in all shapes and sizes. Nevertheless, he was surprised. The woman appeared to be well into her seventies. She looked like the sort of friendly granny who'd pinch your cheek and offer you a sweet from the depths of her handbag—not like a seasoned crook.

There was only a single thing that didn't fit her wholesome image. Her lab coat's sleeves were rolled up, and beneath them, many colourful tattoos covered her arms completely. Even Asen's untrained eyes recognised magic symbols intertwined in complicated patterns on her skin.

She raised her eyebrows over her tortoise-shell glasses. "So, how can I help you?"

Kosara was silent. Asen cast a quick glance towards her and saw her panicked eyes. She'd looked at the jars properly, at last.

He took over the conversation. "A friend sent us over. We don't have anything specific in mind—"

"Feel free to look around. Do you both need a new identity?"

"Potentially. Could you talk us through the process?"

The face merchant rolled her eyes. She was obviously not thrilled with the customer-facing part of her job. "You pick a new face. I give it to you. For a price, of course."

"How?"

"How do you think? Magic."

"You mentioned an 'identity.' Are you able to provide us with documents, too?"

"It depends on how much you're willing to spend."

Asen remembered the significantly depleted supply of cash in his wallet and decided against taking it out. It was unlikely to impress the merchant.

"We're on a budget," he said.

"No shame in that. I can provide you with someone anonymous. There are plenty of unidentified bodies turning up on both sides of the Wall nowadays."

"Turning up?" Asen asked. "How exactly do you procure your . . . bodies?"

He immediately knew he'd gone too far. Chernogradeans could sniff out a copper from a mile away.

"I have my sources." The face merchant said flatly. One of her hands nervously touched her forearm, playing with the lab coat's cuff. "Who did you say sent you here?"

"Roksana," Kosara said, finally returning to the conversation. Her face had gone back to its normal colour. "Roksana Tatarova."

"Ah, the young lady with the yuda lover. I remember her. I've been wondering if she'd come back. Truth be told, I was itching to try transforming a yuda. Faces, I have plenty of experience with. But changing a monster's body? That would have been an interesting challenge." The merchant measured Kosara and Asen with her eyes. "So, what's your problem? Who are you running from?"

"Do we need to be running from someone?" Asen asked.

The merchant shrugged. "Everyone is."

"Konstantin Karaivanov," Kosara said.

Asen frowned at her. She couldn't be expecting the merchant to simply reveal her connection to Karaivanov, could she?

But then, Kosara's shadows unspooled around her, and Asen realised she was trying to intimidate the old woman into spilling everything. Kosara—or Kosara's shadows—must have got tired of small talk.

It didn't pay off. Hearing Karaivanov's name was enough to make the merchant close off completely. Her fingertips ran along the magic symbols on her forearm. At first, Asen had taken it for a nervous gesture, but now, following the pattern of the merchant's hand, he realised what it was. She was triggering an alarm.

Was this why Kosara had decided to cut to the chase?

Before either of them could react, the door opened. A familiar figure stood at the threshold, wrapped tightly in a fur coat. The bright lights of the room reflected in his glasses.

Malamir.

Malamir turned and ran. Asen dashed after him. Some animal part of him couldn't resist the chase.

Asen was a good runner, but Malamir had the advantage of knowing the terrain. While Asen slid and nearly fell on a patch of ice,

Malamir avoided it easily. When Malamir suddenly swerved into a side street, Asen crashed into a wall. He managed to turn in the last moment and hit it with his shoulder instead of face-first, but it cost him a few seconds.

Finally, Malamir disappeared into what appeared to be a blind alley. Asen slowed down, exhausted, letting out clouds of breath into the cold air. His superhuman eyes got used to the darkness quickly. The snow had covered the dingy cobblestones in a pristine white veil, but it could do nothing to hide the overflowing rubbish bins or the heavily graffitied walls.

There was no sign of Malamir.

Asen squinted, tracing where Malamir's steps led. A rusted metal door was ajar at the bottom of the alley, leading into a dark basement stinking strongly of fermented cabbage.

Asen hesitated, but not for long. He had the superior strength and senses of a varkolak now. Malamir wouldn't be a match for him. Asen was certain no one else was in the basement—his ears strained, making out only a single heartbeat, a single gasping intake of breath.

He descended the stepladder into the darkness, and again, his improved vision worked to his advantage. Once he reached the bottom, in the almost complete absence of light, he saw his surroundings clearly.

The basement was bigger than he'd expected. Until recently, it had been used according to its original purpose—Asen's nose told him as much. It wasn't only the barrels of cabbage he smelled, but also sour home-brewed wine and jars of fruit compote.

Currently, the room was empty, save for Malamir, with his glasses glinting in the dark. Asen had prepared for an ambush, but it didn't come. Malamir appeared unarmed.

"I don't want to hurt you," Asen said, spreading his arms, showing he, too, didn't carry a weapon. "All I need to know is where Karaivanov is hiding. If you give me his location, I'll let you walk free."

It hurt Asen to make this bargain—he wanted to strangle Malamir for all the problems he'd caused. At the same time, he knew it was the sensible thing to do.

He wasn't an animal. He could be sensible.

Instead of replying, Malamir took several steps forwards until he was close enough to touch Asen. Was he trying to intimidate him? It didn't work. With his varkolak strength, Asen could flatten him against the wall with a single, well-aimed punch.

Malamir was so close, Asen saw the pores on his face, the little chip in his glasses' arm, the fine hairs between his eyebrows. He looked completely real—and yet, he smelled all wrong. Under the thick after-shave Malamir always wore, Asen caught a whiff of something terribly familiar.

Before Asen could react, Malamir placed a hand on his shoulder. The pain was instant and blinding.

"Freeze," came Malamir's voice.

Asen's chest flared in pain, and he found he had no choice but to obey. He couldn't take a single step. His arms were pinned to his body, and as much as he wanted to curl his hands into fists, he was unable to.

He realised now what the trap had been—except, it was too late. He'd been caught.

"Asen!" came Kosara's voice a second later. Her steps crunched in the snow outside, drawing closer and closer. "Are you down there?"

Asen wanted to scream, to tell her to run, but his mouth was glued shut. The enchantment had stolen his voice, too.

28

Kosara

Kosara had never been a fast runner, but she got there, eventually. She followed Asen's and Malamir's steps in the snow until they led her to the open door of a basement. She clicked her fingers, and a blue flame materialised in front of her. Kosara gripped it in her hand before plunging into the darkness below.

As she descended the stepladder, the first thing she spotted was the glint of something metallic. A gun.

Kosara jumped onto the floor, mumbling a spell, and when she stood back up, she cradled a much bigger fireball between her fingers. It crackled, spitting sparks in the air.

In its light, she saw the basement clearly. Her flame reflected in the lenses of Malamir's glasses and the barrel of his gun, pressed into Asen's temple.

Kosara swore under her breath. Another trap. And, once again, she and Asen had sauntered right into it. How the hell had Malamir managed to overpower Asen? A varkolak's strength was nothing to sneeze at.

"Asen?" Kosara asked.

Asen's mouth remained shut. He didn't move. Malamir must have been holding him with an enchantment, though Kosara could see no talisman in his hand. Only the gun.

"If I were you, I'd put that away," Malamir nodded towards the fireball in Kosara's hands.

"What the fuck are you doing?" Kosara didn't make to extinguish the ball. Its flames hissed between her fingertips. She was so angry, as if the fiery inferno burned inside her own chest.

"What does it look like?" Malamir said, digging the barrel of the gun deeper into Asen's skin. "Put the fire out. Then, we can talk."

Kosara looked at the gun and at Asen's terrified face, and then, with a loud swear, she extinguished the fireball. Complete darkness surrounded her.

"Talk," she spat out.

"Do you want him back?" Malamir asked, as if offering Kosara a book she'd let him borrow. She couldn't see Asen now, but she heard his fast, panicked breathing.

"Yes," Kosara said.

"Very well. You can have him if you give me your shadows."

"What the fuck, Malamir?"

Kosara had accepted Malamir worked for Karaivanov. She'd come to terms with his betrayal. Through it all, in the back of her mind, she'd kept finding excuses for him. His mother was ill, and she needed treatment. People did stupid things for the ones they loved.

But this? This was unexpected. Malamir had never been one to brandish guns and make demands.

"You know a witch's shadow can't be stolen, right?" Kosara asked.

"I know. But I also know these shadows aren't truly yours. I've seen you use them. And if they aren't *yours,* they are free for the taking."

"So what? Karaivanov thinks he can convince them to work for him?"

Malamir let out a barking laugh. "You know he can be very persuasive."

Something about his laugh hadn't sounded right. Kosara had known Malamir for many years, and she'd never heard that cruel tinge in his voice.

"Malamir, what's wrong?" she asked, squinting, trying to see him better now that her eyes had started to adjust to the dark. "If this is about your mother—"

"Give me your shadows now," Malamir said through his teeth. "Or the copper dies."

Kosara hesitated. If she gave up her shadows, *she*'d die. "How about you let me keep mine? You know that's the one no one else can control."

"We'll see about that. In any case, you're not in any position to bargain. Give me all your shadows."

Kosara felt them floating around her, sliding past. There was no way out of this, she realised. She and Asen had got themselves into a right mess. They'd both grown too confident, that was the trouble. Asen, with his supernatural senses, and Kosara, with her damned shadows she'd never learned how to control.

With a sigh, she began folding them. She grabbed them blindly out of the air, feeling their slick bodies between her fingers. They pushed against her in a desperate bid to escape, trying to twist away like angry snakes, but she didn't let them.

Slowly, one by one, she turned them into black beads.

Somewhere in a deep, shameful corner of her mind, Kosara had to admit the prospect of releasing the eleven shadows of the Zmey's past brides felt like an enormous load being taken off her shoulders. Their murmurs in her mind finally went quiet.

Kosara's own shadow came last. It didn't fight. It peacefully melted into her hands, transforming into a little circle of darkness, just as small and innocent as the others. As soon as Kosara's fingers had finished shaping it, she felt its absence, pulling sharply at her navel. She wanted to retch.

"Place them on the floor," Malamir said.

Once again, Kosara hesitated. As soon as she'd parted with the shadows, she'd be susceptible to the sickness again. What Malamir was asking her to do was to hand her life away.

"Malamir, how many years have we known each other? This is not like you—"

"Put them down!"

With a sigh, Kosara did. What choice did she have? Malamir had a gun pointed to Asen's head. This was the problem she had to solve immediately. The shadow sickness would be a problem for later.

Besides, despite his recent behaviour, she knew Malamir. He wasn't a complete monster. Once he'd realised how useless her shadow was to him, he was likely to let her have it back. Once he was sure she wouldn't use it to save Asen and escape.

The shadows rolled out of her hand and spread on the floor like the marbles in a children's game. Making sure the gun still pointed at Asen's head, Malamir fell to one knee to collect them.

The shadows rolled away from his outstretched fingers.

Malamir swore. "Tell them to obey me."

"I can't do that," Kosara said. "They were never truly mine, re-member?"

They hadn't been hers, and they weren't Malamir's, either. After years of living with the Zmey, avoiding his orders to the best of their abilities, fighting against him in their own way—they were nobody's. Kosara had seen the Zmey's desperate attempts at controlling them, and she'd also seen how that had ended for him.

The shadows had grown into their own masters.

"Tell them to come here!" Malamir shouted, still on the floor, and if he wasn't holding a loaded gun, Kosara would have found the situation funny.

Except, the gun was there, and the angrier Malamir got, the more likely he was to pull the trigger.

Malamir finally reached the shadows, gathering them between his fingers, and Kosara exhaled deeply. That was it. She'd lost them again.

She met Asen's eyes, panicked and urgent. There was something he was trying to tell her—something obvious she was missing.

Kosara had been aware that once her shadows were gone, she'd be helpless. That meant she couldn't guarantee that once Malamir got what he wanted, he wouldn't shoot both her and Asen and let them rot in this stinking basement. Her one hope had been that Malamir wouldn't have it in him.

But then, Malamir laughed that unnervingly unfamiliar laugh of his again, and Kosara realised her mistake. She'd heard that laugh before, last winter on the bridge when Karaivanov had used the brand on Asen's chest to torture him.

Too late, it all clicked in her mind: Malamir's unusual behaviour, his strange tone of voice, and now that Kosara looked at him properly, that shapeless fur coat. Her body went cold.

"You're not Malamir, are you?" she asked.

For a moment, he stared at her. Then, he must have decided there was no harm in one last moment of gloating, because he dislodged Malamir's face with his hand and dropped it to the floor. It remained there, frozen in the same haughty expression. On the underside, it was white and shiny, made from polished bone.

Konstantin Karaivanov looked at Kosara over the barrel of his gun. Whatever enchantment the face merchant had woven into the mask slowly unravelled. His general height and shape remained the same, concealed beneath the fur coat, but other, smaller changes took place. Malamir's dark curls retreated into Karaivanov's skull, and his salt-and-pepper hair emerged instead, cropped short. His fingers, which had been long and delicate, shortened. His nails grew yellow from cigar smoke.

Kosara watched him in terror, but also in awe. She'd never witnessed magic like this before. She hadn't thought it possible—even after seeing the heads floating in their jars, she couldn't imagine someone might manage to breathe life into the dead features so convincingly.

Then her gaze fell on Malamir's unmoving face lying on the floor, and her stomach churned. His eyes were glazed, staring at the ceiling behind the thick lenses of his spectacles.

Malamir. Poor, naïve Malamir. If his head had been harvested by the merchant, what had Karaivanov done with his body? Kosara sincerely doubted the smuggler had bothered with a proper burial. It was much more likely he'd thrown it in the river.

Had Malamir's mother even been told her son was dead, or did she still hope he might come home every night?

"How long?" Kosara asked around the lump stuck in her throat. Had Malamir been himself the last time she'd seen him?

"Does it matter? It's not like it changes the current situation, does it?"

Asen's eyes were still on Kosara, large and tense. He'd known, she realised. As soon as Karaivanov had got close enough to him, Asen must have smelled him.

He'd known, but he'd been helpless to warn her.

"How long?" Kosara repeated through gritted teeth. She knew what Karaivanov was like. He loved to gloat.

"Oh, a few days. Let's say, I did not appreciate his conduct the night Sokol was stolen from me."

The night Sokol was stolen? When Malamir had led Kosara straight into Karaivanov's trap?

"What are you talking about?" she asked.

"Weren't you there? He tried to betray me. Good thing I'd been expecting it. I'd been testing him when I revealed the location of the yuda and, needless to say, he failed the test. I'm sure I don't have to tell you this, but the boy couldn't be trusted to wipe his own arse."

Kosara frowned. Could Karaivanov be telling the truth? Was it possible Malamir hadn't known about the trap?

Now that she thought back to that night, Kosara realised it wasn't only possible, but likely. Malamir really had looked close to death when Roksana had brought him to Kosara's workshop.

Despite the dire situation she was in, Kosara couldn't help but smile.

"What are you laughing at?" Karaivanov barked.

"Nothing," Kosara said quickly, aware antagonising the smuggler further was a dangerous idea.

Malamir hadn't betrayed her. Not this time. The only trouble was, he'd paid for it with his life.

If she ever made it out of this basement alive, she'd have to make sure his mother was taken care of. Perhaps she'd see if Dancho Krustev could arrange for her to be admitted to the hospital early. There were two ways to make anything happen in Chernograd: money and nepotism.

"Well?" Karaivanov said. "Which one of you would you like me to shoot first?"

He swung the gun back and forth, back and forth between Asen and Kosara, obviously enjoying watching her squirm. The twelve shadows remained unmoving in his fist.

Ungrateful bastards, Kosara thought bitterly. She'd let them make a fool out of her multiple times, and they wouldn't so much as attempt to save her. When she thought she was giving them to Malamir, she'd harboured hope she might get them back. Now that they were in Karaivanov's greedy hands, she knew the smuggler was unlikely to ever part with them.

Kosara bit the inside of her cheek. She looked at Asen with his arms pinned close to his body, just as the fluorescent face of his watch came alight. It quietly, almost imperceptibly, buzzed.

Ten to midnight.

Kosara inhaled sharply. They might need Asen's distraction, after all. It was a gamble, and gambling had landed her in deep water before—but she was all out of better ideas. If only she could stall for a little longer . . .

"Wait," she said. "You can't kill me. Who's going to teach you how to use the shadows?"

"Believe me, I'm well aware. Otherwise your brains would be decorating the walls by now. However, I can shoot him." Karaivanov's gun moved back to Asen's temple.

Asen's face was ashen. He looked like he might have been sick if he wasn't paralysed by Karaivanov's magic.

"That's not what I'm saying at all." Kosara scrambled for what else she could say to him—anything to keep him from pulling that trigger. "Do you really want to begin our professional partnership with a senseless death?"

Karaivanov laughed, making it perfectly clear how little he cared about senseless deaths. "You'll have to try harder than that to convince me. What can you offer me for his life?"

Kosara struggled to come up with anything. What did she have to offer?

Nothing. Without her shadows, she was a nobody.

"Why did you summon the mratinyak?" she asked, in a desperate bid to stall.

"The mratinyak?" Karaivanov lifted his eyebrows. "Oh, you mean that giant cockerel. Why do you care?"

"Idle curiosity. Please, indulge me."

For a moment, she thought it wouldn't work. But then, Karaivanov gave her one of those smiles that made it difficult to believe he was the most notorious smuggler in the city. He looked too much like a friendly uncle.

"If you must know," he said, "it was an accident. I'd tasked Natalia with bringing me monsters so I could sell them across the Wall, but believe you me, I was less than thrilled with her when she turned up with that thing. That's when I realised she was more trouble than she was worth."

Kosara swallowed hard, acutely aware that Karaivanov could make the same decision about her and Asen at any minute.

"Is that why you killed her?" she asked.

"I killed her because I figured someone wearing her face would have a much better chance convincing those two idiots, Sofiya and Irina, to part with their shadows."

"Why go to all this trouble, though? What are you collecting shadows for?" Then, it hit her. "It's for the ritual, isn't it? You truly have rediscovered the ritual that was used to build the Wall."

Karaivanov let out a laugh. "You seem to be under the impression you're the one asking the questions here, and you couldn't be more wrong. Now, answer me this: What can you offer me for his life?"

Kosara's heartbeat grew so deafening in her ears, she found it difficult to concentrate on her thoughts. "He could be useful to you. He was useful once before, wasn't he?"

"He was, until he betrayed me. I lost my daughter because of him."

"You lost your daughter because you murdered her in cold blood."

"I lost her when I permitted her to marry this bastard." Karaivanov's face twisted in uncharacteristic anger, but then he took several deep breaths, his features smoothing once more. "Listen. You know I'm a practical man. I'd never waste something—or, indeed, some*one*—who might be useful to me. You two, however, have proven to be nothing but thorns in my side." Karaivanov's finger inched towards the trigger.

Kosara tried peeking at Asen's watch, but its face had grown dark once more. It must have been close to midnight. Must have been. Kosara felt as if they'd been talking for hours.

"Come on, Konstantin, be sensible—"

Somewhere in the distance, the clock tower chimed. Kosara barely breathed, counting the bangs. One, two, three, four, five . . .

A scream sounded outside. It must have been one of the goons who were undoubtedly hidden nearby, guarding the entrance. Karaivanov frowned, looking out into the night.

Six, seven, eight, nine . . .

Another scream, this time closer. Then, the shuffling of feet in the snow. Kosara finally allowed herself to exhale—a moment later, she remembered just how wrong things could still go.

Ten, eleven, twelve.

Boryana's face appeared in the open hatch above, pale and gaunt, framed by her blood-red hair. Her scream made the fine hairs on the back of Kosara's neck prickle.

The kikimora grasped at the edge of the opening with her talons, propelled herself on scraggly legs, and plummeted downwards.

29

Asen

Asen's scream was trapped in his throat. No matter how much he wanted to run, his feet were glued to the floor. He watched, helpless, as Boryana descended into the basement.

For a second, Karaivanov stared at his daughter wide-eyed. Then, he lifted his gun and fired. The bullet sank into the kikimora's chest with a squelch. The stench of gunpowder filled the space, equal parts rotten eggs and metal.

Boryana paused, an arm's length from the two of them, her fingers caressing the bloody bullet hole in her dress. The snarl on her face didn't waver. Her amber gaze moved between Asen and Karaivanov. Asen swallowed hard.

He desperately hoped that he'd been right—that given the choice between him and her father, Boryana would choose Asen every time. If he'd been wrong, he was about to die a very painful, very bloody death.

Then, the kikimora moved. She was so fast that Asen barely registered what happened. He heard a loud thud, followed by a desperate scream.

Karaivanov lay on the floor, with the kikimora on top of him. Her arms were a blur as she swiped at him again and again. Her talons opened the fur coat, then slashed through fabric, skin, and flesh. Blood splattered the walls.

If he wasn't still rooted in place by the brand on his chest, Asen would have let out an exhale.

"Help me!" Karaivanov wailed. "Help me and I'll make you both rich!" His words were punctuated with loud sobs, a sound completely unfamiliar coming from the smuggler.

Asen expected one of Karaivanov's minions to rush inside to check on the commotion. The smuggler surely had more people guarding the area than the two they'd heard die at the hands of the kikimora. He was too paranoid not to.

No one came. They were either all dead, or they'd run—and who could blame them? That was the problem with surrounding yourself with the opportunistic and the desperate. They were unlikely to risk their necks to save yours.

"Help me! Help!"

Asen and Kosara couldn't, no matter how much he pleaded. Asen, because he was still trapped by the enchantment. Kosara, because Karaivanov had stolen her magic, her shadows still gripped tightly in his fist. The smuggler had brought this onto himself.

But then, Asen felt the spell over him weakening. As Karaivanov's life seeped out of his body, his magic lost its power. First, Asen managed to move his fingertips. Then, he opened his mouth, and a whisper came out: "Kosara?"

He met her eyes over the bloody scene on the floor, and realised even if she still had her magic, Kosara wouldn't interfere in Karaivanov's death. She'd made a promise to Boryana, and she wasn't about to break it.

Slowly, his every muscle fighting against him, Asen kneeled next to the smuggler. Boryana was still on top of Karaivanov, slowly excavating her way through his chest with her talons. The smell of fresh blood rushed Asen, and he had to take several deep breaths so it wouldn't go to his head. He couldn't afford to turn now.

His voice came out hoarse. "Give me the secret to how the Wall was built, and I'll help you."

Karaivanov didn't hesitate. "The key is in the ring! Just take it!"

The same diamond ring Karaivanov used to punish his minions? The one that had left Sokol's lip bloody?

Asen tried to pull it from his finger, but Karaivanov shook his head. "Not that one!"

Next to the enormous diamond, on his pinkie, there was a second ring, old and patinaed, appearing to be made of simple brass. When Asen removed it from the smuggler's finger, he noticed an engraving on the inside: "Ownership of Master Kliment."

"How do you use it?" Asen asked.

"You know the book?" Karaivanov's gasps were growing shallower and shallower. "The *Magus Liber*? Use the ring on it."

"Konstantin, you're really wearing my patience thin. How?"

"Just look through it! I'm not sure how it works! Do I look like a witch to you?"

"Most certainly not," Kosara muttered under her breath.

"Help me!" Karaivanov shouted again. "You promised!"

Asen popped the ring into his coat's inside pocket and buttoned it shut. Then, he stood up and dusted his knees with his hand. "I lied."

His promise to Boryana meant much more than his promise to Karaivanov.

Karaivanov's eyes widened as the realisation that no help was coming hit him. He opened his mouth again to say something—to plead or to threaten, but the kikimora struck him again, and only a pained moan escaped his lips.

It seemed Asen had been just in time retrieving the ring. A moment later, the pain proved too much, and the smuggler lost consciousness. In the absence of his screams, silence descended on the basement, only the wet squelching of the kikimora's nails digging around Karaivanov's chest remaining. Asen could swear he saw a rib protruding out, white among the gore.

He wanted to turn away, but he knew it would be a cowardly thing to do. Instead, he watched as Boryana reached inside Karaivanov's rib cage, her hand plunging within its bloody depths. She pulled out his heart, raising it high above her head in triumph. It looked purplish red, the colour of a bruise, and it beat slowly, dripping blood on Boryana's face.

She opened her mouth so wide her jaw would have dislocated had she been human, and she took a large bite, as if it were an apple.

Asen had no doubt that scene would plague his nightmares for years to come, much like Boryana's death.

While the kikimora chewed on the heart with a satisfied smile on her face, Karaivanov's body spasmed on the floor until, finally, it stilled. The fist clutching the shadow beads went slack, and they rolled out onto the floor once again.

Kosara was obviously expecting trouble, because she rushed to collect them, muttering something under her breath and rolling them between her fingers until they surrounded her in a black mist.

Once the kikimora was sated, she looked at Asen, her bright eyes contrasting against the dark blood covering her face. She swallowed her last bite and stood, wobbly on her knees.

"I really don't think so." Kosara stepped between Asen and the kikimora with her fists clenched.

Boryana, without ever moving her eyes from Asen, slapped her on the cheek so hard, Kosara flew across the room and hit the wall. Three bloody lines bloomed red on her skin.

Swearing, Kosara stood up again.

"Wait," Asen said. He didn't think he'd imagined the softness in Boryana's eyes.

At least, he hoped he hadn't.

Boryana took another step towards him, slowly, as if he were an animal she was trying not to startle. When he didn't move, she grew braver. Finally, she stood a hair's breadth away, their noses almost touching.

She leaned in and her lips, covered in blood and gore, touched his. They remained like that for a second. Asen was too afraid to breathe, and Boryana didn't have to. Finally, she pulled back, still staring at him with those eyes he'd loved so much, and then, without saying a word, she melted away.

He blinked, and she was gone, only the warmth of her kiss still lingering on his lips, and the smell of blood still hovering in the air.

"What the fuck," Kosara muttered under her breath.

Asen touched his mouth. His fingertips came back red.

He looked at Karaivanov's body on the floor, and all he could think about was how small the smuggler appeared. Like a child wrapped in that enormous fur coat.

Kosara kneeled next to Karaivanov and carefully placed the mask of Malamir's face onto his. A second later, the two fused together, and the corpse looked like Malamir's.

"Why?" Asen asked.

"So his mother can bury him."

"I see." Asen gestured at her cheek, red with blood. "Are you all right?"

Kosara ran a finger down the three slashes cutting across it. "I'm fine. They're not deep, just scratches. We have to get out of here. We're both covered in his blood."

Asen nodded, but for a second, he didn't move.

"Asen?" Kosara said. Thankfully, she didn't ask if he was all right because he didn't know the answer.

This was it. Boryana's murder had been avenged. Chernograd's most notorious smuggler was dead. Asen had expected to be happy— instead, he felt nothing but emptiness.

But then, Kosara's hand found his. Karaivanov and Boryana might both be dead, but he was still here, and so was Kosara. At the end of it all, it wasn't happiness he found, but a strong desire to leave this blood-soaked room behind.

"Let's go," he said, pulling her towards the basement's door.

Kosara flicked through the *Magus Liber*, occasionally lifting the brass ring to her eye and exclaiming loudly, startling Asen every time. It wasn't just the schematics for the ritual used to build the Wall that old Kliment had woven inside the piece of jewellery: it hid all sorts of interesting notes and useful insights.

The spell for building the Wall—and indeed, for destroying it—was just where Kosara had originally guessed it would be. Hidden on the page discussing embedding magic.

While Kosara worked on noting it down, Asen scrubbed the floor. They didn't need the rune circle that had trapped Boryana any longer. The ink had already started to run and smear by the time they'd got home.

At one point, the invisible cat came to check what he was doing—he could tell by the inky paw prints left on the floorboards. It sniffed his hand before retreating to its bed. Perhaps it was starting to get used to him.

He and Kosara had barely talked all evening. He'd taken a shower first, washing Konstantin's blood off himself, and then she'd disappeared for a long bath. Now, they shared a room, but each was busy with their own thoughts.

What was there to talk about? They'd seen a man die. Asen had promised him help, only to watch in silence as a kikimora feasted on his heart.

All along, Asen's plan had been to hand Karaivanov to the authorities—and now, thinking back, he'd been an idiot to ever consider it. The smuggler had people everywhere. He wouldn't get arrested, and if he did, he wouldn't get charged, and if he did? He'd get out of jail within days.

Asen wasn't sure why he was so full of guilt. The old smuggler was dead, so what? Good riddance. Boryana had finally found peace.

Maybe that was it. Maybe Asen felt so awful because he knew he'd never see her again, not even in the form of a bloodthirsty apparition. He'd never got the chance to apologise properly. But then, she seemed to have understood. She seemed to have forgiven him.

He scrubbed the floor harder, watching the ink disappear. It reminded him of how the blood had come off his hands earlier, pink and diluted with water, running between the grimy bathroom tiles.

He looked up and saw Kosara watching him over the leather-bound cover of the massive magic book.

"Are you okay?" she asked.

"I'm not sure," he said truthfully.

Kosara put the book down. She kneeled on the floor next to him. "You did nothing wrong. The bastard deserved to die."

"Who are we to decide who deserves to die?"

"It wasn't us who decided it. He was the one who brought this onto himself when he murdered Boryana."

Asen sighed. He knew Kosara was right.

"You did the right thing," Kosara said. "You never let your anger take over. You never transformed."

For a second, Asen was stunned. The thought of transforming had barely crossed his mind. "Well, I did spend most of the encounter paralysed by magic."

"Yes, but even after that ended, you kept your head, despite the stench of blood all around. That's impressive."

Asen shrugged. "While we were waiting for you to come home the other night, Dancho taught me some breathing exercises. I think they've been helping."

"That's good." Kosara gave him a warm smile, and he couldn't help but return it.

Dancho was convinced that the varkolak curse could be managed, if the one cursed was willing to put in the effort. He'd proposed group therapy, a good diet, and a healthy exercise routine—well, and some medication as needed, in the form of wolfsbane potions. Asen hadn't believed him at first, but now, he was starting to consider that the doctor could be right.

"Listen, I know how you feel," Kosara said, scooting closer to him, letting him rest his head on her shoulder. "When I trapped the Zmey in the Wall, I thought: I'm washing my hands of it all. They say getting embedded is worse than being dead since there's never any peace in it, but I didn't care. I couldn't kill him. I didn't want to be the one to do it. It seemed so . . . final, you know? No way to change my mind. No way to redeem myself. If I killed him, I told myself, I'd become as bad as him."

Kosara paused, but Asen said nothing. She looked like she needed a second to gather her thoughts, and his questions wouldn't help.

"I couldn't kill him," she continued, "because if I'd done it, I would have been guided by nothing but bitterness. I didn't know, back then, that the cost of saving this damned city was his death. It's the same for Karaivanov. If he hadn't died, he'd have kept undermining any chance Chernograd has of rebuilding itself."

"It's not the same. The Zmey is a monster. Karaivanov was human."

"Was he, though? Because he seemed pretty monstrous to me."

For a moment, Asen remained silent. Once again, Kosara was right.

"Still," Asen said. "I'll ask you again. Who are we to decide who lives and who dies?"

"We're nobodies. That's not the point, though. This isn't our decision." She smiled, and suddenly, Asen had to fight with himself not to flinch away from her. There was something of the Zmey in that smile, something vicious and bloodthirsty. "Both the Zmey and Karaivanov sealed their fates many years ago. Let them face the consequences."

"So what? You see yourself as the hand of fate?"

"Someone has to be."

Her shadows unfurled around her, half-hiding her from view. Asen shuddered. They were filling her head with their murmur, he knew, because he recognised that faraway look in her eyes.

Then, she shook her head, and when she looked back at him, she was herself again, an exhausted witch who'd bitten off more than she could chew. A strand of blonde hair fell in front of her eyes, and she blew at it to get it to move. Asen resisted the urge to tuck it behind her ear.

"I should prepare for the ritual," she said tiredly.

Asen didn't reply. He couldn't tell her what he was truly thinking. He didn't trust her shadows. Kosara planned to use them to destroy the Wall, and that would only give them a chance to prey on her again. Asen worried what they'd take from her this time. Little by little, he was losing her to the shadows. She was losing herself to the shadows.

He had to do something. Kosara insisted she had to do it all alone, but he simply didn't believe her.

His eyes snagged on her address book, lying next to the mirror she used to communicate with Vila. Kosara's eyes followed his gaze.

"Do you think you can do it?" he asked, trying to distract her. "The ritual?"

"I don't have a choice, do I?" She laughed, but it sounded hollow. "The shadows of your past are all dead. Tomorrow, it's time to deal with mine."

"Why tomorrow?" Asen asked. "Why not wait for a day or two, give us the chance to regroup . . ."

"And while we regroup, people will keep dying. No. It has to be tomorrow."

Asen swallowed in a dry throat. The Wall was going to fall tomorrow. The monsters would be free to ravage Belograd, a city he still considered home.

"What of Belograd?" he asked, his voice coming out strained.

"We'll have to broadcast a warning. Make sure everyone stays inside while it all goes down. If my plan goes right, it will only be a few hours."

"And if it goes wrong?"

"If it goes wrong, we'll all be dead, so we won't care anyway."

30

Kosara

The shadows wouldn't shut up. Their murmurs filled Kosara's head as she tried to concentrate on reading the *Magus Liber*. In the corner of her eye, she saw different iterations of the Zmey, plucked from their memories—his clothes changed, but his face remained just as she remembered it, pale and perfect.

She ignored it all: the voices, the visions, the thumping of her heart. She tried to ignore Asen too, reading by the hearth, a frown on his face. She had too much work to do, too many steps in this plan she'd devised, too many opportunities for it to go wrong.

First, she had to make certain she prepared the ritual that would destroy the Wall correctly, following Master Kliment's notes exactly.

Then, she had to be sure she had the right runes for a magic circle, similar to the one she'd used to trap Boryana, in order to confine Lamia. It had been strong enough to contain the kikimora for days— she sincerely hoped it would be strong enough to withstand one of the most powerful monsters in the city.

Finally, she had to enchant a pair of wedding rings. She'd stolen the idea from Boryana. As Master Kliment himself must have known, rings were perfect to weave spells into: a circle, symbolising perpetuity. Wedding rings were even more powerful. There was deep, ancient magic in a marriage, tying one person to another.

Kosara fished inside her pocket for the two rings she'd taken from her mother's jewellery box. They were identical, two simple silver hoops: one marked with her mother's name, the other with her father's. It had been a miracle she hadn't melted them into silver bullets in the years since her parents had passed. She'd always been a sentimental fool, she supposed. It occasionally proved useful.

She quickly hid them in her pocket before Asen saw them and started asking questions. He seemed so out of sorts already. Kosara wasn't sure what she'd expected his reaction to Karaivanov's death to be—happiness? Relief? Instead, Asen seemed to be racked with guilt.

Kosara, herself, was glad Karaivanov was dead. Getting rid of the smuggler had been long overdue. She'd feel even better once the Zmey faced a similar fate.

Asen had asked who she was to decide who lived and who died. He'd acted as if she had a choice. What else could she possibly do? Watch the monster realm engulf Chernograd before they were both devoured by the nothingness beyond? Run, like Vila had suggested?

Someone had to choose the Zmey's death. Who, if not her? She was the one responsible for trapping him in the Wall. She was the one burdened with the twelve shadows. She'd been dreaming for years of ridding her city of the monsters, and now, finally, she had the power to do it.

Choosing to do nothing was worse.

Somehow, through the constant muttering of the shadows, she heard the Zmey's laughter ringing in her ears. *Are you coming for me, little Kosara?* he asked in his soft voice, and something about it felt so tangible, she was certain she caught his scent drifting through the room. *You could never stay away from me for long, could you?*

She had to keep her gaze pinned forwards, at the diagram in the *Magus Liber,* so she wouldn't focus on one of the many Zmeys the shadows conjured in the corners of her vision. They were all nothing but spectres of the past.

The Zmey was trapped. At least for the time being, at least until tomorrow, he couldn't hurt her.

I'm waiting, Kosara. I'm waiting for you.

"Shut up." A second too late, she realised she'd said it out loud. Asen gave her a look over the pages of his book. Unlike Kosara, he wasn't poring over an ancient tome—instead, he'd started the second instalment in the *Monster Lover* series, *A Day of Delights With a Voracious Varkolak,* and only his slightly arched eyebrow betrayed what he thought of the plot so far.

"Is he talking to you again?" Asen asked.

"Who?" She knew very well who Asen meant. There was only one person who caused that murderous glare in his eyes, and besides, there was only one person who was a frequent guest in Kosara's head.

"The Zmey," Asen said. "Is he talking to you?"

"He's not talking to me," Kosara said, trying to sound as if she found the idea preposterous. "He's trapped in the Wall. How could he possibly be talking to me?"

Asen's mouth became a thin line. "In the last few days, I've seen a gigantic cockerel murder a woman and a baker snap a chicken's throat with his teeth. Everything is possible in this city."

"Don't be silly. I'm nervous, that's all. Nervous and tired." She stood up from the table and, out of habit, almost stepped over the empty space where the kikimora had been trapped. "We should both get some sleep. It will be a long day tomorrow."

Asen's eyes flicked to behind her back, like how they'd done when he'd been searching for Boryana's ghost. Evidently, he wasn't the only one who'd momentarily forgotten that the kikimora was gone.

Kosara's stomach twisted. She wasn't sure what she'd expected— that once the kikimora stopped haunting him, Asen would forget all about his wife? These things took time.

"I figured it out, by the way," she said, in an attempt to distract him. "What the shadows changed this time."

"Oh?" He raised his eyebrows. "What is it?"

"My left pinkie toe. It's a nice olive brown now. The nail came painted too, in a lovely shade of pink."

"Why did they do that?"

Kosara shrugged. "The shadows are the shadows. I've given up on trying to figure out their motivations at this point."

The first thing Kosara and Asen did the next morning was contact all the radio stations and newspapers on both sides of the Wall, so they could broadcast an emergency message: *A dangerous monster could attack the city tonight. Stay inside. Keep alert.*

There had been questions, of course, which they'd answered with as many evasions and half truths as they could get away with. They hadn't been met with as much doubt, however, as Kosara had expected. In a way, she was grateful to Konstantin Karaivanov for instilling a fear of monsters into many Belogradeans.

She was pleased to see that Chernograd had heeded her warning, and she could only hope Belograd would do the same. By lunchtime, the streets were full of people preparing to barricade inside for as long as was necessary. They had plenty of experience doing so, after all.

As the hour drew closer to midnight, she and Asen made their way across the quiet city. It gave her a sense of déjà vu: six months ago, she and the Zmey had walked to the Wall through the gently falling snow. Now, the snow was heavier. The cold clawed at her skin and burrowed inside her bones.

With every step, the tension inside Kosara grew tauter, until she felt as if any minute, she might snap.

Last winter, Kosara and the Zmey had performed the ritual together. This time, she was on her own. Just her and twelve unruly shadows. She tried to suppress the voice in her head insisting she was making a mistake. What else could she possibly do? She'd asked Vila for help, and she'd been rejected. Surely, no one else was foolish enough to risk their own neck to save the city. Kosara couldn't ask them to.

When they approached the Wall, barely visible through the snow, Kosara noticed a bright light flickering nearby.

"Is that the bakery?" she asked.

Asen gave her a sheepish look.

"Why is the bakery open?" Suspicion crept into her voice.

"Come." Asen gestured at her to follow him.

Kosara had visited Ibrahim's bakery many times, but she'd rarely seen it so full. At first, she couldn't figure out what was going on: a name-day celebration? A late St. Enyo's Day party? Surely, they must have heard the warning on the radio.

Then, she noticed the placard hanging over the entrance to the kitchen. Kosara squinted, trying to make it out through the snowflakes caught in her eyelashes, quickly melting in the heat.

The placard read: "The Witch and Warlock Association."

"What the . . ." Kosara muttered under her breath.

The crowd must have noticed her and Asen standing at the threshold, because their conversations quieted down. She recognised everyone: Yovana the seer, old Ivan the herbalist, Siyana, Ayshe, and a dozen other young witches.

At a table to the side, Roksana sat with Sokol and Vrana. When Roksana thought no one was looking, she added a few drops from her flask to her mug of coffee.

"Ah, Kosara, finally." Ibrahim walked in with a tray of hot chocolate. "We've been waiting for you."

"What is this?" Kosara asked. Her name-day wasn't until September, and she'd never liked surprise parties, and besides, this seemed particularly inappropriate on a night like this. She had more important things to do than to sit around, drinking hot chocolate. She heard her voice getting angrier: "Asen, what the hell is going on?"

"It's an emergency meeting of the Witch and Warlock Association," Siyana said. "Didn't you read the placard?"

"Why?" Kosara asked.

"I told them about the ritual," Asen said.

Kosara turned to him, indignant. "When did you manage that?"

"Last night. Once you fell asleep with your head on top of the *Magus Liber*. I thought you'd need all the help you can get. They all volunteered."

"I don't need help," Kosara spat out.

"Ah, yes," Ivan chimed in, slightly too loud because he'd grown deaf in one ear. "You want us to let you perform a dangerous ritual that might release a terrifying beast on the city completely on your own. Such a brilliant idea."

"I know what I'm doing," Kosara said, her shadows unfurling around her and looming over the crowd.

"That might be so," allowed Yovana, "but I've seen my fair share of magic circles in my time. Come on, girl, sit down. Let us have a look at your schematics."

Asen stepped closer to her, so she'd be the only one who heard him when he spoke. "Kosara, listen to me. I talked to every single one of these people. They are all here because they want to help. They don't have any ulterior motives."

"How could you possibly know that?" Kosara snapped.

"I told you, I talked to them. Call it copper intuition." He smiled brilliantly at her. "Will you trust me on this?"

Kosara hesitated. Why was she fighting him? Ivan was right. The ritual *was* dangerous. Asen was right, too: she needed all the help she could get, even if it came from a group of elderly witches and children.

She hadn't wanted to put anyone else in danger, but wasn't it more dangerous to attempt to perform the ritual alone and risk releasing Lamia?

They can't be trusted, hissed the familiar voice in her head. *No one can be trusted.*

Except, Asen had vouched for them all. She didn't believe her own judgment any longer, but she believed his.

All the witches in the room were there out of their own free will, because Asen had asked them, not because Kosara had forced them to come. Not because she'd threatened them with her shadows. They were there because, just like her, they'd chosen it.

Even so, there was one person in the room Kosara knew for a fact couldn't be trusted. That person had shown her as much repeatedly.

"What is she doing here?" Kosara asked, pointing to Roksana with her chin.

"I want to help," Roksana said, uncharacteristically quiet.

"Help?" Kosara laughed. "Help with what? Releasing the Zmey so you can sell me to him again?"

Roksana shook her head. Her eyes were slightly glassy from the drink, but when she looked up at Kosara, her gaze was determined. "I have no loyalty to the Zmey. He promised me the Wall will fall if I help him. That was all I ever wanted."

Everyone watched Kosara. She felt as if she was a part of a dramatic scene from a play. She knew what they all wanted to see: her forgiving Roksana, tearfully embracing her like an old friend.

Kosara couldn't do that. The monster hunter had sold her to the Zmey.

Finally, breaking the tense silence, Vrana spoke, "If Roksana attempts to free the Zmey, I'll bite her head off. You have my word."

"Bloody hell," Roksana muttered. "Thanks, sister."

"We don't want him back," Vrana snapped without looking at Roksana. "None of us do. The monster realm is falling apart without him, and even so, it's better than living under his rule. If only we'd realised what he was doing sooner, we would have stopped him."

Kosara paused, digesting Vrana's words. She'd never considered how the monsters felt about the Zmey. As long as Kosara had been alive, he'd been their Tsar. She hadn't thought some of them might be unhappy with that fact.

"What has he been doing?" Kosara asked.

"That thing he does to the girls he kidnaps from Chernograd? He's been doing it to all of us. He's been sucking our magic dry, taking it all for himself."

Kosara shuddered. "Why?"

"Greed. What else? He's always been the most human among us."

"He claims he's protecting us," Sokol said. "For the longest time, I believed him. It's true in a way, except if he hadn't taken it all, we wouldn't need his protection."

Kosara sighed loudly, to cover up how the realisation had rattled her. This whole time, the Zmey hadn't only been feeding on his brides. He'd been feeding on his entire realm.

"Fine," she said. "Roksana can stay. But only if you promise to keep an eye on her."

Vrana smirked. "I promise."

"Well, gather around, everyone," Kosara said awkwardly, feeling like a schoolchild asked to read her homework in front of the entire class. She pulled a stack of pages from her satchel and spread them over the table. "Here they are. The schematics for the magic circle to trap Lamia."

The other witches gathered closer, peering at the pages.

Yovana ran her hands over the paper, feeling the ink. "I have a few suggestions, if you'd allow me." Without waiting for an answer, she pulled a pencil from behind her ear, and began jotting notes around the symbols. She crossed out a few runes and drew new ones.

"I've been doing some reading on magic circles," Ayshe said while Yovana worked. "I have a theory they're more stable if they're octagonal."

"Octagonal?" Ivan snorted. "No need for fancy maths. We should do a pentacle."

"What do you think this is, old man? Tarot?"

Kosara let them argue. This was the problem with gathering a large group of witches in the same room. It only took minutes before they went for each other's throats.

"There," Yovana said finally. "I believe this will be more stable."

Kosara examined the additions to the circle. Yovana was completely right. Her changes had made the circle more stable, but also much faster and easier to draw. They were so simple and elegant, they looked obvious—how come Kosara hadn't thought of them earlier?

Because she'd been scrambling to get everything ready on her own, that was why. She'd taken it upon herself to learn three separate, complicated spells in one night. It had been foolish.

"Thank you," she said sincerely.

"No need to thank me." Yovana's voice rose over the clamour of the arguing witches, making them quiet down. "Now, Kosara, do you want to share your plan with us?"

Kosara paused. All the witches in Chernograd who were willing to help her were in this room, but there was one notable absence.

She turned to Asen, trying to sound casual. "Did you speak to Vila?"

He looked down at his hands. He'd been biting the skin around his nails again, and it was raw and bleeding. "I did. She . . . um, she said she was busy."

"Busy," Kosara spat out, equal parts disappointed and angry. What could the old witch possibly be doing that was more important than this? Washing her hair? "Busy with what?"

"She didn't say."

Kosara took a deep breath. Fine. She didn't need Vila. She had herself, and her shadows, and now, a room full of allies. The old witch could spend her evening drinking tea and knitting, for all Kosara cared, while the rest of Chernograd's witches saved the city.

Kosara waited until the room had quieted down again. Then, she leaned forwards over the schematics for the ritual. "The plan is simple. First, we drag Lamia out of the Wall, so she is contained within the city. Next, we trap her in a magic circle and deal with her. Then, once the Wall has been destabilised, we pull the Zmey out and let it crumble around him."

"And then?" asked Yovana.

Kosara hesitated, not wanting to admit that after that, her plan got shaky. She knew one thing: the Zmey had to die. It was the *how* she needed a bit more time to figure out.

Her fingers found the two silver rings in her pocket, and she gripped them tight.

"Sokol, Vrana, can I have a word with you?" she asked.

The two yudas exchanged glances before following her to the empty kitchen.

Kosara leaned forwards so her words wouldn't carry. "What can you tell me about the Zmey's weddings?"

31

Kosara

When Kosara had performed the ritual with the Zmey last winter, every rune had been a battle. Every spell word—a struggle. She and the Zmey had never worked together; they'd competed against each other, raced to the end of the spell.

Now, working with the other witches, she could almost forget they carried out a dangerous ritual that could either destroy or save the city. It felt just like a regular New Year's Eve.

She would have managed to do the ritual alone. Of course she would have—she'd prepared for it so carefully, aware she could afford no mistakes. She'd have been perfectly fine on her own. Perfectly fine.

However, she didn't need to be on her own after all, and she was grateful for it. For the first time in days, she felt as if she could breathe more easily. She had to admit she was glad Asen had asked the other witches for help.

Kosara drew the runes for the magic circle, following the notes Yovana had modified. Her shadows, understanding the gravity of the situation, followed in her step without protest.

In the meantime, the rest of the witches copied the embedding spell from the *Magus Liber,* adding the changes Master Kliment had recorded in his magic ring. Except, since they were hoping to demolish the Wall rather than raise it, they had to do it all in reverse order: read every word back to front, make every gesture the wrong way around, draw the symbols on the ground upside down. It made the ritual look even more uncanny, though the young witches didn't seem to mind. They all laughed loudly as they stumbled backwards in the snow.

Eventually, Yovana's voice came from behind Kosara's back. "We're ready."

Kosara turned on her heel. "So soon?"

"Many hands make light work. You?"

Kosara looked down at her runes glistening on the cobblestones. She didn't feel ready, but at the same time, she knew they had no time to lose. It was almost midnight, the hour when spells were strongest.

"I'm ready."

Yovana nodded at Ayshe. The girl, with her glittering ink, put a final flourish on the last rune, closing the circle.

The witches held hands, and their shadows mirrored them, a circle within a circle within a circle. They all pronounced the spell into being together, their voices rising over the wind—an eerie, slightly out-of-tune choir.

Once they fell silent, for a few tense heartbeats, nothing happened. The wind kept howling and whistling, pulling at their clothes. The snow fell, piling on top of their runes and catching in their hair. Kosara's hands grew so cold, she worried her fingers might drop off one by one, like rotten fruit.

Then, the Wall shook. Its dark expanse swayed and lurched, looming over them, casting long shadows on the ground. Its surface bubbled as though hundreds of hands were trying to push through from within.

A roar sounded, followed by a wet sound, and somewhere high above, the silhouette of a monster separated itself from the Wall.

To Kosara's left, one of the young witches gasped.

Lamia's wings were the size of a warship's sails, stretched so thin under her arms, they let starlight through. Her golden scales glinted in the moonlight as her body twisted and wove through the clouds. Her three heads scanned the city below, searching for prey.

She opened her mouths, and three forked tongues protruded,

lashing at the moon. For a bizarre second, Kosara wondered what would happen if the monster swallowed it.

Then, Lamia's eyes fell on Kosara and the rest of the circle of witches, standing in the square, perfectly visible against the snow in their dark clothes. There was something of the Zmey in her gleaming gaze—something of his uncontrollable fury. Lamia flapped her wings and roared again, making the hairs on the back of Kosara's neck prickle. The low, rumbling sound triggered a primal instinct in her. It took all her self-restraint not to run like a terrified animal.

To Kosara's right, Yovana let out a juicy swear.

Kosara clicked her fingers, and a flame materialised in her hand. She encouraged it with magic words until it grew so big, she could barely contain it between her outstretched arms. It sizzled and smoked when the snowflakes landed on it.

To Lamia's eyes, it must have looked like nothing but a firefly, flickering far below. Nevertheless, it attracted the monster's attention. She turned all three of her heads towards it and flapped her wings, causing a gust of wind to tear through the city, making the windows rattle in their frames.

Kosara's heart hammered against her rib cage, a staccato rhythm almost in time with the beating of the monster's wings.

As Lamia's shadow fell over the square, Kosara realised her mistake. She'd thought the mratinyak was large. Compared to Lamia, the cockerel was a fly next to a great bird of prey.

The magic circle would fit one of the monster's paws at best.

"Run," Kosara muttered under her breath.

"What?" shouted Ivan over Lamia's deafening roars.

"Run!" Kosara screamed, dropping her fireball to the ground where it melted in the snow.

Kosara pulled the two witches on either side after her by the hands, dragging them to Ibrahim's bakery. They'd had the sense to draw wards and hang talismans around the building before all of this had started—and thank God for that. Kosara hoped they would hold, even when faced with a monster like Lamia.

Once inside, they found the two yudas at the window, watching Lamia with wide eyes.

"I'd heard she was big," Vrana said quietly. "I had no idea she was this big."

"What's happening?" Asen asked, helping Yovana inside. The seer's bad knee had started aching while they were drawing the circle, and the dash through the square likely hadn't helped. "What's wrong?"

Kosara took a deep breath so she wouldn't immediately snap at him. Couldn't he see? "She's too big for the circle," she said, leaning her back on the wall. She was out of breath and the cold air had scratched her throat so bad, her words came out barely a whisper. "She's too damned big!"

The building shook as Lamia landed at the foot of the Wall. Then, her heads turned to the bright windows of the bakery, and she crawled towards them on all fours. Kosara swore, already shaping a fireball between her fingers. Roksana took her gun out, as if that would do anything.

Lamia's tail dragged behind her, clearing a path in the snow, and Kosara spotted one of her glistening runes uncovered on the cobblestones. She crossed her fingers tightly and quietly prayed under her breath to whatever god was currently listening.

Provided Kosara had done her job properly, that should have been enough to trap the monster.

Please, please let it be enough.

A second later, Lamia screeched, a high-pitched sound that resonated in Kosara's teeth. The monster froze in place for a moment and then, pulling at the ground with her talons, digging into the soft snow, she tried to drag herself forwards.

She couldn't take a single step. The magic circle had worked—albeit not fully as intended. It had only caught the end of the monster's tail.

Realising she was trapped, Lamia threw her heads back and roared. Kosara allowed herself to exhale. This would win them some time, though it wasn't ideal. Even restricted by the radius of her tail, Lamia could still do a lot of damage. Besides, Kosara wasn't sure how long her magic circle would hold with Lamia fighting against it. As the monster thrashed, the runes on the ground quivered, threatening to turn into liquid once more.

"I have to go out there," Kosara said. She looked around, making sure everyone was safe inside, and turned to the door.

Asen stepped in her path. "Why?"

"I need to take care of Lamia."

"How?"

Kosara hesitated. Her plan wasn't fully formed, but she thought she might rely on what she usually did. "Fire?"

"Her scales are made of metal, Kosara."

"*A lot* of fire."

"We should all go," Ayshe said. "We'll have a better chance as a team."

"Yes," Siyana agreed. "We'll surround her."

"Excellent plan," Yovana chimed in from the chair in the corner where she sat and massaged her bad knee.

Kosara opened her mouth to argue, but then, she realised, they were right. This was their best chance. Now wasn't the time for her to play the hero, and God knew they'd made a good team when they'd been preparing the ritual.

What would Kosara do out there alone, anyway? Asen was right— her fire would be useless. All it would achieve was to make Lamia frenzied enough to free herself from the circle.

She could either accept the help of the other witches, or she could let Lamia destroy Chernograd. The choice seemed obvious. There was no shame in admitting it.

"What about your bad knee?" She turned to Yovana.

The older witch reached to the corner behind her and produced a long, gnarly willow branch. "I've brought my walking stick." She brandished it in the air. "It doubles as a stake if push comes to shove."

"Right. Anyone else have any secret weapons?"

Ayshe gripped the muska amulet around her neck, and Siyana's bracelet of horseshoe nails chimed as she lifted her hand.

One of the other witches, Elif, kicked an elaborately gilded sabre from under the table. "I've brought my mum's yatagan. She's a monster hunter."

Now we're talking. "Do you know how to use it?"

"More or less."

"If you distract her with those fireballs of yours," Ivan said to Kosara, "we can get the youngsters close to her without her catching us. I've read tales of the great Lamia. She's got a weak spot on her chest, near her heart."

Kosara had to admit it sounded like the best plan they had.

"Deal." She took another step towards the door. Asen remained in her way. "You can't come," she told him. "This is witch business." The last thing they needed was for Asen to turn in the heat of battle.

"And yuda business," added Vrana.

Kosara wasn't about the argue with a bloodthirsty bird, so she simply nodded.

Asen sighed. "I know. I'm not coming."

Kosara had to look away. She couldn't take the sadness in his eyes. This was what his new world was, much smaller than his old: trapped inside the bakery while danger lurked outside. Trapped within the Wall until she managed to tear it down.

"Will you promise me to come back inside if Lamia frees herself?" he asked. "You'll all have to come back inside."

"I promise," Kosara said, still looking away. It was easier to lie that way.

She felt his fingers on her chin, gently guiding her to face him. When she did, he leaned in and kissed her.

It was a quick kiss, barely a brush of his lips against hers, but Kosara was stunned. For a second, she stood there, unsure what to do or say. Behind her, a few of the witches whooped. Yovana, completely unbefitting her age, was the loudest.

Kosara's blood rushed to her cheeks.

"For luck," Asen said and stepped out of Kosara's way.

She cleared her throat. "Thanks," she mumbled and rushed outside.

It was all hopeless, that much became clear fast. Kosara did her best
to distract Lamia, forming fireball after fireball with the help of her
shadows, but the monster's body was made of metal. The more flames
Kosara shot at her, the hotter her scales grew, until the air around them
rippled. The snow at the monster's feet melted and ran in streams over
the ground, cascading over Kosara's magic circle.

So far, the runes were holding, though Kosara suspected they
wouldn't last much longer. Their edges were already growing blurry.

Vrana and Sokol circled Lamia. Occasionally, while one distracted
her, the other managed to strike. Their nails and teeth screeched
against her scale-covered face.

The other witches tried again and again to get closer to the monster,
but Lamia spotted them every time, and it was pure luck she hadn't
managed to sink her talons into one of them yet.

All they'd achieved was to make the monster angrier. She looked a
lot like her brother now. Every time her feet hit the ground, it shook.
Whenever she raised her heads to the sky, the wind picked up, strong
enough to lift Kosara off her feet. The snowstorm grew worse, as more
and more clouds gathered on the horizon.

Kosara clicked her fingers again, producing another fireball. Her
shadows watched her, and she felt their scorn. In all her years of training, she could have learned a hundred attack spells more useful than
fire.

She hadn't. Fire was all she had.

It wasn't going to be enough. Just like it had never been enough to
defeat the Zmey.

He'd remained silent all night, but she heard him again now, repeating the familiar refrain: *Stupid witch. Useless witch.*

"Shut up," Kosara hissed and used her anger to power her fire.
The flames between her hands grew so hot, they sizzled. Her fingers

started to blister. Her shadows had been getting paler in the gloom of the evening, but now, in the bright light, they regained some of their power.

Kosara threw the fireball at the monster. This time, the fire was too strong even for Lamia. The fireball hit her square in the face, slamming against her scales, causing them to melt and run down her chin. The stench of burning bone drifted in the wind.

When the flames dissipated, all that was left of the monster's middle head was a calcified stump, shiny with molten gold.

While the monster was distracted, Elif managed to find Lamia's weak spot. Kosara watched as she climbed the monster's long tail, and then leg and torso, until she reached the heart. She tried to dislodge one of the monster's scales with her sabre.

She wasn't fast enough. The next moment, Lamia screamed in pain. The stump of her neck enlarged, shapeless, like a tumour. Then, it split in two. Quickly, both parts grew jagged bones, bulging eyes, and a teeth-filled mouth. Once the transformation was complete, two more horned heads protruded from the monster's body on long, flailing necks.

Lamia roared and shook the young witch off. Elif landed in the snow with a loud thud. Thankfully, she immediately jumped up and ran to hide. There were advantages to having young, sturdy bones, Kosara supposed.

She swore under her breath. Hopeless, all of it. They couldn't fight Lamia; the monster was too big and too powerful.

Just as Kosara came to this realisation, Lamia thrashed again, slamming her paws against the ground. Her talons caught on one of Kosara's runes.

This was all the magic circle could take before it finally snapped. The runes melted, their ink sinking into the mud between the cobblestones.

It took Lamia a second to realise she was free. She extended all four of her heads forwards, smelling the air, snapping her teeth.

Kosara needed to run. She'd promised Asen. They all needed to run.

She couldn't run. With her gone, Lamia would turn on the city. Kosara couldn't allow it. She clenched her fist so tight, her nails dug into her skin, and she tried to order her shadows, *Stop her.*

The shadows watched as Lamia took a deliberate step forwards. Sokol and Vrana kept biting and scratching her, but the monster ignored them. The other witches huddled behind a barricade of snow, their eyes wide. Lamia's gleaming gaze was on Kosara.

Stop her!

A few shadows, feeling charitable, made a half-hearted attempt at it. The monster flicked them away like they were flies.

Lamia was so close now, Kosara spotted the weak spot Ivan had mentioned. The monster's scales all overlapped in a perfect, impenetrable armour—except for one at her chest, which was slightly askew after Elif had nearly managed to dislodge it.

It was, however, still there. It would still protect the monster from Kosara's fire.

Lamia leaned one of her middle heads forwards and opened her mouth. Her breath was putrid, sweet like rotting meat. She had at least three rows of glistening, sharp teeth stretching into her throat, disappearing into the darkness within. They dripped saliva so hot, it hissed as it dripped on the ground.

Kosara saw herself reflected in Lamia's eyes: a tiny, dark silhouette lost in their amber expanse.

This was it. This was how she was going to die.

It was a fitting end for a witch. She'd much rather die fighting monsters than in her bed from old age.

Even so, Kosara couldn't look. She squeezed her eyes shut and waited for the sound of broken bone as the monster's mouth closed around her body. She knew it wouldn't be painless, but she hoped it would be quick.

A drop of something scorching hot landed on Kosara's hand, and she frantically shook it off. Saliva?

Any second now, Lamia would bite. Any second . . .

"Hello, old friend," came a voice Kosara recognised.

She frowned, not daring to look. She was clearly hearing voices again. The panic had gone to her head, there was no other possible explanation.

"It's been a while," said the same voice.

This couldn't be real. Couldn't.

As the heat of the monster's breath retreated, Kosara risked opening one eye. Lamia's head still filled her vision, but it wasn't facing her anymore. It had turned to look behind the monster's back.

Lamia roared and whipped around. In the last moment before one of the monster's gigantic legs swiped her, Kosara managed to jump to the side, landing painfully on her behind in the snow.

As she rose on shaky feet, she saw Lamia facing a familiar figure. A house on chicken legs.

"Did you miss me?" came Vila's booming voice, projected straight from the house's open door.

Lamia let out a screech. She slammed her hand over the house's roof. A single ceramic roof tile rolled down, fell on the ground, and shattered.

From inside came Vila's laughter. "You'll have to try harder, friend." The house jumped and pushed Lamia back with both its feet. Kosara's fireballs and the yudas' attacks had done nothing to the monster. The house's chicken legs, however, wedged their talons into Lamia's scales. The weak one, the one Elif had nearly managed to remove, finally came loose.

Lamia screamed so loudly, Kosara's eardrums threatened to tear. The ground shook as the two giants clashed. The house fought as a hen would, jumping and kicking, using its much smaller size to its advantage. Lamia whirled around, trying to catch it, but the house was faster.

Lamia twisted, revealing the soft flesh of her chest where the missing scale had been. Seeing her chance, Sokol flew to the monster, trying to reach the vulnerable spot. With one paw, Lamia pushed back the house on chicken legs, and with the other, she batted the yuda away, sending her tumbling to the ground. Sokol didn't move.

Swearing, Kosara rushed towards the yuda. Lamia stepped in her way, her feet thundering against the ground, her mouth gaping open.

Kosara lifted her hand in the air, desperately trying to come up with a defensive spell instead of another goddamned fireball. Her mind was completely, perfectly blank.

The next moment, the house on chicken legs rushed past her and slammed its roof against the monster's body.

Its cockerel-shaped weather vane pierced Lamia's chest, aimed precisely at her weak spot. Blood rushed down the roof tiles, thick and red, painting the house's white walls.

Lamia produced a bloodcurdling screech. Then, with a thud loud enough the whole city likely heard it, her body collapsed to the ground. She let out a deep breath, blowing off a few more tiles from Vila's roof, and then, she stilled. Her gleaming eyes fluttered shut.

For a few seconds, Kosara didn't dare move. Was this truly it? What if the monster was playing a trick on them? What if she was going to wait until the witches drew closer, only for her eyes to snap open again?

Vila's house, however, seemed to believe the danger had passed. It plonked itself onto the ground, its legs stretched to either side of it.

The door to the bakery slammed open.

"Sokol!" Roksana rushed out, still holding her pistol, followed closely by Asen. Her voice shook. "Sokol, are you all right?"

"I'm okay," came Sokol's muffled voice from the ground, somewhere behind the scaly, unmoving mass that had become of Lamia. "I think I broke a wing."

Kosara exhaled deeply. Thank God. She couldn't lose Sokol. She couldn't lose anyone else. There had been too much death recently.

She made to go to Sokol, but Vila's voice stopped her in her tracks.

"Kosara?" it boomed through the house's door. "Kosara, are you there?"

The window shutters opened and closed, as if the house was blinking, trying to seek her out.

Kosara hesitated. What if Sokol needed her?

"I'll take care of her," Roksana said, producing a vial from her coat's inside pocket. Kosara recognised it. She'd brewed it for the monster hunter herself, many years ago, when the two of them had still been close. An anaesthetic strong enough to knock out most people, provided they weren't Roksana's size—or monsters, like Sokol.

"Kosara?" Vila said again.

"Go," Roksana urged.

Kosara took a deep breath and nodded. She climbed the creaky stairs. At the door, she looked back at Asen for encouragement.

"Do you want me to come with you?" he asked.

Kosara shook her head. "This is between me and Vila."

The house was dark. It smelled familiar—slightly fusty, of dried herbs and old dust, but there was something else there too, drifting along the hallway. A stench Kosara had become terribly familiar with recently. Death.

A lump got stuck in Kosara's throat. Vila's house was small, and the corridor was barely the size of a large cupboard. Kosara still felt as if crossing it took years. Her feet were leaden, every step an effort.

At the end, Kosara wavered. She heard the fire crackling in the kitchen and saw its pale light trickling under the door.

She considered knocking but decided against it. Slowly, she opened the door.

At first, she didn't see Vila. The fire smouldered in the hearth, casting deep shadows over the room. After the cold outside, the air was suffocatingly warm.

The smell didn't dissipate. It only grew stronger.

Something in the corner moved. A pile of blankets resting on Vila's cot, where she slept during the winter so she wouldn't waste wood heating the bedroom.

Kosara rushed to it. In between the blankets peeked Vila's face.

Kosara had never seen the old witch looking so sick. Her skin was ashen, greyish, like an upir's. Her eyes were deep hollows rimmed with dark circles. Her white hair stuck to her sweaty forehead.

"Kosara," Vila said again, her voice barely audible, "you came."

Kosara hesitated. She'd been angry at Vila, but seeing her like this, her fury quickly faded. She'd prepared what she was going to say, so the words tumbled out anyway, though tinged with worry. "You said you'd be busy tonight."

"I am."

"Busy with what?"

Vila barked a laugh. For a moment, she sounded like herself again. "Isn't it obvious? Dying."

"You foresaw this?" Kosara asked, realising a second too late it was a stupid question. Of course Vila had foreseen this. She was the best seer in the city.

How long had she known? Months, most likely. The last time they'd met, she'd said nothing, letting Kosara assume the worst of her. And for what? So Kosara would run, assuming Vila had done the same?

Kosara's eyes filled with tears. "Vila, why didn't you tell me, I—"

"No tears," Vila snapped. "That's why I didn't tell you. I'm dying, so what? Everyone dies. I've had more time than most. Stop making a big deal out of it."

"But I—"

"But *you*, exactly. You're afraid of death? It reminds you of your own mortality? That's fair. That's the prerogative of the young. You'll miss me? Good. I like the idea of being remembered."

Kosara opened her mouth to say something, to assure Vila she'll never forget her, but the old witch didn't give her the chance.

"Now, listen. I have left a detailed will, knowing what witches are like. I didn't want them fighting over my dead body for who gets to keep the silver tea serving set." Vila nodded to the table where a pile of papers rested, filled with her wonky handwriting. "You have to make sure I don't turn. When you bury me, place silver coins on my eyes and an aspen stake through my heart, and—"

"Vila, I know. I know how to bury you."

"Just making sure." Vila produced a yellowed handkerchief from somewhere in the depths of the blankets and blew her nose loudly. At her feet, Moth the cat woke up with a start and meowed. "What do you want, old terror? I'll be silent forever soon, and then you'll miss me!"

"What should I do with him?" Kosara asked.

"Leave him. He doesn't need an owner."

"And the house?"

"I hope you can use it for the Witch and Warlock Association. We need a better library, don't we? All my books are here. It's all in the will."

"How long do you have left?"

"Truth be told, I was supposed to be gone yesterday. Good thing I've got a few favours to call in with the old grim reaper."

Kosara remained quiet, unsure whether Vila was joking. The silence stretched.

"Oh hell," Vila said. "I've never been good at goodbyes." One ashen hand emerged from between the covers and found Kosara's. "You're doing a good job. You still have a lot of work ahead of you, however. Don't let the shadows get to your head. Stay focused."

"Have you seen—"

"I've seen nothing of the future. That's how it works—once I'm gone, it's all black for me."

Kosara's tears threatened to escape her eyes again, and she blinked fast, not wanting Vila to see them.

"What will I do without you?" Kosara's voice came out hollow. Vila's hand was clammy under hers, cold as a corpse already.

"Live a long and fulfilling life, hopefully. Or die tomorrow, who knows. Not me." Vila snorted. "One last thing. The Zmey's shadow. It is on an island in the ocean."

"Where?"

"Do you still have Blackbeard's compass?"

"I do."

"Come here, I'll tell you the magic word."

Kosara leaned closer. The sweet smell of death filled her nostrils. Vila whispered a single syllable in her ear.

Outside, in the distance, the clock tower struck midnight. Kosara squeezed Vila's hand as the old witch's breathing grew shallower.

By the twelfth chime, Vila was gone.

32

Asen

As the clock tower struck twelve, the Wall frayed at the edges.

Asen frowned, unsure whether he was imagining it in the gloom. He looked around to check if anyone else had noticed. Vrana and Roksana were both kneeling next to Sokol, bandaging her broken wing. The two worked together, for a change—shame it took Sokol getting hurt for them to stop arguing.

The witches had gathered around Lamia's corpse. On one side, Yovana made sure the monster was dead. On the other, old Ivan picked the gold scales off Lamia's body with his penknife and stuffed them deep in the pockets of his greasy trousers.

Lamia was a terrifying, dangerous monster—Asen was very aware of that after he'd watched the witches fight her. If they hadn't stopped her, she would have destroyed the city. Nevertheless, it seemed like such a shame the great beast was dead. She was probably the last of her kind.

Her bones would probably end up in the museum, together with the remains of other mythical monsters. In a hundred years' time, she'd be remembered as nothing but a legend from an old book—again.

The twelfth chime sounded, and this time, Asen was certain: the

Wall was slowly, almost imperceptibly, fading. Pulling Lamia out must have destabilised it more quickly than Kosara had expected.

He looked at the house on chicken legs, where the light still flickered in the kitchen. There was no sight of Kosara.

When he turned his gaze back to the Wall, he spotted the silhouette of a man emerging from it. He kept close to the dark surface instead of crossing the bright, snow-covered square, likely hoping he wouldn't be spotted. Asen probably wouldn't have seen him if it wasn't for his enhanced vision.

"Hey!" Asen shouted at the man, but he didn't turn. "Hey!" He tried to attract the attention of the witches. The howling of the wind drowned his voice.

Asen hesitated, but he couldn't waste any more time. The man had already disappeared in the distance.

Swearing under his breath, Asen followed him.

At first, Asen hadn't been certain. The man could have been a lost Belogradean traveller. He could have been a Chernogradean, sneaking back into the city after a rowdy night on the other side of the Wall.

Now, as the storm finally started to die down, the full moon peeked through the clouds, and its light illuminated the man, with his glinting golden hair and his confident stride. Even while scurrying away, the Zmey had the walk of a predator, like a wounded beast seeking shelter until it could strike again.

The Zmey didn't only keep close to the Wall because it provided him with cover. In the moonlight, Asen noticed its dark substance still clinging to the Tsar's skin. Black wisps of it wrapped around his wrists and pulled on his torso, trying to drag him back inside.

The Zmey must have been thinking he'd manage to free himself of it, eventually, once he got away from Kosara and the other witches. The Wall was large, encircling the entire city. He could easily hide somewhere along its length for a few hours without anyone finding him.

Not on Asen's watch. He rushed after the Zmey, squeezing past decrepit buildings and weaving through dark alleyways. The area around the Wall had recently begun to liven up, but even so, the years of abandonment would take a long time to erase. The streets were quiet, and most windows were dark. The ground was thick with snow. While the Zmey seemed to glide across its surface, Asen trudged, sinking to his ankles.

Even as the Zmey increased the distance between them, Asen wasn't worried. He could smell him—that darkly sweet, sticky odour he knew too well. He remembered it surrounding Kosara every time she'd returned from one of her visions.

Asen heard a low, rumbling noise, and it took him a second to recognise it was him, growling under his breath. When the tip of his tongue touched his canines, he found them long and sharpened to a fine point.

Bloody hell. Asen pulled out the amulet Vila had given him, the one stuffed with dried wolfsbane that Kosara had refreshed. He pushed it under his nose, inhaling its woodsy scent. He felt like the heroine of an old novel, calming herself with smelling salts—but it worked. His teeth shrunk back to their normal size. The question was, how long would he be able to contain the beast?

As he walked, he counted to a hundred under his breath, following a calming exercise Dancho had suggested.

Eventually, the Zmey reached a dead end. He stood in front of the crumbling wall of an old redbrick factory. It disappeared right into the Wall, split in half by the Council's spell.

The Zmey threw a frenzied look at the Wall, considering returning inside it, and Asen quickened his pace. The Zmey, however, seemed to decide against it. He reached for the frame of a shattered window and tried to hoist himself upwards, in vain. The window was too tall, and the Zmey was too weak.

The months he'd spent in the Wall had clearly taken their toll on him. When Asen got closer, he saw how sick the Tsar of Monsters looked: his skin was pallid, almost translucent, stretched over his sharp cheekbones like it didn't quite fit correctly.

"Good evening," Asen greeted him, and the Zmey jumped like a frightened animal. He hadn't heard him. This whole time, Asen had been chasing after him, and the Zmey had been none the wiser.

"Ah, Kosara's pet dog," the Zmey said, his voice level, but Asen smelled his fear, sweet and cloying. "Well, what are you waiting for? Come and get me. Take me to her."

Asen took a careful step forwards, ready for an attack. Even weak and wan, the Zmey struck an intimidating figure as he drew himself upwards, his eyes level with Asen's.

"She never got over me, you know that?" the Zmey spat out. "I was always in her head, watching. That time you kissed her on the kitchen floor? She was looking at you, but she was thinking of me."

Asen's teeth grew again, bulging against his cheeks. He fought against his urge to bare them.

So, this was the Zmey's plan. Get him angry enough to turn, and then, the two of them would be on the same level: beast against beast.

The Zmey knew his fight against Kosara would be doomed. He must have thought he had a chance against Asen.

"You might be hers," the Zmey snarled. "But she's mine."

Asen clenched his fist with the wolfsbane amulet still in it. He wasn't going to turn. Becoming a monster was a choice.

The Zmey could talk all he wanted. What did he think? That Asen hadn't dealt with countless thugs trying to get a rise out of him over the years? Words couldn't hurt him.

Asen took another step until his chest almost touched the Zmey's. "Chatty, aren't we?" He grabbed the Zmey's arms, twisting them behind his back with a practised move. "Come on, Your Majesty. It's time we see who's whose."

He'd expected the Zmey would fight. Instead, he let himself be led back through the dark city. Thankfully, he'd stopped talking. Asen couldn't guarantee he'd be able to resist smacking him across the all-knowing mouth if he hadn't.

Asen had no illusions this would be the end of it. The Zmey must have had some sort of plan, or else he wouldn't have allowed himself to be captured so easily.

The trouble was, when he'd insisted Kosara was his, Asen had heard the sincerity in his words. The Tsar of Monsters truly believed he still had a claim on her.

It was a ridiculous idea, Asen told himself. A complete absurdity.

Except, he had recognised some truth in it, too. That night they'd kissed on the kitchen floor, he'd smelled the Zmey on her, stronger than ever.

Asen and the Zmey reached the square just as Kosara emerged from the house on chicken legs. Her eyes were red as if she'd been crying.

First, she spotted the group of witches gathered near the house. "She's dead," she mumbled so quietly, Asen wouldn't have made out the words if it wasn't for his improved hearing. "She wanted to make sure we remember the silver coins—"

"Please, girl." Yovana rolled her eyes. "I know how to bury the dead."

Kosara sniffled. "That's what I told her, too."

Then, Kosara's gaze shifted, finding Asen and Zmey. The Zmey straightened, trying to appear unperturbed, despite his arms being twisted behind his back. Asen resisted the urge to kick him in the back of the knees.

Kosara's eyes widened. She rushed forwards, stumbling through the snow.

The rest of the witches turned to Asen and the Zmey, too. Their whispers filled the square. Yovana crossed herself. Ivan pulled his neckline forwards and pretended to spit inside it three times, to ward against evil.

Kosara stopped just a step away. Her breath came out in plumes in the cold air, fast and panicked, and yet, her face betrayed no expression as she faced the Tsar of Monsters.

The Zmey said sweetly. "My little Kosara . . ." This time, Asen did kick him in the back of the knees.

Ignoring him, Kosara moved her gaze to Asen. "What happened?"

"He tried to run away. I stopped him."

For a moment, Asen felt like the dog the Zmey had accused him of being. He'd brought the Tsar of Monsters to her without hesitation, like a well-trained pet.

But then, what else was he supposed to do? Attack him, like the Zmey had tried to coax him into doing? Jump straight for the Zmey's jugular?

Better a trained dog than a feral one.

For a moment, Kosara stood there, her eyes fixed on the Zmey, and Asen wondered what she'd do. The Zmey had to die, she'd told him as much, but she'd never elaborated on how she planned to do it.

It couldn't be as simple as stabbing him with the kitchen knife protruding from her boot, could it? Nothing in Chernograd was that simple.

Kosara kneeled down, and for a moment, Asen thought she was going for the knife, after all. But then, she gently pulled on the Zmey's arm until Asen, begrudgingly, released it.

She took the Tsar of Monsters' hand in hers. He raised an eyebrow staring at her new fingers, unscarred by his fire, and Asen wondered whether he recognised them.

Kosara took a deep breath, looking up into the Zmey's eyes. "Let's get married."

33

Kosara

Kosara felt terrible seeing Asen's face. She would have warned him what she'd planned, if only she wasn't certain he'd try to stop her.

There was no other way to go about this. She had to give the Zmey what he'd wanted for the past seven years. She had to agree to let him take her back to the monster realm. Back to his palace.

There was power in the ancient ritual he'd used when he'd married all his brides—Kosara had seen it in the visions the shadows had shown her. There was power in the wedding rings she'd enchanted, too.

The only way to end him was to marry him.

She tried to ignore that tiny, embarrassing voice in her head, constantly pestering, *Is it, though? Is this the only way? Or are you doing it because you want to? Because you want to see what it could have been, seven years ago?*

"Kosara . . ." Asen trailed off, his face scrunched in confusion.

Kosara had to look away. "Let him go."

"But—"

"Let him go."

Asen did. The Zmey stepped closer to Kosara, looming over her as she still kneeled in front of him in the snow. Then, he pulled her up by the hand. He didn't let her step away from him. Instead, he leaned in and pressed his lips against hers.

Several of the witches gasped. Yovana swore.

Kosara didn't move. She remained perfectly still, her face betraying nothing, waiting for the theatre to finish. The Zmey wasn't doing this for her. He was doing it for Asen—one last attempt to get a rise out of him—and for the other witches, because he knew they'd spread the gossip all over the city by tomorrow.

The Zmey wasn't an idiot. He must have realised Kosara hadn't had a real change of heart. Though, perhaps, his ego made him believe that she might. That even if she hadn't yet, he still had time to convince her.

Finally, the Zmey took a step back. Kosara watched him flatly. "Is this a yes?"

"What if I refuse you?" he asked, the corners of his lips twitching. "Will you have your dog gnaw me to death?"

Kosara had no time for this. It seemed the Zmey's attention was split, half on making her uncomfortable, half on tormenting Asen. "I might."

"Not much of a proposal then, is it? More like coercion."

"I learned it from you. Well, is this a yes?"

The Zmey smiled that smile of his, the one that used to make her knees weak. It did nothing for her now. Nothing at all. The tiny, embarrassing voice could stuff it.

"Yes," said the Zmey. "Yes, I will marry you."

Kosara lifted her hand into the air and snapped her fingers. Her shadows whirled around her in the snow. Behind the Zmey, the Wall shook like thick fog blown in the wind.

It only took a second. One moment, the Wall stood there, dark and solid—the next it was gone, leaving nothing but dried land and the gutted corpses of ruined buildings behind it.

The wind quickly picked up the dust settled over the old streets, revealing cobblestones no one had walked over in a century. In the distance, Belograd's lights flickered, barely visible through the curtain of snow.

Kosara had often imagined a day when the Wall finally fell. She'd thought it would come with cheers and celebration.

No one cheered. No one even moved. Everyone watched her and the Zmey.

He brushed off his arms with his hands, like he could still feel the Wall's residue clinging to his skin. Then, obviously enjoying the increasingly panicked gazes of the witches gathered at the square, he began his transformation.

It was always uncanny watching it: his form twisting and stretching, expanding until it filled Kosara's vision; his skin becoming too taut, cracking and splitting, revealing his true shape beneath.

His body, large and covered in golden scales, mirrored his sister's, lying motionless on the ground. The Zmey gave her one last look, seeming unperturbed. So much for brotherly love.

He extended his hand to Kosara. Without giving herself the chance to hesitate, she took it. It was the hand of a monster now, with long, curved talons and covered in scales, but it felt just as familiar under Kosara's own.

"Kosara, don't do it," Asen said, and she recognised the hurt in his voice. There was something else in there, too. Something low, rumbling, and dangerous.

She didn't look at him. Without saying a word, she climbed onto the Zmey's back.

Kosara grasped the Zmey's scales as they flew over the city, holding tight onto him with her knees. Her shadows floated around her. They'd grown uncharacteristically silent after their initial panic, watching what her next step would be.

The whole thing felt oddly intimate. She wished there was more between his scorching scales and her body than a pair of trousers and several layers of thermal underwear. She wanted to stop hugging his neck tightly, but she couldn't, in fear she might fall. His flying had always been chaotic, but today he seemed particularly reckless.

He was doing it on purpose, she knew: flying high, then suddenly pivoting downwards, letting her almost slip off his back. Firstly, because he knew it would scare her, and he liked smelling her fear. Secondly, because he was enjoying himself.

After months trapped in the Wall, he must have been glad to be free again.

"What was it like?" she shouted so he'd hear her over the wind's howling. "Inside the Wall?"

"Quiet. It gave me a lot of time to think."

"About what?"

"You."

Kosara hit him across the neck, and he laughed.

"Did it hurt?" she asked. "Being trapped in there?"

"Not at first. Not physically. It was complete and utter darkness. Complete and utter quiet, so quiet I could hear my bones grind. There was no way to tell how much time had passed, no one to ask about it—no one but Lamia, and she . . ." The Zmey took a deep breath, and if Kosara didn't know him, she'd think it hurt him to talk about it. "She wasn't herself. I believe it had broken her, after a hundred years."

Kosara shuddered. She'd always heard how terrible embedding was, but there were no known details. She hadn't considered what fate, exactly, she'd sent him to six months ago.

Back then, she'd thought whatever it was, he deserved it. Now, Asen's words echoed in her mind: *Who are we to decide?*

"I—" she began.

"Don't tell me you're sorry. I know it's not true."

Kosara shut her mouth again.

"I wouldn't have been sorry, either," the Zmey said. "We're very much alike in that regard. We do what we have to do. Life gives you bad cards, you have to keep playing bad hands, right? What would regret change after the fact?"

Kosara remained silent, not wanting to agree with him. She was nothing like him. He was a cold-blooded murderer.

And she was the witch who'd embedded him . . . and planned to kill him.

She shook her head. She had to keep focused. This was like during one of their card games, when he'd say anything to knock her off-balance.

In a way, the card game never ended with him. She'd play what she thought was an unbeatable hand, and he'd somehow still manage to slither away from the trap. He was always a step ahead. Never unprepared.

He must have thought it would be like that this time, too, or else he would have never agreed to her proposal. He must have thought he had one last ace up his sleeve.

Kosara hoped he was wrong. Because the truth was, in her bitter experience, the Zmey always won.

Kosara had never seen the Zmey's palace so empty. When he'd first taken her there, seven years ago, it had been during the feast, the three days when all monsters crowded inside to celebrate their ruler. Three days that had felt like they lasted months.

Now, as they landed at the palace steps, there was no laughter or music coming from the halls. No monsters, drunk on moonlight, stumbled through the grass.

The air wasn't pleasantly warm—it was just as freezing as it had been in Chernograd, and bitter wind tore through the garden. The branches of the trees were bare. Feathery snow fell down, piling on the ground.

Kosara squinted upwards and, with a start, realised it wasn't only snow she was seeing. It was fragments of sky too, midnight blue and covered in stars, gently floating down before they crumbled to ash as they approached the ground.

The Zmey shifted back into his human form and stood there, naked in the snow, completely unperturbed. The snowflakes hissed as they touched his burning skin.

Kosara didn't look at him. Why would she? He had nothing she hadn't seen before.

Except, she couldn't help but notice the amulet at his chest, a locket made of gold and glass, hiding something black inside.

"What's that?" she asked, nodding towards it.

The Zmey smirked. He'd hoped she'd notice. He'd hoped she'd look at him. "This?" He opened the locket, revealing several strands of hair tied with golden thread.

Bile climbed up Kosara's throat. It was her hair. The locks he'd won from her over the last seven years, every time they'd played cards. He'd had an amulet made out of them. Who knew what he'd been using it to do to her? Was this why bad luck seemed to constantly follow her?

Was this why she'd heard his voice so clearly over the last six months?

Kosara shook her head. It didn't matter anymore. Soon, either she or the Zmey would be gone, and small trinkets like that amulet wouldn't make a difference.

The Zmey grabbed her by the hand and dragged her up the stairs. His brows were furrowed in frustration. What had he been expecting? A welcoming committee?

To Kosara's surprise, the committee appeared a few seconds later, in the form of a flock of servants. They descended the stairs to meet her and the Zmey, led by a short man in a smart waistcoat.

As he drew nearer, Kosara saw his eyes, bright like smouldering coals. A fire spirit.

"Your Radiance." He took a deep bow, and the spirits behind echoed him. Then, he draped a thick blanket over the Zmey's shoulders. "At last, you return."

The spirit wasn't happy about the Zmey's sudden reappearance, Kosara could tell, as expertly as he tried to hide it. There was an almost imperceptible nervousness to his gestures, a twitchiness she knew too well.

His eyes moved from the Zmey to Kosara, and then to Kosara's twelve shadows. "Am I to understand . . ."

"Prepare for a wedding," the Zmey said. "As soon as possible."

"Oh thank the gods." This time, the spirit's relief seemed sincere. His gaze darted to the sky, where the stars twirled in between great, dark cavities of nothingness.

The spirits turned around as a group, just as they'd arrived, and rushed up the stairs to the gate.

"Come on." The Zmey pulled Kosara sharply after him.

The entrance hall was dark, covered in a thick layer of dust. Kosara felt the Zmey tense under her fingers.

The fire spirit was prepared, however. He clapped his hands, making the chandeliers come alight. As they walked, he clicked his fingers at the nooks and crannies where the dust was thickest, making it disappear. Soon, the palace returned to its former state, just like Kosara remembered it: pristine white.

It was disorienting. Every step sent her further into the past. She blinked, and when she opened her eyes, she could swear she was sixteen again, visiting the Zmey's palace for the first time, full of awe.

"So, the wedding," the fire spirit said. "Any special requests? Or just the usual?"

The usual. They were all used to this, Kosara realised, having to organise a wedding nearly every year. Some of the spirits were already hurrying to the kitchens downstairs to prepare a feast, or to the garden outside to gather flowers.

"Nothing usual for my Kosara," said the Zmey, and she wondered if this was a line he used every year. "Only the best."

"Of course, of course." The spirit bowed with every step. "Should we prepare the great hall?"

"The garden," Kosara said, and the spirit raised his eyebrows. He hadn't expected her to speak. "It needs to happen in the garden."

The Zmey narrowed his eyes at her.

"It's an old family tradition," Kosara added quickly.

The spirit looked at the Zmey, who benevolently spread his arms.

"The garden, then." The spirit clicked his fingers again, and this time, a woman appeared at his side. She didn't look human: her eyes were just as bright as the fire spirit's, though her hair was silver, like a samodiva's.

"You know what to do," the fire spirit barked at her.

Before Kosara could react, the woman was dragging her away by the elbow down a long corridor.

"What are you doing?" Kosara tried to twist away. "Where are you taking me?"

"You need to get measured for your dress."

"What dress?" Kosara snapped, increasingly irritated. "I'm not wearing a bloody dress!"

The woman fixed her with pleading eyes. "Please. Don't be difficult. Or he'll take it out on me."

"The Zmey?"

The woman only nodded.

Kosara looked back at him, standing in the hall, ordering the spirits around. When he saw her looking, he blew her a kiss.

34

Asen

As he watched Kosara and the Zmey disappear into the distance, Asen was hurt and confused, but he was also furious. It was an unusual feeling for him, tinged with the danger that at any minute, it might cause him to turn. He had to keep forcing his teeth to retract back inside his mouth. Occasionally, a patch of fur appeared on his hands as he clenched and unclenched his fists—he hid them in his pockets, so the witches wouldn't see. He'd counted to one hundred at least one hundred times at this point.

He was angry at Kosara for blindsiding him, but he was angrier at himself for never insisting on finding out what, precisely, her plan was. He'd trusted her to do whatever was necessary. He hadn't expected her to allow herself to be taken to the monster realm, completely alone.

The witches were gathered in a tight circle, muttering between themselves. As he paced past them, Yovana called after him, "What do you look so angry for? What else did you expect her to do?"

Asen stopped in his tracks. "Excuse me?"

"How else did you expect her to fix things? The barrier between the realms depends on the Zmey. And the Zmey always needs a bride."

"She could have told me earlier," Asen muttered under his breath.

"You could have used your head."

This wasn't helping his mood in the slightest.

He found Roksana with the two yudas inside the bakery. Sokol sat at the table, her wing still twisted in an unnatural position and covered in bandages, while Vrana and Roksana stood over her, arguing. Of course they were. This time, it seemed to be about how they should try to straighten the wing out.

Sokol watched them, smiling, mildly delirious after whatever anaesthetic Roksana had given her.

"What happened?" Vrana asked when she saw Asen's face.

Asen told her, as briefly as possible, what had occurred outside.

"What did you expect?" Vrana asked in the end. "Of course she has to marry him."

"Was anyone going to tell me?"

"I thought you knew."

Asen remained silent for a moment, wishing his canines would stop elongating inside his mouth. He took a deep breath, and then he asked, "Will you take me there?"

"I will," Vrana said without a moment's hesitation. "I knew you were going to ask. Just let me take care of Sokol—"

"I can handle it," Roksana said. "I know what to do."

Vrana turned to Roksana. Asen saw her preparing to object.

Before she'd managed to open her mouth, Sokol interrupted her. "Please go. Roksana knows what she's doing."

Vrana frowned, but nevertheless, she nodded. "Fine. I hope you're right." Then, she turned to Asen, "It'll be a long journey. I might need to take breaks. You're quite heavy."

Asen tried not to take that remark personally. "I understand."

"Wait!" came Ibrahim's voice from the kitchen. He rushed in, carrying a fabric bag. "I've prepared you cake. Chocolate and walnut."

Asen could relate to his desire to be helpful, but at the same time, he could hardly see how a cake would help. "We don't need—"

"It'll be a long journey," Vrana repeated.

"You can't function on righteous anger alone," Ibrahim added, pushing the bag into Asen's hands.

Asen took it without more protest. Ibrahim was simply trying to help. He, Sokol, Vrana, even Roksana—they were all on his side. He'd never expected to find so many allies in a city like Chernograd.

"Come on," Vrana said. "Or we'll be late."

35

Kosara

The fate she'd managed to escape seven years ago had finally caught up with her. Even more frustratingly, she'd done it to herself. She'd returned here completely of her own accord.

Even though she knew it was the only way, she couldn't silence her doubts. Had she made a mistake? Had she ended up exactly where the Zmey wanted her?

She let the spirits dress her, silently enduring it all, as they placed layer upon layer of white and red on her. Her shirt was linen, covered in elaborate embroideries to protect her from evil eyes. On top, she wore a woollen pinafore, decorated with stylised animals and birds, symbolising fertility. Then, came the gold adornments: strings of coins at her neck, large teardrop-shaped buckles at her waist.

They braided her hair so tight, her temples throbbed. Finally, with great care, one of the spirits covered her face with a red veil, kept in place with a wreath of roses plucked from the Zmey's garden. Their thorns scratched her skin. Their scent made her dizzy.

In a daze, she allowed the spirits to usher her through the door. Her veil made everything red-tinged, as if covered in a veneer of blood.

While she'd been getting dressed, the palace had transformed. It was bright, decorated with flowers, almost welcoming. Outside, in the garden, the spirits had cleaned the snow, piling it around in great heaps, so that Kosara felt as if she'd walked through a crater. Her shadows followed at her feet, murmuring and muttering, growing increasingly more restless.

The Zmey was waiting for her, standing in the snow, surrounded by monsters. He had changed into the appropriate attire, too: embroidered shirt covered in magic symbols, just like hers, a thick woollen belt, a pair of dark trousers. His sheepskin cap was white, decorated with an amulet to protect him from evil—a branch of boxwood tied with a red string.

He looked handsome. It made Kosara even more furious. In some other life, in a parallel universe where the Zmey wasn't the Tsar of Monsters and Kosara was just a girl, she might have been happy to find him standing there, her golden-haired groom. In a world where they hadn't been pushed into this by circumstance, where the snow didn't keep relentlessly falling in June, and where the garden was full of happy relatives, not monsters.

They'd all come: the samodivas on their gold-horned deer, the yudas circling high above, the rusalkas, the karakonjuls. The spirits from Chernograd had started making their way to the palace too, landing in the snow and rushing in from the woods.

They weren't all there yet, but the Zmey didn't want to wait. He seemed, just as Kosara, eager to get it over with.

Kosara stepped towards him, alone. It wasn't right. She should have been led to him by family—her father, an uncle, or at least a friend.

"Wait!" someone shouted, somewhere high above.

Kosara turned her gaze upwards. A large cauldron crossed the sky, and then, screeching, crashed into the snow at the foot of the palace stairs. It rolled several times until it finally came to a stop.

The kitchen spirit of Kosara's own home jumped out of it, triumphant. Her shoes, her apron, and even her hair were covered in snow. She must have flown right through the storm to get to the palace on time.

"Thank God," she said, trying and failing to clean the snow off her clothes. It was caked on. "I thought I might miss it."

She walked to Kosara and took her by the elbow. Once they reached the Zmey, he extended a hand forwards. Kosara made to take it, but the kitchen spirit stood between them.

"I'm not giving her away," she said seriously.

Kosara knew her protests weren't real. It was all a part of the ritual, the pretence that the wedding might not occur after all, unless the groom convinced the bride's family he was worthy.

The Zmey rolled his eyes, but he couldn't argue with tradition. He undid the strings of gold coins decorating his belt and handed them to the kitchen spirit. "Enough?"

The kitchen spirit shook her head. "For my Kosara? No way."

The Zmey took in a deep breath. Kosara felt his growing frustration, and so did the monsters gathered around. Their murmuring ceased. They all watched him, waiting for his outburst.

Kosara squeezed the kitchen spirit's arm and whispered, "Aunty, please . . ."

"Give me your amulet," the kitchen spirit demanded. "There's nothing to protect yourself against here. We're all friends, aren't we?"

The Zmey muttered a swear under his breath, but he undid the boxwood branch clipped on his hat and threw it at the spirit. She caught it, a smile splitting her face.

Kosara wondered just how powerful that amulet had been. She'd thought it nothing more than a part of his costume, an ornament rather than a functional object. Would it have protected the Zmey from the spell she'd woven into the wedding rings? Would the embroideries on his shirt?

It was too late for her to do anything about it, no matter the answer.

The kitchen spirit retreated to stand with the monsters, surrounding Kosara and the Zmey in a circle.

This was when Kosara noticed how much hungrier the monsters looked compared to when she'd last seen them in the winter. The ribs of the karakonjuls poked through their skin. The samodivas' faces were gaunt, and the rusalkas' scales had lost their lustre. As the sky kept falling, she wondered how much the monster realm had already lost to the nothingness beyond.

The Zmey grabbed Kosara's hand and squeezed her hard. Too hard. His nails dug into her skin. "That was very brave of your household spirit," he hissed in her ear. "She should be glad I'm in a good mood."

He didn't look it. If anything, he seemed irritated, like this was nothing but a trifle to him, which—Kosara supposed—it was. He'd been married hundreds of times before. Married, and then widowed.

To her, this shouldn't have been a big deal, either. This wedding was a sham, a means to an end. She, however, found herself oddly giddy. Part of it was nervousness about what was to come. Part of it was the eyes of the monsters, triggering her stage fright.

And part of it was the fact that she was marrying the Tsar of Monsters, and once she'd got her enchanted ring on his finger, he'd be *hers*.

The Zmey led her to a samodiva, standing in front of a table on which she'd arranged a cob of bread, two goblets of red wine, a pot of honey, and two elaborately decorated gold crowns. The samodiva was tall and veiled, an imposing figure dressed in white, looming over them. She spoke in a singsong voice, and though Kosara only caught an archaic word here and there, she recognised the ritual.

Kosara had thought her wedding to the Zmey wouldn't resemble anything she'd seen at the local church. The monsters, she'd imagined, would have their own rituals to follow.

She'd been wrong. It made sense, she supposed: the Zmey took brides from Chernograd, who would have demanded things were done the proper way. Besides, the human rituals worked. They might have taken place in a church nowadays, but they were much older than that, dating to a distant past only Vila and the Zmey remembered.

Or, Kosara thought, a lump forming in her throat, only the Zmey did now.

First, the samodiva handed Kosara and the Zmey two lit candles, tied together with a golden string. Then, still singing, she brought out the wedding rings. Two golden hoops: one empty, the other inscribed with the Zmey's name on the inside.

Kosara swallowed hard, imagining how many different fingers that gold hoop had wrapped around. It made her sick.

The Zmey must have sensed her discomfort, but he misunderstood it. He leaned in and whispered, "I'm sorry. I didn't have time to get your name engraved on my ring. I'll get it done after the wedding."

Kosara suppressed a nervous smile. If things went her way, there wouldn't be an *after* the wedding for him.

If things went wrong, there wouldn't be an *after* for her.

"It's not that," she said. "I proposed to you, didn't I? I'd hoped to use the rings I brought. They were my parents'. It would mean a lot to me."

Kosara rummaged inside the pocket of her pinafore and took out the two silver rings.

The samodiva abruptly stopped singing. Her face was invisible behind the veil, but Kosara thought she felt her indignation.

The garden grew quiet. The monsters stared and muttered between themselves. The tension hung heavy in the air, and Kosara forced herself to take deep breaths. She squeezed her thumbs in her fists so the trembling of her hands wouldn't betray her anxiety.

It was too late to change her mind. Whatever was to happen would happen.

"For a fresh start," she added quickly. "You understand, these two golden rings, they've seen so many failed marriages. My parents were together for decades before they died."

Without saying a word, the samodiva turned to the Zmey.

The Zmey impatiently waved his hand. "Yes, whatever. Use hers."

Kosara didn't dare breathe until the samodiva grabbed the two silver rings. Only then, she allowed herself to relax a little. So far, so good.

The samodiva took up her droning chant again. She presented one of the rings in front of Kosara's face, waiting for her to kiss it, and then did the same to the Zmey. Then, the samodiva swapped them around three times until Kosara lost track of which ring was which.

She caught the Zmey's eyes on her. The corner of his mouth twitched.

He thought he'd foiled her plan, she realised. He must have figured out why she'd wanted to use her own wedding rings—he wasn't stupid—but he'd assumed she'd only enchanted one of them. The one that was supposed to go on his finger.

Kosara hadn't. The enchantment wouldn't have worked as planned if she had. They were wedding rings, a matched pair. If one of them tied the Zmey to her, the other tied her to him.

As the samodiva finally pushed the ring onto her finger, Kosara felt the spell begin to take hold. When the second ring slid onto the Zmey's hand, the air stank of magic so strongly, it made her eyes water.

The Zmey must have felt it, too. The enchantment was too powerful for him not to, brewed by Kosara and her twelve shadows.

There was no way he hadn't felt it. Why, then, was he still smirking?

Next, the samodiva took the two gold crowns from the table and performed a similar series of gestures with them. Kosara was too nervous to pay attention. She kissed the gold when it appeared in front of her and watched in a daze as the crowns got swapped.

The monsters' eyes were on her, like hundreds of spotlights. She could swear they traced every drop of cold sweat rolling down her face, even though they shouldn't have been able to see her behind her veil.

As the crown descended on her head, Kosara wanted to scream. The magic in the air grew thicker yet, the pressure making her ears pop.

She hadn't been the only one who'd hidden an enchantment into the wedding ritual. The Zmey had done it, too. It had been so foolish of Kosara not to consider he would. It wasn't his first time, after all.

Kosara had enchanted the wedding rings, and the Zmey had enchanted the crowns. They were tied together now, with two powerful spells, not just one.

The rest of the ritual was a daze. Kosara drank the wine from the goblet. She took a piece of bread dipped in honey, and though she swallowed it, she thought she still felt it there, stuck in her throat.

Finally, the Zmey lifted her veil and leaned in for a kiss. All Kosara wanted was to get away, and yet, she couldn't. The monsters watched them in silence. There was no cheering and no clapping—nothing but wide, hungry stares, tracking the Zmey's forked tongue as it slid between her lips.

He tasted good—that was the most offensive part—sweeter than the honey-covered bread, tangier than the wine. She'd remembered his taste occasionally over the years, like a craving for a dish she could no longer have, and it had always filled her with guilt. Today, it only added to her sense of disorientation.

She'd done it. She'd married the Zmey.

The enchanted crown was heavy on her head, trying to drag her down like an anchor. She wanted to be sick, to kneel in the snow and heave, but she wouldn't give him the satisfaction.

Once he'd had enough of her, he stepped back. He grabbed her hand again, lifting it in the air, and turned her around to face the monsters.

"I've brought you a new Tsaritsa!" he shouted.

The monsters, knowing what was expected of them, finally cheered.

He looked down at Kosara, and she saw something unexpectedly human in his eyes: there was satisfaction he'd tricked her into wearing the enchanted crown; there was fear of what was to come; but there was hope, too. Hope that, together, they'd save his realm.

"Are you ready?" he asked, moving his gaze upwards to the cracking sky.

"What?" Kosara sputtered. "Right now?"

The Zmey cocked an eyebrow. "When would you rather do it?"

He was right, Kosara knew he was. This was why she'd come here in the first place, and why she'd gone through with this damned wedding.

But now that she'd tied herself to the Zmey, and he'd tied himself to her, she found herself hesitating. She wasn't certain she'd walk out of this alive. Kosara had been happy to sacrifice him to save the monster realm and her city. She wasn't prepared to be the sacrifice herself.

She didn't have a choice. The Zmey's fingers were already intertwining with hers. He was in no mood to wait.

The warmth from his hands spilled into hers. She hadn't realised how cold she'd grown, standing there in the snow, but now, the blood rushed back to her fingertips and her cheeks.

Their clasped hands began glowing.

Immediately, one thing became obvious. When the Zmey had told all his previous brides they needed to give up their shadows to perform the ritual, he'd lied. Kosara's twelve shadows only bolstered her magic. As they surrounded her in darkness, the light pouring out of her grew stronger.

Together, she and the Zmey guided it upwards, towards the gaps in the sky. At first, it seemed hopeless. The light was too dim, and the darkness—too vast. Then, slowly, under the widening eyes of the monsters, Kosara and the Zmey shone brighter.

They'd always been so good at burning together.

Kosara caught the Zmey's eyes again, and she didn't think she'd imagined the pride she saw in them.

He stepped closer, so close she felt his warm breath on her ear. "I knew you'd be good at this."

She was. For once, she'd found a type of magic that came to her naturally. There was no need to memorise magic words or click her fingers. There was no need to push herself to the limit of her powers or to force her shadows into submission.

She and the Zmey worked together, but, as usual, they also fought against each other. While Kosara's wedding ring prevented the Zmey from taking her over completely, his crown stopped her from doing the same. They each pulled the spell towards them—one moment, Kosara prevailed, guiding his light towards the sky; the next, the Zmey was victorious, leading hers upwards.

As she watched their magic repair the tears in the realms, Kosara realised she was having fun. Bizarrely, ridiculously, she was enjoying herself.

The Zmey leaned into her, and she thought he might kiss her again. She found herself not entirely opposed to the idea. He'd tasted so good. She couldn't quite remember why she'd felt guilty about it before. The crown weighed heavier on her, pressing the wreath of roses into her skull, but Kosara had never felt lighter.

She shook her head. This wasn't right. What had Vila called it? Spell drunk. She was getting spell drunk again.

"Look what you're wanting to give up," the Zmey whispered, so quietly only she heard him.

"Excuse me?"

"I know what you're planning. I can feel that enchanted ring on my finger. Are you really ready to sacrifice me?"

"I wouldn't—" Kosara hesitated. Was there a point in denying it? He knew.

"No one else can give you this. I'm your one equal."

"I've no idea what you're talking about." It was a lie. She knew very well what he meant.

Vila was gone. It was just the two of them left now, Kosara with her twelve shadows—and the Zmey.

"Say I'm gone." The Zmey's fingers squeezed her hand. "Then what? Will you truly be happy returning to your role as the village witch? Curing people's bad backs and prescribing potions for sore throats? Aren't you going to miss me? Miss this?"

Kosara wanted to look away, but she couldn't. She was mesmerised by the fire burning in his eyes.

His hands gripped hers even tighter. "I can give you so much more. If only you agree to stay here, with me. Be my Tsaritsa."

Kosara knew what this reminded her of: being trapped in one of her shadow's visions, unable to leave. She wished, just like back then, Nevena would come and save her. Though she couldn't look away from the Zmey, she thought she saw her sister's silhouette in the corner of her eye, standing in the snow, apart from the monsters.

Nevena. The thought hit Kosara straight in the chest. This was why she'd felt guilty kissing the Zmey. Because he'd murdered her sister. Had she really forgotten?

The guilt was back now, and so was her anger.

"Never," she said through her teeth. With the strength of her twelve shadows, she pulled on his magic sharply.

The Zmey must have truly been distracted, because, unbelievably, it worked. She grew brighter, while the Zmey's light dimmed. She remembered watching him as Tsveta lay on the ground bleeding light, dying, and her determination only grew.

She wanted to see him there in the snow, helpless. She tasted his impending death on the tip of her tongue, metallic like blood.

Except, the Zmey wasn't going to give up without a fight. He snarled, "As you wish."

Kosara's heart beat faster as she recognised the look on his face. The last time she'd seen it, she'd been sixteen, and his fingers had been digging into her throat. That had been the face she'd seen right before she passed out, unsure if she'd wake up again. The face that had finally convinced her to leave him.

He opened his mouth, revealing his forked tongue and his sharp teeth, and he inhaled deeply. With every breath he drew in, Kosara's magic left her.

No! she screamed in her mind, trying to hold on to it, but it was all in vain.

What had she thought would happen? This had been a mistake. She wasn't the Zmey's equal. He was the Tsar of Monsters, and she was a useless witch.

Her shadows were just as helpless, as hard as they tried to hold on to her magic. It was no wonder—they were eleven other witches who'd already lost their lives to him. They hadn't been able to fight him back then, when they'd each been alone. Kosara had hoped that now they were all together, they'd find the power to defeat him. She'd underestimated him.

As black spots danced in front of her eyes, Kosara was sure she saw Nevena again, standing there with her eyes wide. She thought she spotted the faces of the monsters change—from the nervous trepidation they'd shown before, to worry, even fear. They wouldn't help her and risk the Zmey's anger, she knew, but she wondered if they wanted to.

And then, she thought, she must have finally lost it, because she could swear she saw Asen. He drifted into her vision on the back of a yuda—no, not any yuda, Vrana.

Kosara realised a second too late her surprise must have shown on her face, as the Zmey frowned and turned around.

Before the Zmey could react, Asen smacked him across the face with something made of fabric.

The Zmey stumbled backwards, only managing to keep himself on his feet because he held on to Kosara's hands. The crown, however, slid off his golden hair and tumbled to the ground, disappearing in the snow.

Kosara took a deep breath, the enchantment around her loosening.

The Zmey must have felt it too, because he tried to pull his hands away from hers and dive down after his crown. She didn't let him. She kept him there, partly by the grip of her hands and partly by the force of her magic, enjoying the growing panic in his eyes.

Kosara wanted to wait until her head stopped spinning and her breathing normalised, but she had no time. Asen had, somehow, managed to buy her a few seconds—she couldn't squander them.

It was her turn to feed on the Zmey, and she did so hungrily, sating herself with his magic. His breathing grew faster. His perfect face blurred, like he struggled to keep the illusion of it—like it was going to melt from his bones like wax.

High above, the sky was almost whole. Only thin fissures remained where the gaps had once been.

Kosara fed on him until she'd sucked in every last drop of his magic. The light filled her, rushing inside her veins, making her lightheaded. The fire in the Zmey's eyes died down, leaving them blue. Simple, ordinary, greyish blue, the sort of eyes you wouldn't look at twice.

Only then did she let him go. He stumbled to the ground on his knees.

He wasn't dead, not yet. Kosara knew, somewhere in the corners of her spell-drunk mind, that she shouldn't have let him go. She could keep him in place with the power of her enchanted wedding ring, but for how long?

And once he'd freed himself, what would he do to her? What would his monsters do after she'd repaired the gaps in their realm, and they no longer depended on her?

She had to kill him. She had the power to do it, and he had to die. It was either him or Chernograd. Either him or Nevena.

He looked at her from the ground, still on his knees, more pathetic than ever. "Kosara, please don't . . ."

Inside her mind, the shadows whispered, *Burn him.*

Kosara felt the fire building at her fingertips.

Burn him.

She squeezed her eyes shut, until the fire had grown bright and strong, powered by her magic and the Zmey's combined. They'd always burned so well together.

Burn him.

Kosara threw her head back, raised her hands to the sky, and let her fire out. She thought she heard the Zmey's choked inhale, but she ignored him. She poured all her fire upwards, into the sky, filling the last remnants of the cracks between the realms.

Slowly, the sky wove itself back together. Stars, split in two, became whole. The constellations gathered themselves and continued on their tireless journey, as if they'd never been interrupted.

The snow finally stopped falling.

The Zmey remained on the ground. Kosara had expected him to strain against the power of her enchantment, but he didn't. It was as if the fight had finally left him.

Kosara wouldn't let him fool her. She knew all his tricks. He thought that by staying there, defeated on the ground, by looking helpless and alone, he'd stir some sympathy in her. He thought she'd let him keep his life, if only he didn't look like a worthy opponent.

"Kosara, please . . ."

She hated to admit it, but it was working. She couldn't kill him when he looked this helpless.

Burn him! screamed the shadows.

He reached for her, and she took a step back. The spell had drained her so much, her knees were weak. She looked around and found Asen standing together with Vrana, surrounded by the Zmey's monsters.

Except, seeing the monsters' faces, she wasn't convinced they were the Zmey's any longer. They all watched her standing over him as he kneeled. She'd expected them to fight her for his life, but they didn't seem to care what she did with him.

Could it be they'd had enough of him?

Kosara realised she had to know—or else, all of this would have been for naught. If she ever hoped the monster realm and Chernograd could coexist, that once the Zmey was gone the monsters wouldn't pick someone just as bloodthirsty to be their Tsar, she had to give them the chance to dethrone him.

She couldn't bear looking at his grovelling any longer, in any case. She couldn't believe that was the man who'd haunted her nightmares all those years. The man who'd killed Nevena. He deserved no more of her time.

Without saying a word, she turned her back to him. Her eyes met Asen's.

"Let's get out of here," she mouthed so quietly, she worried he might not have heard her.

He did. He rushed to her side, and she leaned on him.

No! screamed the shadows in Kosara's mind. *Don't leave him! Burn him!*

She ignored them. They were like kikimoras, in a way: nothing but spectres from the past, hatred and hurt frozen in time.

Before Kosara left the Zmey's garden, she found the single golden seed in her pocket. Making sure no one noticed, she dropped it to the ground, burying it with her foot.

As she walked away, she heard the roars of karakonjuls and var-kolaks, the gurgle of rusalkas, the creaking of the samodivas' bows being drawn. She didn't want to look—didn't want to see what fate she'd left the Zmey to—but she had to.

She only turned around for a second. It was enough to see his monsters swarm him.

A silhouette stood apart from them, familiar with her long hair and her short jacket. Nevena. As Kosara's eyes fell on her, she thought she saw her sister draw her old monster-hunting blade and join the monsters.

Kosara blinked, and Nevena was gone.

36

Asen

There was a moment of confusion about how Kosara and Asen were going to return to Chernograd, until the kitchen spirit came running through the garden and ushered them both towards her giant cauldron.

"Thank God," Kosara muttered under her breath. She swayed on her feet and Asen hurried to catch her by the waist. She must have been exhausted, because she didn't protest, nor did she insist she was fine. She leaned her head on his shoulder. "Imagine leaving the Zmey to his fate and walking away dramatically, only to have to hitchhike your way home."

Asen suspected that after what she'd just pulled off, plenty of monsters would have gladly transported her back to the city.

She still wore her bridal clothes, though she'd taken the red veil off. The wedding ring glinted on her index finger.

He wondered if she'd ever take it off, or if she'd leave it there as a reminder, like how she'd kept the scars on her cheek left by Boryana's hand. She hadn't dyed over the strands of blonde hair the shadows had given her, either.

"It'll take me a wee while to fire the old clunker up," the kitchen spirit said, while she repeatedly pressed on a pedal with her foot and pulled on a series of levers. "But once it gets going, we'll be back in the city in no time."

Vrana came to see them off, and the three of them made small talk for a while, as if they were still in Ibrahim's bakery. Kosara and Asen both pretended not to notice the Zmey's blood on the monster's face. In the background, the kitchen spirit kept swearing under her breath, pressing buttons and pulling on levers as smoke wafted up in clouds from hidden valves.

It was only when Vrana turned to leave that Kosara said, "Wait."

Kosara stood there, playing with the elaborate embroideries on her wedding shirt, looking nervous. It didn't suit her. She was the witch who'd brought down the Tsar of Monsters. The witch who'd torn down the Wall.

Her shadows circled her, restless, probably filling her head with murmurs.

"Thank you," she said to Vrana, and the yuda nodded. Then, Kosara's gaze moved to Asen and the kitchen spirit. "Thank you all. I wouldn't have managed alone."

She said it casually, but Asen knew how much that admission must have cost her.

"Thank you for saving the monster realm." Vrana's lips twisted into something that Asen, after some consideration, decided must have been a smile.

Kosara laughed. "Well, someone had to, and it wasn't going to be the Zmey, was it?" She paused, suddenly serious again. "Do you know what will happen with the barrier between our two worlds now that the Zmey is gone?"

Vrana shrugged. "I haven't seen the future, if that is what you're asking, but I suspect it will weave itself back together, like it does at the end of every Foul Days. Though this time, it might take longer. It wasn't just a crack, it was a proper tear."

"Would you like me to warn Sokol? If she doesn't want to get trapped down in Chernograd . . ."

It was only then that Asen noticed Sokol's absence. The other monsters had all returned from Chernograd to attend the Zmey's wedding. All but Sokol.

Vrana shrugged, faux casually. "Oh, she knows. She's made her choice."

"Ah." The corners of Kosara's lips twitched. "I see. Well, we'll see you next Foul Days."

"I'll see you then. I suspect, by then, you'll find the monster realm a very different place."

"Let's hope you're right."

Vrana turned and hurried back towards the garden. Asen could tell she must have been eager to see what she'd missed.

Asen, himself, had no doubt what had occurred once they'd left. He'd seen it in the gazes of the monsters. He'd smelled it in the wind, carrying the stench of the Zmey's blood.

Finally, the cauldron made a loud rumbling noise and rose from the ground.

"Now we're talking!" shouted the kitchen spirit, reaching to pull Kosara in by the hand. "All aboard!"

They whizzed straight upwards at an ungodly speed. Asen's hair— which had grown even longer in the last few days—flapped in the wind. His ears popped.

After a minute of frantic ascent, the cauldron stabilised high up in the sky, and proceeded to glide forwards at a much more reasonable pace.

Kosara spent most of the journey sleeping with her head against Asen's chest. He barely moved, too afraid he'd wake her up. At the same time, if the constant swearing of the kitchen spirit as she navigated the clouds didn't awake her, nothing would.

Kosara abruptly opened her eyes once they reached the Zmey's sea. Asen was surprised to find it there outside of the Foul Days—but then, if the monsters had returned, why wouldn't it?

It stretched far below, with the white crests of waves running over its dark expanse, disappearing somewhere beyond the foggy horizon.

"Damn it," Kosara muttered, her eyelids still half-shut. She pulled a compass from her pocket. Asen recognised it—it had once belonged to Blackbeard, the sea captain. "I almost missed it."

"Missed what?" Asen asked, as Kosara studied the compass intently. "I thought we were going back to Chernograd."

"We are. But first, I need to do something else."

She leaned closer to the compass and whispered a single syllable into it.

The compass led them to an island—nothing more than a patch of rocks and sand in the middle of the sea. The kitchen spirit categorically refused to step foot on it, so they left her floating on the sea to knit and guard the cauldron until they returned.

The coast was full of rusalkas, lounging on the sand and feasting on beached fish and unfortunate seagulls. As they saw Kosara approach surrounded by shadows, they scattered away, diving in the waves.

"Where are we?" Asen asked.

"It's the island where Vila buried the Zmey's shadow. It can't be found unless you have Blackbeard's compass and you know the magic word."

Asen stiffened. She hadn't come here so she could dig it out, had she? She couldn't have finally buried the man, only to uncover his shadow.

Surely, she had enough shadows whispering in her mind.

Tense, Asen watched her as she kneeled in the sand. Then, she folded up eleven of her shadows—all but her own. He'd seen her do it before; usually, they'd fight her, trying to slither away between her fingers and escape.

This time, they submitted without protest.

"They'd be able to leave, if they wanted," Kosara said. "They're not mine to control. They're nobody's."

"But?"

"But I have the feeling they're ready to rest."

She made a hole in the sand with her hand and poured them inside.

They remained there, nothing but black beads in between the sea-shells and the rotting seaweed.

Kosara stared at them for a second, biting her lip. Then, she buried them. Asen let go of the breath he'd been holding.

She got up and brushed the sand off her pinafore. As she walked to the cauldron, she didn't look back at the island. Her steps seemed to have grown lighter.

The kitchen spirit pulled them inside once more. While the cauldron warmed up, Kosara turned to look at the sea, stretching dark into the distance. She took the compass out of her pocket and weighed it in her hand.

Then, she threw it. It plunged between the waves.

She leaned back with a satisfied smile.

They flew for what felt like hours, though the sky didn't get brighter. Kosara drifted in and out of sleep with her head on Asen's shoulder. Above, the constellations twirled.

When the lights of Chernograd emerged in the distance, the moon still hung low over the city. Asen wasn't sure why he was surprised. He'd known time passed differently in the monster realm.

"What did you hit him with?" Kosara mumbled, startling him. He hadn't realised she was awake.

"Sorry?"

"When you and Vrana swept down from the sky, you smacked the Zmey's crown off his head. What did you use?"

"Oh." Asen still felt bad about that. He'd lost the bag in the snow after it had hit the Zmey. "Cake."

"Cake?"

"Chocolate and walnut, if I remember correctly."

Kosara laughed. It was funny, he supposed—the fact that the Tsar of Monsters had been defeated by a well-aimed bag of chocolate cake.

As they cleared the sea, the crashing of the waves quieted. The smell of seaweed grew less thick. When Asen turned around, the Zmey's sea was gone. All that remained was a shallow pond. In it glinted the scales of goldfish, not rusalkas. A rusty pedalo rested on the shore.

In the sky over the city, fireworks blazed. Somewhere in the distance, music could be heard.

"What's happening?" Asen asked.

"I think it's a celebration," Kosara said, sounding more carefree than he'd heard her in months.

"You youngsters go," said the kitchen spirit. She landed her cauldron on a dark side street and ushered them to leave with a gesture. "I need to rest. I've had quite enough excitement for one night."

"Thank you for your help," Kosara said, though the kitchen spirit waved her off.

"Yes, yes. I'll see you two in the morning, though you might not see me, depending on how far the barrier has stitched itself."

With a great rumble, the cauldron rose into the air, and clinked and clanked its way through the narrow alleyway, bouncing off the walls.

"Well, should we?" Kosara asked, and though Asen had also had plenty of excitement for one night, he couldn't refuse her once he saw the light in her eyes.

She walked a step ahead of him, eager to see what had become of her city, and at her feet, her single shadow followed her.

Asen hurried to catch up, weaving his fingers with hers. Finally, with the shadows buried safely in the sand and the Zmey gone forever, with Boryana's spirit resting peacefully and Karaivanov dead, it was just the two of them. No more ghosts.

37

Kosara

The ground where the Wall had once stood swarmed with people—not only Chernogradeans, but Belogradeans, too. Everyone had come: festivalgoers in elaborate costumes, musicians and street performers, amateur theatre troupes and puppeteers. Wine-sellers and pastry-makers pushed their trolleys through the crowd, and sausages and koftas sizzled at every corner, filling the air with smoke. Fireworks popped, illuminating the sky in a multitude of colours.

Kosara had been worried what the Wall falling would mean for both cities. She remembered the gathering of angry people she'd seen at the square a few days earlier, stirred up by the Belogradean mayor.

They were probably still there, hiding in their houses, watching the celebrations from behind twitching curtains. They'd likely crawl back out the next morning with their placards and their signs. There was still a chance the mayor would get reelected, even now that she didn't have Karaivanov's money and influence propping her up.

Kosara could do nothing about any of it. She'd done all she could—it was the two cities' turn to decide their futures, just as the monsters had decided theirs.

Kosara and Asen wove through the crowd until they found Rok-sana and Sokol. The couple was easy to spot, being a good bit taller than everyone around. Sokol's bandaged wing was hidden under a big jacket. She'd wrapped a shawl around her head in an attempt to disguise her feathers, but it wasn't too convincing.

Nevertheless, Kosara suspected Roksana standing there with a gun at her belt would protect the yuda from too many invasive questions.

When she saw them, Roksana grabbed two glasses of wine from a street seller and handed them to Kosara and Asen.

"I don't—" Asen began, but Roksana interrupted him.

"I know. I asked for nonalcoholic."

"I'm so glad you both made it back!" Sokol unexpectedly crushed both of them in a tight hug. Her feathers had lost their otherworldly scent and acquired some of Chernograd's smoke.

"Well?" she asked. "What happened?"

Kosara recounted what had occurred in the monster realm, Asen filling the gaps where she'd been too panicked—or too spell drunk—to remember.

"So, he's dead," Roksana said at the end.

"He's dead."

The monster hunter lifted her glass in the air and splashed some of her wine on the cobblestones. It was an old tradition, spilling wine on the ground so the spirits of the dead could have a drink. "May the soil be light over him."

At first, Kosara was taken aback. Then, she realised she harboured no ill feelings towards the Zmey, now that he was gone at last. He'd got what he deserved. No point in wishing him a restless death after his terribly long, terribly restless life.

She followed Roksana's example, watching the red liquid sink between the cobblestones. "For Vila. And Malamir. And for Sofiya, Irina, and for Natalia Ruseva."

"For Boryana," Asen said, tilting his glass.

Finally, Sokol let out a few drops from her cup. "For everyone we've lost."

They downed the rest of their wine in silence, and then Roksana, who'd never been one to stay still for long, shouted, "Enough doom and gloom. Let's go dancing!"

She hooked her arm around Sokol's waist and the two of them disappeared in the crowd.

Kosara watched them, shaking her head, a smile tugging at her lips. She was too tired for dancing. She enjoyed simply being there, drinking wine with Asen at her side. Despite the fact she was surrounded by noise, she was at peace.

The Zmey's voice in her head was finally gone.

She'd thought him defeated forever last winter, and she'd been wrong. This time, however, she felt he had been silenced at last. That dark little corner of her mind where he liked to lurk was blissfully quiet.

"Asen!" someone shouted, and Kosara saw Rosa Bakharova elbowing her way through the crowd.

"Mum!" Asen rushed to meet her.

Rosa's face was wet with tears. "I didn't believe it when they told me. The Wall is gone! It's finally gone!" She cupped his face in between her hands and stared into his eyes. "You need a shave."

"I know, Mum, I know . . ."

Kosara walked away. She didn't want to interrupt their reunion. They didn't need her there—a grumpy, tired witch. Besides, she had so much work to do. A witch's work never ceased. She was sure there was already a queue forming in front of her workshop, of people who'd drunk too much and were desperate for a hangover cure, and others whose stomachs hadn't agreed with the sausages they'd purchased from a street cart.

No matter what the Zmey had told her, this was her job: curing people's bad backs and prescribing potions for sore throats. She wouldn't change it for anything.

A hand wrapped around hers, stopping her in her tracks.

She turned to find Asen standing there, out of breath. He must have chased her through the crowd. "My mother asks if you'd come to hers for dinner."

"I—" Kosara almost said no. Old habits died hard. "I'd love to. How about tomorrow?"

"Can we do the day after?" Asen said, looking sheepish. "I have my book club tomorrow."

Kosara couldn't help but let out a relieved laugh. Deep down, so deep she didn't even want to admit it to herself, she'd been worried now that he was free to return to Belograd, he'd forget all about her city. He'd forget all about her.

"So, you've decided to go?" she asked.

"I didn't read the entirety of *A Night of Passion With the Upir Lord* for nothing! Anyway, where are you going? I heard that band you like is playing nearby."

"The Screaming Rusalkas?"

"The Rotting Upirs. There's a rumour going around that the vocalist is a real upir, can you believe it?"

"I bet you he started it himself." Then, she suddenly remembered. "That was Nevena's favourite band."

Kosara was surprised that thinking about her sister no longer brought hurt and guilt. Only a pleasant warmth, tinged with a grief she suspected would never fully fade.

Asen pulled her after him. "Come on or we'll miss them."

Kosara opened her mouth to argue. She had so much work to do. Besides, she was worried about all that would come tomorrow, when the celebrations died down and the city's new problems became evident. The Zmey's death would have repercussions in both the monster realm and the human one.

But then, her eyes met Asen's, and she thought instead of worrying about things she couldn't control, she'd check if that last kiss they'd shared was a fluke. She leaned in slowly, to give him a chance to step away if he didn't want it.

Kissing him was nothing like kissing the Zmey—none of the sweetness, none of the tang. All she tasted was cheap nonalcoholic wine, little different from grape juice, and the scent of smoke caught in his hair and stubble. Above them, the fireworks kept popping, illuminating the city.

A wild, impossible-to-suppress smile split her face. She grasped Asen's hand tighter and let him lead her through the crowd. Tomorrow, she could worry about what happened next.

Tonight, it was time to celebrate.

The Chernograd Witch and Warlock Association

P R E S E N T S

A PRACTICAL GUIDE TO MONSTERS

(Foul Days edition -- Now reprinted)

Dear denizens of Chernograd and visitors to the city, the Foul Days are nearly upon us! And what better time is there to re-familiarise yourself with Chernograd's monsters: from the common upir to the cruel samodiva; from the prophetic yuda to the bloodthirsty karakonjul. We know what you're thinkin--everyone knows the monsters of Chernograd. Everyone has a story of how their great uncle's cousin's friend defeated a karakonjul with a clever riddle or fought a varkolak with their bare hands. However, at the WWA, we believe a quick refresher is never amiss. We have deliberately written this guide to be accessible to all ages and levels of knowledge, and we encourage you to distribute it widely among your family and friends. Remember: to be safe is to be prepared. (For those looking for a refresher on the Foul Days themselves, we recommend you turn to the "Back to Basics" section below the monster listings.)

Upir

WHAT IS IT: The restless spirits of the dead who rise from their graves to torment the living. Can be encountered year-round but are especially active during the Foul Days.

HOW TO RECOGNISE IT: Upirs resemble walking corpses in various stages of decay, often with partially decomposed flesh and bloodshot eyes. Upon encountering a living person, an upir will attempt to puncture their body with their needle-sharp teeth and drain the person of blood. During the Foul

Days, they tend to rise from their graves en masse and are more likely to move in groups.

HOW TO PROTECT YOURSELF FROM IT: To prevent your loved one from rising as an upir, be sure to follow the appropriate burial rituals. Being vigilant begins at the wake: it is imperative not to let any household cats walk over the body of the deceased! The burial includes the following precautions: placing a coin in the deceased's mouth, burying them face down, trapping them with a sickle or other agricultural implement, cutting their head off, placing an aspen stake through their heart, and severing the tendons of their knees to prevent them from rising. It sounds like a lot, but it's better to be safe than sorry!

In the event that a person is bitten by an upir but manages to get away, they should be treated by a professional as upir teeth often contain venom. Upirs possess a unique brand of illusory magic by which they are able to make their victims believe they are hearing or seeing people or scenes from their own memory. This magic is intensified when many upirs gather in a single area.

There are many stories, some of which you'd have undoubtedly heard in your local pub, about upirs returning from the dead and attempting to resume their normal life, going home and greeting their family as if nothing has happened. If you suspect your recently buried but now mysteriously resurrected relative to be an upir, do not panic. Upirs hate garlic and holy water, so it is especially important to keep these substances on hand during the Foul Days to serve as a repellent. If worst comes to worst and you have to fight, an aspen stake through the upir's heart or cutting their head off has proven sufficient to kill them.

Varkolak

WHAT IS IT: Varkolaks are people who transform into large wolves during the full moon. Lycanthropy is a contagious disease, transmitted through biting, and there is no cure. There are folk stories recording cases where angry varkolaks caused an eclipse

by biting off a piece of the moon, but the authors have no conclusive evidence to either prove or disprove such occurrences.
While varkolaks are a common threat during the full moon all
year, they become particularly aggressive during the Foul Days.

HOW TO RECOGNISE IT: Varkolaks tend to be larger than normal
wolves, and besides, there have been no wolves in Chernograd
for hundreds of years, so spotting one is a pretty good indi-
cation you need to stay far, far away.

HOW TO PROTECT YOURSELF FROM IT: If you suspect a friend or
a relative has been bitten by a varkolak, you have to follow
the appropriate quarantine procedures. First, lock them in
a cage in the basement. Secondly, immediately contact a licensed witch or warlock.

If you suspect you've been bitten by a varkolak, hand yourself
over to the nearest witch or warlock's workshop. It is not
wise to attempt to hide your condition, as keeping varkolaks
contained requires rune circles and talismans only available
to licensed magic practitioners.

Remember, varkolaks have superhuman strength, sight, sense of
smell, and hearing. You can't outrun a varkolak. You can't
hide from them. Their one weakness is silver, but we recognize
in these trying times, access to the precious metal is highly
limited. Singing has been found to temporarily distract them,
but it does not work for long. The best thing to do in order
to keep yourself and your fellow citizens safe is to remain
vigilant and watch out for signs of the varkolak infection in
your immediate circle. A varkolak bite doesn't have to be the
end of one's life if all appropriate precautions are followed.

In fact, many people have gone to live long, fulfilling lives
after having been bitten, with their condition only a minor
inconvenience during the full moon.

If all else fails, a varkolak can be killed with a silver
bullet. The WWA would like to make it clear that this should
be a last resort. Varkolaks are humans and they deserve to be
treated as such.

Household Spirit

WHAT IS IT: Also known as "stopani," the household spirits are
the echoes of a family's ancestors, trapped between the realms
of the living and the dead due to their love for the family
home and their desire to protect the household. While their
presence can be felt year-round, they are usually only spotted
during the Foul Days.

HOW TO RECOGNISE IT: Household spirits resemble the dead an-
cestor they've originated from, but with exaggerated features
related to their abode. Thus, hearth spirits often have fiery
red hair and eyes like burning coal, while the spirit of the
stable might be wearing riding clothes and be armed with a
crop. Some spirits can transform into snakes, which makes it
particularly important to be gentle with any snake found near
the threshold.

HOW TO PROTECT YOURSELF FROM IT: They are generally benevo-
lent if prickly. The best strategy is to keep on their good
side by making sure the house is kept clean, tidy, and well
maintained. If they demand food, feed them. If they want a
drink, pour them one--they tend to like milk. If the spirits
like you, they're known to help with household chores, such
as keeping food from spoiling too fast. Never, no matter what
happens, laugh at them, as it angers them. While household
spirits can't generally do much harm, they can cause enough
minor inconveniences in your home to make your life miserable.

Kikimora

WHAT IS IT: The spirit of a murder victim rising from the pool
of spilled blood. Their weapon of choice is their long nails,
which they use to dig into people's chests and pull out their
hearts. Kikimoras do not technically have to eat, but when
given the chance, they are quite partial to a human heart.
Due to the general rise in violent crime during the Foul Days,
kikimoras rapidly increase in frequency during this period.

HOW TO RECOGNISE IT: Kikimoras resemble the murdered person, except often covered in copious quantities of blood and with long, strong talons.

HOW TO PROTECT YOURSELF FROM IT: While kikimoras are the victim's anger and hurt personified, and are thus very volatile and aggressive, they usually aim their wrath at their murderer and anyone else standing in their way from reaching said murderer.

If you find yourself cohabiting with a kikimora, it is important to leave it plenty of space, as they are prone to violent fits. Never fall asleep in the same room as a kikimora; they have been known to enjoy sitting on their victims' chests while asleep, getting progressively heavier and heavier, until the victim wakes up and discovers they are unable to move.

Karakonjul

WHAT IS IT: A small, vicious creature with an omnivorous diet, which more often than not includes human flesh. Karakonjuls are only found in Chernograd during the Foul Days, when they are a common sight, rummaging in rubbish bins and chasing stray animals up the streets.

HOW TO RECOGNISE IT: These are small monsters, the size of large dogs, with thick fur, yellow gleaming eyes, and curved horns. They have donkey-like ears and flat snouts with protruding curved fangs.

HOW TO PROTECT YOURSELF FROM IT: Karakonjuls are, notoriously, the least intelligent of the monsters, and it is tempting to treat them as nothing but rabid dogs. However, their capability for understanding human speech should be kept in mind. In fact, your best weapon against karakonjuls is to ask them a riddle: due to their limited intellectual capabilities, they can rarely come up with an answer, which means they tend to freeze, with their small brains overheating, allowing you to run away. At the same time, there is something to be said for

the very human reaction of becoming petrified upon spotting
a pair of lantern eyes staring at you from a dark alley and
being unable to come up with a riddle. We suggest preparing a
few before venturing outside after dark.

There have been reports of karakonjuls being able to transform
into common objects, such as shrubs or large boulders. At
present, the evidence remains inconclusive, but we nevertheless recommend not approaching suspicious large boulders
after dark.

Rusalka

WHAT IS IT: The spirits of drowned people, rusalkas are omnivorous creatures that sustain themselves on a diet of fish,
seagulls, and lost sailors. Rusalkas are only encountered in
Chernograd during the Foul Days.

HOW TO RECOGNISE IT: Rusalkas are generally human-shaped but
often have fish-like features, such as tails, scales partially
covering their bodies, and hair resembling seaweed.

HOW TO PROTECT YOURSELF FROM IT: Stay away from water, any
water--running or stagnant, including canalisation and sewers. Rusalkas have an unusually long arm span, which means
they can reach their victims easily. If you do need to go near
water, remain vigilant: do not allow yourself to be tricked
by lights flickering in the distance. Those are not the lanterns of lost fishing boats, but the spotlights hanging from
the foreheads of rusalkas. What makes rusalkas particularly
dangerous is their ability to steal a person's voice: if you
hear someone crying for help from the water during the Foul
Days, chances are, the person is long dead, and the only
thing that remains is their voice, stolen by the rusalkas to
use as bait.

Yuda

WHAT IS IT: Yudas are monstrous birds who feed on carrion and have prophetic abilities, commonly spotted in Chernograd during the Foul Days.

HOW TO RECOGNISE IT: Yudas resemble large birds with human faces and a beak instead of a mouth. They have a crown of feathers, large feathery wings, and taloned feet. Similar to the samodivas, they are almost always female, for reasons we can only speculate. For example, some theorise the female yudas are the only ones who leave the nest while everyone else stays behind to look after the young, somewhat similar to the bee social structure.

HOW TO PROTECT YOURSELF FROM IT: Yudas are largely harmless to the living as their primary source of nutrition is half-spoiled human meat. They can, however, be rather distressing and it is highly recommended that they are avoided, especially by children, the elderly, and those weak of heart. They have the ability to foretell the future and a penchant for screaming the names of people who are soon to die, sometimes accompanied by other gruesome details, such as the time, place, and cause of death.

Samodiva

WHAT IS IT: Forest spirits known for their cruelty and bloodthirst. Unlike other monsters, they tend to kill not for feed, but for fun. Thankfully, these vicious monsters are only able to cross the boundary between the monster realm and Chernograd during the Foul Days.

HOW TO RECOGNISE IT: Samodivas resemble young women, long-haired, usually barefoot and dressed in white linen, with a semitransparent veil covering their faces. They have bright, impossibly white skin; gleaming hair the colour of moonlight; and large, completely black eyes with no whites. When on the hunt, they ride gold-horned deer and are armed with bows.

HOW TO PROTECT YOURSELF FROM IT: The first and most obvious
thing you can do is to avoid the places where samodivas dwell.
Those are usually recognisable, as they resemble thick for-
ests, sprung among the city overnight. Whatever you do, do not
play music or sing near a samodivas' den. They adore music,
and have been known to kidnap musicians, forcing them to play
until they drop dead from exhaustion.

If you ignore this advice and meet a samodiva, the rules are
simple:

• Don't drink the wine she offers you.
• Don't look her in the eyes.
• If she calls your name, don't answer.
• Don't accept her invitation to join the samodivas' dance,
  as once you dance with the samodivas, you can never return
  home.

Music is a way to attract a samodiva's attention, but it is
also a great way to distract her if you've been captured.
While you play or sing, the samodiva will not kill you. If
you find yourself trapped by a samodiva, the only way to free
yourself is to take her "bulo" (veil) and hide it, so she
can't retrieve it. This is where she keeps her power. However,
care should be taken when attempting this, as samodivas do
not take kindly to attempts to steal their power, and their
arrows tend to be very, very deadly.

The Zmey

WHO IS HE: The Tsar of Monsters

HOW TO RECOGNISE HIM: When he descends to Chernograd during
the Foul Days, the Zmey usually takes on the shape of a handsome man with bright-blue eyes and golden hair. In his monster
form, he is enormous, with a body covered in golden scales,
wide bat-like wings, and a horned head. It is best not to encounter this form, as he only shifts into it when angry. This
is also the form capable of breathing fire.

HOW TO PROTECT YOURSELF FROM HIM: Young women between the ages of sixteen and twenty are at particular risk, especially those who have been conceived or born during the Foul Days, and those who show a penchant for witchcraft. Women moving in groups are safest. The Zmey tends to lurk in places where he might catch his victims alone and unprepared: near a water fountain so he'd offer to help her carry water back to the house; near a library so he'd assist with her books. He is charming to a fault, and oftentimes no amount of prior warning makes a difference. It is possible he enchants his victims, though no conclusive evidence has been found.

Once the victim has been taken to his palace, your chances of recovering her are drastically lower, especially once she's drunk his moon wine and eaten the enchanted fruit he offers her. Do not let him take her to his palace. Once the Zmey marries his victim, you might as well consider her dead. She most likely will be within forty days.

Lamia

WHO IS SHE: The Zmey's sister, Lamia is just as dangerous and vicious. Unlike her brother, she has the ability to control the weather.

HOW TO RECOGNISE HER: Identification is straightforward, as Lamia has three heads on long necks, and three mouths full of teeth the size of swords. She's so large, her every step sends the ground shaking. When her horns pierce the clouds, they cause thunder and lightning, and when she tosses her heads, she brings gales and storms.

HOW TO PROTECT YOURSELF FROM HER: Run.

Back to Basics

What are the Foul Days? They are the twelve days between midnight on New Year's Day and the first rooster's crow on Saint Yordan's Day, after the new year has been born but before it has been baptised, when monsters, ghosts, and spirits roam the streets freely. Here are the fundamental rules to ensure your survival during those twelve days:

1. <u>Do not</u> go outside after dark, as this is when the monsters are awake.

2. <u>Do not</u> wash your clothes--the water is unbaptised!

3. <u>Do not</u> wash yourself. (Yes, for twelve days . . . do you want to protect yourself from the monsters or not?)

4. <u>Do not</u> host a wedding, an engagement, or a funeral-- essentially, any large gathering is asking for trouble.

5. Make sure you do not conceive, as any child conceived during the Foul Days will become a drunk and a rascal, and/or will catch the eye of the Zmey.

For the WWA, prevention comes first. Our advice will always prioritise making sure you avoid the monsters as much as possible. However, in order to account for all possible turns of events, we've also added tips for distracting the monsters so you can run away, or, if all else fails, for fighting them. May God help you.

! IMPORTANT NOTICE !

Please remember, the witches and warlocks of the WWA are available for hire to cast protective wards on dwelling places. Contact your local witch or warlock for more information.

ACKNOWLEDGMENTS

As always, huge thanks to the team at Tor, including my editor Sanaa Ali-Virani, cover artist Rovina Cai, jacket designer Jamie Stafford-Hill, interior designer Greg Collins, managing editor Rafal Gibek, Emily Honer and Emily Mlynek in marketing, production editor Jeff LaSala, production manager Jacqueline Huber-Rodriguez, publicist Caroline Perny, associate publicist Jocelyn Bright, copyeditor Sarah Walker, and proofreader Satchel Joseph. Thank you for making this book the best version of itself.

Thanks to my amazing agent, Brenna English-Loeb, as well as to the rest of the team at Transatlantic Agency and coagents, including Laura Cook from the Transatlantic contracts department, Júlia Garrigós Martí and Irene Merino Jiménez at the Foreign Office, Katya Ilina at the Elizabeth Van Lear Agency, Megan Husain and Sarah Dray at the Anna Jarota Agency, Renata Paczewska and Martyna Kowalewska at Book/lab Literary Agency, and Erica Berla and Elisabetta Romano at Berla & Griffini Rights Agency.

Thank you to my ever-patient beta readers, A.C. Moore, Angelika Anna, Anna Makowska, Ashleigh Airey, and Bori Cser. To Sandra Salsbury for being amazingly talented, to Cee Jordan, Andrea Max, Amber Frost, and to everyone from the Aubergine Salon for the support, wisdom, and frequent excuses to procrastinate.

Finally, thank you to my partner, Kenneth—for everything.

ABOUT THE AUTHOR

Julie Broadfoot

GENOVEVA DIMOVA is a fantasy author and archaeologist. Originally from Bulgaria, she now lives in Scotland with her partner and a small army of houseplants. She believes in writing what you know, so her work often features Balkan folklore, the immigrant experience, and protagonists who get into incredible messes out of pure stubbornness. When she's not writing, she likes to explore old ruins, climb even older hills, and listen to practically ancient rock music.

X: @gen_dimova
Instagram: @gen_dimova